Praise for Timothy S. Johnston's
The Savage Deeps

"Reading *The Savage Deeps* is like watching a movie ...
mesmerizing ... Torpedoes, mines, imploded subs, and bodies litter
the ocean floor ... Johnston is an author skilled in bringing life to
his characters through dialogue, engaging readers' emotions by
their behaviors and thinking, and creating brilliant settings, all of
which play out like scenes in a movie."
— Five Stars from Readers' Favorite

"*The Savage Deeps* delivers on every level."
— SFcrowsnest

"*The Savage Deeps* is like a futuristic *Das Boot* with a lot of intense
action and some interesting technology ... full of spine-tingling
thrills ... I give *The Savage Deeps* a five star rating."
— A-Thrill-A-Week

FATAL
DEPTH

THE RISE OF OCEANIA

Fitzhenry & Whiteside

Published in Canada by Fitzhenry & Whiteside
195 Allstate Parkway, Markham, ON   L3R 4T8

Published in the United States by Fitzhenry & Whiteside, 311 Washington Street, Brighton, MA   02135

2 4 6 5 3 1

Fitzhenry & Whiteside acknowledges with thanks the Canada Council for the Arts and the Ontario Arts Council for their support of our publishing program. We acknowledge the financial support of the Government of Canada through the Canada Book Fund (CBF) for our publishing activities.

Canada Council   Conseil des arts
for the Arts   du Canada

ONTARIO ARTS COUNCIL
CONSEIL DES ARTS DE L'ONTARIO

an Ontario government agency
un organisme du gouvernement de l'Ontario

Design by Ken Geniza
Printed in Canada by Houghton Boston

Propeller Model from the U.S. National Archives
Schematics designed by Cheyney Steadman

Library and Archives Canada Cataloguing in Publication

Title: Fatal depth / by Timothy S. Johnston.
Names: Johnston, Timothy S., 1970- author.
Description: Series statement: The rise of Oceania ; book three
Identifiers: Canadiana 20210111569 | ISBN 9781554555574 (softcover)
Classification: LCC PS8619.O488 F38 2021 | DDC C813/.6—dc23

Publisher Cataloging-in-Publication Data (U.S.)

Names: Johnston, Timothy S.,1970-, author.
Title: Fatal depth / by Timothy S. Johnston.
Description: Markham, Ontario : Fitzhenry & Whiteside, 2021. | Series: Rise of Oceania. | Summary: "THE MISSION: Sink an unsinkable submarine. Truman McClusky, Mayor of Trieste City on the shallow continental shelf just off the coast of Florida, has given his team an impossible task: infiltrate an enemy submarine, blend in with a hostile crew, damage the vessel from within, and hope to hell they can escape before it takes them all down. The stakes are massive, for if they don't succeed, its next target will put an end to the peaceful colonization of the ocean floor once and for all: Trieste City itself" -- Provided by publisher.

Identifiers: ISBN 978-1-55455-557-4 (paperback)

Subjects: LCSH: Submarines (Ships) -- Fiction. | Espionage -- Fiction. | Thrillers (Fiction). | Fantasy fiction. | BISAC: FICTION / Thrillers / Military.
Classification: LCC PZ7.J646Fa | DDC 813.6 –dc23

fitzhenry.ca

TIMOTHY S. JOHNSTON

FATAL DEPTH

THE RISE OF OCEANIA

Books by Timothy S. Johnston

The Rise of Oceania

THE WAR BENEATH
THE SAVAGE DEEPS
FATAL DEPTH

The Tanner Sequence

THE FURNACE
THE FREEZER
THE VOID

Timeline of Events

2020   Despite the fact that global warming is the primary concern for the majority of the planet's population, still little is being done.

2055   Shipping begins to experience interruptions due to flooded docks and crane facilities. World markets fluctuate wildly.

2061   Rising ocean levels swamp Manhattan shore defenses and disrupt Gulf Coast oil shipping; financial markets in North America become increasingly unstable due to flooding.

2062-2065   Encroaching water pounds major cities such as Mumbai, London, Miami, Jakarta, Tokyo, and Shanghai. The Marshall Islands, Tuvalu, and the Maldives disappear. Refugee problem escalates in Bangladesh; millions die.

2069   Shore defenses everywhere are abandoned; massive numbers of people move inland. Inundated coastal cities become major disaster areas.

2071-2072   Market crash affects entire world; economic depression looms. Famine and desertification intensifies.

2073   Led by China, governments begin establishing settlements on continental shelves. The shallow water environment proves ideal for displaced populations, aquaculture, and as jump-off sites for mining ventures on the deep ocean abyssal plains.

2080   The number of people living on the ocean floor reaches 100,000.

2088   Flooding continues on land; the pressure to establish undersea colonies increases.

2090   Continental shelves are now home to twenty-three major cities and hundreds of deep-sea mining and research facilities. Resources harvested by the ocean inhabitants are now integral to national economies.

2093   Led by the American undersea cities of Trieste, Seascape, and Ballard, an independence movement begins.

2099   The CIA crushes the independence movement.

2128   Over ten million now populate the ocean floor in twenty-nine cities.

2129   Tensions between China and the United States, fueled by competition over The Iron Plains and a new Triestrian submarine propulsion system, skyrockets. The USSF occupies Trieste following The Second Battle of Trieste.

Winter, 2130   Trieste Mayor Truman McClusky begins a new fight for Independence against the United States. With new deep-diving technology, he defeats French and US warsubs in battle in the Mid-Atlantic Ridge, killing Captain Franklin P. Heller and sinking a hundred USSF submarines.

"The hazards of colonizing the ocean floor exist in every possible corner of the watery world, regardless of depth. The slightest breach, caused either by design or manufacturing flaw—or perhaps by weapon—is likely to spell certain doom to the colonists below. Water is a heavy blanket, but it is not comforting.

It is relentless."

— Frank McClusky, Freedom Fighter and once Mayor of Trieste

2130 AD

Prelude:
The Weapon

Location: USSF ATLANTIC HQ
                   Norfolk, Virginia, United States

Latitude: 36° 56′ N
Longitude: 76° 17′ W
Time: 0825 hours
Date: 18 April 2130

THE ALARM BLARED FROM THE SONAR console just as USSF Lieutenant Cathy Lentz was lifting the mug of coffee to her lips for the first sip of the morning. It was still early, the sun was rising over the Atlantic waters to the east, and the sky was a brilliant blue. Tearing her gaze from the panoramic floor-to-ceiling viewport, she shot a glance to the display. There, on the holographic image, a brilliant white orb glowed ominously only two kilometers east of the United States coast.

She half choked as she pulled the mug away.

Damn. She'd just burned her lips.

She thrust the thought aside immediately. The large sonar return had puzzled her.

The United States Submarine Fleet HQ was located at former Naval Station Norfolk, Virginia on the Hampton Roads peninsula—Sewell's Point. Originally built for the US Navy in 1917, the USSF had converted it for exclusive use in the late Twenty-first Century. Housing over eighteen kilometers of pier space on the water and an additional thirty *under* the water, the facility was the single most important base for the USSF in the Atlantic. It serviced and maintained an immense fleet of over a thousand warsubs and countless other support craft. Hundreds of buildings containing engineering divisions, personnel offices, medical facilities, and even nuclear plant maintenance stretched across acres of land. Roads connected all the buildings on the surface, but of course there were few people currently on them. Just a few trucks and topside dwellers walking around performing routine work on the asphalt and building exteriors.

Most of the base personnel were *inside* at that moment, and they would remain that way. Every building and facility in the area maintained a constant four atmospheres of pressure, standardized across the world for ocean dwellers for easy travel to the undersea colonies. If the base didn't do this, it would be a nightmare of logistics and wasted time as crewmen sat waiting in decompression chambers. Umbilicals connected warsubs to buildings, and USSF sailors moved around the base in this manner. The fiberglass tunnels were either above ground, on the ground, or under the ground. Each building and tunnel was airtight to maintain pressure throughout the base.

Due to rising waters decades earlier, the USSF nearly had to evacuate the base and pick an alternate location farther inland. Instead, the US Army Corps of Engineers had built a massive seawall surrounding Sewell's Point, which held the waters back. From Lentz's current perspective in Sea Traffic Control, five stories up with an excellent view of the entire base and the ocean beyond Willoughby Bay, the wall was there, rising from the water and stretching far to the north and south, connecting Virginia to Delaware at Wise Point, offering them the barest hint of protection. As much as stone and concrete could give, anyway. The rising waters due to Global Warming were inexorable. Nations could only adjust their own structures and keep up with the advance. Water would top the wall eventually, unless of course the Army Corps added to it within the next five years.

Lentz's duties that day were the same as every other day since she'd arrived at the base three years previously: she monitored the sonar screens to watch for incoming subs. Her team of five, currently sitting at consoles in the small room, studied signals from the east continuously, backing up the monotonous work of computers as every noise from every bit of sea life and mechanics made its way to a vast sonar array, through fiber optic cables, and to that very room. Lentz had spent some time on warsubs and in the three US underwater colonies of Trieste, Ballard, and Seascape before the USSF transferred her to HQ in Norfolk. She had a grim sense of foreboding that her career was on a downward path. Instead of moving into larger and larger warsubs and working in their sonar divisions, she had now ended up on land—*on land!*—which for an officer in the USSF was not ideal. Lentz wanted to be in the water.

Under the water.

Cruising the world at immense depths, extending the power and grasp of the United States to the new and exciting frontier, listening to the sounds of ventilation systems and ballast pumps and the ocean sliding past a thick titanium-alloy hull.

But she was in Norfolk, in a pressure-controlled building, watching the ocean and sun out the viewport and staring at a sonar screen. To make things worse, she couldn't even go outside Atlantic USSF HQ to feel the sun on her skin.

Commanding officers had repeatedly told her that she just wasn't calm enough in tense situations. That she panicked easily.

She pulled herself back to the situation. The sonar was ringing, and she stared in fascination at the contact on the screen, not fully comprehending the situation.

"What is it?" Seaman Collins muttered at her. He had said it with an air of nonchalance. After all, alarms weren't rare. Whenever any unidentified contact appeared off the coast, the alert ended up at that room, for that team to determine its source. Usually it was nothing. An errant boat. A fishing trawler, perhaps.

"It's—it's—" Lentz trailed off, staring at the contact. *That can't be right*, she thought. The label above the glowing white cloud showed its speed, depth, and exact location. "It's traveling at over 450 kilometers per hour," she whispered.

"Say again?" Collins face was a mask of confusion as he stared up from his own console, the glow sending ghostly shadows up his face. "Underwater? It's a sub?"

"You heard me," she snapped in reply. She glanced again at the image. The contact was only two kilometers from the seawall and closing fast. It would impact within seconds. But how did it get so close without an array detecting it or a warsub intercepting it? *And how the fuck was it going so goddamned fast?*

An instant later she slammed her hand on the red base master-alarm button. For emergencies only, and she'd never had to hit it.

She had no choice.

She stared out the viewport in shock. The seawall was there, a white line above the blue ocean.

But not for long.

——••——

CALLS WERE BEGINNING TO COME IN now, most of them frantic.

Most recently on the base, the mysterious loss of nearly a hundred warsubs somewhere in the Mid-Atlantic Ridge had consumed Lentz's commanding officers for days. But now that she had hit the alarm, they were wondering just what the hell was going on. They had their protocols, she thought. They should just follow them, lock the base down, and wait for instructions.

From her.

The sonar was showing the contact now only two hundred meters from the wall. The white glow coming from it was incredible, an indication of the immense sound the vessel emitted. Usually sonar returns were mere points of light, a result of the stealth capabilities of most subs designed to contain as much noise as possible. This vessel didn't seem to care.

Then Lentz noticed its specifications.

And she swore.

"It's huge," she gasped.

"Say again?" Collins asked.

She shot a look at him. He still didn't understand what the hell was going on.

"Why'd you hit the alarm?"

She turned back to the display.

The impact was an instant away.

The vessel slowed to a full stop. It was a more abrupt deceleration than she'd ever witnessed. Then again, she wasn't used to seeing a ship travel so fast underwater. Perhaps it was using a supercavitating drive, she reminded herself. She'd been hearing rumors about that technology for the past year.

A screech sounded from the display an instant before programmed algorithms shut it down.

The screen flared white as the mysterious vessel emitted a sound louder than the sonar arrays were prepared to handle.

The sonar net had just shut itself off to protect its delicate equipment.

Was that deliberate? Lentz asked herself. *Subs are supposed to be quiet.* She frowned as she studied the screen.

It was like watching a train wreck, she realized dimly. She understood what was happening, but things were moving too fast. There was nothing she could do.

"Look at that!" Seaman Bishop cried out. She was pointing out the viewport toward the seawall.

Lentz squinted. There was something rising on the other side of it. The white concrete was in silhouette now, with blue water *behind* it, a delicate line tracing across the scene from north to south.

From Virginia to Delaware.

"Oh fuck," she groaned.

Tsunami.

—••—

BUT IT DIDN'T MAKE SENSE. THERE was no tectonic zone this close to the coast. There hadn't been a quake. There wasn't even a tsunami warning system in the Atlantic. The most dangerous area of the world for seismic events was the Pacific Rim, she thought. Not the fucking Atlantic coast!

And then, right before her eyes, the seawall holding back the might of the ocean gave way.

—••—

SHE REALIZED WITH A PIT OF hot fear in her gut what had happened.

"It's an attack," she said. Then louder, for the first time during incident, which had now only lasted thirty seconds, she shrieked, "We're under attack, goddammit!"

When the seawall gave way, the ocean wouldn't just swamp USSF HQ.

It would flood the entire coastal area of Virginia.

There were millions of people in the water's path. People who lived in Norfolk would just be the beginning. Hell, Portsmouth was downstream.

Lentz scrambled to grab the mic and she pulled it savagely to her mouth. "How do I do an all-call?" she yelled. She'd never had to do it before. No one on her team answered. They were standing in half crouches, frozen in place as they had been rising from their consoles to stare out the window at the scene before them.

Below the tower, land personnel were running from the piers. But there was no place for them to go.

The water would catch them.

It was just a matter of time.

—••—

F<small>INALLY,</small> L<small>ENTZ LOCATED THE BUTTON AND</small> pushed it with so much force she cut her index finger on the metal edge. She ignored the blood. "Listen to me!" she cried. She had given in to terror now, there was no containing her fear.

Or her fate.

"Listen!" she continued. "We're under attack. The seawall is crumbling. There's a massive ship out there . . ." It was all she could manage. She dropped the mic and stared out the viewport.

—••—

T<small>HE SEAWALL, TWENTY METERS WIDE AND</small> thirty meters deep, rooted to the bedrock below and reinforced with two-inch metal rebar, had held the rising waters back for decades. It had cost hundreds of millions of dollars and only protected the coastline along Virginia at USSF HQ Command. Other defenses protected other areas of the country, such as New York and

Washington, but the government had abandoned most places and allowed them to flood under nature's merciless onslaught. It had been an exercise in triage. They couldn't afford to save everything. There wasn't enough money for that, for the economy was suffering now too. Save the most important places, let the others flood. People can move.

But now the seawall was under severe stress. The weight of trillions of liters of water pushed against the structure in a sudden compression wave.

Nature was violent, but not like this.

Concrete fractured at the first stresses. Rebar bent. The ocean began to worm its way in.

Water is relentless.

First the ocean began to flow through minor cracks that had existed for years but which the engineers had said were not important enough to fix immediately.

The cracks widened as the wave pushed. They expanded slightly and more water found its way in.

The pressure increased.

There was no holding it back now.

Trickles grew to streams grew to torrents grew to a flood.

But it wasn't enough. Not yet. It wouldn't cause enough damage.

That would come within a minute.

— •• —

THE OCEAN ROSE RAPIDLY ON THE leeward side of the wall. Water flooded in and waves that always lapped at the eighteen kilometers of piers quickly climbed the steel and washed across the docks. Land crew were sprinting from moored vessels, water at their ankles and moving upward fast. Waves flooded Massey Hughes Drive and Rodgers Ave, which were right on the coast. Just south of them were the buildings, hangars, drydocks, and facilities of the base.

Vehicles were idling motionless in the streets now, abandoned. Water coursed around their tires and began to carry them away, down the streets, crashing them into each other and into the structures. Glass shattered, horns blared, and metal wrenched under the stress.

Lieutenant Cathy Lentz watched in horror as the water continued to flood in. Dread filled her. She could only stare, openmouthed, at the scene. Still, she thought, it wasn't the end of the world. Engineers could rebuild the seawall. Pumps could remove the water. Things could be fixed.

Then they would figure out just who the hell had done—

Then the bomb detonated.

————••————

IT WAS A NUCLEAR-TIPPED TORPEDO. Fired from a stern tube of the departing ship that was now powering away at over 400 kph. But the sound disruption was continuing, and forensic investigators wouldn't uncover this detail until days after the destruction of Atlantic USSF HQ at Norfolk Base.

No sonar could tell precisely what was occurring at that exact moment because of all the noise.

The bomb detonated underwater at the base of the seawall halfway between Virginia Beach and Delaware at Wise Point, at the inlet from the ocean into Norfolk. The water amplified the blast, as it does with underwater detonations, and the last retaining force of the wall finally gave way.

The sea flooded in, shoving enormous blocks of rubble aside and tearing through the rebar—and it wasn't just a trickle. It was a massive wave, caused not just by the weight of the ocean, but of the nuclear blast.

The bomb's yield wasn't huge—it wasn't even a hydrogen bomb—but it was enough. Just.

The enemy had calculated it perfectly, based on the seawall's specs—stolen years earlier—and tests on the concrete itself surreptitiously performed by agents under the cover of darkness.

A wave fifty meters high was on its way to the base.

————••————

LENTZ SHIELDED HER EYES WITH AN outstretched hand as the blast rose from the ocean, and a cascade of water began to rain down on the base.

"Holy fuck!" she cried out. "It's going to—"

Before she could finish, the wave hit the first line of piers.

The advancing water tossed the boats like toys. They banged into the docks, and ropes mooring them in place snapped under tremendous pressure. Some capsized immediately, others were pushed aside like so much rubbish in a giant's hand.

The water hit the first building and—

The windows fronting the water blew inward as the wave hit them.

A choking gasp worked its way up Lentz's throat. The buildings at the base were at four atms. If the pressure bled out to the environment . . .

"Oh no," she gasped.

Her heart strobed.

The atmospheric pressure was constant so crew and officers could come and go easily. But with the viewports blown out, it meant the personnel would instantly go from four atmospheres to one.

And they would all experience The Bends.

She grabbed the mic frantically to warn them—

But then the water hit the base of her tower.

The Sea Traffic Control tower that she monitored.

She was in charge there.

Lentz swallowed but her throat was too dry. She'd just witnessed the destruction of Atlantic USSF HQ.

And any personnel who could not get to emergency shelters to maintain their pressure were not going to survive.

No one had anticipated a scenario of this sort.

Viewports in the lower levels exploded into the tower. The air inside the control room flash-condensed as pressure exploded outward. Lentz stared in horror around her as she covered her mouth and struggled to hold her breath.

But it was no use.

Bubbles were fizzing on her tongue.

Her heart fluttered as she staggered toward the stairs that led down to the shelter. Dizziness overcame her and she reached out to grab the handhold, but she missed it and fell against the concrete wall. The sound of screams and rushing water surrounded her. The fog was everywhere; it was impossible to see.

She fell to her knees.

Everything turned black.

Air bubbled from her tissues, clogged her circulatory system and began to choke off her brain. She gasped to breathe, and pain overwhelmed her ability to comprehend what was happening.

Convulsions overcame her as she died on the cold floor.

——••——

THE WATER OF THE ATLANTIC PUMMELED the base buildings, shattering viewports and flooding the streets and ripping airtight doors off hinges. Inside the structures, alarms raged and USSF crew and officers sprinted toward the cores of the facilities where emergency shelters could house them.

Many found the hatches already locked.

The first people to seek shelter had already hit the emergency buttons to close them, for rapid decompression takes an almost immediate toll. The first people to arrive had realized with a sense of doom that if they couldn't increase pressure fast, they'd quickly fall unconscious. And if no one was awake to close the hatches . . .

The fight-or-flight instinct kicked in, and they closed the hatches before most people had arrived. It was contrary to every drill they had run in preparation for decompression emergencies.

And on the base, in the span of only minutes, eighty percent of all the personnel were dead.

Water destroyed and inundated every single building.

The advancing ocean flooded thousands of hectares and killed thousands more people before natural topography could stop the onslaught.

And after the first day of disaster relief, as teams pulled bodies from the debris, some bloated from drowning and others bloated from The Bends, investigators finally got to work to figure out exactly what had happened.

To identify the enemy who had declared war against the United States.

Part One:
Wake

The Ridge

Latitude: 28° 05' 13" S
Longitude: 17° 23' 58" W
Depth: 3,782 meters

In the Mid-Atlantic Ridge

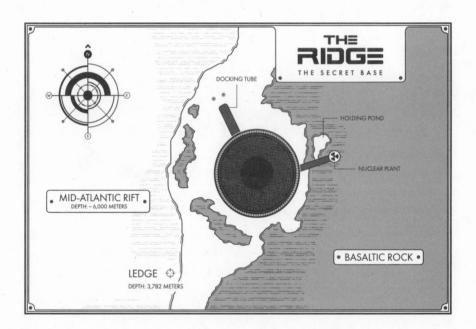

Chapter One

THEY ATTACKED OUR SECRET FACILITY DEEP in the Mid-Atlantic Ridge almost immediately after Kat's funeral.

The troops cut into the hull and invaded with the intent to kill us all.

We had needed to say goodbye to her. We'd had the celebrations following the battle, we'd banished the traitor Robert Butte to his uncertain and lonely future, and we realized that we had to do something for the person who had given us the supercavitating drive. Had to give her an appropriate farewell. Kat had loved the oceans. She'd dreamed of them before she'd even seen them. During her years caring for her sick dad, all she'd wanted to do was live in the water. It had given her meaning through all the years. And now that she was dead, killed during the battle to help gain freedom for Trieste and to create the free seafloor nation of Oceania, I decided to give her body back to the oceans.

She would have wanted it this way.

In the Mid-Atlantic Ridge, that canyon that sliced through the Atlantic Ocean and cut nearly right to the molten mantle at the hot interior of the Earth, I decided to take her body as deep as we could possibly go and let nature and the undersea elements do what they wanted with her.

My sister Meg and I wrapped her body in a white sheet and tied it with rope. It wouldn't last long out there, we knew, for the ocean would eat away at the coverings quickly.

But that was the point.

And there, in the rift zone, we could make it to the very bottom: 6,000 meters. Six kilometers under the ocean, where magma rises from even deeper and creates new ocean crust, where ash plumes and clouds of sediment leak continually from the seafloor and fill the crevasses with murky blankets of dark clouds.

It was deeper than any other sub could go, which is perhaps why I had picked it.

No other human would ever see Kat again.

We boarded her seacar—me, Meagan, Johnny Chang, Manesh Lazlow, Richard Lancombe and Jessica Ng—and departed the stealthy and silent dome where we had staged the battle only a few days earlier. Where we had crushed the USSF and French forces that had tested our new fighter subs, the *Swords*. The fight had also damaged *SC-1*, but we had repaired her and had even made a few additions. She was back to full operation.

The pressure in the airlock rapidly built until it equaled the exterior, the outer hatch opened, and I piloted *SCAV-1* outside, banked her smoothly to the port, crested the ledge over the three-kilometer abyss, and pointed her nose down.

We dove at low thrust—ten percent only—and I watched the readout cautiously. Under normal conditions, the deepest the vessel could go was 4,000 meters, but at that point we had a new technology that could aid us in going even deeper.

The hull creaked and groaned and the others looked around, uncertain. The Acoustic Pulse Drive still wasn't completely familiar to us. But our acoustician Doctor Manesh Lazlow had invented it, and it had been the single most important factor in our stunning victory.

The readout was at 4,000 now, and I thumbed on the APD and kept my speed at fifty.

The *thrum* of the sound pulses echoed through the hull. Johnny, my best friend and former partner in Trieste City Intelligence, was sitting in the co-pilot chair to my right, and he glanced at me.

"It still doesn't feel safe," he muttered.

"You know it works."

"It's new on this ship."

I grunted. He was right. But the sound pulses that were radiating out from the blunt bow of *SC-1* were sending compression waves *away* from the sub, and we powered into the lower pressure tunnel that they created. As they rebounded back to the source, as sound waves do, we'd already moved away. They were not able to cause damage. It was a brilliant method of forcing the pressure back upon itself, allowing us to go deeper. Using the APD, we could descend right to 6,000 meters at the bottom in the rift.

I glanced behind me at the living area of *SC-1*. Katherine Wells' wrapped body lay on the deck. Sitting to either side, on the couches, were Doctor Lazlow, my twin sister Meg, and the elderly freedom fighters Lancombe and Ng, who had fought in the early days of resistance with my father.

They were all staring at the body.

Then Meg turned to look at me. Her eyes were moist. Even though we'd had a few days to grow accustomed to the notion that Kat was dead, it still hadn't helped.

"How are you doing, Tru?" she asked.

My name is Truman McClusky. I was currently mayor of the US undersea colony Trieste, but I was also covertly leading Trieste City Intelligence in a war of independence against the superpowers of the world. Using new technologies like the supercavitating drive and the APD, we had just won our first major victory, but there was still so much to do. My plan was to forge the new nation of Oceania, comprised of all the undersea colonies, because we were tired of the land nations using us for resources and not compensating us for our efforts. In the ocean depths, we struggled enormously. There were deaths due to the extreme hardships. We loved what we did and we wanted to contribute, but we were through with the abuse by the land nations and their submarine forces like the USSF, the FSF, and the Chinese Submarine Fleet.

Our new technologies would help us achieve independence, but our cities were so vulnerable. We would have to change that.

I blew a breath out as I brought our seacar down into the depths. "I'm all right. Managing."

Meg shook her head at me. I knew what she was thinking. Kat's death had hurt us all. She had died in a torpedo blast and a shattered control console aboard that very seacar. She had been a crucial part of the fight, and now she was gone. Meg didn't want me to just ignore the pain, as sometimes I did. Push it down deep and just forget that it had happened.

But Kat would live on, and our fight would continue.

Then I realized that I was pushing her body as deep as I could to leave it on the bottom of the ocean. Was I physically doing exactly what Meg silently accused me of emotionally?

I snapped a glance at my sister as realization hit.

She was glaring at me.

—••—

WE HAD TO KEEP MOVING AT fifty kph or the sound waves would rebound and the seacar would hit crush depth instantly. I set the autopilot to follow the rift and stepped back into the living area. Johnny followed. Upward-moving thermals buffeted the seacar and we all braced ourselves as we stood in silence. *SC-1* jerked up and down and from side to side, and inside the seacar it was a rough ride.

The body was at my feet, and I knelt beside her. Placed my hand on her head, closed my eyes. She had convinced me to rejoin the fight over a year ago. I had given up and was working at Trieste farming kelp. Then she had come into my life, I'd rejoined the resistance, and within weeks had not only become its leader, but was also elected Mayor of Trieste. The election had occurred more because my dad had been an important figure in the city—a former mayor whom the CIA had assassinated in 2099 because of *his* efforts to achieve independence—and the citizens had elected me in a landslide vote. But Kat was the emotional core of the movement, and her death was a monumental loss despite our victory.

I looked up at the others. At the tears on their faces. Even Johnny was crying. "She's the reason I rejoined the fight," I said, my voice husky and faltering. "I realized that she was right. We can't sit back and let them use us for labor. We're not their slaves. We're going to fight for our independence, and we're not going to stop until we've got it."

They were nodding as I spoke, perhaps realizing the colossal impact this decision would have on the oceans and the colonies and on the superpowers of the land nations. "We're going to press on," I continued, "because if we don't, then her death will be in vain. This is what she wanted. It's what my dad wanted." I gestured at Lancombe and Ng. "It's what you two have been preparing for more than thirty years." I sighed and then slowly rose to my feet. We were going to put Kat in the airlock and flood it while piloting just over the seafloor near a series of thermal outgassing vents.

There was a pit in my gut. I felt hollow.

"Let's do this," I whispered.

—••—

CRUISING AT FIFTY KPH JUST A meter or two over the bottom, we carried Kat's body into the airlock and set it down gently. We sealed the inner hatch and then, without fanfare or any other speeches, we opened the outer hatch. On the video monitor, the water rushed in and carried the body out into the depths.

She was now truly and utterly gone.

—••—

BACK AT THE RIDGE, THAT DOME nestled on a ledge just above conventional crush depth and half buried in the cliff face, the place where we had secretly constructed almost a hundred *Swords* to fight in the battle, we surfaced in the docking pool and climbed onto the hull of *SC-1*. I noticed absently that countless scrapes and pits from the fighting of the past few weeks still marked her hull. I would have to get them repaired eventually. Each could represent a tiny flaw that might eventually cause an implosion. Besides, it would have horrified Kat if I didn't fix her seacar.

Jackson Train, the manager of the facility, was standing on the steel mesh dock beside our berth. In the Olympic-sized pool were other moored seacars; they bounced in the waves we had created from surfacing. There was a murmur of white noise from the sloshing against the docks and catwalks. The air was cold and moist and I took a deep breath. I loved it. I'd been living underwater now for over thirty-five years.

The colonies were my home.

"What's next, Mac?" Jack asked me. His voice was soft; he knew what we'd just done. Others had died in the battle as well, but their bodies had been immediately sacrificed to the deeps due to torpedo or mine detonations. Kat's body had been the only one to return with us.

I looked up at the ceiling and around at the little fighter subs. They were all in good working order, having weathered the battle better than anyone had predicted. There were forty more of them in the holding pond, behind the cliff face near the base's fusion reactor.

I pursed my lips. "We continue building ships I guess. Get ready for the next battle."

He blew his breath out and looked at his feet.

"What's wrong?" I asked.

"It's just that we've been here for a year. And everyone wanted to do it, don't get me wrong. But we've just won our first battle, and a break would be . . ." He trailed off and looked away again, as if in shame.

I couldn't help but chuckle. "Jack. No worries. We'll get everyone home now. You're right. I'll arrange a new crew to come here."

A look of panic suddenly crossed his face. "That's not what I mean!"

"No?"

"This is my base. Don't take it away from me, Mac!"

"I'm not—"

"I'm in charge here! I just need a break. We've been working nonstop, not even taking a day off in a year. I just want to see my family back at Trieste. They think I'm dead, Mac! Died a year ago. Let me get back to them for just two weeks."

I laughed louder this time. "How about a month?"

"I have to keep building ships. Two weeks is enough." He thrust his chin in the air, as if that was his way of saying the discussion was over.

"Good enough," I said, slapping his shoulder. "Done."

At that moment, one of the Triestrian workers at The Ridge sprinted across the flimsy mesh catwalk. It had some give to it, so each step he took made him rebound slightly. He appeared to be moving faster than otherwise he would have. It was like running on a trampoline, I realized. Was he doing it for enjoyment? I wondered.

But the expression on his face said otherwise.

"Mac!" the man cried out. "Ships, a bunch of them! It's an attack!"

—••—

U<small>P IN THE DOME'S CONTROL ROOM</small>, on the uppermost level, we stared at the display screens anxiously. The dome was dark, hidden amongst a jumble of rocks and boulders and half carved into the cliff face. And we were deep. I knew they wouldn't be able to see us.

Anechoic tiles also covered the hull, each pitted with random geometric shapes that rebounded sound in all directions. They would make us seem like a giant boulder to any sonar crew searching for us. Our double hull was vacuum within, to cut down on errant noises of the assembly machinery, so I wasn't worried that they'd hear us. And we had no communication ability in The Ridge, so no stray transmissions could have led them to us. But still . . .

How did they know where we were?

Or were they just searching the area cautiously?

"Maybe it's the French or Americans, looking for their lost ships," Johnny muttered. The light from the displays shone up at him, sending twisting shadows across his face.

"Maybe." I studied the readout. Sonars studied the sounds of vessels and the database held information on every known warsub and seacar in the oceans. It should have been able to detect these, but it couldn't. Each point of white light on the screen had a label over it which read:

```
Unknown signature
Depth: 3,312 meters
Speed: 3 kph
```

I shook my head. They were going slow. As if they knew exactly where we—

There was a shout from outside the control room. One of the workers.

Then another.

I straightened suddenly and listened to what they were saying.

"Sparks from the bulkhead on the first level! They're cutting their way in!"

My gut tightened. Oh, *shit*. "Get some weapons," I snapped. "They've found us."

Chapter
Two

I SPUN ON JACKSON AS THE others ran from the control room to organize some resistance. The mysterious ships had not only found us, but one had positioned itself outside the main dome, had attached an airtight umbilical, and troops were cutting through our hull.

A flood of soldiers would enter in just a few seconds, and they would likely be well armed.

It's the same tactic the CIA had used to kill my dad, I thought dully.

"Listen to me," I rasped. "They've got us."

"But who?"

"Doesn't matter. They're going to try to kill every one of us. We have only one play here." I was thinking furiously as I spoke. "Get some rations. Go to the holding pond, behind the cliff face. Are you able to seal it?"

He nodded slowly. "I can close the hatch, lock it. But they can just cut through—"

"Can you collapse the tunnel on this side of it?"

He stopped suddenly and his mouth fell open. "Yes. I suppose I can."

"We have to protect this facility. It's our only way of fighting right now. All our *Swords* are here." There were forty back behind that cliff as well. They were essential to the fight. "Barricade yourself in. Protect the reactor as well. Keep it running."

His face had paled. He knew what I was asking him. If we failed and died in the attack, he could survive until his rations ran out. Perhaps a few weeks. Maybe months. It would be a lonely and miserable time.

"What will you do out here?"

"I have a plan. You've got three minutes." His face registered shock as I told him.

Then he ran from the cabin, terrified at what I was about to do.

I punched a series of commands into the panel.

— •• —

OUR BUNKS WERE JUST OUTSIDE THE control room, each separated by a curtain. The curving dome was overhead, and the steel deck rang with each step I took. Shouts were floating up from the level below. I cursed. I might not even have the three minutes I'd given Jack.

I grabbed a needle gun from my bunk. Its square barrel was black steel with protruding and glinting needles. Each was twenty centimeters. They traveled better underwater than in air, but they were effective nonetheless.

I had a bag of personal items that I slung across my back, and with one last look, I turned and marched down the ladderwell.

Toward the fight.

— •• —

JOHNNY HAD TAKEN CHARGE AND WAS coordinating our people in the assembly area of the dome. Around us, half-finished seacars hung from harnesses. When the plant was in operation, these would move down the line of workers as they installed electronics, mechanics, and control surfaces, and my people used riveters and welders to connect the hull pieces.

But the tools were quiet now. The only noise was the sound of an arc welder and the spray of embers into the chamber.

Everyone was focused on the exterior hull near the fusion assembly station on the line. The weld scar stretched in a large semicircle from deck to ceiling and then back to the deck.

It was nearly finished.

Alarms started blaring.

The welder had severed the vacuum seal between the two hulls, air from the facility had rushed into the opening, and automatic vents had opened to maintain the pressure in the dome. The noise was deafening.

Johnny was handing out weapons—the few that we had—and others were setting up barricades to offer protection. I surveyed the scene and couldn't help but swear. We only had thirty people.

The attackers had *warsubs* out there.

They outnumbered us a hundred to one.

Johnny could tell by the look on my face. He knew me well. We had been on many missions together, infiltrating other cities, stealing tech, recruiting spies for Trieste. We were involved in a cold war on the ocean floors that was rapidly turning hot. We had struggled for years to keep Trieste at the forefront of technology and resource exploitation on the ocean floor. To keep her growing and advancing, we'd had to use espionage as a tool to survive and prosper. But Trieste wasn't unique—other cities had intelligence agencies too. We had pared ours down in recent months after discovery by the USSF and Captain Heller, but I had dealt with that issue over the past few weeks.

I'd killed Heller, along with his fleet of a hundred warsubs that he had ordered to do the same to me.

We waged a silent, hidden war across the oceans to keep Trieste successful, and to increase her power so we could cut loose from our mother nations. The people wanted independence, and I was actively fighting for it.

Then I looked again at the sparks flying into our dome, and my heart sank.

"Don't give up," Johnny muttered.

"They outnumber us."

"We'll fight them off."

"No, we won't."

He shot me a look. His expression said it all. "Don't tell me we're going to surrender?" He grabbed my shoulders. "Mac, I know Kat is gone now, but—"

I shook him off. "No. It's not that." I snorted. "We have to know when we've lost. But I have a plan."

His eyes lit when I outlined what I had arranged with Jackson Train only minutes earlier. Then I turned to the others. "Listen to me!" I called. "They'll be inside in a minute. We have to be ready."

"But who is it?" a voice called.

The truth was, we didn't know. But it didn't matter. I ignored the question.

"We need to cause as much confusion as possible for the next few minutes." I pointed at three of the workers, hunched behind an overturned barrel. They had needle guns and were taking aim at the exterior hull. "Go get a torpedo. It's our only hope right now."

Their faces remained blank for an instant. Then, as one, their jaws dropped.

—••—

WE POSITIONED THE TORPEDO JUST INSIDE the hull where the welding cut was nearly completed. It was a SCAV weapon, full of rocket fuel. It was essentially a missile that traveled underwater and carried its own oxygen supply for combustion. It was two meters long and the three men had used a cart to move it as quickly as possible. It had come from the docking pool and our currently moored *Swords* in the next chamber over.

We set the weapon for IMPACT detonation, and hauled it up on a hoist so it pointed straight down at the deck.

When we released the chain, the torpedo would fall, nose-first.

It would be an epic explosion.

We waited.

The lights in the facility suddenly turned blue and began to flash.

Klaxons rang out.

These were pressure alarms and warning lights.

The base was beginning to flood.

The others looked at me with shock on their faces.

We were abandoning The Ridge.

—••—

I ORDERED ANOTHER GROUP OF WORKERS to go cut the moors in the docking pool. As the water rose, we needed those *Swords* to stay on the surface.

The water was rising in the facility now. The outside pressure was enormous, but the pumps were allowing it in only very slowly. Once the dome was completely full to the ceiling, then the secondary program would kick on—it would rapidly increase pressure until it matched the exterior. When that happened, we *had* to be inside our vehicles and prepared to leave, for our bodies could not withstand the weight of nearly four kilometers of water.

Not without having an equal pressure in our lungs, that is. As it stood now, the exterior would squash our chests as flat as paper. It would crush ribcages, and shattered bone would tear lungs and hearts to shreds.

The water was up to our knees, and people were looking around with worried expressions. The weld was only inches from finishing.

Before I could give the order to evacuate to the docking pool, the cut section of steel fell into the dome.

It revealed a nightmarish scene for just an instant before all hell broke loose.

Troops in black wetsuits. They held long rifles and had knives strapped to their thighs. They wore face shields which no doubt doubled as masks.

They were shock troops for war, underwater.

An immediate shower of needles shot from our people through the opening in the hull and cut down the soldiers at the front of the line. They spun away as spurts of arterial blood sprayed across the interior of the umbilical. I grimaced at that, but there had been no choice.

There were no markings on the troops. *Who were they?*

The water was at my waist and it was freezing. Four degrees Celsius. We were all shivering and mist formed as we exhaled.

"Now!" I cried out.

I couldn't believe that the troops hadn't had some sort of explosive of their own planned. That they were just standing in the umbilical waiting for us to attack.

Did they think we'd just surrender?

"Evacuate to the docking pool!" I yelled.

Three things happened simultaneously only seconds after my command, as my people were sprinting away, each event so stunning that it was hard to keep track of the chaos.

From behind, along a different section of hull, a new weld started and sparks sprayed into the facility, each sizzling as it impacted with the water flooding the base. This weld was moving ten times faster than the first, which clearly had been diversionary.

A series of explosions rocked the dome and a cloud of rock dust churned into the assembly chamber. It was the collapsing roof of the tunnel that led to the storage pond and the fusion reactor. An acrid, burning smell hit me, and it made me cough involuntarily.

It was Jackson, who had followed my order and barricaded himself. His explosives had sealed him in.

Perhaps forever.

And then our own weapon detached from the hoist and fell to the deck, seemingly in slow motion.

Its nose disappeared below the water as it plummeted.

I screamed, "Everyone get—"

And then the SCAV torpedo, meant to explode outside under tremendous pressure, detonated *inside the dome.*

Our own people had been half-swimming, half-sprinting away and had managed to throw themselves behind solid objects which protected them from the flying shrapnel and pieces of our own deck and hull. These tore outwards to become jagged missiles which would shred flesh. Each was glowing white hot as the expanding fireball filled the dome. In the umbilical, where the diversionary troops were attempting to keep us occupied, the ragged steel filled the tunnel like buckshot in a shotgun barrel.

It reduced them to *meat.*

Chunks of flesh and limbs sprayed the interior of the umbilical.

On the far end, where the umbilical entered the black hull of the enemy warsub, the seal shuddered as the vessel bore the brunt of the impact.

Water started to spray from the edges of the umbilical, cutting inward and slicing into the bodies, sending up new fountains of blood.

The water was up to my neck and the explosion had dazed me.

I shook my head. My ears were ringing as I stared at the horrific scene in the umbilical. Smoke was pouring from it, but the flooding water at high pressure and the pieces of corpses were impossible to miss.

The water had turned red.

Behind me, the second cut in our dome—the *real* one—was nearly complete. An instant later, the steel fell with a splash and troops began spilling from the opening.

Shots rang out and I threw myself under the water and started to swim with everything I had.

—••—

E VEN UNDERWATER I COULD HEAR THE chaos above. The pressure alarms, machine guns, explosions and screaming. I hoped my people had made it far enough from the assembly chamber to avoid the enemy onslaught.

At least Jackson had collapsed the tunnel, I thought. He would be safe.

The cold was so painful that it nearly overcame me. I was used to it, however, from my training in Trieste City Intelligence and from previous missions with Johnny. Clamping down on my discomfort, I thrust it aside as I swam. Eventually I needed a breath, and I burst to the surface to gulp air before darting down again to stay under the surface, where I hoped at least the water would provide a little safety.

The ceiling was now dangerously close—it was only half a meter over the water line.

Water nearly filled the first level of the dome.

Not much time left.

The enemy hadn't expected to be under water inside the dome, and so didn't have needle guns with them. Finally, I reached the hatch to the docking pool and looked back into the assembly chamber. There were more troops than I could count, approaching fast.

Grabbing the needle gun from my thigh, I held it steady under the water and fired in rapid succession at the invading soldiers. The first line of them convulsed and thrashed in the water as the needles sliced bone and muscle and arteries.

Then I slammed the hatch closed and spun back to the docking pool.

—••—

THE *SWORDS* WERE FLOATING NEAR THE ceiling, banging into one another. I groaned at the potential damage that the impacts were having. There wasn't much time left. We needed to board the ships before water flooded their upper hatches.

There was only about a minute left, for the water continued to enter the dome.

As I had programmed it to.

The others clustered together near the ceiling in the center of the chamber, swimming frantically. Nearly everyone was there, and suddenly I realized that I had forgotten about one very important person.

"Where's Manesh?" I cried.

Meg heard me and snapped her head around. Her blond hair, even soaking, was impossible not to notice. "He's here! Almost everyone is except Jackson and two others!"

Manesh was eighty years old. His gaunt face, white beard and hair bobbed next to Meg. Johnny was on his other side, holding him between them, and the old man wore a life jacket. Smart move, I thought dully. Meg and Kat had recruited Doctor Manesh Lazlow a few weeks earlier to develop technologies for us. He had abandoned his life in the States for this; he'd wanted nothing more than to join our fight.

The cold was nearly debilitating.

The ceiling was right over our heads. People were reaching up to grab light fixtures to keep themselves in place. Mist from our breath filled the space; it was growing foggy.

"Listen up!" I called. As one, the group turned to look at me. "This is a controlled flooding. But we only have seconds left to board the ships. As soon as the dome is full, valves are going to open in every area of the facility. The pressure inside will skyrocket. Once it does, turn on the SCAV drive and get out of here."

"Where to?" a female worker called out. Her words were a splutter as a wave washed over her face.

"Meet at zero degrees latitude, in the Rift."

Right on the equator.

Get the hell out and go north.

And we only had seconds to escape.

Chapter Three

JOHNNY, LANCOMBE, NG AND LAZLOW SWAM for *SC-1*. I brought up the rear. Together we helped Lazlow pull himself up on the horizontal stabilizer and stumble and slip over to the top hatch. Water was spilling into the seacar as waves washed over her, and with each liter the vessel dipped lower. The situation was dire.

And the water continued rising in the dome.

The seacars were crashing into each other and I flattened myself on the top of the hull to watch the others board their vessels. Each person was entering their own so we could save as many as possible. The smaller fighter craft were the same size as *SC-1*, roughly that of a recreational vehicle topside. Meg had entered one on her own.

Finally, as the dome nearly finished filling and water was *gushing* down the upper hatch and into the seacar, I pulled myself over the edge, collapsed down the ladder, and lowered the hatch. Pumps worked furiously to clear the water and I could hear Lancombe and Ng in the pilot chairs firing up the systems.

"Prepare the SCAV drive!" I yelled.

"From inside?" Ng said, staring at me in shock.

"There are enemy subs out there. We have to blow past them and get away before they know what's happening."

The buffeting stopped at that point, and I pulled myself to my feet, dripping wet and wiping my face. The dome was completely full. "Get ready," I muttered. "The airlock hatches are about to open."

We flooded the ballast and moved the vessel to the bottom of the docking pool. The lights were still on—a strobing blue that illuminated green water and cast a ghostly ephemeral glow over everything—and the other seacars lined up nearby. The scene out the canopy was surreal. Thirty fighter subs submerged in the docking pool, all just waiting.

I sat in the pilot chair and stabbed at the fusion controls. Behind us, in the engineering compartment, the reactor powered up and its dull roar filled the seacar.

It was a comforting sound.

Before us, the airlock hatch was a solid steel barrier.

Any minute now . . .

It slid aside and a torrent of high-pressure water cascaded inward. It threw *SC-1* to the side and the jolt shook everyone.

The pressure rocketed up until it matched the exterior. Nearly 380 atmospheres.

The troops back there would be gone, I thought. Crushed.

I slammed the SCAV drive on full. Seawater boiled instantly in the fusion reactor, and a wake of steam shot from the rear of the seacar.

We powered through the airlock hatches, through the docking tube that was fully open to the outside, and into open water.

The passive sonar screen filled with contacts the second we were past the confines of the docking tube. Ten warsubs surrounded our facility. Umbilicals connected two to the dome, though one was foundering. As I watched the screen, it tore away and a flood of bubbles rushed out of the vessel. It drifted back, listing to the starboard as water flooded in.

The torpedo blast down the umbilical had damaged this vessel beyond repair, I realized. The sudden detonation had likely killed all the troops and ripped the umbilical from its seal. Perhaps the airlock hatch had been blown open.

The ship continued to drift toward the abyss. It scraped the rock for an instant and then a second later went over the edge.

Stern down now, the warsub tipped and plummeted into the depths, bubbles churning out as it sank past crush depth.

Behind me, *Sword* after *Sword* swarmed out of the dome and followed me on the journey north, to the equator, where we would meet and decide the next plan of action.

I couldn't help but wonder whose ships those were. The sonar couldn't identify them. They looked unfamiliar to me. And the troops we'd fought hadn't said a word.

Who the hell had done this to us?

———••———

WITHIN MINUTES WE WERE MOVING AT maximum speed—for *SC-1* that meant 450 kilometers per hour. It was the supercavitating drive. As the ship moved forward, the blunt bow created a low-pressure zone which caused dissolved air in the water to bubble outward. Cavitation. As the vessel moved, this air stretched back to encompass the entire vessel, effectively reducing friction to almost nothing. This allowed tremendous velocity underwater—*supercavitation*. The previous limit of a conventional drive was eighty kph, due to friction of steel with water. But this technology, invented in the Twentieth Century, was exclusive to torpedoes until Kat had taken the notion and, combining it with a fusion reactor, adapted it for crewed vehicles underwater. It had changed the balance of power in the oceans, for until recently only Trieste had it. I had just given it to the French colonies to convince them to join us in the fight to create Oceania, and I had also offered it to the Chinese underwater cities as well as the American colony, Ballard. I suspected the USSF had it as well, since they had captured some of our supercavitating seacars after the battle in the Gulf of Mexico a year earlier.

Traveling at 450 kph meant we would arrive at the Equator within hours instead of days. The attacking ships fell behind us quickly. I felt a pang of regret as they disappeared from our scopes. We could have turned to fight and easily destroy them, striking from the depths as we had earlier against the FSF and the USSF, but our munitions were low. Many of our subs were not armed at all.

Finally, we arrived at zero latitude and I hauled back on the throttle. It had been a tense trip. Someone had taken our base. The positive was that we had cut it off from further infiltration; at 380 atmospheres, they likely would not risk going in again.

But Jackson was still there, I knew.

I was the *only* one who knew, in fact.

We would have to go back for him.

The other *Swords* were on my scope and they too had stopped and were holding with station-keeping thrusters over the giant abyss. There were twenty-eight of them; we'd left two behind in the docking pool, and forty in the holding pond now behind tons of collapsed tunnel.

The comm beeped and I thumbed it on. "This is Mac."

"What now, Tru?" It was Meg, in a *Sword* just to my port.

I glanced out the canopy and the virtual display showed the white lines of her vessel in silhouette against a dark blue simulated background. The computer took information from the sonar and translated it into computer-generated images projected just over our heads. More and more militaries were using the technology in their warsubs to give a visual of what was happening in the dark and dangerous waters that enveloped their ships.

"We go back to Trieste. We continue our efforts."

"Doing what exactly?"

"Building alliances with other undersea cities. Keeping the USSF off our backs. Same as the past year."

There was a building murmur of voices on the channel, and I struggled to make out what they were saying. Then I realized.

Those workers had been at The Ridge for a year now, working alone. I had sent them there following the battle in the Gulf the year before, and their families thought they were dead. No one knew where they had gone; I had told everyone that we hadn't been able to recover or find their bodies in the destruction. A lie, but for a greater purpose.

Now, their families were going to discover the truth.

I smiled. "Yes, we're going home. You've done a great job. Time to rest."

There was a silence at that. Johnny flashed me a look, the hint of a smile on his face.

Then a voice from the comm, "But Mac. What if I want to come back here to The Ridge? To keep building *Swords*?"

Jackson had said the same thing to me, just an hour or two earlier. "We can arrange something," I said.

Cheers sounded from the comm, and it made me grin widely. You couldn't beat that kind of optimism and morale.

—••—

WE SET COURSE FOR TRIESTE, STRAIGHT west along the equator. Johnny and I chatted about our options, wondering exactly what would happen at Trieste now that Captain Heller and *Impaler* were gone.

Just a few days earlier, Heller had led an invasion force to the Mid-Atlantic Ridge to find our base and kill me. I had been too clever for him, however. I'd anticipated his move and had manipulated him into a battle versus the FSF in the wrong location over the deep abyss in the rift zone. Using the *Swords*, with the supercavitating drive and the deep-diving acoustic technology, we had crushed both the USSF and the FSF forces.

I had to say it to myself over and over, as if it hadn't really happened and our success had amazed me.

Impaler was gone.

Heller was gone.

We had defeated him.

Trieste no longer had to endure his dictatorial demands. But despite this, a feeling of dread overcame me whenever I thought about the battle. Yes, it had been a resounding victory.

But I'd had to do something for which I might never forgive myself.

The victory was bittersweet.

And besides, I thought, someone else might just replace him.

— •• —

RICHARD LANCOMBE, JESSICA NG, AND DOCTOR Manesh Lazlow had made themselves comfortable in the living area just aft of the control cabin. They were discussing the recent battle and our near-death during the invasion of The Ridge. They too were wondering who it had been, and how they had found us. Then something they said caught my attention, and I turned to them. "Say that again."

Richard glanced up at me. He was seventy-three years old and had been my father's close advisor and friend back during their days in Trieste running the independence movement in the late 2090s. When the CIA had assassinated Dad in 2099, people had presumed Richard and Jessica dead. But they had shown up just recently after spending thirty years in Ballard living as a married couple and working the farms.

"Renée Féroce," Lancombe said. Sitting across from him, Jessica nodded.

I mulled that over. Renée was a captain in the French Submarine Fleet. I'd held her prisoner after she'd tried to kill me, then had let her go just before the battle. "You think she led those ships to us?"

Lancombe shrugged. "It's as good a guess as any. Those weren't Chinese or American. I'm not familiar with the configuration of the hulls."

Lazlow said, "The sound of the screws was off too. Not American."

I shot a glance at him. "You could tell through the hull?"

He snorted as if my suggestion insulted him. "Of course. I've been listening to them for decades. From an office on land, granted, but still."

I studied him for a moment. He had been a professor at Berkeley working as an acoustician. He was an expert in the field—an acoustical engineer.

I considered what Lancombe had said as well, about the hull shape. Each country had a unique placement of thruster pods and horizontal stabilizers. The American ones were close to the stern, very wide and essentially straight lines out to the pods. Chinese stabilizers swept forward to the pods. The French variety were much longer, sometimes occupying the entire length of the hull from bow to stern. But these subs had possessed *double struts* connecting thruster pods to their hulls, and had no real horizontal stabilizers. They likely used dive planes at the bow

...perhaps gimbaling screws to maneuver. Lazlow had requested that I take detailed sonar readings as we'd left The Ridge; he would investigate them later to see if the sound emissions could provide an identity.

"You think Féroce left The Ridge, joined up with that mysterious force of subs, and led them straight to us?"

He snorted. "There's a strong possibility."

"I disabled all her nav and communication capabilities. She couldn't have known."

"Not the exact coordinates. But the general location. It would have given them something to go on, anyway."

I leaned back in the pilot seat. "You might be right." Still, something didn't ring true with it. She'd indicated empathy with our struggle just before she'd left.

There were also numerous agents of foreign cities—Chinese, perhaps— that would be eager to see Trieste fail in the oceans. Hell, it could even have been another American undersea city, out to hurt us. Seascape, perhaps.

But there was another strong possibility, I knew.

I just hoped that wasn't it.

After a minute, Ng sighed and looked at the deck. "I feel like we're running away and licking our wounds. Yet we won a massive battle."

"We didn't lose anything," I grunted.

Richard gestured at me. "He protected The Ridge. Saved it for later. Flooded it for safe keeping"

"Along with all the *Swords* there," Johnny said.

Ng hesitated and then nodded slowly.

I couldn't help but agree with her, in part. It did feel as though we were licking our wounds.

—••—

FOUR HOURS LATER—OVER 1,600 KILOMETERS westward—a loud PING reverberated through the hull of *SC-1*. Johnny swore and I jerked my hand over the throttle and pulled us out of SCAV drive. The other *Swords* followed suit.

"Who is it?" I asked. The sonar wasn't showing any other ships, but then again, its passive range was only thirty kilometers.

Johnny shook his head. "No idea. Perhaps an active pulse of our own?"

"Do it."

He pressed the button and our own ping shot outward into the ocean depths. It returned seconds later, lighting up ships on the surface and underwater. There were a few sailboats up there, some commercial transports, four submarine freighters travelling between ocean colonies, and some civilian transports to the north.

And one USSF warsub, between us and the Gulf of Mexico.

Between us and home.

—••—

THE LABEL OVER THE CONTACT SAID:

```
Registry: USS Devastator
Terminator Class SSBN, USSF
Depth: 237 meters
Speed: 0 kph
```

I swore. The warsub was the largest in the USSF fleet. She was 261 meters long. A missile boat with eight torpedo tubes, thirty-six missile tubes, a crew of 210, and one giant screw that could push it up to forty-six kph.

I knew this warsub, but I thought she had been in the Pacific dealing with Chinese in the Iron Plains and expanding US influence over the newly discovered resource field just east of the Philippines.

It was Admiral Benning's flagship.

He'd been waiting for us.

"What's our depth?" I muttered.

"Two hundred and thirty-seven." Johnny blinked at the realization.

A prickle worked its way up my spine. My fists clenched unconsciously. Johnny was watching me, worried. He knew what Benning meant to me.

"Do we run?" he asked in a quiet voice. I understood his silent plea:

Don't attack this vessel.

My forehead crinkled as I thought it over. Then, "No."

"But Mac, they'll sink us. They won't let us go back. We destroyed their fleet at the Ridge. We killed Heller."

I snorted. "They don't know that, Johnny. We defeated them, yes. But it was in the rift. No one heard. No one knows what happened to them." I paused. "Let's see what they want."

Chapter Four

I ORDERED THE *SWORDS* TO HANG back while we took *SC-1* toward the massive USSF warsub.

Admiral Benning.

The man who had killed my father thirty years earlier.

My hands were tight on the yoke and sweat beaded my forehead. I'd clenched my teeth and I could barely speak.

Meg had pleaded with me not to go, not to see what they wanted, but I'd ignored her. It made her furious, but she'd get over it.

Johnny said, "It's not time yet, Mac."

I worked my jaw. He knew what I'd been thinking. What I'd been planning. I glanced at him. "I know."

He nodded, then said nothing. But if the opportunity presented itself, I might just do it, I thought. And I had a SCAV drive. I could just run.

But what would I do after? I'd be on the run, forever.

We looked out the canopy. The warsub was there, hovering silently before us.

I pulled next to it, connected umbilicals, and the airlocks on both vessels opened, joining the subs in an open corridor where we could cross freely, for all ships were at four atmospheres.

He appeared on the other side of the umbilical, and my heart caught in my throat.

—••—

HE MARCHED CONFIDENTLY TOWARD US, TWO officers trailing slightly behind. They were staring at me, ice in their eyes, and I matched the glares perfectly.

I thought of my father, killed at this man's hands. It would be so easy, I thought. I could end him in an instant, even with his two thugs. Snap his neck.

"Easy," Johnny whispered.

He was in his early sixties I guessed, but he didn't look it. He'd been a major force in the USSF since the 2090s. He'd been a part of the attack on Trieste in 2099 that had killed my dad along with the entire city council to end their bid for independence. The US had regarded him a hero. The USSF had promoted him repeatedly and recently had given him control over the Pacific fleet. But here he was in the Atlantic, which made me wonder.

There were a lot of rumors about him. He wasn't volatile like Heller had been. He was calm, cool, and collected. He thought over options before he acted. He always applied consequences to those who angered him, including other nations. I had heard about him executing criminals—mutineers—by attaching balloons and letting the victims soar to the surface.

Death by The Bends.

It was a horrific reputation to have, but from his point of view, to make him seem more menacing was probably a good thing.

His family was from Charleston, South Carolina, long since flooded by the rising waters of Global Warming. They'd been forced to move from ancestral homes, and this had caused an underlying bitterness that he had directed at the ocean colonies of the world, including the US cities of Trieste, Seascape, and Ballard. We existed due to the rising temperatures because we were a new source of resources for the topsiders—including fish, kelp, methane, and minerals—and he had translated his anger to us. He'd lost Charleston, but the US had gained the undersea colonies. He resented us.

Or so the rumors went.

They seemed plausible.

He stopped before me. We had a similar build and height. His hair was gray, there were deep lines in his tanned face—most likely from underwater lights which provided much-needed Vitamin D—and he was heavily muscled with square shoulders and a matching jaw.

This man was a warrior, I thought. It's the first time I'd met him, though we had communicated over the comm during the battle in the Gulf.

I'd surrendered to him, in fact.

His full name was Admiral Taurus T. Benning.

"Mayor McClusky," he growled.

"Benning."

His face hardened at that. "I offered you the courtesy of the title. You could do the same."

I remained silent.

He grunted. "Very well." He glanced at the couches in the living area, just forward of our airlock. "Shall we?"

Lancombe, Ng, and Lazlow were in the engineering compartment, where I had asked them to remain quiet. No need to make Benning wonder more than necessary.

He sat down without waiting and I followed suit, just across from him. Johnny stood beside us, next to the two officers.

I locked eyes with Benning. He returned my gaze, and then snorted. "You seem angry."

"With the USSF? Perhaps. It's warranted."

"Because of how we treat your city?"

"Heller isn't an understanding occupier."

"You say *occupier* as if you're the enemy. You're American too. The USSF is just watching, don't forget."

"Your troops harass our people. You steal our produce."

"Your purpose is to provide resources for the mainland. Warming temperatures are hurting all nations. Don't forget your place."

"There are muggings. Even rapes."

This stopped the man. "Pardon me?"

"Your troops have hurt our people in more ways than you can imagine."

He looked genuinely shocked. "There have been sexual assaults? Have you told Captain Heller?"

"Multiple times."

He looked away as he processed that. "I see."

"He ordered a ten percent increase in output. It's put a lot of strain on us."

Benning turned back to me. "You have to put it in context of what's going on at the surface. Bangladesh just disappeared you know. There are riots. Economies are crashing. Nations are going to war. Russia is disintegrating again. You are our nation's quest to expand our borders. Our power."

I remained silent at this. I didn't want to tell him what I really thought.

His mouth twitched as he watched me. I realized that he might be trying to goad me into talking about independence. To see what I thought about current events.

"It doesn't excuse how USSF troops behave," I managed.

He paused, then, "I agree, actually." He glanced around at the interior of *SC-1*. "This is the famous seacar."

I frowned. "Famous?"

"It has the first working SCAV drive in a crewed vessel. Correct?" He gestured aftward at engineering. "The fusion reactor flash-boils seawater to propel the vehicle at fantastic speeds." He winced. "You could outrun my missile boat easily."

"Perhaps. But why would I?"

"Well, you don't seem to like me, do you?"

"You don't give many reasons to."

"I'll consider your claims." Then he paused. "Where have you been?"

"Prospecting." It was the common answer I'd been giving when asked. And since the USSF was asking for more resources, it even made sense. I gestured to Johnny. "This is my geologist."

Johnny kept his face passive, which was a lucky thing.

He didn't know a single thing about minerals or mining.

"I see," Benning said. "I'm looking for Heller, in fact."

"He and *Impaler* are positioned outside of Trieste. Running war games. As usual."

"He's not there now."

"No?" I raised an eyebrow.

"He left several days ago. Called every warsub around him into action, without senior permission, I might add. There were nearly a hundred of them. They went east."

"And?"

Benning sighed. "Disappeared, I'm sorry to say."

My guts were quivering. *Does Benning know?* I said, "We haven't come across them."

"We fear the worst."

I frowned at that. "A hundred warsubs and you fear the worst? But why?"

"Because of what happened at Norfolk just two days ago."

—••—

THIS CAUGHT ME OFF GUARD. I had no idea what he was talking about. "I'm sorry?"

Benning swore. "Someone attacked us, McClusky. Atlantic USSF HQ. Devastated us."

I leaned forward on the couch. "But that would mean war. Another country attacked the mainland USA?" There were always incidents occurring underwater. It was a new cold war, after all. The undersea colonies were engaged in espionage and attempts to one-up each other in the quest to capture as many resources as possible. The US was trying to gain control over The Iron Plains in the Pacific, while we were developing technologies to give us the greatest advantage in the oceans. It meant sabotaging other cities' efforts, stealing technologies, and even the odd assassination. Johnny and I had been partners in TCI years ago, and we were back together now, working to help Trieste. As Global Warming caused catastrophe on the surface, nations had realized that the oceans were the future.

"They even used a nuke."

"On the mainland?" I repeated.

"Not technically." His brow crinkled and he looked away as he processed the events in Norfolk. "They had a unique technology. It's confused our forensics experts."

"What was it?" I was now on the edge of my seat. My anger at Benning had transformed to curiosity.

"A vessel approached at over 400 kph."

"Supercavitating drive."

"Yes. Like this one. But it approached the seawall quickly, seemingly appeared from nowhere. We didn't have time to react. It then stopped, almost on a dime. Caused a tsunami."

I shook my head. I'd never heard anything like it.

He continued, "The tsunami hit the seawall, crumbled it."

"And Norfolk is right behind that wall."

"Yes. Our people are in pressure-controlled buildings at four atms."

I hesitated. "They were . . . exposed?"

"Yes."

"From a tsunami?"

"There's more. A nuclear-tipped torpedo, which the sub fired as it departed. Detonated underwater. It wasn't huge, only a fission bomb. But it broke the seawall right through. Water is still flooding in. It's affected millions, McClusky."

I shook my head. "I had no idea. We've been cut off. Prospecting where there are no junctions on the fiber optic lines."

"We still don't know who operates the ship."

"There is a sonar trace of it?"

"Yes, but much of the information is gone. It destroyed servers. The tsunami was a brilliant weapon." He leaned back and sighed deeply. "Nature is a more potent force than technology, it seems. We've been dealing with Global Warming for so many decades now. There's no avoiding it. And this attack used nature against us. A tsunami and the destruction of a seawall." And then he clenched a fist and stared at his white knuckles. "But we'll discover who did it. And we'll pay them back in kind."

It would mean outright war. So far, the tensions had been relatively quiet, confined to the fighting under the seas and on the seafloors. But this was something different.

I glanced at Johnny. The news had shocked him as well.

Benning said, his voice coarse, "I was hoping you might have heard something. That you might know who did this to us."

"Heller? But I told you—"

"And the attack on Norfolk. We need your help."

I stopped suddenly at that. We had been involved in a struggle against the USSF for thirty years. During the occupation, we'd been trying to keep them off our backs and their troops from harassing our people. To keep them from asking for too much. I looked at Johnny again; he was staring back at me. This might give us a way out of the situation. A way to escape the occupation.

And the attack on Norfolk would be a good way to explain what had happened to Heller and his ships.

I said, "I'll ask around. I'll investigate. If I hear something, I'll let you know."

"There's more," he said abruptly.

I stopped at that. "Go on."

"The ship that attacked."

My eyebrows raised. "You said there wasn't much information on it."

"Other ships gathered some data. It was hard not to notice, in fact. It had a SCAV drive after all."

It was difficult to hide a vessel that used it. They were so loud that ships appeared as white flares on sonar screens for kilometers around.

"The vessel was over 400 meters long, McClusky. *Four hundred*. It's a dreadnought. With a supercavitating drive."

———••———

I NEARLY CHOKED AT THAT. I knew what vessel he was referring to. Weeks earlier, while traveling the Mid-Atlantic Ridge with Johnny, we had come across it. It had been cutting across our path, and we'd stopped to watch and take sonar readings. It was 414 meters long, a hundred high with thirty decks, and was traveling at 467 kph. The ship had been using supercavitation to travel, and its wake had churned sediment from the seafloor kilometers below. The ship had perplexed me and Johnny. No superpower had such a vessel. The next largest in the oceans was the one Benning currently commanded, and it was half the size without such a drive.

I stared at Johnny. He had matched my look.

"What is it?" Benning growled.

I wondered for a moment if I should tell him. But there was no reason to keep it a secret. This ship would be a threat to us all.

And if we could connect that ship in any way to the ships that had just attacked us . . .

"I've seen this warsub," I whispered. "The dreadnought. We both have."

He rose slowly to his feet. "Where?"

"On a prospecting trip. A few weeks ago. Near the Mid-Atlantic Ridge. It was powering westward at 467 kph."

Benning swore. "I can't believe it. And you didn't tell anyone?"

"I told my security chief."

"But not Captain Heller?"

I snorted. "He's not approachable." I made sure to speak about him in the present tense.

Benning grunted. "Understandable." He thought for a minute before, "Listen to me, McClusky. This ship is a threat to us. To you too. *No one* fucks with us and gets away with it! We've lost HQ, a hundred warsubs, and there's a disaster underway in Virginia. We must find out who it is. It might also solve the mystery of Heller."

I started at that, but kept my cool. This man who was always so composed was showing a crack now.

The Admiral continued, "We need to work together. It could prevent us from establishing our influence on the ocean floors. Keep us from getting the resources that belong to us. The oceans are ours!" His face suddenly grew hard, and emotion that he held below the surface began to boil out. "We've worked hard to maintain a grasp on the seafloor resources. Our colonies represent our reach outward. We can't let go of those things, goddammit, and this ship is an obstacle. We need to find it. Find it, and destroy it."

He lurched toward me and thrust his face into mine. "And you're going to help."

Interlude:
Sheng City
Intelligence
Sheng City, China

Location: Sheng City Intelligence,
                   City Council Chambers
                   Sheng City, in the Taiwan Strait

Latitude: 24° 37′ N
Longitude: 118° 30′ E
Depth: 30 meters
Time: 1313 hours
Date: 22 April 2130

AGENT LAU OF SHENG CITY INTELLIGENCE gritted his teeth as the hatch swung open into the city council chambers. He had not been looking forward to this meeting. Although he was the grandson of Lau Tsi City's founder, he had no real prestige in any of the undersea cities anymore, a fact which still annoyed him after all the months since he'd lost the SCAV drive following the Johnny Chang debacle. The city leaders had blamed him for losing the technology, had accused him of conspiring with the mayor of Trieste City, and had even threatened him with execution for treason. It was all nonsense, of course. Lau had tried his best to steal the tech. He'd fought hard to bring the secrets of the supercavitating drive back to the Chinese underwater city, but he'd been unable.

Truman McClusky had proven too intelligent, too cunning, and too good in hand-to-hand combat. He'd matched Lau at every move until Lau had had no other option but to retreat.

It had happened a year earlier, and he had paid a price for his failure. His superiors had ridiculed him, assigned him low-level jobs like security for visiting dignitaries, and had even demoted him. And all of this despite the fact that his family had settled one of the Chinese underwater colonies in the previous century!

But Lau had endured the stress. He'd dealt with the consequences. His family had been forced to leave their city of Lau Tsi. He hadn't been happy—it wasn't an ideal situation—but he'd vowed that if he ever met up with Truman McClusky and Johnny Chang again, he would get revenge for what they had done to him.

Johnny had pretended to be a Chinese agent. He'd defected from the US colony of Trieste, professing his desire to return to his heritage and work for their underwater cities and not the Americans.

But it had been a lie.

He'd joined up with his former partner McClusky and had run back to the US colony at the first opportunity.

Yes, Lau thought. *If I get my chance, I'll kill them both.*

But no time for that now, he reminded himself. The city council had called him for a meeting. It couldn't be for another useless assignment. His immediate supervisor would have done that, as per the normal procedures.

No, he thought. It was probably much worse. Maybe execution for his failures, finally.

Or, he pondered with a glimmer of hope, maybe it was to finally send him on a real mission, one that involved protecting the city, something which he had wanted all along. To help the city prosper.

Sheng City was doing quite well, in fact. Produce increased every year, as did immigration applications. That part wasn't odd, for the environmental destruction on the surface was progressing at a rapid pace. But the economic indicators all showed the city as one of the fastest growing municipal economies in all of China, not just in the oceans. There were only six Chinese colonies in the oceans, but Sheng was the most powerful in terms of total revenue and produce generated. Located in the Taiwan Strait just off the coast of Kinmen Island, China had chosen it to bring Taiwan back into the Chinese sphere of influence. No more pushing for independence by them, he thought.

And yet . . .

So many places now seemed to be clamoring for it. Hell, even the underwater cities had been speaking of it. Of course, not in open audience or in public spaces. Only in private. Only at city council meetings, or at

Sheng City Intelligence sessions.

Lau didn't really have much say in such things, however, and he wasn't really interested. He just wanted to work hard and see the city prosper, as with most undersea inhabitants.

But now Lau marched into the council chambers and noticed the fifteen people seated at a curving desk against the exterior bulkhead. Behind them, a panoramic viewport stretched around the chamber, showing the beauty of the undersea environment. Kelp swayed in the distance, fish darted about, sun beams sliced through the ocean from above, and vessels and scuba divers cut through the water easily, going about their business.

The fifteen councilors were on a raised platform, where they could look down at him.

Literally as well as figuratively, he thought with an inward growl.

"Agent Lau Hwuan, we called you today to speak with you about an urgent matter."

Lau dipped his head slightly. "The honor is mine. Do you have a mission for me?" He addressed the man in the center, the one who had spoken. He was the leader of the council, the oldest serving member, and effectively the mayor of the city.

He also led the intelligence agency.

"For a year now we have been in discussions with Trieste City Intelligence."

Lau nearly choked at that. He wanted nothing more than to destroy that city along with its mayor. He managed to keep his face stony. Somehow. "And?" he finally managed.

"They have offered us a gift in exchange for joining them in their struggle."

"Struggle for what, exactly?" Though he already knew the answer. Inside, his guts tightened. He wanted to scream.

The elder said, "Independence. They want to fight their colonizing nations and win their freedom. They want us to join them."

Lau snorted. He had been involved in the battle in the Gulf of Mexico when Truman McClusky had surrendered to USSF Admiral Benning. He'd just given up then. He had offered a great gift to the Chinese underwater cities as well; in fact, Lau had helped set up the communication at the time.

"Yes, you were there. You relayed the message to us."

"It was a foolish thought. It went nowhere."

A deadly silence settled over the chamber. The lights were low. Each council member had one on his desk, illuminating any papers they might have, and there was one large dome light over Lau's head, right above the center of the floor.

Lau was starting to sweat from the heat, in fact.

"Why foolish?" came the rumbling voice. "And watch what you say to us, founder's grandson or not."

He swallowed. "I meant no disrespect. But it was a ploy to get us to leave the battle. Instead we could have—"

"It was no ploy, as I said. We've had meetings with Trieste's emissary, Johnny Chang."

Lau hadn't known this. His face flattened in surprise. "You have?" *And why didn't you tell me?* he wanted to yell.

"He has even brought the supercavitating vessel to our city for us to examine. The technology and the vessel impressed our scientists."

Lau had the sudden urge to ask if he could just go steal it, then he realized that he and Johnny had already tried that. And failed. He studied the elder's face. His name was Chan Ho Lee, but everyone just referred to him as 'Sir,' 'Mayor,' or 'Elder.' "And?" he prompted.

The elder looked to his right and left, at the other councilors. "We have been discussing it. It would mean war, of course, but we would have a distinct advantage. The vessel goes nearly 500 kilometers per hour. We could also adapt it to our own warsubs. Already we have a better hull technology and can dive deeper than most other nations. But with that sub . . ." He trailed off and looked down at his papers.

"What do you want of me?" Lau asked, exasperated. He didn't want anything more to do with McClusky and Johnny Chang of Trieste. Unless it meant their deaths, that is.

"Go to Trieste. Speak with their mayor. Agree to their demands and get us that SCAV drive."

Once again, Lau wanted to scream, but he could only comply. He clenched his teeth and forced himself to respond. "I will do as you ask."

"Get it here as soon as possible."

There was something in his voice, Lau thought. It had changed slightly as he'd said it. "Why the rush?" Lau asked.

The elder glared at him. "Are you questioning me?"

"No. But as your agent, I need to know if there is a time factor involved here."

There was a long, painful break. And then, "We are worried. The attack on Norfolk."

Lau blinked. "What does it have to do with us?"

"We've heard that the warsub was larger and more powerful than anything else currently in the oceans. A dreadnought. And the oceans are our salvation." He sighed and leaned back, closed his eyes and put his head back on the chair's headrest. "Mayor McClusky was right. Things are coming to a head. The superpowers of the world have realized how important the resources of the ocean are. We need to carve our piece of them."

"But China is doing that already."

"We will not work for other people!" the elder cried. Then he took a deep breath, as if he had to calm himself. He continued, "We work hard in the colonies. We want what's best for our people. For undersea dwellers. Not topsiders, even if they are Chinese. For us, it is to work for ourselves." There was another long and horrible silence as the elder seemed to ponder the dilemma. "This powerful warsub is a problem. It attacked the United States. It has incredible technologies. Our spies in America tell us that it has confused them as well. But if it attacked them, it will surely attack us. We must prevent that. Things are too precarious now. The seawalls that surround Chinese coastal cities are easy targets, as this dreadnought proved. We have to strike out on our own, try to make a place for ourselves in the oceans."

"Have you discussed this with the other colonies?"

"Yes. The emissary went to them as well. Some are with us, some are still undecided."

"But what happens when China learns what her undersea colonies are doing?"

The elder paused again. "Hopefully by then it will be too late."

"They'll crush us."

He raised a finger. "Only if it serves their purpose, Lau. Only then."

Lau felt like laughing, but one glance at the guards flanking the door he'd entered convinced him otherwise. "How wouldn't it?"

"If they need something we have, of course."

"And that is?"

The elder shrugged. "Technology. Resources. Minerals. Food. If we can still provide all that to them, and more than we have before, then we can survive as an independent nation."

"Allied with . . . allied with . . ." He couldn't even say it.

"With Trieste? And the other US cities? If need be. Now go do your job, before we find someone else who can."

Lau could barely nod his head.

"And if you fail again," the elder grated between clenched teeth, "then this time you *will* end up dead. If not by them, then by us."

Part Two: Missions

Trieste City,
United States
Continental Shelf
30 Kilometers
West of Florida

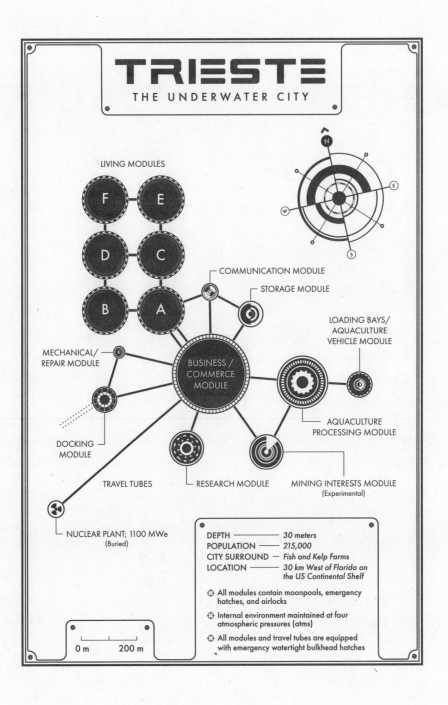

TRIESTE
THE UNDERWATER CITY

LIVING MODULES

F E
D C
B A

COMMUNICATION MODULE

STORAGE MODULE

LOADING BAYS/
AQUACULTURE
VEHICLE MODULE

MECHANICAL/
REPAIR MODULE

BUSINESS /
COMMERCE
MODULE

AQUACULTURE
PROCESSING MODULE

DOCKING
MODULE

TRAVEL TUBES

RESEARCH MODULE

MINING INTERESTS MODULE
(Experimental)

NUCLEAR PLANT; 1100 MWe
(Buried)

N
E
W
S

DEPTH —————— *30 meters*
POPULATION ——— *215,000*
CITY SURROUND — *Fish and Kelp Farms*
LOCATION ——— *30 km West of Florida on*
the US Continental Shelf

⊕ All modules contain moonpools, emergency
hatches, and airlocks

⊕ Internal environment maintained at four
atmospheric pressures (atms)

⊕ All modules and travel tubes are equipped
with emergency watertight bulkhead hatches

0 m   200 m

Chapter Five

BENNING DEPARTED THE SEACAR WITHOUT EVEN looking back. He'd had incredible composure during our discussion—until the very end, that is.

"He cracked a little bit there," Johnny said. "I've never heard of him being like that."

"The attack on Norfolk really rattled him," I said. As well it should have, I thought. It signaled a tremendous weakness to the land nations of the world. Seawalls could hold back rising waters, but not for long. Or not safely, at least. Eventually they could give way, due to a natural disaster like a hurricane or an earthquake.

Or a tsunami.

It was odd though. How did the warsub do it? Even though the vessel was large and fast, something still seemed off about it.

Benning had sent us away with one final request: wait for orders. He was going to investigate more, study the forensics of the sonar signatures that other ships had captured, and then contact us again. In the meantime, we were to continue researching to see what we could discover.

Lancombe, Ng, and Lazlow had returned from the engineering compartment, we'd sealed our airlocks, detached umbilicals, and continued to Trieste. The *Swords* were with us, and we all traveled with conventional drives now. No need to further attract Benning's attention, I thought.

The others had heard the entire conversation. Lancombe said, "Do you think he could be lying? Could they know what really happened to Heller?"

"I don't think so," I answered. "They would have just arrested us on the spot."

"Who's operating the dreadnought?" Ng asked. "If it's not American, is it Chinese?"

"It's possible," Johnny said with a shrug. "Although Mac and I saw the thing. It didn't look like any Chinese design."

A long silence stretched over us. Lazlow was deep in thought. He wanted to get back and start reviewing the tapes of my previous encounter, as well as the recordings of the invading force at The Ridge. If anyone could figure it out, he could. I had faith in him.

Whatever the case with Benning, one thing was certain—it was a stroke of luck that he hadn't suspected us of destroying Heller and his fleet of a hundred warsubs. It was probably unthinkable, anyway, which is why it had never occurred to him. How could the mayor of a small undersea colony have destroyed so many USSF vessels?

We traveled slower toward Trieste, more anxious than ever to arrive.

—••—

IN TWO MORE DAYS OF TRAVEL, Trieste finally appeared on our scopes. It was beautiful. With a central module for commerce and command, and others for living or for work radiating out along travel tubes with transparent ceilings, it was stunning. The central unit had a clear skylight as well, and an atrium that led right to the bottommost level. Natural light penetrated to the lowest deck as a result; it was the most beautiful module in all the undersea cities.

The other sectors of the city included docking, mining interests, aquaculture, storage, repair, and communications. There were some other smaller ones as well. The city was at a depth of thirty meters. Each ten meters of water was one atmosphere, and with one natural atmosphere *above* the waterline, that equaled four.

Each module had moonpools at seafloor level, for easy entrance and exit—one could dive right into open water and swim out into the ocean—and there were airlocks on each level in case of catastrophe.

I recalled the depressurization emergency a few weeks earlier. The French had caused it—somehow—to capture or kill me. I hadn't been back since, and so didn't know if my security chief Cliff Sim had been able to catch the culprits. I'd have to ask him.

I gave orders to the *Swords* to dock in the storage module, where we could lock the vessels away from prying eyes. I then swung *SC-1* around to the west side of the city, and with Sea Traffic Control's permission, entered the docking module. Grant Bell sounded thrilled at my arrival, was intensely curious about the twenty-eight other vessels, but kept the commands professional and directed us in.

Making the ballast positive so the seacar was lighter than the water we displaced, the vessel rose to the surface, I piloted her into our berth, and shut the thrusters down.

Home.

—••—

IT WAS A BITTERSWEET FEELING. I hadn't been prepared for it. After all, this was where I'd spent the last year as mayor with Katherine at my side.

And now she was gone.

I'd lost her, and I was going to have to get used to it.

Along with that, there was something else gnawing at me, but I was keeping it hidden just below the surface. But soon I'd have to deal with it.

There was a pit of dread in my gut.

I glanced at the others; they all had smiles on their faces. "Back to business, I guess," I muttered.

Lazlow grinned even wider. Despite his expression, he didn't look good. He'd lost a lot of weight and his face was skeletal. His beard was growing unkempt.

He said, "If you don't mind, Mac, I'd like to get to work on those signals immediately."

I plucked the chip from the console and held it up. "Here's the sonar data. Cliff Sim has the other one for you to study." I was referring to the one of the dreadnought, which Johnny and I had recorded weeks earlier.

He snatched it from my grasp and turned to ascend the ladder. His spidery fingers wrapped around the first rung, and I stopped him with a cough. "Uh, Lazlow."

He looked at me. "Yes?"

"How do you feel?"

"Never better. I love this life."

"You do?"

He chuckled. "Of course. I spent decades on land conducting acoustical experiments, just dreaming of coming here. To the undersea world."

"I realize that. But—"

"But what?"

I sighed. "Nothing. Just take care of yourself."

"I always do! That's why I'm here, isn't it?" And with that he climbed the ladder and was on the hull in a flash. His agility for a man of eighty surprised me.

Lancombe and Ng had watched the entire exchange. "He's looking like he's lost weight," Ng muttered.

I waved it away. "Let's check on him later."

She nodded. "We're going to get to work now, Mac."

I blinked. She was referring to the improvements to city defense we'd been planning. "Already? Don't you want to rest?"

"We've been resting for thirty years! Time to start!"

—••—

ONCE IN THE MODULES AND TRAVEL tubes of Trieste, I looked around and took several deep breaths. I felt more comfortable there than anywhere. It was a feeling of familiarity for me. I'd lived there since the early 2090s, when dad had brought the family during the escalating environmental crisis on the surface. He'd had the foresight to look ahead and predict what would happen. Once in Trieste, he had entered city politics and

Triestrians soon elected him mayor. His warnings and fears about the USSF taking over had clearly appealed to the citizens. He had been very open about his desires. And then—

The shit hit the fan, to be blunt.

He got involved in the move for independence from the States, and they killed him to stop it.

I'd spent thirty years believing that he'd been naïve and ignorant of the reality of the situation. About what the States would do if they felt he was going to take Trieste away from them. My worries had been borne out, but all was not as it had seemed, for I had just found out that he'd known the assassination was going to happen. He'd *let it happen* so people would resent our colonizers even more. To delay the independence movement until we had more power, better technology, and until we could fight back and win. The simmering desire for freedom had burned for years, just under the surface.

Until his son was in charge, that is, and Trieste had weapons powerful enough to fight.

The city's travel tubes were three meters high with transparent, curved ceilings that showed an incredible array of life surrounding the city. The sun was high in the sky far above, and its rays cut downward toward us, shimmering and shining over the modules of Trieste. There were also divers and vessels out there, and no matter the direction I looked, it was like a scene from a storybook.

Some of the travel tubes were so long that conveyers were needed to move people quickly to and from work shifts. Triestrians wanted to work, wanted to succeed. Even though we only required them to do one eight-hour shift and then have two off, people routinely did a shift at their regular job, then a half shift at a volunteer job.

I took another breath.

It had been a tough couple of weeks, but we had persevered. The city was still there, her citizens were happy, and we had scored a tremendous victory.

From the docking module, I moved into the central commerce and economic module, the largest in the city. People I passed smiled and waved. They were thrilled to be underwater, excited to be pushing the frontier outward.

At the uppermost level, I stood at the balcony and looked down nine stories to the lowermost deck. Trees and vines ringed the rails. The ceiling was transparent and natural light illuminated the entire facility. We'd dug five stories down through the sediment into bedrock, and four stories up— we could go no higher for fear of large surface vessels scraping the top of the module—and the atrium was fifty meters across. It was a large open area, sunlit and shimmering, with stores and businesses and administrative offices fronting the balconies, along with cafes and restaurants and pubs. Triestrians marched around the perimeter, on their way to work, many carrying scuba gear and dripping water onto the deck—there were drains everywhere for just such a thing—and some were sitting in chairs and taking a moment to relax, drinking kelp tea and eating lunch from resources we'd farmed just outside.

Yes, I thought. Without exception, the people were happy.

Then something else occurred to me, something odd indeed: There were no USSF troops. They'd all boarded *Impaler* days earlier and had left for the battle.

An uncomfortable blanket settled over me, nearly suffocating. I stared down at the levels surrounding the atrium, at the people who moved about.

My heart pounded.

It took me a moment to catch my breath.

— •• —

WITHIN A FEW MINUTES, THE EPISODE had ended. Dizziness had almost overwhelmed me. If it had occurred the year before, I would have wondered what had caused it.

But now, after all that had happened, I knew.

Admiral Taurus T. Benning was also on my mind. The man had assassinated my father, I had just come face to face with him, and I hadn't killed him.

I knew I would have to deal with it when the opportunity presented itself. When I next saw him, perhaps. But there was a massive dilemma confronting me: Would I sacrifice all that I had created for Trieste, and throw away the independence movement and the struggle for the new nation of

Oceania for something as basic as *revenge*?

He'd also spoken about the militaristic and colonial demands of the USSF. It had pissed me off. He'd been quite open about extending US control over the oceans of the world and using Trieste to achieve it.

We would not let them use us.

We were not his *tools*.

The evidence of their inability to extend their reach into the oceans safely was all around. Industrialization on the land had scorched the Earth, had turned arable land to dust, had changed the atmosphere and melted ice caps. Whole countries had disappeared and refugees flooded the interiors as fast as water flooded the coast. It was a global disaster.

But despite that, he'd been right about one thing: The dreadnought was the priority. We had to figure out who operated it and decipher their motives.

And hope they didn't strike again.

—••—

THE TRIESTRIANS WHO HAD BEEN WORKING at The Ridge constructing *Swords* were now back home. They had docked in the storage module and I assumed they were in the process of finding their families and explaining where they had been. I had given them strict instructions: They were not to discuss independence, not to mention the battle in the rift, and were not to mention what they had been doing for the past year. They were to say only that they were away working for the city, had been out of communications reach, and they were sorry but could say no more.

I knew it wouldn't satisfy the families who had been grieving for their missing people for the past year, but it was the best we could do.

Thinking about The Ridge brought Jackson Train to my mind. He was still there. Trapped behind the collapsed tunnel and a watertight hatch. He'd been there now for three days.

There was also another mission I had to launch soon, and I would combine the two when I could.

Chapter Six

THE CENTRAL MODULE ALSO CONTAINED TRIESTE'S control center. It was a large room with consoles to monitor and control every aspect of the city's engineering demands, from the nuclear plant to pressure control to water traffic surrounding our modules. My staff was there, light from their consoles shining up in their faces, headsets on, all murmuring commands over the comms to others around the city. Along one entire bulkhead was an expansive map of the Gulf and Caribbean region with all traffic in the area—generated from sonar information from our monitoring stations as well as from other vessels. There were three large blue stars on the map, each just off the coast of the States. These were the three underwater colonies of Trieste, Ballard, and Seascape.

My staff looked up as I entered, and their faces erupted into surprise and happiness. It made me smile. They wrapped up their work and rose to their feet.

"Mac!" called Joey Zen. She worked the Pressure Control station. "Where have you been?"

Kristen Canvel at City Systems Control marched toward me. "You can't just take off like that!" I couldn't tell if she was angry or not; her tone was harsh, but the smile on her face said otherwise.

I said, "I told you when I left. I put Cliff Sim in command." He was our security chief.

"You also took our deputy mayor with you! Cliff doesn't know squat about politics."

I frowned. "Why? What's going on?"

Braeden Staple shrugged. "Just the usual complaints from the kelp farmers. The repair module is also overwhelmed. Cliff doesn't know what to do. He just delayed them all, saying you'd be back soon."

I recalled that I had taken some workers from the repair docks to work the fields. The USSF had demanded more production from all sectors—we provided fish, kelp for methane and food, as well as many minerals from deep-sea mining ventures—and it had been the only way to help the aquaculture division.

"I'll take care of it."

"And where is *Impaler*? Have you noticed that there are no USSF troops here right now?"

"I did, actually."

Grant Bell from Sea Traffic Control, still wearing his headset, said, "*Impaler* left here when you did. She was following you. All the troops boarded her just before. She still hasn't returned."

"I'm sure they'll be back," I muttered. But I didn't say it with much conviction.

The others just stared at me.

"I guess we should just be happy for as long as they're gone."

"Agreed." I gestured to my office. "I'll be catching up on work."

"Wait—where's Deputy Mayor Butte?" Kristen asked.

"He won't be back." I said no more.

There was a long pause as my command staff looked at each other in bewilderment. Then I turned to leave and I heard, "Good to have you back, Mac!"

—••—

MY OFFICE WAS MOSTLY BARE STEEL and bland, with gray rivetted bulkheads and a tiny viewport. There were no amenities. I remembered the other mayoral offices I'd seen on my trip to Seascape and Ballard. Mayor Winton's had been significantly nicer, with painted bulkheads even, and Mayor Quinn's at Seascape was simply opulent, complete with an oak desk.

A wood desk, underwater.

It was unheard of, but it spoke to the power of his city due to the tourism industry.

I sat at my metal desk and with trepidation, checked my mail.

I swore.

—••—

HOURS LATER, I WAS STILL SIFTING through the messages and doing what I could to assist department heads and managers who were asking for—or *demanding*—assistance. Soon I came across a message from the repair dock; I knew immediately what it was about.

"Dammit, Mac!" an angry voice yelled on the recording from ten days earlier. His face was on the screen. Behind him were berths filled with seacars down for maintenance. Sparks were flying across the scene as workers crawled on hulls and worked on the vessels. The man was Josh Miller, in charge of the repair division. "You took ten people from my docks and now we're overwhelmed!"

Sure enough, behind him each berth was full. Crew were only working on a few of the ships; others were just floating there, untouched.

Miller was wearing overalls with grease stains, there was a tool belt thrown across his shoulder, and his hair was, like most other people in the colonies, shaved to stubble. It made drying easier. He continued, "We're important, dammit! If we fall behind on repairs, what do you think happens to our quotas? No machinery means less produce. Do the math!" Then he stabbed at the comm and the image turned blue.

I sighed. Politics. Miller just wasn't aware of the other issues surrounding the quotas.

I considered my response, and then called the man back. He was on the screen in a few seconds, from a different angle this time, though I could still see some of the same ships floating behind him. There were new vessels there as well now too—many of these hung in harnesses over the water. There was no room for them.

"Josh," I said.

"You're back." His voice was hard, his face lined and angry.

"Yeah. I hear your concerns, trust me. I agree with you. But you have to realize that yelling and getting angry isn't going to solve much."

He snorted. "It's pretty clear to me though."

"And it's obvious to me too. I understand the issue." I sighed and leaned back. "The quotas went up ten percent."

He paled. "What?"

"The USSF demanded more."

"Then get more workers—"

"I did. From you. I couldn't bring any more from the mainland."

"But we don't have enough—"

"Exactly. We don't. Which is why I had to transfer a few people." I hesitated and he mercifully remained silent while I considered. "The good news is that our quotas might come down a bit now."

He frowned. "But you just said they went up ten percent."

"But *Impaler* has disappeared. Heller too. No one knows where they are." I tapped a pen on my desk. "I'll move a few people back to the docks from the kelp farms. Send me five names. You'll get them before tomorrow."

His face lit up. "That'll really help. Thanks, Mac."

I leaned forward. "No worries. And listen to me for a second—screaming and yelling isn't going to get your point across as effectively as plain talking with some logic behind it. We're better than that."

He sighed. "Sorry, Mac. I'm just passionate about Trieste."

You and everyone else here, I wanted to say. "I know."

He offered a slight smile. "Thanks for your help. I really appreciate it."

I nodded and cut the transmission. Damn. Now I would have to call Rebecca Hartley in aquaculture and give her the bad news.

But the positive was that with Heller gone, the increased quota might no longer even exist.

Being a politician was a tough gig. I used to be a spy. Hell, I still was one, but politics and managing were more delicate skills. Spying and espionage were clear. There was no dealing with emotional and overly sensitive people. Still, I understood Miller's passion. I held it too.

—••—

AN HOUR LATER I DECIDED TO visit my security chief, Cliff Sim. His office was just down the corridor from City Control. He was everything that a security chief should be, I thought as I marched in and saw him at his desk: He was gruff, big, and tough. He was a former USSF soldier and understood the importance of discipline and the chain of command. He was loyal and trustworthy—so much so that I'd left him in charge during my recent trip to The Ridge. There were no viewports in the office; like mine, his was basic and gray. He likely thought a port might allow someone to spy on him.

"Hi, Boss," he said as I entered.

"Cliff. Good to see you." I sat across from him. "You're not surprised I'm back."

"I've known for hours."

That startled me, but I should have expected it.

"How was your trip?" he asked.

"Great, actually."

He eyed me. I noticed the scar that cut through his eyebrow as he studied my facial expression, which I kept stony. He said, "You're back."

I frowned. "I think we've established that."

"Without Robert Butte."

"Yeah. He won't be returning."

Cliff looked away as he processed that. He lowered his voice. "Dead?"

"No. Just . . . sent away."

"I see. Good choice." Cliff had known about Butte's traitorous activities with Captain Heller. In fact, he had monitored the man at my command, and he'd gathered video evidence of Butte traveling to *Impaler* to inform on my activities. "And Heller?" he asked, voice even lower.

"Won't be back. Ever."

His eyes went wide momentarily. It was more emotion than he usually showed. I wasn't worried about anyone overhearing us. Cliff routinely swept my office for bugs; I knew his office would be safe.

"Interesting," was all he said.

"Tell me what happened while I was gone."

He nodded and gave me a detailed summary of the demands and complaints of the city's divisions, the routine city maintenance that crews had completed, and finally news of the depressurization incident that had forced me from the city a few weeks earlier. He had located the cause of the failure in the pressure equipment that had led to the module's environment plummeting to only one atm. It meant the ocean had flooded in through the moonpool and into the upper decks.

"But how did they flood? The airtight hatches—"

"They sabotaged that system too. Some closed, some didn't."

I sighed. I hadn't seen my living compartment yet.

He noticed me mulling that over. "Don't worry. It's all cleaned up."

I blinked. "Great work."

"I had a volunteer crew do it in their off time. They understood the importance."

"And the culprit?"

He paused. "French. Infiltrated a day before. Left using the same method."

"Let me guess. Through a moonpool."

"You got it."

I swore. It was a big problem for the undersea colonies. People were free to come and go as they chose. Some entered through the docking module where they parked their seacars. Some, however, swam up to the city, leaving personal scooters or vessels drifting outside, and entered through a moonpool, which each module had. The moonpools were at seafloor level and since the air pressure within exactly balanced the pressure outside, the water couldn't rise into the city. It was an easy way to sneak in. In fact, I had used it multiple times to infiltrate other cities throughout the world. English, French, Chinese.

"There's no way to stop that," I said.

"No. Not unless you want to close the moonpools and make everyone enter through one common module."

"Not going to happen." I wasn't even going to entertain that. We were not a police state. We'd just have to do a better job at monitoring sea traffic approaching Trieste, and keep the moonpools under video surveillance. I considered how to broach the next subject. "Listen, Cliff. I have a problem. I left someone behind."

He tilted his head. "Where?'

I hesitated. Cliff was totally loyal to us, but he didn't know much about the independence movement. In the past, he had mentioned his interest in helping, but I hadn't taken it any further than that. Until now. "Back at our base in the Mid-Atlantic Ridge."

He hesitated before a simple, "I see."

"It's Jackson Train. He's trapped."

"But he died in the battle last year. We never found—" Then his forehead flattened. "You're full of surprises, Boss."

"Thanks."

"And I have to say, nice going. I'm impressed." He had obviously put two and two together and now realized what I'd been doing and what had happened to Captain Heller.

"Thanks again. However, someone attacked us." He listened to the story in rapt attention. He remained quiet as I told him about the *Swords*, The Ridge, and the mysterious vessels. At that point, he broke in.

"Sounds like that other ship you mentioned to me."

"The dreadnought."

"The one that can't exist."

I frowned. "Why do you say that?"

"It's too big. It's too fast. I just can't buy it."

"Did you hear about Norfolk?"

He blinked. "Of course. We all have. Seawall broke."

"It was the dreadnought."

There was a long stretch as he stared at me. "How do you know?"

"Admiral Benning."

Cliff swore again. "Things never seem to settle down."

"No, they don't." I glanced around the sparse office as I thought about my next course of action. There was a sealed hatch in there; I knew that it led to a corridor with a series of prison cells. They were rarely used, however, for people in Trieste were there to work hard and not cause trouble. There was drinking, of course, and the odd issue that resulted from it, but it was rare. The USSF caused most of the problems in the city, not her citizens. "Tell me," I continued, "did Doctor Lazlow come to see you?"

"Yes. A few hours ago, right after you arrived from your trip. I watched him exit your seacar and come straight here."

My forehead crinkled and I gestured to his video screens. "You saw it there?"

"I did."

"Good. And did Lazlow tell you what he needed?"

"I set him up in the research module. Seemed appropriate. He said he wanted to review some sonar records."

"He's an acoustician. Thanks."

"I hope he can help."

"He already has," I muttered. Cliff raised an eyebrow at that, but I didn't say more about the man. "I ordered our *Swords* to dock at the storage module."

"I noticed that too." I couldn't help but laugh. But before I could ask him, he continued, "I've secured the module, posted guards, and the moonpool there is closed. No one will be able to get to them."

No wonder he was my security chief. He was not only effective and professional, he was intuitive. I said, "I need your help now, Cliff, more than ever." He listened to my request without saying a word.

Chapter Seven

KAT AND MEG HAD RECRUITED DOCTOR MANESH Lazlow to join our efforts months earlier. His arrival had been a mystery, for I just couldn't understand why we needed an eighty-year-old man in the movement. But once I'd taken him to the ridge and he began his true work on the *Swords*, he'd amazed me. His Acoustic Pulse Drive had allowed them to dive deeper than any warsub or seacar on Earth. The USSF didn't know about it yet, for we had destroyed Heller's entire fleet. The FSF, however, was now aware of it. We had let some of their vessels escape. I hoped they would get the message and stop chasing me, but I sincerely doubted it. They had proven that they were quite determined to catch or kill me.

Or both, probably.

They would catch me first, followed by months of torture, then a painful death.

I found Lazlow in a darkened chamber in the research module. I hadn't been to that area very often. There were teams of people there who operated on their own and preferred it that way. They worked at improving our scuba technology, our hull designs and sonar systems, along with anything else that would assist our colonization attempts under water. They were invaluable to Trieste.

In fact, I thought with a sense of anticipation, the APD would astonish them when they finally learned about it.

Lazlow was hunched over a desk in front of multiple monitors, some holographic, some flat screen, and wearing headphones. There was a look of intense concentration on his face. His eyes were closed. I hated to disturb the man, but he didn't yet know I was there.

"You really should keep this hatch locked," I said.

No reply. His eyes remained shut. I glanced around. There were empty shelves lining the small chamber. There were no viewports; it was an interior cabin roughly four by four meters. He had folded himself into the chair with elbows on the desk; he looked like a twig bent at right angles.

I opened my mouth to say it again and—

"I heard you," he whispered.

"Even with the headset on?"

"Yes. I'm listening to your recording."

I pulled a chair up to him. A series of graphs, tables, and fluctuating readings and charts lit the screens. It was gibberish to me. "I could have provided a nicer lab."

"I chose this one. Your security man Cliff was quite accommodating. He showed me a few others before this."

"But why an interior—"

"Less noise. I don't want to hear the ocean except for what's on these recordings. There's still a lot of ambient interference. Ventilation machines, pumps, announcements on the comms, mayors barging in. It's distracting. I completely sealed my lab topside so no outside sounds could penetrate."

"We're thirty meters below the surface, Lazlow. We need equipment to keep us alive. A lack of sound means danger here."

"I'm not complaining, just stating facts. Maybe I can soundproof this lab." And then he wrapped his long fingers around his headset, pulled it off in one quick movement and turned to look at me. "The recording is fascinating."

"Which one?" There were two: one of the dreadnought, and one we had just captured during our escape from The Ridge.

"The large warsub. You weren't lying, and Admiral Benning has a right to be scared. It really is over four hundred meters long."

"Yes."

He whistled. "More than four football fields. Wow. It's almost a hundred meters longer than the *Ford* Class aircraft carriers."

"And to be moving at 467 kilometers per hour underwater is just . . . astonishing."

"I would have said impossible a few months ago. But supercavitation has changed everything." He shook his head. "Katherine Wells impressed me. She'll go down in history, Mayor. She was one of a kind."

"Yes, she was," I muttered.

He pressed on as if he hadn't noticed the impact his words had had on me. "Her mind was remarkable! To use a micro-fusion reactor to flash-boil seawater for thrust. Just amazing. It wouldn't have occurred to most people. It's like the old days of steam engines on locomotives!"

"Produces lots of noise though. Hard to hide."

"True." He pointed at his screens. "But the way the water moves over the hull and any projections—like the thruster pods—sends acoustic signals out for us to decipher."

I blinked. "You can separate that from the noise of the SCAV engine?"

"Yes. *I* can, anyway. I've trained my brain, and I've created algorithms to help me along."

"So, you have an answer for me?" I leaned forward.

He hesitated. "An answer to what?"

"Who is operating the vessel?"

He shook his head. "I'm days away from that. I'm still investigating."

"Oh."

"But don't worry. I'll keep working."

I looked him up and down. "Make sure you get some sleep, Lazlow. And a meal."

He pointed behind him. "I'm sleeping there."

I glanced in the direction he'd indicated—steel deck and bulkhead. "Where?"

"There." He pointed again.

"On the deck?"

"Sure, why not?" He grinned and his cheeks sunk farther into his skull. "I've dreamed about this for decades. I am loving this experience, McClusky!"

I rose to my feet. "I'll make things more comfortable. But promise me you'll eat and have a shower."

"If I have time." He turned back to his work and put his headset on.

—••—

OUTSIDE, IN THE CORRIDOR, I CONTACTED City Control on a bulkhead comm. Kristen Canvel was on the screen in a flash, staring at me with bright eyes and a smile on her face. She wasn't hiding her happiness that I had returned safely to the city. "Hi, Mac."

"Please send a cot with blankets to this location." I recited Lazlow's lab number. "Also call someone to deliver some meals."

"Which ones?"

"Breakfast, lunch, and dinner."

"Got it." She reached out to terminate the call.

"And some snacks," I blurted as an afterthought. "Mid-afternoon and late evening." I mulled something else over and then shook my head. Too bad I couldn't deliver a daily shower.

—••—

I LEANED AGAINST THE BULKHEAD AND pondered the situation. The dreadnought had attacked the United States and caused enormous devastation. It had destroyed USSF HQ in the Atlantic. It had even used a nuclear torpedo to break through the seawall! A nation that did such a thing was not afraid to provoke a war. Only a nation that thought it could win would have done it.

Could it be the French? It was possible, but it didn't make sense. They had been after me for months. They'd tried to assassinate me, sink me, and had even used an EMP in the Gulf to disable SC-1. But if they had really wanted to kill me, they would have just sent that dreadnought to destroy the entire city.

Still, I realized that Johnny and I had come across that ship in the Atlantic by accident. They hadn't been searching for me.

Or had they?

It was a possibility that I hadn't considered before, but I shrugged the thought aside. It was an interesting theory, but I just couldn't picture the French using a nuclear bomb against a seawall to destroy USSF HQ.

Checking the schematics of the research module, I located a lab that I wanted to visit. It was one deck up and adjacent to the outer bulkhead. I only had to ascend one ladder, and as I did so a feeling of loss came over me. Lazlow had mentioned Kat without really acknowledging what had happened to her only a few days earlier.

We'd only just had the funeral.

Everywhere I looked, I saw her. She loved this city, I thought. She lived for this struggle.

I sighed and pressed on.

—••—

THERE WAS A SIGN ON THE HATCH that said NUCLEAR RESEARCH. I rapped on the steel and it slid open. There were three people within—two women and one man—and their eyes widened when they saw me.

I waved their reactions away and sat down. Like Lazlow's lab, there were shelves on the bulkheads and everything was bare steel. But this one had a viewport with a view of the open water to the south.

It took a moment for the three to find their voices. The man had a pencil behind his ear; the two women had clipboards and were reading numbers from charts and tables of some sort.

"Mayor McClusky," the man finally said.

"Hello. And you are?" I recognized him, but didn't know the name. There were over 200,000 people in the city, after all.

He swallowed and then shook himself out of it. "I'm Frank Walls." He gestured to the others. "These are Doctors Li and Williams."

I nodded at them. "You are a doctor as well, I take it?"

"Yes."

"Of nuclear physics?"

"Yes."

I studied our surroundings. "What do you do here?"

All three remained silent, confused by my question, until Doctor Li, a plump Asian woman with short spikey hair, cleared her throat. "Uh, we study the output of the fusion reactor at Trieste, research, and try to improve performance for our portable reactors that we send out to our mining interests in the area."

"Good. I need your advice."

——••——

BACK IN CITY CONTROL, I ENTERED my office and called the mining interests division. They were responsible for our efforts to extract minerals and send them topside. Some of the deposits were nearby, some much farther out. They prospected as well as mined; it was a difficult and dangerous profession, but they were passionate about what they did and preferred it if I left them alone. It wasn't our principal method of earning income for the city—this division was still in the research and development stage. But each month their output increased. Soon it would be just as important to us as the kelp farms.

The director came on the comm and smiled at me. "Mac. Good to see you again."

It was Laura Sukovski. She was direct and to the point, and totally competent at her job. She pushed for safety, which I appreciated for there had been too many mining accidents in the years while Shanks had been the director of TCI. After the battle and the USSF had taken Shanks— for probable execution—I'd replaced the previous director of mining with Sukovski. Since then, production had increased and accidents had decreased. Still, it was the most dangerous profession underwater, and injuries were unavoidable.

"Hello, Laura."

Her smile faded as she realized that it wasn't a social call. "Oh, shit. You're not calling to tell me the quotas are up again, are you?" Her eyes narrowed. "We're already—"

"No. It's not that. It's something else."

"Oh, good. We're really pushing our people."

I said without preamble, "I need you to start up a thorium venture."

She frowned. "What for?"

"I want you to mine some for me. I know you don't currently have a deposit in operation."

"No, but we do have a deposit."

"But you're not mining it."

She shrugged. "It's not necessary. There are other minerals that make more money. Iron, gold, titanium, molybdenum."

"I need thorium."

She frowned as she considered the request. "It's that important?"

"Yes."

"What's it used for?"

"Gas tungsten arc welding." That's what the nuclear research doctors had told me.

She frowned. "And it's just occurring to you now? We reported on the find months ago."

"I remember. But it's too expensive to import from land." It would also set off alarms at the USSF, I wanted to add.

She continued to mull it over, and then nodded. "Okay. I can do it. When do you need it?"

"Yesterday."

"Come on, Mac! Be serious. It takes time to set up an operation."

I sighed. "All right. How about two weeks?"

Her face remained blank. "Is that a joke?"

"I'm deadly serious right now."

She swore. But then, "Okay, okay. I think we can manage that. Barely. I'll be in touch."

"This is high priority, Laura. We need it."

She pursed her lips and stared at me in a long, painful silence. "It's dangerous. We need to take precautions."

"It's not harmful until refined and concentrated. You know that. I'm sure you'll be careful with it."

"Hey! I didn't agree to that! Only extracting—"

"Good luck," I said. Then I cut the comm before she could say more.

—••—

A minute later, Meagan walked into my office in a huff. It was easy to tell when she was angry. Twins always knew what the other was thinking, after all. Meg had been angry for a big chunk of her teenage years, following Dad's murder when we were fourteen. As soon as she hit eighteen she'd fled the city and had ended up at Blue Downs, the Australian underwater colony in the Tasmanian Strait. During her life there she had picked up a new occupation—seacar maintenance—had become proficient and in fact had started a thriving business. During it all I had joined TCI and made Operative First Class—but in secret. I'd had to lie to Meg during that period of my life, and of course she had suspected. It hadn't fostered a great relationship between us. That and the issues surrounding our early years. Dad's death had devastated our mother, who had never recovered and died a few years after Meg left. When Meg had returned to Trieste and discovered that I was in the intelligence business and running the independence movement—as Dad had—she'd been furious. But after seeing the supercavitating drive in action, she'd realized that we had a chance at it after all, and she'd joined up. Since then, our relationship had rekindled and we had grown closer. Closer than even before Dad's death.

But when she stormed into my office, I could tell that she was *pissed*.

"Hi Meg," I said with a grin. I knew it would just anger her more. I was her brother, after all.

"Fuck off," she growled. "What are you thinking?"

"Pardon?" It confused me; I had no idea what I had done.

"You went and connected to that USSF warsub and let Benning board *SC-1*!"

Ah. Of course. "I had to speak to him."

"He could have taken Kat's ship!"

"He didn't."

"He killed Dad!"

"I know that."

"He deserves to die, that son of a bitch!"

"I know that too."

"He could have captured you and ended the movement! He could have killed you for what we did to Heller and his fleet!"

"Yes. But he doesn't know what happened to Heller."

"You didn't know that."

"I took a chance."

Her face flushed and her blonde hair spilled across it. She brushed it aside angrily. "Shit, Truman!" It was all she could manage, and it made me smile.

"I really needed to talk with him. To find out what he knew."

She hesitated. "And?"

I smiled. "See? You're curious too."

"But you put yourself in tremendous danger! Trieste is depending on you!"

"We needed to know. Now we do."

"But after Kat—"

She dissolved into tears and I frowned. "What?"

"I loved her too, Tru. I can't lose you as well. You're the only family I have left. Dad's gone, Mom's gone, now Kat. Don't you understand?"

I sighed. Of course. It made sense. "I'm sorry. Really. You're the only person I have left too, other than Johnny. But everything hinges on hiding our activities from the USSF. We had to know. Trieste depends on it."

She wiped a tear away angrily. Then she jabbed a finger at me. "Don't ever do something like that again without clearing it with me first!"

I wrapped her up in my arms. "Okay. I promise."

Meg had been piloting a *Sword* at the time. She'd been forced to watch the meeting from hundreds of meters away, not knowing what was going on. No wonder she was acting this way. I filled her in on the dreadnought and USSF HQ and what Benning had asked of me.

"He wants you to investigate?"

"Yes. The dreadnought."

"Why you?"

"Lazlow is studying our readings now."

She sighed and stepped back. "It was still too dangerous."

"You've seen what happened to Virginia. The dreadnought did it."

Her face remained blank. "I didn't know that."

"We're going to have to deal with it soon. It represents a major shift in the balance of power in the oceans, Meg."

"I know." She tilted her head as she studied me. "What are you planning?"

I paused. "Right now I'm taking care of mayoral stuff. But soon . . . soon we're going to have to deal with the dreadnought. And Benning."

Her face grew hard once more. "And are you going to kill him?"

"You want me to?"

She gave a sharp nod. "Yes."

I stared at her for a long, silent stretch. Such a request was unlike her.

Chapter Eight

BENNING ARRIVED AT TRIESTE THE NEXT day.

It was the last thing in the world that we wanted at that point.

We had only just rid ourselves of Captain Heller, USSF troops, and USS *Impaler*, and then before we knew it another warsub showed up.

And this new one was significantly larger than Heller's.

Impaler had been a *Reaper* Class nuclear SSN attack boat. Two hundred and fifty meters long, with a max speed of seventy kph. But *Devastator*, Benning's command vessel, was a missile warsub. Two hundred and sixty-one meters and an SSBN, meaning it had ballistic guided nuclear missiles.

It was larger and more menacing in nearly every single category, with one exception: *Impaler*'s crush depth had been 3,850 meters, while *Devastator*'s was 3,000 meters.

Following my discussion with Meg, I'd gone for a walk around Trieste to clear my head and focus on the city's critical needs for both the short and long term. The people smiled and waved at me as I passed, children swarmed my legs at times, wanting high-fives and words of encouragement, and there was even the odd smile from a pretty lady as she wandered past. But I couldn't shake Kat from my thoughts. I hadn't really had a long-term loving relationship before her. Just casual sex and companionship. Other than that, Dad had set up me up for a history that was just too consuming. He'd sacrificed himself for his passion—*independence*—but his early death had thrown our family into disarray. Meg and I were only just coming to terms with it, and rediscovering our sibling love for one another, but it had irreparably hurt our mother. The whole incident made me curse when I thought about it.

He hadn't even said goodbye to me.

He'd walked away from our living compartment that night, knowing what was going to happen, and he hadn't even looked back.

Nothing.

He'd had a plan, as Lancombe and Ng had pointed out, but for the past thirty years the incident had left us all suffering.

I studied Trieste as I moved through it, almost on autopilot. It never ceased to astonish me. The transparent ceilings in the travel tubes. The expansive viewports in bulkheads showing the brilliant view outdoors. Daytime, with sunlight slicing downward to the sandy bottom and the kelp fields as seacars powered through the water, bubbles from cavitating screws soaring upward, and nighttime, which was even more stunning, as the city lights shone for a hundred meters or more around the city, attracting swarms of creatures that clouded the water. Seacars with blinking navigation lights, the bright blue light on the top of the commerce module, and the blinking lights leading to the docking tube and module.

We were an island of light in the night.

Everyone who lived in Trieste loved the city and understood that it was more than a grand experiment run by the United States. It was our life. Colonization had taken hold of us and each day we worked as hard as possible to make the city a success. The USSF occupation had smothered us slightly, but we had persevered. People went to work each day to produce kelp, methane, fish, minerals, and a host of other resources that we shipped topside. We even made tea, beer, and alcohol from kelp! We used to sell to countries around the world, but lately Heller had forced us to send it exclusively to the US for less money than other nations would pay. That was going to change.

Soon I found myself back in my living compartment, in Module B, and with trepidation pushed the divider aside. I'd expected to find a ruined living space, which was only four square meters, but the interior pleasantly surprised me. Sheets were back on my bunk, cleaned and folded. There were a few pictures in frames that volunteers had replaced. The only real damage the flood had caused was to electronics. Wires spilled from the comms on the wall and the desk, presumably to let them dry, and my computer was gone. The IT division had left me a note in its place, telling me it would be back in a few days.

There was no way to communicate with anyone, which might be a good thing, I thought. I might get a good night's sleep for a change.

It was a tiny area, with a small desk fronting a bunk. Above the bed were some shelves and drawers for clothes and personal items. There were no viewports and no bathroom—that was down the hall. It was for communal use.

I sat on the bunk and stared at the bulkhead.

Kat had visited the compartment numerous times in the past year.

—••—

A BEEP DISTURBED MY REVERIE AND I looked up, startled. The comms were not functioning, so where—

Damn. There was a Personal Communication Device under the pile of blankets. The IT people had probably put it there so Control could contact me in an emergency.

There goes my quiet night, I thought.

Kristen Canvel's voice floated to me as I pushed the button on the small device. "Mac, sorry to bother you."

I grunted. She was one of three people in charge of City Systems Control; they were also considered the mayor's assistants. All were completely competent and professional, and I relied on them for much of the administrative tasks the office required. "Go ahead."

"There's a call for you I thought I should put through."

I checked the time. It was 1900 hours, the sun was just setting up top, and I needed a break. "Can't it wait?"

"It's Mayor Winton of Ballard City."

I paused at that. Weeks ago, I had visited her and opened up about our independence movement. She had confessed her own plans to me, and it was there that Lancombe and Ng had approached and requested a meeting. This was an important call, after all.

"Good job, Kristen," I said. "Please put it through."

An instant later Grace Winton said, "Hello, Mac?" It was not a video signal—voice only.

"Hi, Grace, how are you doing?"

"Fine. You?"

"I'm all right."

She hesitated. "You don't sound convinced."

"It's been a tough couple of weeks. I just got back and it was a long day of city business."

She chuckled. "I know how it is." There was a pause and then, "I was thinking about our last meeting."

"Yes." I stopped at that. We had to be safe with this type of transmission. There was no telling who might also be listening.

"How did things go?" she asked finally.

"Things are good. No more *Impaler*. No more Heller as far as I can tell."

There was another long period of silence. "Do you know where he is?"

"No. Benning doesn't either. He thinks it's connected to the attack on Norfolk."

"When did you see the Admiral?"

"He stopped me while we were out on a prospecting mission. Told me Heller was missing, along with a hundred warsubs."

"Missing, huh?" She hesitated. "And what do you mean, *attack*?"

"Norfolk wasn't natural. Someone smashed the seawall on purpose."

She swore. "I can't believe it."

"Things are escalating, Grace."

"I can tell." She clicked her tongue several times and then said, "When we last spoke, you had mentioned needing my help. You were going to send us a vessel . . ." She trailed off.

I knew what she was referring to. I had offered her the supercavitating drive if she joined us in the struggle. She was now agreeing to the plan.

Perhaps it had been my honesty with her, or perhaps USSF troops in Ballard had pushed her too far as well. Then again, maybe she was just realizing that I hadn't been joking, that we were serious, and that Heller's disappearance had been at my hands.

I swore inwardly. Of course. Richard Lancombe and Jessica Ng had lived in Ballard for thirty years. They'd been part of the independence movement there, and had contacted me when I had visited Mayor Winton.

They were probably still in touch with that movement—and Grace Winton— and had told her about the battle in the rift.

I said, "Yes, I'll have one delivered immediately. But I could use some help from you as well."

There was a drawn-out hesitation. "I would be happy to join efforts on that project."

"Great. I need a specialist for our fusion plant. Do you have someone you can spare?"

"I do, actually. I'll send her over to you tomorrow."

"Is she . . . *trustworthy?*"

"Absolutely. In every way."

"Thanks, Grace. I see great things for our two cities in the future."

"Me too." She sounded genuinely thrilled.

If only Reggie Quinn at Seascape had shared our view of the looming struggles with the world's superpowers. We needed all the US underwater colonies on board if this was going to succeed.

—••—

As I LAY IN MY BUNK, the sounds of the ventilation fans and the air pumps whispering in the dark, I wondered if I was safe. The French saboteurs had depressurized the entire module to kill me, putting thousands of others at risk. We had been lucky that it hadn't killed anyone, but those spies had escaped.

They could return at any time.

I thumbed on the news feed as I tried to sleep. It was nonstop coverage of the escalating disaster in Virginia. Engineers were having difficulty shoring up the seawall, and water continued to flood the state. It had displaced millions, left citizens stranded on rooftops, and had killed thousands, not to mention the devastation at USSF HQ in Norfolk.

I drifted into a fitful sleep filled with nightmares of sinking ships and drowning crews.

—••—

THE NEXT DAY, I SENT JOHNNY to deliver a *Sword* Class vessel to Grace Winton. We were in City Control and staring out the viewport at the lightening water as the sun rose overhead. There were a few sharks circling the city, but our wildlife management division had already spotted them and had gone out to chase them away. I could see them, in bright orange wetsuits and scooters.

Johnny grinned at my request and said, "I hope I won't be gone for another year."

He was referring to the mission I'd sent him on to the Chinese underwater cities to do something similar. It had had mixed results. Some interest, but not much. Many of those leaders were too frightened of mainland China and the CSF to risk their lives on an independence plot. I would just give it time. I felt in my heart that things were going to turn in the oceans, eventually.

"Don't worry. You'll be back by evening. Unless you want to stay there for a day or two."

"No thanks, I'm anxious to start our plans here."

I grabbed his shoulder. "Thanks, partner."

"I'll work with Lancombe and Ng when I get back."

I frowned. I hadn't communicated with them since our return; I'd been too busy. But they had mentioned that they were going to get to work immediately. "What are they up to?"

Johnny blinked. "They're in the research module. Cliff Sim set them up."

I snorted. Of course. My security chief had taken care of it. "What are they doing?"

"They have a lab. They're arranging defenses."

I made a mental note to touch base with them later in the day.

An alarm sounded and I turned to Grant Bell at the Sea Traffic Control station. "What's up?"

He looked at me and shook his head. "Big contact coming into passive range."

That was thirty kilometers. "From which direction?"

"Straits of Florida."

I glanced at the large map on the bulkhead. Sure enough, there was a blinking light approaching on the course he'd indicated. It was USS *Devastator.*

Benning's warsub.

"Shit."

—••—

"MAYBE THEY'RE JUST PASSING BY," I muttered.

But Grant was speaking with someone over his headset and he grimaced. "Nope. She's coming here. Requesting to dock via umbilical."

The vessel was way too big to enter our docking module. Umbilical was the only way to dock, unless she wanted to send runabouts over.

"Shit," I repeated.

"You already said that."

"I know. But I was hoping . . ."

"I hear you."

We watched the blinking spot of light on the map slowly approach Trieste. Her speed was only thirty, so it would take a full hour before arrival. I considered my options. I couldn't prevent the boarding, and I couldn't keep her crew out.

I just hoped it wasn't a continuing occupation. Benning and I had spoken, and I thought I'd gotten my point across. At least, he had agreed with me about the required behavior of USSF troops.

In my office, I keyed the comm for Cliff. He answered in a flash. In fact, I realized, he seemed to always be there. I wondered absently if that's where he slept. "Go ahead, Boss."

I filled him in on *Devastator* and he swore.

"That was my reaction too."

"How many troops are they offloading?"

"They would never tell me something like that."

He remained silent as he considered it.

I said, "How is the storage module?"

"Under guard, though Johnny just took a vessel, as per your command."

"Yes. Please increase security there, but not visibly."

"Aye, aye."

It made me smile inwardly. He was former USSF, very military in his style and bearing.

I said, "Can you send a warning to Lancombe and Ng? I understand you set them up in the research module."

"I did."

"Also warn Lazlow. He's still studying the sonar recordings."

"Aye, aye."

I cut the comm and went back out into the control room to watch the map.

It was a *Terminator* Class vessel. There was a reason they had given it such a name.

Chapter Nine

WITHIN THE HOUR, THE ENTIRE CITY had heard about *Devastator*. I'm not sure how, but news travels fast, and it wasn't exactly secret. It made my heart sink. There had been a lessening of tension after Heller had pulled out—it had thrilled Triestrians, actually—but now the USSF was back.

Meg was at my side in a flash after she'd heard, and her face was drawn and tight.

Outside the viewport, the vessel powered slowly into view, a massive shadowy shape, and it ground to a halt next to the docking module. Hatches for torpedoes, grapples, mines, countermeasures, and airlocks covered her titanium-alloyed hull. There were also thirty-six missile hatches on the vessel, in two rows of eighteen.

Now it was Meg's turn to swear. "That is one hell of a weapon of war. Why didn't he stay in the Pacific to deal with the Iron Plains issue?"

"That ended after the Norfolk attack."

Maneuvering thrusters powered up to maintain station-keeping and an umbilical stretched toward the city. An anchor fell from the stern and hit the seafloor, causing sediment to rise like a mushroom cloud over the warsub.

I grunted at the visual and turned from the scene. "I guess I should go meet him."

"I'll come with you this time," Meg said, her eyes narrowed.

"Just be calm, okay? Trieste's future is on the line here."

"Since when are you lecturing me about being calm?"

"Since right now."

"You know what I think of him."

"I feel the same. But we need his help and support right now. He needs ours too."

"You're not going to give it to him, are you?"

"Absolutely I will. If he gets *Devastator* out of here."

"And what about—"

I didn't let her finish the sentence. "In time. In time."

We marched from City Control to *welcome* the USSF Admiral.

—••—

TAURUS T. BENNING WAS THE FIRST person through the umbilical, flanked once again by his two guards. Their faces were stony.

All three wore the blue uniform of the USSF. Crisply pressed, sleek, complete with sidearms on their belts and knives on their thighs. This was a symbolic weapon—scuba divers universally carried a knife in a thigh holster—though still deadly. It was always easily accessible to get one out of a tricky situation. I had used blades on countless occasions underwater, but as an operative in TCI, I had used my knife to kill and injure enemy combatants more than anything else.

I squared my shoulders as the man marched toward us.

Beside me, Meg growled.

"Easy," I whispered.

Benning stared at her as he stopped before us. "And you are?"

"Meg McClusky."

He blinked and looked at me and then back to Meg. "You two are married?"

"This is my twin sister," I said.

His eyes registered understanding, but they remained riveted to Meg. She was beautiful and men generally approached her daily around the city.

It wasn't just because of Dad and the fact that he was considered one of the most important figures in Triestrian history. With blonde hair and blue eyes, she was fit and an air of authority and intelligence radiated from her.

"Pleased to meet you," he finally said. His interest was obvious. Then he turned to me. "Mayor McClusky. I am formally requesting permission to dock at Trieste."

This made me frown. It was something that Heller had never done. The USSF did not have to follow such a tradition. I swallowed, caught momentarily off guard. Then, "What are your intentions, Benning?"

Now it was his turn to look surprised. It wasn't the answer he'd expected. "R and R for my crew. And I would like to converse with you about the dreadnought."

"Do you have more information?"

He hesitated and glanced around. "You could say that."

Meg and I locked eyes, then I turned back to Benning. "Very well. You are welcome to brief us."

His eyes narrowed slightly. "And my crew?"

"How many, exactly?"

"An entire shift. Eight hours. Then rotating to the next."

I calculated the number in my head. There were 210 people on his sub, working in three shifts, as at Trieste. It meant seventy USSF, stalking the travel tubes and modules of the city, probably drinking and causing havoc. I didn't have much say in the matter, however. "And what of the issues I mentioned earlier to you?"

"I spoke with the crew. They understand."

I cleared my throat. "On behalf of Trieste, I welcome you to the city."

It was painful to say it.

—••—

B<small>ENNING RETREATED TO HIS WARSUB TO</small> begin preparations for his crew to debark; we arranged to meet in my office an hour later to go over his news on the dreadnought. Meg and I marched immediately to the research module, to see Richard Lancombe and Jessica Ng in the lab Cliff had set them up in.

Perhaps we were feeling that with *Devastator* now hovering next to our city, we needed to discuss military measures and defenses to ease our worries.

Lancombe opened the hatch and smiled at our appearance. "Welcome, Mac."

"How are things progressing?" I asked. Meg and I entered and sat on stools surrounding a desk in the corner. Printouts and charts and video screens displaying schematics of our plans cluttered the lab already.

Jessica said, "Your man, Cliff, arranged this space for us. Thank you."

I studied her. She was an older Asian woman, quite pretty, and her hair was lighter from living underwater and frequent immersion in salt water. There were a few strands of gray, but not many. The salt had affected it more than age had. There were crow's feet at the corners of her eyes, her hair was short, but despite her age she was still lithe and graceful when she moved. It made me wonder what she had been like thirty years earlier, fighting for independence with my father. She and Lancombe had escaped when the CIA made their move, and people had assumed them dead, though no one had known for sure. Their appearance weeks earlier had shocked us.

"No problem," I said. "Have you heard the news?"

"No, what?" Lancombe said. He was older, with a lined face, but his eyes were sharp and bright and his movements swift and deliberate. Many years ago, when he was a younger freedom fighter, he would have been a formidable adversary.

"Benning is here. And *Devastator*."

His face paled. "They don't suspect, do they?"

I shook my head. "They still have no idea where Heller is. I want to keep it that way."

Ng said, "Then what is he here for?"

"To discuss the dreadnought." Then I snorted. "And for his crew to *relax*."

"Are they occupying Trieste again?"

I sighed and Meg and I looked at each other. "I'm not sure at this point. He wasn't clear. But he's acting . . . different, I'd say. More respectful than Heller."

"That's a good sign."

"It could be an act. We're meeting him in less than an hour. Meg and I wanted to check in with you, see if you need anything."

Lancombe smiled. "Let me show you what we're doing."

—••—

THEY WENT OVER THE PLANS IN detail. Meg took notes on what they needed, and what work crews we could spare to help them out. The biggest effort was going to be the false fish farms—bubble fences, which normally acted as enclosures to keep fish inside to raise for export, but these would contain torpedo launchers with conventional and SCAV torpedoes. If enemy vessels approached, we would target them from City Control, then launch from behind the shroud of bubbles. Since we had numerous other farms around the city, it would take an invading force time to identify which farms the torpedoes were coming from. If possible, anyway. Warsubs would be busy maneuvering and launching countermeasures to spend too much time watching our fish farms.

It was a fantastic idea, which we had come up with a few weeks earlier. It was now time to get moving on the plan.

There was also the anechoic tile strategy—to cover our modules and travel tubes to make it more difficult for sonar to lock onto us. Geometric indentations scattered sonar signals. Since we were a stationary target these made less sense than for warsubs, but Richard said, "Every bit helps, don't forget."

"There are viewports all over our bulkheads. The travel tubes have transparent ceilings. We can't cover those."

"No. But we can put the tiles wherever we can." He shrugged. "If it confuses an incoming torpedo just a bit, it might help our countermeasures."

Which brought up his next idea: countermeasure launch points around the perimeter of the city.

I gave the go-ahead on all three strategies, which they would start on immediately. Meg would arrange the work crews, led by Lancombe and Ng.

As I moved to depart the lab, I stopped and turned to look at the two.

"Are you still in touch with Grace Winton by any chance?"

Richard looked up from a clipboard. Then he set it down and pursed his lips. "That is a loaded question."

I sighed. I had to be delicate. "I know you're part of Ballard's independence movement, Richard. That's how you contacted me. But Mayor Winton seems to know more about Heller's disappearance than she's letting on."

He glanced at Ng. "Yes, we filled her in on the battle. She's running the intelligence agency at Ballard, along with the independence movement. She needed a little . . . *nudge*, shall we say, to move her along."

"She still wasn't sure about joining up with Trieste," Ng interjected. "But after we told her about the *Swords*, Lazlow's Acoustic Pulse Drive, and the major success you scored in the rift, she immediately joined."

"It blew her away, Mac. You and TCI have really impressed her."

I considered that. "Thanks for helping. But listen to me. *I'm* in charge. Only *I* decide what info goes out to others. I know that you've been with their movement for thirty years, but either you're working for us or you're not."

Lancombe frowned. "But we're all together on this, aren't we?"

"Yes, but the USSF thinks the dreadnought destroyed Heller and his warsubs. I want to keep it that way. If rumors start to circulate about us and the battle in the rift . . ." I trailed off and stared at them.

Eventually he nodded and again looked at Ng. "He's right. We can't be acting as lone wolves. We're here at Trieste and Mac's in charge."

Ng said, "I didn't think it would be a huge issue. We were just letting our people there know about the victory."

"I understand," I said, "but there will be time for that later. And you really should go through me first."

They nodded understanding. "Sorry, Mac."

"It's not a problem. Yet. Let's just work on these defenses."

Lancombe said, "I should ask, then, if you're okay with me sending these plans off to Ballard? They need to start similar defenses too."

I wondered absently if he had already decided to do that, but now realized he should clear it with me first. "Go ahead. Sounds fine."

He grinned. "Good."

Meg and I left the lab.

—••—

LAZLOW WAS DOWN A LEVEL TOWARD the interior of the module. The deck rang with each step, the ladders were steep, and every surface was gray steel. Muted commands over the comms echoed down the corridors. There was grating at our feet for water to slip through should there ever be a depressurization incident, or should a scuba diver walk by, dripping water. It was standard to all modules in all areas of the city.

The hatch slid open and Lazlow looked up from a computer. He still wore the same headphones. I absently noticed some dishes on the floor near the hatch.

"Are you getting your meals?"

He cleared his throat. "Yes, thank you. That was considerate."

"How are things progressing with the dreadnought and the mystery ships?"

He frowned. His usual smile was absent. "Interesting, you could say."

I filled him in on Benning and the fact that we would be getting more data for him within the hour. But when I asked about his progress and what new information he'd discovered, he remained tightlipped and turned back to his work.

He would say no more.

—••—

MEG HAD BEEN QUIET FOR A long time now. We marched together to my office in City Control and once inside, sat around my desk. Something was clearly bothering her.

She cursed under her breath. "It's just Benning." She ran a hand through her hair, exasperated. "That bastard has the gall to bring his ass here and come over like a welcomed guest! For Christ's sake, Tru, he murdered Dad! He cut into the travel tube, shot him in the head, then flooded the tube around him just to make sure."

I watched her silently for several moments. Like me, she had thought it had been a cut-and-dry assassination. "Dad knew it had been coming, Meg. He let it happen."

She snapped a look at me. "Or so Lancombe and Ng would have us believe."

"They knew him. They worked with him."

"And now we're trusting them with our defenses!"

I frowned. "You're saying you don't? Dad did. With his life."

"That's the problem! They let Dad go through with his hare-brained scheme! And then those two mysteriously got away."

"They left to plan for another day. *This* day."

"Did they?"

I blew my breath out in a rush. I understood where her skepticism was coming from. After all, they had waited a long time to reveal themselves to us. But I trusted them. "They were waiting until we had the ability to defeat the USSF. Now we do. Thanks to Kat."

She mulled that over. "The SCAV drive."

"And *SC-1*, yes. Now that we have it, and with Lazlow's pulse drive, we can beat them, Meg. And Lancombe and Ng know it."

She sighed. "I hope you're right, Tru. I really do."

My comm interrupted us. "Mac, Admiral Benning is here to see you."

"Shit," I muttered.

Chapter Ten

BENNING MARCHED INTO MY OFFICE AND barely looked around before he sat. Meg captured his attention, but only briefly. He nodded at her and then turned to me.

His guards waited outside, watching the controllers with narrowed eyes. The hatch closed.

"There's been another attack," he said without preamble.

It made me blink. "Where?"

"San Diego. The seawall is broken. Water spilling in now."

"Why haven't we heard?"

"Only just happened." He checked his watch. "Thirty minutes ago."

I exhaled. This was bad news. "Did they use another bomb?"

"Too early to say. But Pacific USSF HQ is there."

"You think that was the target." It wasn't a question.

"It's the common thread between San Diego and Norfolk."

I pursed my lips. Meg's face had gone white. I stared at her for a minute. "The dreadnought? Any more information on it?"

Benning growled, "They used the exact same strategy. Came up at over 400 clicks per hour. Stopped on a dime. Tsunami broke through."

"And the USSF buildings?"

He nodded, grim. "Windows smashed, pressure lost." He slammed a fist on his thigh. "That's the problem with our admin offices on the mainland. We have to keep them at four atmospheres, but it's a weakness. I don't like weakness." And then he looked around the office pointedly. "It might be better to have USSF HQ underwater. I've argued that for years, actually."

My blood ran cold. "You mean in an underwater city." *He couldn't mean Trieste.*

He shrugged. "Perhaps. Or some other facility, on the continental shelf somewhere."

A long, awkward silence ensued. Meg narrowed her eyes and glared at the man. It was a death stare, I thought. Thankfully, he didn't notice.

I flicked on the topside news and sure enough, every channel was running stories about San Diego. There were aerial drone views of the seawall, a hundred-meter section blown to rubble with bent rebar stretching upward like fingers grasping at the sky, water spilling through, and streets flooded, sending debris like cars and garbage and boats and seacars hurtling past buildings.

Fires were burning, smoke rising, and people had already climbed to rooftops and were waving their arms at the cameras, begging for help.

Benning swore at the images. "Goddammit! This is the last thing we need! For Christ's sake, we have to take that dreadnought out!"

"Do you have sonar readings of it yet?"

"From the Norfolk attack, yes. Not from this one though. But I will."

"Did you bring me the copy for my expert to examine?"

He reached into his breast pocket—hidden behind a series of medals pinned to his chest, which made me shudder—and removed a datachip.

"Listen, Mac." That made me frown, for only my friends called me that. He continued, "We need to work together on this. The dreadnought has changed the balance of power in the oceans."

"You don't need to convince me. I already agreed to it."

He offered a tight grin, but there was no mirth there. "Good."

I rose to my feet, thinking furiously. I had been mulling it over since our last meeting, in fact. "If we are going to defeat this mystery ship, we need to know more about it." I held up the datachip. "This will help. But we are also going to need others on this."

Meg was looking at me, worry on her features. I ignored her. On a sudden whim I said, "The USSF is desperate to stop this, right?"

His eyes narrowed. "The whole of the United States is, of which you're a part."

"I need to talk to some people. See if we can come up with a strategy."

"Not on your own. The USSF is very much involved."

I hesitated. His inclusion was the last thing I needed. However . . .

I shot a look at Meg, at her questioning gaze. "Of course," I muttered finally. "I'll keep you in the loop. Give me a few days first though. Then I'll fill you in."

—••—

FIVE MINUTES LATER, MEG WAS SCREAMING at me with fists on her hips. Her face was red. Benning had already left and I was sure the staff outside could hear her.

"What the fuck are you thinking?" she yelled.

I knew my sister, however, and I understood how not to escalate the situation. I sat back in my chair and let her rant until she'd exhausted herself.

She continued, "That bastard *cannot* be part of this! You can't let him in, goddammit! Now he's in the city, with his fucking troops, and you're inviting him to join up with us! What the—" She stopped and glared at me. But her breathing grew shallower. She tilted her head. "Unless . . . are you planning to take him out? Get him out of the city somehow and then . . . and then . . ."

I raised a hand. "Easy now, Meg. I'm not planning that just yet."

"But—"

"If we take him somewhere and he dies, then the USSF will most definitely reoccupy us."

"They already have!"

"We don't know that yet. It's just rest and relaxation, as Benning said."

"You trust him?"

"No. But there's no rush."

She swore. "I swear you infuriate me sometimes."

"Just hang tight. I have a plan."

—••—

KRISTEN POPPED HER HEAD IN A few minutes later, after the yelling had died down, and said, "Mac, you have an appointment I didn't know about?"

I turned to her. "Say again?"

"Someone's here to see you. You asked for her, apparently."

I glanced at Meg, who was now significantly calmer and sitting opposite me at the desk. "I don't recall."

"She's from Ballard City."

A light bulb went off in my head. "Yes! I forgot. Send her in." Meg was staring at me with a crinkled forehead. I said, "Mayor Winton sent her to help out."

"With what?"

Before I could answer, a tall woman entered. She had pointed features and medium-length brown hair. She was in her late thirties. "Mayor McClusky?" she asked.

We shook hands and I introduced her to Meg. Her name was Irena Rostilov, and she was a nuclear engineer from Ballard.

Her eyes remained riveted to mine as I thanked her for coming on such short notice. In fact, I realized, she hadn't even volunteered for this.

"I'm sorry," I muttered. "I didn't even ask you to come. I was speaking with Mayor Winton—"

"No problem at all!" she interrupted. "I'm thrilled to be here." She shot a look at Meg and back to me. "And to meet both of you. It's an honor."

I suppressed a smile. "Thanks." I considered something as I studied her. "What is your background? Your last name?"

"Estonian. We emigrated when I was young."

"Did you grow up in Ballard?"

"Yes. My entire life."

"Good."

She leaned back and said, "Now, what can I help you with?"

"I have a team of nuclear researchers here. Doctors Walls, Li, and Williams."

"I know all three." At my questioning glance she continued, "At symposiums. The reactor staff in all three US cities meet regularly to talk research and update each other on operations." She paused and then, "And since the USSF hit your reactor in the . . . *incident* last year, and crews had to rebuild it, we spoke quite a bit."

"We buried the plant this time. To protect it."

"Yes." She nodded. "A great idea. We've been pressing Mayor Winton on the same thing."

"Good. I've posed a dilemma to my team, but I need additional help. I was hoping you could assist."

———••———

T<small>HE NEXT ITEM ON MY LIST</small> for that day was a meeting with Cliff Sim. I gestured to Meg and she accompanied me on the short trip to his office. Her face was a picture of confusion. She had no idea what I was doing.

"What the hell did I just witness?" she muttered. "Why do you need a nuclear engineer or whatever she is?"

"Can't talk now," was all I said. We were outside of my office, and I always had to be aware of others listening in to delicate conversations.

Cliff was at his desk as we entered. He glanced up at us and then raised his eyebrows. "Everything okay with the USSF?"

Meg snorted and I shot her a glance.

"Don't tell me there are problems already."

"Not with the troops. They haven't come over yet, but they're going to—one shift at a time."

He sighed. "So that would be . . . seventy USSF personnel in Trieste?"

He had known the crew complement of a *Terminator* Class warsub without looking it up.

Meg said, "But just wait—soon people will be calling with complaints, the troops will be drinking, it'll be a total cluster—"

"Easy," I said. "Let's see how this plays out." I put my hand on her arm and studied her for a moment. This wasn't like her. In fact, she was behaving more like Kat than my sister.

The thought made me frown.

I leaned back and sighed. "Cliff, how are the preparations for your mission going?"

"I'm ready to go." He was referring to the job I had asked him to do. He wasn't technically part of TCI—he wasn't an agent of our intelligence agency—but I was short on people. The French had tortured and killed the last two I'd sent out, meaning I was down to five now. Five plus Johnny and myself, that is.

"I'd like you to come with us, first. We have to try to get more help before we deal with the dreadnought."

He blinked but remained silent for long heartbeats. Then he crossed his thick arms on the desk in front of him. "Mac. You don't think you can take out that warsub by simply shooting torpedoes at it, do you?"

"What do you mean?"

He glanced at Meg. "You tell him. You're a sub engineer."

She took a deep breath and pursed her lips. She was noticeably pulling herself back from the brink of rage, and this was something she could focus on. Something she knew about. Facts and statistics and engineering. "You say this dreadnought is over four hundred meters long? And thirty decks, meaning the height is a hundred meters?"

"Yes."

"Then Cliff is right. It's too enormous to sink with explosions. It's likely heavily compartmentalized. Hit the hull, puncture it, flood a few compartments. Big deal. Then you hit it again. And again. In multiple places over the exterior. But the fact is, even with every cabin near the hull flooded, watertight hatches will seal and the warsub will still be seaworthy."

"Because the interior is so damn big," Cliff added. "It'll have a positive buoyancy."

"It has ballast tanks," I said. "What if we flooded those too?"

"And how do you arrange that?"

I shrugged. "I'm just saying that with every exterior compartment flooded, *along* with ballast tanks, it might sink to crush depth."

"*Might.* But you don't know. It's a huge gamble. It would mean an enormous battle involving every torpedo you've got. And even then, it doesn't guarantee anything. It has countermeasures, and probably a complement of fighter subs."

I smiled at the two of them. They didn't know.

"What?" Meg snarled. "You don't seem convinced."

"Are you saying this warsub is *unsinkable*? We've heard that before."

"This isn't *Titanic*. And it's not even *Bismarck*. It's nearly two hundred meters longer than both of those ships."

"I have a different plan."

"To sink the dreadnought."

"Yes."

"What is it?"

I rose to my feet. "In time, Meg. In time. For now, we have to go meet some people, try to arrange help. Then we'll come back." I looked at Cliff. "Except you. You'll continue on, and return when you can."

Meg looked back and forth at us, not understanding.

—••—

Back at City Control, Grant Bell pushed his headset up and said, "Mac. A ship just signaled. The pilot is asking for you."

Meg had left to go pack a bag and prepare *SC-1* for another voyage. I was checking in with my controllers to prep them before I departed as well. I also had another dilemma—no deputy mayor, and Cliff was coming with us so I couldn't leave him in charge. I'd have to find someone else.

I marched over to the Sea Traffic Control station. Grant had the sonar screen zoomed on a single target. The label over the point of light identified the vessel as a seacar from Sheng City, one of the Chinese underwater colonies.

"What the hell?" I grumbled. The last time a ship from those colonies had been in our waters, they had been involved in a massive battle. But we'd convinced them to leave. Bargained with them, really.

Then I frowned. "Can I speak with him?"

Grant passed me a headset and indicated the button to speak. "Do you want video?" I nodded and he brought up a holographic screen over the sonar image.

"This is McClusky," I said. "Who is this?"

"Hello, Mac," a familiar voice rumbled in my ears. "This is Lau." Then there was a long pause before, "Can we talk?"

Chapter Eleven

"Is Johnny back?" I asked Grant.

I'd sent Johnny to Ballard to deliver a *Sword* to Mayor Winton, and I hadn't heard from him yet. And now Lau had arrived.

I hoped Johnny was okay.

Inside, my guts were churning. Johnny and Lau had a tenuous history. They had been partners following Johnny's defection. But when he had decided to come back to Trieste to help me, he'd betrayed Lau. Lau had not taken it well. He'd escaped from us, informed the Australian security forces at Blue Downs, and had contacted Chinese agents. It had forced Johnny and me to fight our way out of the city, following a hand-to-hand confrontation with Lau that I'd almost lost.

"Let me check," Grant said. A minute later, "Yep. He docked late last night."

I blew my breath out. "Good. Please call him to my office immediately." Then I made a sudden decision. Keying a number into my comm, a person I had only spoken with once before appeared on my screen. His face showed surprise and skepticism at my call.

I leaned forward after the pleasantries were done. I didn't have much time; Lau would arrive any minute. "I need to meet," I said.

The person on the line frowned. "When?"

"Tomorrow." I told him the coordinates and this time waves of shock crossed his features.

"Are you serious?"

"Yes. Can you make it? I need help. I'm bringing some people to brief you."

The other man, a mayor, hesitated, then looked off screen for a moment. "We've been talking about you, actually."

I didn't know if that was good or bad. "And?"

"We have questions too."

"Then a meeting is in order. Can you make it?"

After another pause he finally nodded. "I'll be there."

"Can you bring her too?"

A flicker of a smile. "Yes. She's here, and she'll come."

"I have another request. I am going to send a man to your city. Can you lend him a ship and some expertise?"

He hesitated. "But I don't know what you're asking. Military assistance?"

"Perhaps. A ship at the least. Perhaps one or two people to help him. He will do everything needed though. I wouldn't ask you to put your city on the line."

It only took a moment, and he nodded curtly.

I cut the connection and leaned back. Things were moving fast now.

—••—

JOHNNY AND LAU ARRIVED AT MY office at nearly the same time. Johnny looked genuinely shocked at the other's presence. His hand had shot to his waist—

To a holster that wasn't there. Then he said, "What the fuck are you doing here?"

They were facing each other for the first time since the mission a year earlier, when they had stolen the SCAV drive from Kat and I had hunted them down. I'd almost killed them—and they'd almost killed me—but in the end, I'd escaped with the drive, and it had forced Lau back to Sheng with his tail between his legs. He'd no doubt had to deal with that failure. His superiors would not have been pleased.

"I was going to ask the same thing," I said with a glare at the foreign agent.

The tension was electric. At any moment, I thought they might go for each other's throats—

But Lau stepped back and turned his eyes to the deck. Security had checked the man for weapons, and was at that moment going through his seacar. He held his hands out, one toward me and one toward Johnny. "I know the last time we saw each other things were different."

"You betrayed us," I snapped.

"I never joined you in the first place," he said. His face had grown hard, and I could see that he still held resentment for what had happened.

I decided to push him more. "We had the SCAV drive, and you wanted it. You failed. I could have sunk you in the Aleutian Trench. Then you tried to turn us over to security in Blue Downs, but that failed too."

"I was just doing my job, Mac."

"My friends call me that."

He winced. "I'm doing my job now too."

"By coming here? I should arrest you."

"I'm not here as an Agent of Sheng City Intelligence."

That made me pause. "Are you telling me you're a tourist?" I recalled that he had family at Trieste. "Visiting?"

"No. Of course not. I'm here as a Sheng City government representative."

I glanced at Johnny and he shot a look at me. Johnny had spent the last year over in the Chinese cities, trying to convince them to join our movement.

My breath caught in my throat.

Was there a chance?

Lau sighed and looked back at the deck. "They've sent me to discuss your offer."

A silence descended over us. No one spoke for long seconds. Johnny and I just stared at Lau. It was awkward. A year earlier, the three of us had been trying to kill each other. But I knew I had to be careful here; there was still a chance that Lau wanted to assassinate me for what had happened, and that his superiors had sent him to do exactly that.

"And what did they ask you to say?"

He straightened, squared his shoulders, and locked eyes with me. "Sheng

City accepts your terms. We want the SCAV drive and the ship Johnny demonstrated. In return, we will join your efforts to fight for independence. Covertly at first, of course."

A smile crept across my face. Even Johnny looked shocked before surprise replaced his expression.

—••—

FIVE MINUTES LATER, LAU HAD FILLED us in on the Sheng City elders' concerns about escalating tensions in the oceans, the attack on Norfolk and now San Diego, as well as the dreadnought. They wanted to be on the winning side of the fight in the oceans, and they had realized that forming the new nation of Oceania was the only way to achieve it. I felt that Lau wasn't fully on side with the plan—he still had resentment for Trieste, Johnny, and myself—but he was loyal to his city and was doing what they wanted.

"We still have to work out the specifics," I said. "The economic as well as military ties between us."

He nodded. "There's a lot to discuss. How to keep this secret from China for as long as possible. How to interest the other underwater cities. But we can hold talks on those items."

I pursed my lips. I was thrilled beyond words, but couldn't show it. Yet. Sending Johnny to negotiate and demonstrate the SCAV drive had worked. But if I showed too much enthusiasm, it might affect our talks, so I remained cool and collected, as did Johnny.

Something else occurred to me. "Lau, I'm glad your city has seen things our way. We'll have those talks soon. But for now, Johnny and I were just about to depart on a mission." Johnny's eyes flicked to mine; he hadn't known. I ignored it and contacted my assistant just outside the office. "Kristen, can you get Lazlow for me? Have him meet us at *SC-1* in fifteen minutes. With a bag." Then I turned back to Lau. "I want you to come with us."

Lau's face erupted into surprise. "What?"

"We're going to get help. In *SC-1*. You'll join me, Johnny, Meg, Lazlow, and Cliff Sim, my security chief."

"Uh, Mac . . ." Johnny started.

I pressed on. "We need to deal with the dreadnought. Your superiors want that too, no?"

He nodded but didn't reply.

"Then it's settled."

I studied the two men before me. Former adversaries thrust into an uneasy alliance.

And we would be together, back on *SC-1*, joined for another crucial journey.

On a clandestine meeting to a secret facility in the Atlantic.

With one mission: sink an unsinkable warsub.

Interlude:
Cousteau City Intelligence
Cousteau City, France

```
Location:          Cousteau City, Cousteau City
                   Mayor's Office
                   Off the coast of France in the
                   English Channel

Latitude:          49° 39′ N
Longitude:         0° 29′ W
Depth:             30 meters
Time:              2313 hours
Date:              25 April 2030
```

M<small>AYOR</small> F<small>RANCOIS</small> P<small>IETTE</small> <small>STARED AT THE</small> blank computer monitor before him. Truman McClusky of Trieste had just cut the signal after a terse conversation in which he had requested a meeting in the Atlantic Ocean, east of Canada. Renée Féroce, who was sitting across from Piette in his office, had jumped at the coordinates. Now her face had glazed over as thoughts churned through her mind.

Renée had arrived at the city some weeks earlier, after a sudden and shocking development in the southern Mid-Atlantic Ridge. First Mayor McClusky had called, offering a gift of incredible technology should the French undersea colonies join him in his quest to form a new and independent nation of Oceania. Such a notion appealed to Piette. France had been demanding more and more from the colonies as waters rose and climates shifted and scorching temperatures ravaged the European nations. Frankly, he was sick of it. He had heard of McClusky and his struggles for independence—including his father's doomed fight in the 2090s—and had studied it with some interest. As France continued to escalate demands, and as the French Submarine Fleet tightened its grip, Piette had grown increasingly angry at his mother nation.

During the mayor's first call weeks earlier, Piette had indicated his interest in McClusky's proposal, if only to learn more information. He hadn't committed in any way other than to gain insight. Then a few things happened in quick succession: Captain Renée Féroce had arrived in an advanced but mysterious vessel, and reports started swirling about the FSF losing a hundred warsubs or more in a battle in the Southern Atlantic Ocean. Those reports were unsubstantiated, but there seemed to be a connection between Féroce and the missing subs. And then Féroce told a simply incredible story. She couldn't have fabricated it; it was too far-fetched.

Then there were reports of a hundred missing *USSF warsubs* soon after, and the destruction of USSF HQ at Norfolk and San Diego.

And Féroce's vessel was just *incredible*. It could travel at over 450 kilometers per hour. Cousteau's sub engineers had taken it to sea, with Féroce piloting, and the vehicle had shocked and dismayed them simultaneously. If other superpowers of the world had vessels like it, then France would lose the race to develop ocean resources.

And, Piette knew, if France got the technology and *not* the French undersea colonies, then France would further tighten her grip over them. They would never enjoy peace and stability in the oceans.

And now McClusky had just called again.

Piette realized that there was no harm in listening to the man, and had agreed to the meeting at the mysterious coordinates.

And McClusky had asked Féroce to accompany him.

When he'd said that, Piette had seen a fleeting look of joy cross the captain's face. But she had clamped down on it quickly, he thought. She was either hiding it from him, or from herself.

"Are you willing to go?" he'd asked her in a soft voice.

"I'll go." She was back to being impassive.

"What do you think he wants?"

"I assume it has to do with his fight for independence."

"He may be responsible for all these attacks. Should I worry?"

She frowned. "No. He wouldn't kill needlessly. I don't think, anyway."

"What of Norfolk and San Diego?"

"I can't see him doing that."

"And the French defeat in the Southern Ocean?"

She eyed the mayor. "That is possible. Very possible. *They* were chasing *him* after all. They were trying to sink him. He likely fought back."

"But he only has one city on his side. How could he possibly defeat so many warsubs? USSF ones too? A whole fleet."

"He has the SCAV drive. Other technologies as well."

"Still . . ." Piette trailed off. He needed more information. He wasn't a military man, he was a politician. But he understood history and knew about the balance of power. If it truly was shifting, he wanted to be on the right side of the scale.

The one whose power increased.

"And you're sure that you don't want to return to France? You're part of the French Submarine Fleet, not the colony forces."

She frowned. "I used to think that I wanted to be in the FSF forever. But after meeting Mac . . ." She trailed off and said no more. She just looked confused.

Piette sighed. She was a conundrum, he mused. But she could have more time to decide. She had brought them the SCAV seacar, after all. She could have all the time she needed.

There were also two other French colonies to consider, the first two undersea cities the country had settled: Conshelf Alpha and Conshelf Beta. They would want to be involved in this too, he realized.

In time, he thought. In time.

First, he and Captain Renée Féroce would meet with McClusky to see what he was planning. Then Piette would decide how to involve the other colonies, if at all. He had considered keeping the SCAV drive for himself, but of course it was too late for that. Other countries would have it soon, and now his only hope was to simply keep up. Perhaps McClusky would be able to move faster than the others, however, as he'd clearly been doing already.

"Prepare to depart immediately," he told her. "We'll see what he wants."

Part Three: Preparations

Chapter
Twelve

WE BOARDED *SC-1* AND DEPARTED TRIESTE without fanfare. *Devastator* was connected via umbilical just outside the docking module, and her huge shadow fell over us as we turned to starboard and navigated on our way toward the Florida Straits. They had not started offloading the first shift yet, and I was worried about it. Cliff Sim was coming with me, and he had left his senior officers in charge of security. They were effective, but no one could take Cliff's place.

As for me, I could only leave my assistants to run things in my absence. I would try to get back as soon as possible. All they had to do were administrative tasks. Keep Trieste running.

Before we left, a call had come in for Lau, which I had allowed him to receive. When he returned to the seacar, he looked pale and grim. I had not pressed him on it, but inwardly I wondered if Sheng was having second thoughts about their offer to join us. I hoped not.

As we left, I turned the seacar once to view the city, which was magnificent. Lights traced along her modules and travel tubes, and there were bubbles drifting upward from seacars, scooters, and divers. Schools of fish clouded the water, and there were streams of bubbles churning upward from the fish farms.

It made us all smile. Trieste was beautiful.

As for our journey, Lau and Johnny were not talking, and the others could sense the underlying tension between the two. Johnny was in the copilot's chair on the right side of the control cabin, and he didn't say much to me either. I hoped things would ease up a bit before we reached the meeting.

Lazlow had brought a few personal items in a bag, as well as some portable equipment to continue working on the sonar readings. The headphones and squiggles on holo displays completely absorbed him during the trip. Lau watched with interest, not fully understanding what Lazlow was doing or even who he was, but Lau could tell that it was of some importance, and he would likely find out soon.

Cliff Sim had boarded wearing a wetsuit with a watertight bag slung over his shoulder. He was built wide but in no way out of shape. He was all muscle. His lack of hair was likely because he shaved it so it would be one less thing to worry about in the morning. He was all business, all the time. He spent the bulk of the voyage staring at maps and charts showing the bathymetry of the ocean floor. I knew what he was studying—the maps were not of the Atlantic Ocean—but no one else did. He had a knife on his thigh, and I suspected there were a variety of weapons in his personal bag.

As for Meg, Benning had really angered her. She was still stewing about it. I could tell from the way she was marching about the cabin, speaking in terse sentences, jamming her things into drawers near the two bunks. Then she disappeared into the engineering compartment in the stern to monitor systems. I knew she just wanted to be alone to mull over the USSF interference in Trieste. She'd sent one sharp look at Lau, not fully understanding who he was, before she hid in the aft compartment. Had she calmed herself and paid more attention, she would have recognized him from our confrontation in Blue Downs one year earlier.

We powered through the Florida Strait, set course northward, and I fired up the fusion reactor to engage the SCAV drive.

Johnny glanced at me. "Are you sure? People will hear."

"I think we're past that now. Time is not on our side."

I pushed the button and the familiar *thrum* growled behind us. In the reactor chamber, radio waves rapidly turned the fuel—deuterium and tritium—to plasma, a super-hot gas. Plasma had unique properties. The one that was most crucial to fusion was that it was magnetic. A powerful electromagnet compressed the plasma even more. Within seconds the core of the unit hit a temperature to fuse the atoms together, releasing neutrons and energy. The beauty of fusion was that if the reactor ever failed and the magnets shut off, the plasma simply expanded back to normal pressure and temperature. There were no residual issues such as an escalating temperature and a runaway meltdown.

Deuterium occurred naturally in seawater, which we extracted continually, and we had to import the tritium, but we used only small amounts.

The supercavitation bubble began to form around the vessel's bow, and it slowly stretched back to envelop the entire seacar. As it did, friction with the water decreased and our velocity increased. Soon we were at 450 kph and I held the yoke steady in my hands, directing us northward along the coast of the United States.

Lau was behind me, staring out the viewports at the scene. The fluctuating bubble distorted images slightly, so it was like looking at a mirage in every direction. There was a trace of a smile across his face, and it made me frown, for his motivations were still in question.

Then I realized—he had only seen this technology in action once before.

"It's impressive, isn't it?" I asked him over my shoulder.

He stared at me, face impassive once again. "It is," he finally conceded.

Johnny turned slightly to listen, but he was not watching.

"It's why Sheng City wants the technology, and why I'm willing to give it to them. To any Chinese underwater city."

"I thought it was to make them run away and leave you alone."

I frowned. He was referring to the fighting in the Gulf of Mexico around Trieste when I had convinced the Chinese underwater colonial fleets to leave.

"It was that and the dream of Oceania."

He sighed and leaned back, closed his eyes. "Oceania," he whispered. "What's the point?"

I gestured for Johnny to take over in the control cabin, and I squeezed out from between the pilots' chairs to sit on the couch in the living space just aftward. "The point is that the superpowers of the world have oppressed and abused us for far too long."

"That sounds like your dad talking."

"He was right. They take our produce and give us nothing in return. They occupy our cities and treat our people like garbage." I paused and studied the foreign agent. "Your superiors agree with me, right? That's why you're here, Lau."

He looked away as he processed that. "I don't agree with your philosophy, but Sheng City does."

"Doesn't China mistreat your people? Use you?"

His face suddenly tightened; he couldn't answer.

I rose to my feet and returned to the control cabin. There was nothing else to say.

—••—

HOURS LATER, WE ARRIVED AT A major formation in the western Atlantic Ocean between Iceland and the Azores. The SCAV drive had powered us there faster than any conventional sub in the world, and no doubt we had shocked and stunned every surface and subsurface vessel that we passed on our way. Some even sent signals to us, asking who we were, but we ignored them all.

The fracture in the ocean crust was thirty kilometers wide and a thousand long, and some sections were three times deeper than the Grand Canyon. The average depth was 4,500 meters—four and a half kilometers— and the seafloor there was beyond our crush depth, unless we used Lazlow's invention: acoustic pulses to force the pressure away. A river of cold, dense water flowed through the canyon, further eroding and carving its sides, and it tossed the seacar as we slowed to a conventional speed of fifty kph.

Johnny noticed our location and his face paled. "Really?" he asked me.

Lau heard and approached from behind. He glanced at the nav screen. "The guyot?" he whispered.

Sure enough, on the depth finder ahead of us, a flat-topped mountain rose from the seafloor to a depth of a thousand meters. On the top was a dome set on stilts.

The French base.

———••———

It was the same location where I had hunted and trapped Johnny on his run from Trieste with the SCAV technology. Only I hadn't caught him—he had led me there. I had interrupted his meeting with French officials, where he was going to give them the technology, and during our struggle we'd damaged the base, flooded it, and in the ensuing fight I'd sunk a civilian seacar and fired on a French warsub—*Destructeur*.

Renée Féroce had captained the vessel, and it had sent her career on a path of obsession and torment.

I said, "Yes. We're meeting people here."

"Who are we—"

"You'll find out very soon."

He snorted. "You're full of surprises, Mac."

———••———

The base was empty, as I'd expected. It was a small dome, perhaps originally meant for espionage, because its color allowed it to completely blend in with the mountain. After our fight, we had left it flooded with major structural damage. I was curious what had become of the interior, if the French had even invested much effort in it.

I descended to the guyot, lowered the landing skids, and connected the umbilical to the dome. The tube's pressure hit four atms, and the airlock hatches slid aside.

———••———

The last time I'd been in this region, we had almost lost Kat's invention. We'd battled a Chinese *Jin* Class warsub, a French warsub, as well as Johnny's seacar as he continued on his run around the northern coastline of Canada, through the Arctic Ocean, and south past the Aleutians into the Pacific.

Johnny's face was tight. Lau's didn't look much different. He had stabbed me during the confrontation inside that base while I'd fought Johnny.

I rose to my feet and faced the others. Cliff was staring out the viewports, quiet as usual. Meg was now there, also looking outside, although it was too dark to see much. Our exterior lights were off, as were the base's, and sunlight could not penetrate to this depth. "Where are we exactly, Tru?" she asked.

"A French dome in the Charlie Gibb's Fracture Zone."

"You've been here before?"

Johnny, Lau, and I glanced at each other. "Once," we all said in unison.

And then we smiled. It had been enough to finally break the tension. "We have to put it behind us," I muttered. "We have to move forward. To the future."

"To Oceania?" Lau said with a frown.

"Yes. You got it."

"I'm still skeptical."

"There's a nation out there that wants to start a war. The USSF wants to stop them."

He sneered at me. "You're working with them? The enemy?"

"We have a common enemy right now. And if it'll help us in the long run, then yes, I'm working with the USSF. Maybe they'll see us in a different light. Work with us instead of against us."

Meg's posture tightened and her expression turned rigid. "But not for long, right?"

I turned to her. "Let's take one thing at a time. The dreadnought comes first right now." I gestured to them to follow. "Let's go."

Cliff held up a long rifle. "I'll lead the way."

—••—

AS EXPECTED, THERE WAS NO ONE inside. The French had fully repaired the base. It was dry and the sound of ventilation fans and electronics whispered in our ears. The bottommost level contained operational equipment such as waste treatment, recycling, and banks of batteries. The second level contained living spaces, lounges, and games rooms. The upper level held only a few command spaces, such as the communications cabin. *Module de Commande* marked a hatch.

Cliff opened it and looked inside.

Nothing.

Along the exterior of the circular room were consoles and controls and video monitors. The ceiling contained a large skylight, which was intact. There was a conference table under it.

The last time we'd been there, Johnny had fired at the skylight, puncturing it.

Deliberately.

He'd caused a disaster within the base to escape.

He glanced at me as we stepped cautiously inside. His face showed guilt, but there was a trace of humor underlying it. If we had been alone, he probably would have joked with me about the fight we'd had.

We had tried to drown each other.

I turned to Lau. "This is where you stabbed me. Do you remember?"

It took him aback. "Yes. But not in this room."

"No."

A frown crossed his features. "And you are still angry." It was a statement.

I stopped and faced him. "I'm willing to put it aside for the greater goal. You?"

He hesitated. "I'm loyal to Sheng. I'll do what they want."

Meg said, "And what do they want, exactly?"

"To work with you. With Trieste. To build a new nation and declare independence."

I could feel the disdain dripping from his tone.

It was the first time she'd heard his motivations, and her face exploded into surprise. She spun on me. "Tru! Did it work? Did it really work?"

"Seems that way," I said.

"Holy shit," was all she could say.

We all smiled at that. Even Lau showed the hint of one.

—••—

THE BASE'S PURPOSE WAS EITHER FOR clandestine operations, a meeting space, or for research. Perhaps all three. The French had repaired it then left it alone for use at some later time. Our group sat at the consoles, studying the passive sonar display and waiting.

Finally, hours later, a contact appeared on the screen. It was a small seacar, French by its acoustic signature, that drifted to a landing next to the dome, connected via umbilical, and powered down.

"Here we go," I muttered. I gestured at Lazlow, who'd been quiet as he continued working with his headset and portable equipment. "Are you ready, Lazlow?"

He looked up, quizzical. "For what?"

"Why do you think you're here?"

"I have no idea. I'm just working. You asked me to join you, and I did." He looked confused.

"I want you to brief us on what you've discovered. As soon as they get here."

Meg said, "And who are *they*?"

"The mayor of Cousteau City and Captain Renée Féroce. Ballard City has already joined us." I gestured at Lau. "Sheng City has now too. And Cousteau will as well. We're building our alliance."

"And what is the point of this meeting?"

I didn't respond.

Silence descended over the command cabin.

Chapter Thirteen

MAYOR PIETTE WAS THE FIRST PERSON through the hatch. He was tall and fit with weathered features and short hair. There were lines in his forehead and gray at his temples. He did not carry a weapon, but he entered with apprehension at the group who met him. Then he saw me and came to a halt.

Captain Renée Féroce was behind him. She entered much slower than the mayor had, but her eyes fixed on mine and never strayed. It was hard to read her. Weeks earlier, she'd wanted nothing more than to kill me. Then I had captured her, brought her to our base, The Ridge, and forced her on a journey to steal a secret from a facility in the Indian Ocean. In the end, I had let her go with the supercavitating technology. I'd asked her to take it to Cousteau, which she had. She could have returned to the mainland and the FSF, of which she was a part, but she had chosen to join my struggle.

At least, I thought she had. She might have just been weighing her options. Time would tell, I thought.

I nodded at her. "Hello, Captain."

"Mayor," was all she said.

People watched us, curious.

One look around the chamber made me snort. "What is it?" Piette asked me.

"I just noticed that in this command cabin, right now, there are three people who have actively tried to kill me in the last year."

Lau said, "We all failed."

Johnny added, "It's a good thing."

Piette looked confused. "And now you are all together on this journey?"

I said, "They know the future is bigger than one man's death."

"Your dad would have said that," Féroce finally said in a soft voice, eyes still on me.

I hesitated. "Maybe. He started me on this path. And Meg." I motioned to her, and then I realized I should make introductions, which I did. Piette visibly relaxed, and together we sat at the table in the center of the room. It was new—the punctured skylight had broken the last one.

"Now," he said, "Why am I here, Mr. McClusky?" His English was excellent, though he spoke with a strong French accent.

"Mac, please," I corrected him. "First off, did you get the *Sword*?"

A perplexed look appeared on his face. "Pardon me?"

"The ship Renée was in." Now it was my turn to look confused. "With the SCAV drive?"

"Ah, yes. Thank you." He smiled. "I didn't know what its name was."

"It's the class of vessel. It was a gift."

His smile faded. "To join you in your efforts, I take it."

"We're hoping." I gestured around us. The others were watching quietly, not knowing where I was headed with this. "Ballard has joined, as well as Sheng City. I'm hoping you'll be next."

He sighed and leaned back. "It's a big thing to ask, you know. To go against the FSF."

"And the USSF," Féroce said. "And the CSF. All superpowers, all formidable enemies."

"We are powerful too," I said. "But if we can avoid fighting, we will."

"But how could you do it and avoid fighting? I understand you've already been involved in two major battles. Only one was a victory."

Lau darted a glance at me. He didn't know about the fight in the Mid-Atlantic Ridge.

"Yes," I said. "We have fantastic new technologies. If need be, we'll fight."

"What technologies?" Lau asked.

"The SCAV drive propels our ships close to five hundred kilometers per hour. And the Acoustic Pulse Drive allows us to descend to eight kilometers."

His face erupted into shock. It was an interesting reaction from a man usually so guarded. "You're serious?"

"Totally."

"But that would mean . . . it would mean . . ."

"We can fight any fleet from far below their ability to travel. It's like having air superiority on land. It's how we defeated the USSF and FSF in the rift."

"How many warsubs did you beat?"

"Hundreds. We only lost thirty *Swords*."

His jaw dropped and he leaned back. "And are you willing to also give this to Sheng, along with the SCAV?"

"Yes. Since you are with us now."

Piette had watched the exchange with interest. "And us as well?"

"We're in this together—if you agree—and we'll share tech to help us gain independence."

"To fight the superpowers."

I raised a finger. "Only if need be. I would prefer economic partnerships that will benefit all of us. But should a power threaten us . . ."

Piette watched me with a flat expression. Then he turned to Féroce. "He is compelling, I'll give you that."

She nodded slowly. "He convinced me," she whispered, "and I was his prisoner at the time."

"Guest," I corrected. Then I turned and gestured to Lazlow. "The doctor here is an acoustical engineer. He's been studying the dreadnought's sonar traces."

"But why are you so concerned with this warsub?" Piette asked. "It's done you a favor by destroying USSF HQ on both coasts."

I shook my head. "It's disrupted things in the oceans. It's going to cause tremendous problems. The USSF will ramp up activities. The other nations will get involved soon. It's a massive warsub."

He snorted. "There are a lot of large ships—"

"It's over four hundred meters long. With a SCAV drive. It has a fusion reactor. It can go 467 kilometers per hour."

His face paled.

I continued, "It also can somehow create tsunamis to break seawalls and destroy coastal communities. The USSF needs assistance."

"And you think by aiding them you can help yourselves?"

"It's a win-win. It'll stabilize the superpowers once again, and perhaps help us with the USSF. Besides, it's possible the dreadnought will turn its attention to the undersea cities. Those are easy targets. We have to stop it at all costs."

A silence descended over us.

"I have additional information, Mac," Lau interjected.

We turned our eyes to him.

He continued, "The message I received in Trieste just before we left. It was from my superiors. After the dreadnought attacked San Diego, it ambushed the CSF fleet in the Pacific over the Iron Plains."

A tremor passed through my body. I clenched my fists. "And?"

"Sixty-three warsubs destroyed. No evident damage to the dreadnought."

"Oh my god," I muttered. "It's not Chinese then?" A big part of me had thought it a CSF vessel. After all, it had targeted the US mainland.

"No. Could it be French?" He looked pointedly at Piette. "Is there a chance that the mayor here already knows the dreadnought's origin?"

"It's not French," Lazlow said abruptly.

"How do you know?"

The acoustician glanced at me. "Mac asked me to examine the sonar trace we have of the dreadnought. I've been doing that for the past few days. Admiral Benning just provided me the record from the Norfolk attack. I've been using that too."

"And?" I asked.

"They are very different readings. The one from the Mid-Atlantic Ridge is an uninterrupted sonar recording of the warsub at high speed. I've learned much about her SCAV drive, its power output, and the ship's hull. I'm working up a schematic of its exterior which I should have completed soon. But the most important thing for now is the way the conventional thruster pods connect to the hull. It uses a double strut to secure them. No other fleet in the oceans uses such a configuration, as far as we know. French, USSF, CSF, the English, and Germans. Canada and Australia. None of them."

We've seen those before, I thought. In the Mid-Atlantic Ridge.

Lazlow leaned forward. "But there's something more interesting from the Norfolk attack. The ship literally *rocketed* toward the seawall at what we assume is its maximum velocity. Then, when it was only a hundred meters out, it slowed dramatically and triggered a powerful noise emission to confuse and disrupt the USSF's listening devices." He shook his head. "It was tremendously loud, and it worked, to a certain extent."

"What do you mean, 'worked'?" Piette asked.

"There could only have been one purpose to that noise. To mask something else. That warsub's operators didn't want anyone to know what they were doing."

Meg said, "But it's obvious what they were doing. They were attacking USSF HQ."

Lazlow raised a finger. "But they were trying to hide *how* they were doing it." He sighed. "But they messed up. They deployed their weapon *before* the noise, so I can hear what happened."

He had us on the edges of our seats. The cabin was completely quiet except for the hum and sigh of the life support and ventilation equipment.

He continued after a long series of heartbeats, "There is a sound of hydraulics. Of movement. The displacement it caused was *massive*. The drag of this ship against water is larger than any I've ever heard." He shook his head. His next sentences seemed to be meant only for his own ears; we had to lean forward to hear what he was saying. "To deploy such a structure underwater, *while in SCAV drive*, seems ludicrous. It would have caused enormous g-forces in the ship. They must have been strapped in or the force would have crushed them against the forward bulkheads."

"What do you mean?" I asked finally.

He shook himself out of his reverie. "The warsub deployed a structure at its bow. It took precisely seven seconds to extend fully. It was a *plow*, Mac. Pushed outward against the sheer force of the water by powerful hydraulics. It displaced the water before the vessel in the direction the ship was driving. At first the plow moved with little resistance. Into the supercavitation bubble. Probably a few meters to either side of the dreadnought's hull. Then the ship *slammed* out of SCAV and hit the water at 467 kilometers per hour. It would have come to an abrupt halt, transferring its total kinetic energy forward." His face lit now in absolute admiration. "Imagine the force on the crew! To not only come out of SCAV in such a large vessel, but to deliberately transfer your motion into the wall of water in front of you!" He snorted. "As they came out of SCAV, the plow extended even farther. From the noise it created, I estimate it quickly telescoped at least thirty meters *on each side* of the warsub."

The faces around the table remained blank. Lazlow stared back now, a cascading series of emotions tracing across his features: excitement, joy, and fear all at once.

"What are you saying?" Cliff Sim finally asked into the silence. "That the ship literally shoved the water into a tsunami that cracked the seawall?"

Lazlow slammed his hands on the table, making everyone jump simultaneously. "That's precisely what I'm saying! That ship has a tremendous weapon that it can use against any coastal community. Breaking seawalls will also damage inland areas because the water levels are so high now, and they've nearly crested so many current walls. The dreadnought powers toward the coast in SCAV drive, then extends the tsunami plow and simultaneously drops speed to zero. It displaces massive amounts of water forward toward the coastlines."

The rest of us sat in a stunned silence. It was unthinkable, but they had used the weapon twice now. Combined with an underwater nuclear blast at one of the sites, probably both, to open the seawall.

Tsunami Plow, I thought to myself. It was a tremendous weapon against countries flailing to survive Global Warming. And USSF HQ had been especially vulnerable due to the buildings that maintained four atms.

"Lazlow," I whispered. "What were the effects of the noise eruption just after they deployed their plow?"

"I can only surmise that the noise shocked and confused sonar operators. Also, there are warning nets around the coast that listen for very quiet and distant sounds. Their sensitivity is exquisite." There was a look of pleasure on his features now.

His love for acoustics underwater made me smile slightly.

He continued, "This tremendous blast of sound . . . the listening posts—which are automated—and computer algorithms just *shut them down*, automatically. Tripped them off. After that point, Benning provided me with a few more minutes of sonar recording, recovered from nearby vessels that managed to keep their computers going. They were farther away, so the noise didn't affect them as much."

"Wow," Renée Féroce whispered. "Just, *wow*. I can't believe a nation would do that to the United States and the USSF. Not one that wanted to work peacefully in the oceans, anyway."

"That's the point," I interjected. "This nation wants war."

"There's more," Lazlow said. "Even with the noise emission, I was able to decipher something interesting from the feed. Something unique."

"What?"

His face tightened. "The conventional screws. They didn't behave the same as others in the oceans."

"But all screws operate in the same manner. They're propellers basically, but under water, pushing behind them."

"True, but as Meg here knows, the shape of each blade is crucial. If they create too low a pressure around the leading edge, the pressure in the water falls too much and dissolved air bubbles out. This lowers the effectiveness of the screw, creates noise—not good for stealth—and can even damage the blades."

"Cavitation," Meg provided.

"Yes. It's a delicate balance, and a whole field of study unto itself. Designing blades that offer performance without too much cavitation, to remain as silent underwater as possible. But if you want speed, a screw that operates better at lower rpm can be ineffective at higher ones. So, if engineers design a screw for high-speed operation that cavitates less, they can be less effective at lower rpm and lower speeds! It has to do with the shape of each blade, but also the *angle* of the blade outward from the main propeller shaft."

Meg was nodding. "So?"

"The interesting thing is, the conventional propulsion on the dreadnought had very little cavitation from its screws when it was moving slowly."

"How'd you hear this?" I asked. "The noise—"

"I filtered out the noise with the algorithms I invented."

I snorted. Of course. Lazlow was the expert the USSF most likely needed. And Trieste had him.

He continued, "But when the sub turned under high speed, to fire a torpedo as it sped away, the rpm increased dramatically. *But the cavitation, which should have increased as it ramped up its speed, didn't!*"

No one said a word.

"Explain," I said finally. "In English."

"He's saying," Meg supplied, "that if designers create a blade for slow speed stealth, then it would most likely be louder at higher velocities. But this one wasn't."

"There's something unique about the dreadnought's screws?"

"Yes," Lazlow said. "And I know what it is." He sat back and a wide grin spread across his bearded face.

"Well?" I asked. "What is it?"

"I heard a hint of a noise as it increased speed. I had to isolate and study it for a lengthy amount of time. Magnify it. It was hydraulics once again. Mac, this ship can angle its screw blades and can change how each surface and leading edge slices through water. *They're not static.*"

I blinked. Then Meg said, "You mean it can adjust the blade orientation?"

"That's exactly what I'm saying."

She swore. "No ship does that underwater. It's like a helicopter on the surface."

"The point being?" Féroce asked.

"To remain stealthy. Quiet. Not cavitate when it moves, causing bubbles around its blades."

"Seems odd for a ship with a SCAV drive to care about that."

He shrugged. "It means it can approach a coastline quietly. It's a technology we don't have."

And a technology that would be nice for us to acquire. I opened my mouth to speak and—

"I'm not done," Lazlow said. "The ships that attacked us at The Ridge."

A shock jolted through my body, moving upward along my spine. "Go on."

"They also showed the same signals."

Chapter Fourteen

I CLENCHED MY FISTS. "YOU'RE SAYING that not only did the hulls resemble each other—the double struts connecting thruster pods to the main fuselage—but they also had the . . . hydraulic blades that allow more stealthy travel under water?"

"Exactly."

Inwardly, I swore. We needed to figure out who was operating that dreadnought. It was an emerging ocean power, that much was certain. "Listen," I said finally. "The USSF has reached out to us for help. We have to give it to them. We're going to find this vessel . . . find it, and destroy it."

Now the others turned to me, looks of complete horror on their faces.

"What do you mean?" Meg finally asked.

I shrugged. "Simple. We're going to figure out a way to sink it."

"But we've already discussed that." She gestured at Cliff. "We both spoke with you about it. It'll be impossible to put enough punctures in its hull to take it down. It'll be too compartmentalized, too—"

"Sorry, Meg. We're going to do it. We're going to figure out a way, and I need everyone who's here, at this table, to help."

They were silent once more, and those looks of shock continued. They just couldn't process what I was suggesting. Then Lau sighed. "I can say

unequivocally, despite my misgivings, that Sheng City is going to help you
with this, McClusky. They've told me to extend whatever assistance you
need, including our warsubs."

"And the other Chinese cities?"

He shook his head. "I can't speak for them. But I understand you
were already there asking . . ." He sent a pointed look at Johnny, who
merely shrugged.

"They were undecided," he replied.

Lau continued, "Then we'll wait and see about them. But for now, we
will help."

"Thank you," I said. I turned to Mayor Piette. "And you?"

He was staring at me, his face blank. Then he glanced at Féroce. "You've
given us the SCAV drive. You've demonstrated your abilities in battle." He
sighed. "I know that I personally would love to shrug off our colonial past and
move forward as an independent nation, but I have to speak with our council.
There are also the other French undersea colonies—Conshelf Alpha and
Conshelf Beta—to involve." He hesitated and then, "I'll return to Cousteau
and have an answer within a day or two. Is that good enough?"

I nodded. It's all I could have hoped for. I knew they weren't a dictatorship;
his politicians would have to discuss matters. "Are you able to keep this quiet?
It goes without saying that you can't involve the FSF or mainland France."

"Of course."

"Just know that this dreadnought is no one's friend. It's attacked us and
China. France might be next."

"I realize this. And we are extremely vulnerable."

I rose to my feet. "We need to return to Trieste and start working on a
plan. But first—" I turned to Féroce "— can we speak? Before you leave?"

Her face erupted into surprise, then she clamped down on it and nodded.

—••—

FIVE MINUTES LATER, FÉROCE AND I were alone in the cabin. The others had
left for their respective ships and were waiting for us. Mayor Piette had shot
her a curious look, but she didn't even look away from me as they marched

out of the command chamber. Meg and Johnny were confused as well, but they'd understand in a few minutes.

Féroce was studying me. She was a mystery, still. She had tried multiple times to kill me, but had failed each attempt. Then I had captured her and taken her to The Ridge, where I had forced her to stay until I dealt with the French fleet that had been chasing me. Then I'd sent her to Cousteau with a supercavitating ship, as an envoy, to help broker a partnership in independence. I'd asked her to go there, not knowing whether she would or not. After all, she was a captain in the FSF—the mainland submarine force—and was not affiliated with the undersea cities. She had done it though, and had helped me immeasurably.

We were staring at each other in silence, and the electricity was palpable. It made me feel uncomfortable, however, for Kat was still very much on my mind.

Other things weighed on my conscience as well.

She studied my eyes. "You seem sad, McClusky."

I blinked. "Just stress, I think. But I wanted to thank you for taking the ship to Cousteau. You've given me an in with the French cities now."

She nodded. "I had to think long and hard about it, but it was the right decision."

"And the FSF? Do they know you're alive?"

She shook her head. "They believe I'm dead. Along with all the other French subs you destroyed."

"The USSF was involved too."

"You arranged that battle over the rift. *You* did that."

I hesitated. I didn't want to argue with her. "They were chasing me, don't forget. They killed and tortured my two agents. I had to fight them off."

Her eyes flashed and it looked as though she was about to yell at me, then suddenly her expression softened. "You're right. And this struggle you're involved in . . . it seems you were right all along. This dreadnought . . . it's a formidable force in the oceans."

"We have to deal with it."

"You really think you can defeat it?"

"With help."

"Sheer power won't sink it."

"There are other ways."

She stared at me, not fully understanding. "And what do you want of me now?"

"Come with me. To Trieste."

Now a look of utter shock rippled across her face. "Why?"

"To help. You're a captain in the military, currently presumed dead. You have nothing to lose. That ship is working with one purpose—to *destroy*. Our cities are fragile. I need you to join us on the mission."

"To sink the dreadnought."

I nodded. There wasn't anything else to say.

She stared into my eyes, thoughts churning in her head. But it didn't take her long to decide. "Let me get my things."

And as she turned to stalk away, I saw a smile creep across her face.

—••—

"CLIFF," I SAID. WE WERE BACK in *SC-1*, and he was gathering his things. The others were watching, curious. "It's time for you to go. Come back safe."

"Wait a minute," Meg yelled. "Where are you sending him? We need him at Trieste! The USSF troops—"

I turned to them. "Cliff is going on a mission. I'm sending him to Cousteau first. He'll return soon." *I hoped, anyway.*

"Where?"

"Remember the syntactic foam? The French base in the Indian Ocean?"

Meg frowned. "Your two people died trying to steal it last time."

"We didn't have the correct coordinates. We do now. Cliff's going to get it." I was referring to the hull filler that the French had invented. Made up of microscopic spheres, sub engineers sprayed it between the inner and outer hulls of subs during construction. It began as a foam, but hardened to form a super-strong layer that resisted water pressure better than the type that we currently used. We didn't understand why. Renée Féroce had provided me with the proper coordinates when I'd allowed her to leave The Ridge a few weeks earlier; now it was time to send another mission to retrieve it, and I'd picked Cliff Sim for the job.

"But we need him for the dreadnought, don't we?"

I glanced at the security man. "He'll be back before we leave. With the foam."

Lau had watched the entire exchange. "But I thought you had a technology that could take you down to 8,000 meters."

"It has some drawbacks still. The vessel has to be moving at fifty kph for it to work. You can't stop. The syntactic foam will let us descend farther before we need to activate the APD." I shrugged. "It's an extra advance in technology that Trieste needs. For our deep-sea mining expeditions, for instance. You know the game, Lau, and this is how it's played. The CSF already has it. We need it too."

He looked embarrassed, but only for a moment. After all, he and Johnny had tried to steal the SCAV drive from us the previous year.

I clamped my hand on Cliff's shoulder. "Get back soon, Cliff. We'll need you on the mission to destroy the dreadnought."

His expression didn't change; he was focused on his task. "No problem, Boss. I'll get it."

—••—

WE DEPARTED THE FRENCH DOME AND set course south, for Trieste. Féroce—Renée—had boarded SC-1, and she'd looked around for a moment in recognition, for the last time she had been aboard she had tried to take over the seacar. I'd had to blow the airlock hatch, rapidly decompress, and risk The Bends to convince her to surrender.

It made me shake my head. Funny, how the drive to independence and world events can change people. Now she was on side with me, had helped approach Cousteau to inquire about a partnership, and was going to come on the mission to destroy the dreadnought.

Johnny and I sat in the pilot's chairs, and he shot a glance at me. "You think Cliff can do this?"

"Absolutely."

"That base is a research facility. It'll have guards."

"Cliff is a military man. And the base is concealed. Security will be minimal. He'll make it." But I gripped the yoke tighter.

Inside, I was trembling.

—••—

OUR DEPTH WAS 2,000 METERS; I wanted to stay deep in the Atlantic gyre, the global current that travels from the cold, dense waters of the Arctic to the equatorial regions near our destination. The northerly flowing one— warm waters moving from low latitudes to the pole—was much shallower. Our buoyancy was neutral and I reached to activate the fusion reactor and the SCAV drive—

The sonar blared.

Johnny snapped a look at it and swore. "Torpedo in the water! Range—" He gasped. "Only three hundred meters! It's a SCAV weapon, Mac!"

Which meant it would rapidly accelerate to a thousand kph, and we were sitting ducks.

"Eject countermeasures!" I blurted as I slammed the reactor button and pushed the throttle to full. But it needed a few seconds to start vaporizing seawater, and those seconds were going to be precious. The torpedo was only moments away.

"Who the hell is it?" I yelled. I blew ballast and pushed down on the yoke. We could go deep to avoid it, I knew. We had Lazlow's APD to keep us below a level where weapons or other subs could descend.

Johnny ignored me. "Countermeasures are active. Torpedo closing!"

Behind us, the others had sat on the couches in a tightlipped silence. The attack had caught them off guard as well.

The alarm continued to blare, then it doubled in volume. A glance at the sonar screen confirmed my worst fears. "Another torpedo in the water," I hissed. "Target the ship that's firing at us."

"Got it," came the terse response.

"Fire a homer. SCAV."

"Done!"

SC-1 was diving quickly now and the bubble was stretching back from the bow. But the torpedo chasing us was much faster. It was already at

550 kph and still accelerating. "Dammit," I snapped. "This is bad. How'd they get so close to us?"

"Six hundred and seventy-three kph and climbing!" was the only reply. "Bearing three seven two!" Johnny was working the problem, calling out information for me to adjust my heading.

Our depth was now 3,500 and dropping fast. Our speed was over two hundred kph. Within seconds we were at crush depth—4,000 meters—and I reached to trip on the Acoustic Pulse Drive—and Lazlow screamed from over my shoulder. "No! You have to slow to fifty first!"

I swore again. He was right. The APD would let us go deep, but we couldn't be moving fast. It was a dilemma. How was I going to avoid these SCAV torpedoes before I could get to a safe depth?

I had only one option. "Eject countermeasures—a bunch of them! Give these torpedoes no other option!"

"How many—"

"All of them!"

Johnny gritted his teeth and pressed the COUNTERMEASURE LAUNCH button repeatedly. Finally, "All fifteen are away and churning in the same general location, Mac."

I blew ballast and took her up like a rocket. I hoped the mass of countermeasures would be too great a target for the torpedoes to miss.

Our depth decreased rapidly. Soon we were at max velocity and soaring to the surface. The hull popped and creaked as the pressure diminished. Although a bubble of air currently enveloped us, it was at the same pressure as the exterior water. Our hull was compensating for the differential as we ascended.

Behind us, a massive detonation shook *SC-1*. The seacar shuddered and rattled and the yoke jumped in my hands. "Tell me we got them," I rasped.

"Both torpedoes blew! The countermeasures worked!"

But we were out of them now, and I still had no idea who was attacking us.

—••—

I LEVELED US OFF JUST BELOW the surface. The wake from our SCAV drive churned behind us, no doubt leaving a frothing trail across the waves. I had another strategy in case there were more torpedoes on the way, something I hadn't used in a while.

But I wanted to be ready.

"You're going to jump out of the water?" Johnny muttered.

I nodded. "If we have to."

SCAV weapons were so fast that it was the only way to knock them out. The idea was to let them approach, and then leap from the water. As *SC-1* descended back and slammed into the surface, the missiles would follow and detonate at impact. I'd used it before against both the USSF and the CSF, and afterward they had programmed their weapons to never follow into open air above the surface. It might work against these attackers, however.

I risked a glance at the sonar, to locate the source of the torpedoes. There were five subs there, falling rapidly behind.

They didn't have SCAV drive. They couldn't keep up with us.

Then our torpedo caught my attention. It was traveling at 1,000 kph, and it was approaching the cluster of vessels.

I turned *SC-1* back toward the enemy. We were still at 450 kph.

Johnny said, "Are you sure? We're clear now. We can just run."

"I want to know who that is," I said. The label over the contacts read:

```
Unknown signatures

Contact 1:
Depth: 1,150 meters ^
Speed: 24 kph


Contact 2:
Depth: 2,223 meters v
Speed: 47 kph
```

Contact 3:
Depth: 2,578 meters
Speed: 63 kph

Contact 4:
Depth: 3,675 meters ∨
Speed: 33 kph

Contact 5:
Depth: 750 meters ∧
Speed: 30 kph

The arrows indicated whether the contact was rising or descending. All five were dispersing. One was maintaining depth but moving faster than the others.

It wouldn't make a difference.

Contact 3 then flared on the screen in a cloud of white noise and the point of light disappeared.

"We got it," Johnny whispered. A dull thud reverberated through our hull. The sound of the detonation.

"Fire three more SCAVs. All homers."

He grimaced but did it. It was a tough thing to send people to their deaths, but they had started this.

The color out the canopy was a light blue, indicating that we were quite shallow. I couldn't see the contacts because they were all far below us. I adjusted our angle slightly, pushing our bow down, and they drifted into our field of view. The computer projected them as simple white lines on the blue background—the VID system only worked for a five-kilometer radius around us—but I gasped when I saw the warsubs.

They were small, similar in size to the USSF *Hunter-Killers*, and all the same class, all twenty-four meters long.

They had a distinctive double strut connecting the thruster pods to the primary hull.

Chapter
Fifteen

"How are they here?" Johnny asked. "Did they follow us?"

"It's possible, but I don't see how." Unless there was someone informing on us. Again.

Then I took a longer look at one of the warsubs.

The double strut was the same as the dreadnought's.

The same country of origin.

The ships were still scrambling to escape our weapons. I took the opportunity to take us deep again, right to the 4,000-meter crush depth, and then slowed until we were at fifty kph. If they fired again, I would take us down using the APD.

Now we had some breathing space.

I watched the aquanautic gymnastics as the four remaining warsubs fired countermeasures and swerved to keep the torpedoes away from them. Then they fired two more weapons, which locked to us and began to track. They accelerated quickly.

More SCAV weapons.

We dove deep.

The hull groaned and creaked at first, but then stopped suddenly.

As I took *SC-1* below 5,000 meters, and the APD's rhythmic pulses echoed through our vessel, pushing *outward* at the smothering water to create a low-pressure tunnel for us to power through, all three of our weapons made solid impacts.

One by one the vessels stuttered to a stop. Each torpedo vaporized large amounts of water instantly, creating empty cavities that the surrounding seawater pounded into. This created secondary impacts, and two of the warsubs imploded. The wreckage sank quickly as bubbles and oil churned upward.

The third vessel stopped dead in the water, a gaping hole in its rear compartment. It listed backward and sank, stern first, until it hit crush depth of just over 4,000 meters. It crunched like a tin can.

Only one more left.

I had deliberately let it survive.

The SCAV missiles coming for us continued to dive, attempting to follow. But our depth was too great, and each missile faltered, thrust flickering, before it drifted to a silent stop and simply plunged downward into the depths.

Johnny finally leaned back in his chair and sighed. "That was close."

We could relax a bit now. He was right. Now that we were below their weapons' abilities to follow, we were in the clear.

Meg appeared at my shoulder. "Are they the same subs as at The Ridge?"

"Appears so," I said. "Same type anyway."

She studied the last one, projected on the canopy. "Are you recording its sonar trace?"

"Yes."

"I'll want to study it," Lazlow called from the back. "They seemed to sneak up on us easily."

"Our passive sonar didn't hear a peep," I muttered.

"It was their screw blades. Built for silence at low or high speeds."

I shook my head. Then, "Let's see if we can discover a bit about them." I keyed the comm and spoke into the mic.

——••——

"ATTENTION WARSUB. YOU ATTACKED US WITHOUT provocation. We've destroyed the other four. You're next, unless you give us some information."

No response.

Johnny glanced at me. "Let me open the torpedo hatch. Let them know they're only seconds from death."

"Do it."

I pressed the comm. "We're preparing to fire."

Still nothing.

Their sonar signal was steady. They were at neutral buoyancy, neither rising nor falling. Velocity zero.

Just sitting there.

Johnny had a pair of headphones on, and he frowned. "I'm hearing some weird noise," he muttered.

Lazlow rose from the couch and approached. "May I?"

He put the headphones on and closed his eyes. "I hear . . . equipment being moved. Crates or boxes perhaps. I also hear . . . arguing."

I frowned. "They're speaking loudly?"

"Quite loud. Can you bring us closer?"

"I can pull up under them and circle. But I don't want to rise above five kilometers. If they attack again, their torpedoes can't—"

A white flare blossomed on the sonar display. The canopy showed a cloud of white, and simultaneously Lazlow ripped the headphones off his head with a curse.

He was staring at me. "There was no torpedo."

"No."

Meg said, horrified, "Rather than surrender to us?"

I frowned. "What language were they speaking, Lazlow?"

"I couldn't tell. They were quite a distance away. I just heard muffled voices. It wasn't English though." He looked down at the display between the pilot chairs. "I'll review the tapes. I should be able to isolate the words."

I grinned tightly. It was a stroke of luck.

—••—

It would have been a tense last couple of minutes, I thought. As the commander ordered the vessel destroyed, would the crew have objected? Lazlow felt for sure that there had been at least eight people speaking, possibly more. What would it have been like, I wonder, to activate a bomb and set it next to your own hull and wait for it to detonate? What exactly would end up killing you: the explosion, the water flooding in, or the pressure after flooding?

Each soul who navigated the depths risked their lives every single second. Equipment or hull failure, power loss, or some other innocuous malfunction could end it all in a split second.

But to end it all at your own hands . . .

"What do you think they're hiding?" Johnny muttered.

"Their identity."

"It's that important?"

I grunted. "They attacked the United States. If we discover who they are, it might mean war."

"But surely that's what they want."

"Maybe so. Maybe they're not ready for it yet."

A long silence stretched out inside *SC-1*. I continued to stare at the sonar. Fragments of white on the screen grew dimmer as the wreckage drifted downward, toward the choking depths.

"Actually, maybe they are ready for it," Johnny said. "Maybe they do want it. But not on land. Just in the oceans."

I considered that for a moment. He was right.

This cold war we were in the middle of was hardly cold anymore.

—••—

The next day we arrived back at Trieste, to the immense relief of my assistants. Without a deputy mayor, we really needed someone second in command to take over in case of emergency, though all the procedures and processes were already in place and the control staff knew what to do. But it was good to have a leader there, to provide stability and present an air of composure over everything in the city.

I sent Lazlow to continue his work deciphering the sonar and building a picture of the dreadnought, which we would need for our mission. We needed to know how many torpedo tubes that warsub had, along with any other weapons. We also had to figure out what language the mysterious attackers had spoken before they had scuttled their own vessel.

—••—

ADMIRAL BENNING WAS WAITING FOR ME in my office.

He was sitting in my chair, staring at the ceiling as I walked in. I ground to a sudden halt and glared at him. How long had he been there? Had he been going through my things?

Not that it mattered.

I didn't keep anything TCI-related in that office.

I had marched right past City Systems Control; Kristen had been there, but something on the comm had held her attention.

"What do you want?" I growled at the Admiral.

He turned to me, slowly. "You're back. My people informed me, so I came to speak with you."

"You're not welcome to come in without being invited." I gestured to my chair.

An oily grin spread across his features. "But I *did* ask, earlier. You gave me and my crew permission. Remember?"

"Only to visit. Not to invade my privacy."

He glanced around. "What are you hiding here? Why is this a problem?"

"If I went to *Devastator* and sat in your chair, you would have had a similar reaction."

"My crew wouldn't allow you to board, actually." And then that smile again crossed his features.

My eyes were icy as I watched him. I was not going to put up with that kind of disrespect. Not in Trieste anyway. I took a step toward him—

He sighed and rose to his feet. "Very well. I'll give you your desk back."

He shifted smoothly to another chair with a grace that betrayed his large frame and his age.

I stuttered to a halt and said, "Don't fuck with me, Benning. You asked for my help. I'm going to give it to you. But don't overstay your welcome."

"We're all US citizens, McClusky. And Trieste only exists to serve a purpose."

Inwardly, I swore. So here was the real USSF officer, finally coming out. I stood over the man and stared at him for a long, sustained moment. "I mean it, Benning."

He looked up at me with a slight smile on his face. Finally, he whispered, "We'll see."

I remained there for another thirty seconds before I moved to my chair.

He exhaled and then smiled again. "Now, where have you been?"

"I've been digging up help for the dreadnought issue. I think I have a good team now. We're learning more about it. I'll brief you soon. My acoustician needs a few more days on it, then we'll be able to plan."

His face grew serious. "Turns out they did use another nuke against the San Diego seawall. Broke it clean through, just like at Norfolk."

"And the relief efforts?"

"Virginia is settling down. They've shored up the seawall. It's going to take months to pump out the water and for the region to recover, if there is such a thing nowadays." He snorted. "San Diego is a disaster still." He waved his hand. "The USSF lost a lot of people."

"Warsubs? Ships?"

"Some. But most of the damage was to the personnel." He rose to his feet. "I'll be back in two days. Make sure you have something for me by then."

—••—

BENNING WAS GONE AND I KNEW I had to press on with my efforts. First, I got Laura Sukovski on the comm from the mining interests division. It took a few minutes, but finally she appeared on the screen, breathless and tired. "Mac," she said. "Why are you bothering me?"

I frowned. "Checking on progress. The thorium deposit."

"Yes, of course." She swatted my question away. "We're working on it. Automated ships have arrived and settled down. The habitat is under construction. The remote machinery is already digging down to the ore."

"How deep is it?"

"The mine or the ore?"

I shrugged. "Both."

"The mine is 1,700 meters below sea level. The ore is close to the sea-floor—only seven meters of digging needed."

I sighed. It was deep for a manned operation. "Sounds dangerous. I know I put a deadline on this, but I don't want anyone dead. Don't take unnecessary risks."

She glared at me. "Damn you, Mac! I'm doing what you asked—"

I knew when to leave things alone with her. We had a good friendship, and this request wasn't personal. "Thanks, see you." I flashed her a tight grin, then cut the comm at a final image of her flustered and hostile expression.

Before I could take care of the next item, my comm buzzed. It was a direct call from outside of Trieste. I frowned and punched the button.

Mayor Reggie Quinn of Seascape City appeared on my screen. It made me want to yell in shock, but I clamped down on the feeling.

Months earlier, I had contacted him in person to inquire about a partnership in the quest for independence. Quinn had made it clear to me, however, that he wanted nothing to do with it. Seascape was too prosperous, too successful to even consider going against the USSF or the US.

He had kicked me out of his city.

It had occurred during the same trip to visit Mayor Winton, who had joined us willingly.

"Mayor Quinn," I said, guarded. "This is a surprise."

His face remained flat, devoid of expression. "Mayor McClusky."

"How can I help you?"

He sighed. "Things are not good here, Truman."

"Mac, please."

"Mac. You were right, actually."

I frowned. "About?"

"About what would happen to us should the tourists disappear."

His city focused primarily on tourism, while Ballard had a fishing focus, and ours was kelp farming. I leaned forward. "What's happened, Reggie?"

He shook his head and looked away. "I'm sorry I was so rude to you when we met. You came all that way to see me, and I was a jerk."

"You said you didn't want what I was selling." I said it slowly; I realized I had to be careful here.

He stared at me for long moments, his eyes dark and intense. "I do now. I'd like to come to you this time. May I?"

I sighed as I mulled it over. "What's going on, exactly?"

"It's San Diego and Norfolk. Both enormous disasters. Bookings have nearly disappeared. Others have cancelled their trips."

I nodded. As I'd predicted. "Reggie, I'd love to host you here. When can you come?"

We arranged a time and he extended a courteous good bye. Then the screen turned blue.

Interesting, I thought.

—••—

I HAD TO CHECK IN WITH the repair docks to see how their crews were progressing, if the additional workers had lessened the load on the supervisor, Josh Miller. He had been rude to me days earlier, not fully understanding the pressures that the USSF had forced on me and Trieste. I could let it go. He was doing what was best for his division.

Still, I thought, he should invest more thought into the bigger picture at Trieste.

Rather than call him, I decided to physically visit the repair dock. To stretch my legs. It was growing late in the day—we had arrived back from our trip to the French base in mid-afternoon—and the second shift was currently on duty. The sun was setting, dusk was falling, and the lamps outside had come on, casting a massive island of light around the undersea city. Above, on the surface atop thirty meters of water, there were a few ocean vessels passing, their wakes glimmering in the red light of the setting sun and resembling ribbons of churning lava stretching across our 'sky.' I stopped at a vast viewport to stare out at the scene. It never failed to captivate me. Even *Devastator*, moored just to the west, was a fascinating sight. Bubbles escaped from vents in the hull and rose serenely to the surface. Divers moved about, performing routine maintenance, and airlocks opened and closed as scooters entered and exited the warsub.

The umbilical drew my gaze. Lights illuminated it from within; I could see shadows as crew moved back and forth between the city and the vessel.

I grunted and turned away.

Kat was still very much in my thoughts. She'd spent the bulk of her early adulthood caring for a sick father, and it had taken her time to find her way to Trieste and to achieve her dreams of living underwater and helping the independence movement.

At the time of her arrival, I had been very much against her plans. I'd survived the death of my father, then years in TCI, then capture, then imprisonment and torture at the hands of Sheng City Intelligence. I had wanted out, and had thrown myself into menial labor on the kelp farms.

But when I met Kat, everything changed.

She had convinced me.

I lived under the shadow of my father. Meg and I both did. I desperately wanted to achieve the greatness that he had, but had known for so long that his ignominious defeat was something I needed to carefully avoid. Then I'd learned that he had known the attack was coming, and he'd deliberately walked into the trap hoping that it would set up independence at a time when the city was better prepared for it. It made me shake my head. Could I have done that? Could I have let them kill me, hoping that it would change the future for my children and send them on a path to hopeful victory?

The news had shocked Kat as well, but her focus on independence had never wavered. I'd learned from her.

Soon I found myself in a travel tube, stopped dead in my tracks; I was staring up through the transparent ceiling at the darkening sea above.

My heart thudded in my chest, and it felt as though an icy hand was squeezing it.

This was the same travel tube where—

Where the CIA had attacked and killed dad.

Frank McClusky. Mayor of the city, freedom fighter, and Director of Trieste City Intelligence.

It was the tube in the south-eastern sector of the city, connecting the aquaculture module to the central commerce module.

But why was I there? I had been walking to the repair docks, on the *other side* of Trieste!

I must have been in a daze. Events were having a larger impact on me than I'd thought.

Admiral Benning had been the one who had carried it out. The CIA had clearly been working with the USSF. They'd attached an umbilical to the tube. Sealed both ends so once he was in, Dad couldn't escape. Then they'd entered and shot him in the head. They'd planted a bomb and left, sealing the umbilical behind them. The seas had crashed in, crushing his body, just to make sure.

Just to make sure.

At the same time, others had killed the rest of the city council while they slept. They'd killed them all, and had never apologized for it. They simply couldn't lose Trieste, they'd said.

Then people had moved on, but Triestrians had remembered. They'd never forget.

I searched the tube's bulkhead to see where they had cut in, but it was impossible to find a weld where it had happened. Repair crews had likely replaced huge sections to remove the damage.

Just cut out the evidence, replace it, and paint over it.

If only memories were so easy to repair.

—••—

THE HEAVINESS THAT WAS ALWAYS THERE within me, just under the surface, grew harder to suppress and I had to lean against the bulkhead and just stare outside for long moments. People passing by watched, but thankfully didn't say anything. I wondered what they were thinking, but it didn't matter.

Wasn't I just as bad as the people who'd murdered him? I'd killed before. Hell, only weeks ago I'd just—

A choking gasp rose in my throat and I had to smother it. I clenched my fists and closed my eyes.

No. I wouldn't think about that yet.

Later.

I pulled myself together and forced my feet to start moving.

To the repair module, I scolded myself. *Go take care of city business.*

I left the tube, but its invisible hold on me would remain forever.

Until I died, that is. Perhaps as my dad had. Assassinated by the city's enemies in a dark and lonely place.

Chapter Sixteen

JOSH MILLER SAW ME COMING AND stopped what he'd been doing. He was working into the evening, which most likely meant he'd been doing double shifts for some time. He gestured at some workers to continue welding a hull plate to a kelp harvester, and marched toward me.

I groaned. I don't know why I'd wanted to come, but inside I realized it was likely the best thing for a leader to do—to check in with his managers in person, see if they needed anything. Sure enough, he was smiling at me now, which was quite different from his demeanor during our last conversation.

"Hi, Mac," he said. There was a hint of contrition on his face.

"Josh." We shook hands and I pointed at the line of ships in the repair berths. "Seems like you're still really busy."

"We're keeping up now, actually, thanks to the five people you sent."

I attempted a smile. I'm not sure it worked. "And it was enough?"

He frowned and scratched his head. "We can always use more, I guess, but it's worked out well. Thanks."

"Is there anything else you need?"

"We're doing great now. Those ships there are done and ready to go back to the farms. We'll be finished that one by morning. We have some electrical repairs to make on that equipment over there. Should have that done by end of day tomorrow. There are three new repairs we'll start then." He'd been pointing each out as he spoke.

"I just thought I'd come and see how you were."

His smile grew. "Thanks, Mac. And I'm sorry—I'm sorry I was such a dick to you earlier. I realized later that we don't have much control over the USSF."

"I'm trying."

His expression grew serious and he pointed at me. "I know that. Hell, everyone knows it. Don't ever doubt it."

I let that soak in. Then, "Get back to work, Josh. Call if you need more help."

He turned and marched away, but yelled over his shoulder, "Thanks again, Mac!"

—••—

SLEEP WAS FITFUL AGAIN THAT NIGHT. Kat kept coming to me, asking for help with this or that, asking about *SC-1*, telling me to take care of the seacar and to keep fighting for independence. It really was exhausting. I needed sleep, not constant reminders of things I should be doing.

I knew inside that it was my conscience speaking, that I was taking too much on, but Dad was a big part of it too. He'd expected a lot from me, and I couldn't let him down.

—••—

SEVERAL DAYS PASSED, WHICH I SPENT taking care of administrative tasks and managing the divisions and maintaining production. The USSF troops in the city were staying under the radar, thankfully, and there weren't many security issues to worry about. Yet.

Renée Féroce had a compartment in a living module that Kristen Canvel had arranged upon her arrival, and when I saw her, I thought she looked disheveled and tired. She merely shrugged when I mentioned it; she'd been volunteering in the aquaculture module, spending her time working the kelp farms.

"Liking undersea life?" I asked. We were in my office; Lazlow had called to request a meeting, asking if I could assemble the team for a briefing. I'd called the others, and Renée had been the first to arrive.

She grinned and her tired eyes lit up. "I am loving it."

"Miss the military?"

"Maybe. But for now, being outside in scuba gear is wonderful."

I knew how she felt. "Trieste is incredible. I'd do anything for the city."

Her eyes grew serious. "Yes, I know. But something tells me that you're about to reveal the next step."

I hesitated. "I'm not sure myself." I didn't know what Lazlow wanted to share, but he had requested the presence of everyone relevant to the dreadnought. I had decided to include Admiral Benning. That made me shudder, but I knew it was necessary, otherwise he would grow antsy and that dark side might emerge again.

Soon the others had all arrived: Renée, Meg, Lau, Johnny, Benning, Lazlow. I'd also invited Laura Sukovski from mining, and our visiting nuclear engineer from Ballard: Irena Rostilov. Also present were Richard Lancombe and Jessica Ng, the married couple who had been working hard on the defenses surrounding Trieste. Their eyes narrowed when they saw Benning; they knew not to give anything important or incriminating away to the USSF.

Benning also looked around with interest. "Who are all these people?" he asked me.

"My team," was all I said. Then I pointed at Lazlow. "This is my acoustician. He's been studying the dreadnought."

Benning stared at the two Chinese men. "And you?"

"They are geologists," I lied. Beside me, I saw Laura eye me uncertainly.

"Why do we need—"

"I have information," Lazlow interjected.

Thankfully, it attracted Benning's attention. I wondered if it had been such a good idea after all to include him in this meeting.

I studied Lazlow for a moment. I had to admit, he was looking better. His face had filled out a bit, and he didn't look so skeletal. The three meals a day, delivered to his lab, were working.

Meg was glaring at Benning, but I shot her a look. *Don't start any shit,* I signaled.

She nodded imperceptibly.

"Go on," Benning said in his deep voice.

We sat on chairs that I had brought in for the meeting. It was cramped; the office wasn't large, and there were a lot of us in there.

Lazlow inserted a memory chip into my computer, and a projection lit the space between us.

There were gasps.

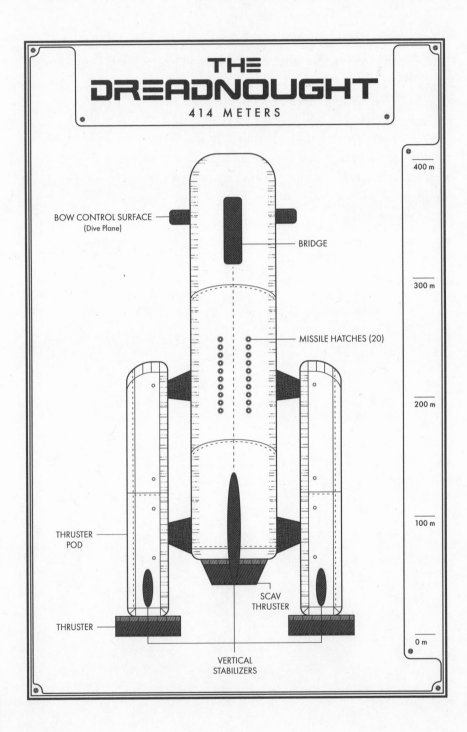

THE DREADNOUGHT
414 METERS

BOW CONTROL SURFACE (Dive Plane)

BRIDGE

MISSILE HATCHES (20)

THRUSTER POD

THRUSTER

SCAV THRUSTER

VERTICAL STABILIZERS

400 m

300 m

200 m

100 m

0 m

"This is a simplified diagram of the dreadnought," he said. "It's the best I can do with only the sound of water passing across its hull to give us clues. But it shows the configuration of the hull, thruster pods, control surfaces, and missile hatches with fair accuracy, I believe." He pointed at the diagram. "It's 414 meters long, with a height of a hundred meters give or take. That gives it thirty decks. Note the double-strut connection to the pods."

"We've seen those before," I muttered. Benning shot me a look, and I said, "Small vessels attacked us a few days ago. The sonar didn't have the ships in its database." I gestured to the dreadnought. "They looked like smaller versions of that. Only twenty-four meters long."

"Why didn't you tell me?"

"I'm telling you now."

He looked like he was about to continue, but then glanced around and realized where he was. He ended up giving a curt nod. "Very well. Go on, Doctor."

Lazlow said, "The ship shows remarkable new technology. The tsunami plow for one. It must be located here, at the bow—" He pointed again. "—but it's not in the diagram because it didn't affect the water as the vessel moved in SCAV drive. It's most likely recessed into the hull. The warsub's top speed is 467 kilometers per hour. There are twenty hatches on the top, presumably for nuclear missiles. I count over fifty torpedo tubes, and *at least* 150 airlocks for troops or smaller vessels." He then brought his long finger to indicate the double struts. "These don't have enough surface area to interact with the water to be control surfaces."

"But it has bow dive planes," Johnny said.

"Not large enough for a ship that size," Meg said. "The conventional screws must be able to gimbal."

She meant that there were hydraulics which could move the direction of the screws, much like a rocket's nozzles, to direct the path of the warsub.

"Anechoic tiles cover the vessel," Lazlow pressed on. "Its maximum conventional speed might be fifty-four kph."

Meg swore. It was fast for such a gargantuan vessel. The screw blades must be massive.

"And it likely also has hydraulic blades, same as the smaller versions. To change their orientation to reduce cavitation at low speeds or high speeds."

"Wait a minute," Benning growled. "Just wait. Two things—what do you mean, hydraulic blades? And how do you know its max conventional speed?"

Lazlow shrugged. "I'm theorizing about the speed. After it created the tsunami in both locations, it turned and powered away under conventional drive. They hid this from us in the San Diego attack better by using a deliberate, loud noise to mask what they were doing. But in the Norfolk attack, we learned more. As it turned and sped away, Admiral, it launched a nuclear-tipped torpedo at the seawall. Do you think they *wouldn't* have used top speed to get away? Eventually they did kick in their SCAV drive to run faster, but while they were launching the torpedo, it was conventional thrusters only."

"Good point," Benning conceded.

"As for the hydraulic blades, they're meant to change each impact angle with the water as they rotate. It can alter this, depending on vessel speed, to lower cavitation and reduce noise. We think it makes the ships stealthier at higher speeds as well as slower ones."

Lazlow paused, and I said, "Do you know the country of origin yet?"

During all this, Irena and Laura were completely and utterly confused. They were watching the entire presentation in a perplexed silence, not understanding why they were there.

Renée was also paying close attention. She was studying the image intently.

"From this diagram, and from the nature of the attack," Lazlow said, "no, we can't tell. But there are clues to which countries it's not from. It's *not* Chinese or US or French. It simply doesn't share any of the same characteristics as warsubs from those nations. Nor is it English, Canadian, Australian, German, or Brazilian. No other nation seems to use the gimbaling thrusters, nor do they use hydraulics to adjust blade orientation to lower cavitation— and noise—with the water. So, we can eliminate those nations."

I sighed. "So still no—"

"But we do have evidence from the smaller warsubs."

That took me aback. I'd forgotten. The arguing on board just before the crew had scuttled their own vessel.

He continued, "If we accept that the smaller versions are from the same country as this larger one, and the language they spoke inside the scaled-down warsub during a very stressful few moments was not a ploy to throw suspicion off them, then I can tell you that I think I know the country of origin."

Benning bolted to his feet. "What? You know who attacked us?" His face was hard and his eyes lasers.

Lazlow turned to me. "Are you sure it's okay—"

"Go ahead," I said with a wave. "Benning is here because we are assisting the USSF with this."

"Very well."

It was clear that I had agitated Benning, for he suddenly realized that he didn't have any power over the people in that room. They deferred to me.

Lazlow said in a curt, abrupt tone: "They were speaking Russian."

—••—

A WAVE OF SHOCK PASSED THROUGH the cabin. Each expression showed complete disbelief and stunned realization as Lazlow revealed the attacker. Even my own. I couldn't believe it.

"But Russia has not been interested in the oceans," Lancombe said. "They're going through tremendous economic despair, worse than any superpower on Earth."

"They're disintegrating right now, breaking apart," Benning said. "How could they have built such a ship? Or a fleet, if what you're saying is true and they have smaller versions of this as well?"

"They've been somewhat interested in the oceans," I muttered. "They have two underwater cities: Gagarin and Gorshkov. They have the RSF too, with eight classes of warsubs and four missile boats. From the *Lenin* Class to *Kirov*, from *Finisher* to *Eliminator*."

Benning stared at me. My knowledge of foreign submarine fleets must have shocked him. But it didn't matter.

"But these new subs don't match any current configuration," Johnny said. "How did they make this leap? And a SCAV drive as well?"

I nodded. "You're right. Maybe there's a new faction. The country is crumbling, as you say, Benning, but maybe they're just realizing the importance of moving to the oceans now."

Lau said, "It would explain why they destroyed the Chinese fleet over the Iron Plains. If they're hoping to make a claim to it."

Benning said, "They did *what?*" His face was white.

Lau nodded. "Sixty-three ships. No damage to the dreadnought." Then he hesitated and sent a darting glance at Benning. "According to my family member in the CSF, anyway."

The admiral hadn't noticed the slip. He clenched his fists. "They are determined to rule the oceans, and they're going to go through anyone in their way to control the resources there."

"But they won't," I said. Silence descended over the cabin. The others turned to me. "Because we, in this room, are going to destroy this warsub. It's why you're all here."

Chapter Seventeen

IRENA ROSTILOV STARED AT ME. SHE had come over from Ballard, and according to Winton, was involved in their intelligence agency. "You're saying that this vessel uses a fusion reactor to vaporize seawater for propulsion?"

"We do it too," I said.

"But that ship is huge." She pointed at it.

"Right. It's partly why you're here. How big would the reactor have to be?"

She frowned. "I'll need more data, but it must be significant. Larger than any reactor in any other warsub, I'm sure. It'd need to power the vessel's systems, provide power for the conventional thrusters, as well the SCAV drive you're talking about." She shook her head. "As large as any nuclear plant that might power a city."

I snorted. Like the rest of the warsub, everything was super-sized on this beast.

She lifted her chin as she studied the diagram floating before us. "Do you have a readout of its emissions?"

"I'm sorry?"

"Every reactor releases neutrons and other particles like gamma rays. If I had a reading of its emissions, it would give me more to go on."

I looked at Benning and raised an eyebrow. He nodded and said, "We have some data that a warsub near San Diego recorded during the second attack. I'll send it to you immediately."

I said, "Now we have to talk about how to destroy this thing."

"There's more than that!" Benning roared. "I have to tell my superiors. We're going to war with Russia!"

"Wait!" I snapped. "Listen to me. We're still not a hundred percent on that. And you can't go starting wars based on supposition."

"*They* started it! They attacked the mainland USA!"

"I know. But it'll be best in the long run for us to just end it before it grows to something we can't handle. The land nations are going through enough right now. Economies are suffering. *People* are suffering. This will just make things worse."

He squared his shoulders and stared at me. "I can't betray the chain of command, McClusky."

"Just hold off until we know more," I said. "Then you can do it. Just give us a couple more days."

"We may not *have* many more days."

"It's better than a land war using nuclear weapons, for fuck's sake."

His face was hard as he stared at the others around him.

"I included you in this," I said. "You asked for help."

He deflated after a few tense heartbeats, and remained quiet.

I hesitated as I considered something. "Let me ask you this. If we needed the USSF to organize a fleet, could you do that? To hunt for this dreadnought?"

His brow crinkled. "Of course. That's what we want to do anyway."

"And could we advertise it somehow? Announce it?"

Lancombe was staring at me. "You're suggesting letting them know that the fleet is out there looking?"

"I am."

His expression flattened. "To lure it in."

"Yes."

Benning looked outraged. "As bait?" Then he scoffed. "We'll be more than bait, I'll tell you that."

Lau said, "This dreadnought blew sixty-three heavily armed Chinese warsubs apart. They offered no resistance. Don't overestimate this vessel, Admiral."

"We'll offer *better* resistance."

I frowned and stared at the man. "Sinking it is going to be difficult."

"Not with nukes."

I shuddered. "That's a last resort, Benning. That'll start a war for sure."

"They already used nukes on us!"

"Only small fission warheads. They weren't hydrogen bombs, right? Tactical nukes only?"

"Yes. And we can use the same on them."

The mood in the office had grown dark. No one wanted to hear about countries using nuclear weapons on one another.

"I have a better idea," I muttered. "Can you give me just a little more time?"

He shot me a look, at the resolve in my face, and then said, "You better have a good plan, McClusky. And you better hope they don't attack while we're waiting."

Then he marched from the cabin.

—••—

MEG TURNED TO ME. HER FACE was red. "Why are you involving him in this? He's a monster. He's going to—"

"I know. I know. But it's politics, Meg. We need the USSF on our side. We need to fight them without letting them know we're their enemy. Heller knew about us, and he made our lives miserable. This way, by including Benning, things might be different."

"He killed Dad!"

The others were staring at us, at brother and sister, hashing it out in front of all to see.

"I have a plan, Meg. He's part of it. Please, I'm asking you to trust me as well."

Silence descended once again. In the middle of the room, that image of the dreadnought remained, rotating slowly.

Laura Sukovsky said, "Mac, why am I here exactly?"

I turned to her. "You're part of the plan. I want you to know the stakes."

"That ship attacked the United States. It's killed countless people. It destroyed USSF HQ on both coasts. I understand all that. But that might be a good thing for Trieste, isn't it?" She glanced around. "I know that sounds heartless, but it's a fact."

"They've attacked us too. In the Mid-Atlantic Ridge, then again when I picked up Renée. Trieste is in grave danger." I pointed at Richard and Jessica. "That's what they're doing here. They're putting defenses in place. Against those smaller ships, we might survive. *Might*. But against that dreadnought . . ." I trailed off. "We don't have a chance. We have to take the fight to them and destroy this thing, and we need to strengthen our ties with the USSF at the same time. They're still our enemy, Meg, no doubt about it, *but I don't want Benning to know that we're his enemy too*. Do you understand that? It's the best thing for Trieste."

They looked around and, one by one, nodded agreement. The pieces had fallen into place for them, and they realized that I was offering the best option.

I sent Laura and Irena to continue their respective work, with a plea for them to remain quiet about Russia and the dreadnought, and turned to the rest of my team.

Johnny said, "Benning saw us all here, Mac. He might put two and two together. He might realize that there's more going on than just this dreadnought."

I glanced at Meg. "He's not going to live long enough, Johnny. This mission is going to kill him."

Lancombe said, "You are full of surprises, Mac."

"You didn't know that about me yet?"

He snorted. "I did. You're like your father."

I stared at the man. "I'm not sure about that. I don't think I would have done what he did."

"He did it—"

I cut him off. "I know what you're going to say. But strategy is one thing." I glanced at Meg. "*Family* is another. What he did had enormous repercussions." And then I waved it away. Now was not the time. "You and

Jessica have been working on our defenses. How are things going?"

They glanced at each other. "We've started installing the remote torpedo launchers."

"And the fences?"

"They're ready to activate."

Johnny said, "Fences?"

"Fish fences. Bubbles. To hide the launchers."

Johnny, Lau, Renée, and Meg were staring at me. Renée said, "You really are surprising," she muttered. There was something in her eyes when she said it.

Her life must be in turmoil, I thought. Ever since we'd crossed paths, she had ended up losing her career in the FSF and was now adrift. She seemed happy at Trieste, but she'd only just arrived. I realized that I'd have to make sure she felt valued here.

I said, "And when will crews install the torpedoes and launchers?"

Jessica said, "A few days. The operator will be here, in City Control. We'll create a new station called City Defense perhaps."

I blinked. "Sounds great actually. Will the launchers also be manned?"

Lancombe frowned. "Automated."

"I'd like them to have secondary controls on site. If we lose control from here. I want a scuba diver to be able to swim over to them, aim and launch manually if necessary."

A silence fell over the pair as they studied each other. Then they looked back to me. "Okay," Lancombe replied. "Sounds good."

Lau swore. "I just can't believe that it's Russia. That they're now getting involved in this cold war."

The Russians had been mysteriously quiet for many decades, focusing on internal issues such as the breakup of the Federation. But they had settled two conshelf cities, years after the other superpowers had started, to keep up. There were rumors that they did not invest effort in maintaining the undersea colonies, did not allow immigration to them, and did not even rely on them for resources to help the mainland. They were for show only.

But now . . . now things were different. Someone else was in charge over there.

"It's another major player in the oceans, you're right. And we need to keep them contained. Are you sure Sheng City will be onboard with this?"

"Of course."

"Will you ask them if they'll provide military help against the dreadnought?"

"I don't have to. I already have authorization. We'll be there in battle if need be."

Johnny said, "Why the mining division, Mac?" He looked perplexed. "Everyone who was present here during the meeting, I understood, but not her."

"Laura?"

"She doesn't have anything to do with the dreadnought."

"She's part of my plan. She didn't even know it until today though."

Johnny snorted. "As is usually your game. You play your cards close to your chest."

I recalled how I had manipulated the FSF and the USSF fleets into the battle over the rift in the Mid-Atlantic Ridge without any of the others realizing it. I knew that sometimes it was better to unveil plans slowly, so no one could cause complications.

"And how is she part of this?" Johnny pressed.

I looked at him and smiled. "Johnny, we're not going to sink that dreadnought with a conventional attack," I whispered. "We're going to use the USSF to lure her in . . . along with any other fleet we can get to help, like the French and the Chinese perhaps, and then we're going to infiltrate that warsub. Sneak aboard, and sabotage her from within."

They looked at me in horror. "*Who* is going to do that?" Meg hissed.

"We are, of course. We're going to announce our search efforts loud and clear so they'll hear. Then when the dreadnought arrives and the battle begins, we'll be prepared. We're going to get aboard her without her crew realizing. And then we're going to sabotage her, somehow, and send her right to the bottom."

Interlude:
RSF *Drakon,*
SSBN
Dreadnought
Class

Location: RSF *Drakon*, SSBN
                   In the Pacific Ocean

Latitude: 11° 09´ S
Longitude: 176° 17´ W
Depth: 813 meters
Time: 1512 hours
Date: 2 May 2030

RSF *DRAKON* HOVERED IN THE PACIFIC Ocean just below a thermal transient—a sharp shift in water temperature that could reflect incoming sound waves. They were naturally occurring and provided protection from discovery. *Drakon* had recently been involved in a major battle against the Chinese fleet, its first real test at ocean battle, and had performed brilliantly. It had survived nearly unscathed.

Nearly.

Captain Ivan Arkady Ventinov stood on the bridge of his warsub, the largest ever put to sea in the oceans—on the surface or below—and felt enormous pride surge through his body. His entire history had led him to this point in his career. Born to government officials, raised in Moscow and socialized around aristocrats and politicians his entire life, he had had a meteoric rise in the Russian Submarine Fleet. His parents and their associates had been his connections, and he had made use of them time and time again. His peers had complained about him having advantages that they didn't, but Ventinov didn't care. He used any method possible to drive himself further in the RSF. During his early years in the fleet, he frequently called on contacts to aid him in his training, ensuring him promotions and opportunities that others simply didn't have access to. Within a few years of his entrance in officer training school, he was a full rank ahead of his classmates, and every year since, the gap widened. Others eyed him with bitterness and envy, but they knew to hold their tongues. Once, early on, a young officer had dared to voice his displeasure, and within days he'd been forced out of the RSF, thanks to a call Ventinov had made to one of his father's political friends.

No one complained openly after that.

He had used everyone he could to increase his status in the fleet, for Russia was too important to leave to the sheep. *Someone* had to lead the others toward strength and victory. To bring Russia back from the dismal cellar of failure, and toward a future that mirrored the strength of history. Ventinov had longed for Russia to return to the greatness of previous centuries, but he knew things on the surface were falling apart. Nations were struggling as ocean levels rose and as temperatures soared and arable land disappeared.

He understood, like others within the ruling class, that the oceans were the newest and most promising frontier for Russia to recover her former glory, and he had fought hard to make this day happen.

The bridge's ceiling was completely transparent, providing a wonderful view of the ocean and the sky far above. When the ship descended too deep for light to penetrate from above, the computer could project images of nearby contacts on the canopy. It was nearly sixty meters long, encompassing the entire command and control chamber on the dreadnought. Around him were countless consoles and stations, where loyal Russians sat and worked on systems; light shone upward at their faces, sending twisting shadows across their features, and there was a pervasive murmur of voices as they gave orders and received information.

Drakon—Dragon in English—was a marvelous warsub. Glorious, even. Ventinov had commanded many different classes of ships in the RSF—*Devil, Leonov, Minsk, Kirov,* and even the missile boat *Eliminator* Class—and had served on others, but this *Dreadnought* was the greatest and most powerful of them all. His background in naval tactics and history and his experience had led to *this* day . . .

The day that Russia would retake its place at the forefront of world events, capture the greatest prize of all—ocean resources that other nations were scrambling to stake claim to—and strike fear in the hearts of all ocean-going nations on Earth. The warsub was a monumental achievement for Russian scientists; senior government officials right at the top had pushed them to create this weapon.

And they had succeeded, brilliantly.

The warsub was unparalleled in undersea travel. It was the largest, most well-armed, fastest and best-armored vessel in the water, without question. Its top speed was 467 kilometers per hour, and was the first—and only—SCAV ship in the RSF. This seemed odd to Ventinov, because the Soviet Union had invented the technology for its torpedoes in the 1970s. Other nations had taken the technology and had improved upon it, leaving Russia far behind, especially after the collapse in later years.

Ventinov unconsciously clenched a fist behind his back. But now, he thought . . . now Russia was *back*.

They had just displayed their power over the Iron Plains region in the Pacific Ocean, east of the Philippines. It was an area rich in iron nodules—deposits precipitated from outgassing vents in ridge axis regions. Geology was a science foreign to him, but the rich iron deposit, stretching across an area the size of Brazil, was what appealed to Russia. They needed resources like this, and others from the oceans, to expand their power. For too long they had succumbed to environmental and economic collapse.

Russia had thrown everything into this quest, thanks to their newest leader Gavriil Ghorzinski, and had created the newest class of warsub, *Dreadnought*. They had also retrofitted earlier versions with newer technologies. They had replaced some altogether, such as the *Vostok* Class vessels, which were now fast and stealthy with a large complement of weaponry. Each only had twelve crew, but the nation had put forty-two of them into service quickly.

Of course, some of the nations west of Russia had suffered for this achievement, notably Ukraine, Belarus, and Poland—all of whom were now part of the new Russian Empire.

Dragons were very much a part of Russian folklore. Most had three heads, walked on hind legs, and spit fire.

Spit fire.

Yes, *Drakon* would spit fire, but from its stern. It used its fire for *speed*.

Dragons also typically represented foreigners in Russian mythology, and they would use its namesake, this massive titanium-alloyed beast, to destroy anyone who stood in Russia's way.

Ventinov stared at the sea over his head. Inside, his guts twisted. The ship had been sitting there, in one place, for too long. He wanted to *move*. To *attack*. Already they had destroyed two USSF bases and over sixty Chinese vessels, but there was so much more to do.

"Give me a report," he said in a quiet tone to his executive officer, who approached silently from behind.

One torpedo had made it through their countermeasure net, and despite *Drakon's* high rate of speed away from the battle, it had impacted dangerously near to her SCAV water intakes. Repairs were necessary. Crews had been working on them since they had found the thermal boundary. They did have a backup system, but the captain demanded that the primary intakes be fixed and the backups used only in emergency.

"Engineers continue working on the intake hatches. Damage is more extensive than previously thought. The intake tubes are also—"

"Just get it done," he growled in response. "Next."

"We continue to hide below the thermal boundary. Chinese warsubs have passed near, but have not spotted us."

This made Ventinov angry. He did not want potential victims to power in and out of their targeting field without *Drakon* acting. He ground his teeth at this news.

His XO, Gregor Sukilov, continued, "The USSF is suffering. Huge sections of Virginia and California are flooding, although they have shored up the Norfolk seawall. We killed many in the attack."

"Vessels?"

"No. Mostly personnel, though there were some hull ruptures. Not many though."

"Damn."

"Captain, the tsunami plow had a greater effect on the buildings in the area. Not on ships that can float or descend under water. And the nuclear bombs were not powerful. They were just enough to break the seawalls."

He snapped a look at Sukilov. "Do you think I'm stupid?"

His XO's face paled. "I did not say such a thing."

"You implied it." Ventinov turned away. "Spend the next two shifts working in engineering. Maybe that will teach you."

He had said it in a calm, yet bitter tone.

There was also the fact that an operator had activated the noise shield too late during the first attack. They had planned to use it *before* they extended the tsunami plow, but this had not happened.

That operator was now dead.

"Aye, aye, sir." The XO's gaze was on the deck.

"What else?"

"The Americans are scrambling to figure out who attacked them and how. We have reports that they have enlisted the aid of Trieste."

Ventinov turned to the man. "Say again?"

"The underwater colony off Florida's coast."

"I know what Trieste is. They were involved in the battle last year in the Gulf of Mexico. They surrendered to the USSF."

Sukilov swallowed. "Yes, sir. But now they are working together, apparently to solve the mystery."

Ventinov suppressed a hollow chuckle. "Perhaps this news will help us pick our future targets."

"Yes."

"It will also please our guest, wouldn't you say?"

"Probably."

The captain paced the long aisle between consoles as he considered the situation. They had made their presence known, there was no doubt of that. They had devastated both coasts of the United States with sudden and unexpected attacks. Then they'd hurt the Chinese.

But there were others who needed lessons as well.

The French, for instance. They had surprised Russia in the last century, building a massive undersea navy despite a faltering economy, and they had more power in the oceans than even Russia. This was disconcerting, especially for the Russian leader, Ghorzinski, because the French had long been a Russian adversary.

But for so many years Russia had been weak, quiet, and a minor player on the world stage.

But no more.

Drakon would turn the tide in the oceans.

More dreadnoughts would soon put to sea. The country had thrown itself into the RSF program, the revitalization and creation of new and powerful technologies. It was just a matter of time.

But for now, for Ventinov, his job was to forge a foothold in the oceans for Russia, and hold onto it, using the dreadnought's might, until the RSF could add to the fleet.

And as for the next target, who would it be?

France, perhaps? China again?

He stared at a map of the region, and at the nearby undersea colonies.

Maybe that was the best course of action after all, he mused. *Take out the undersea cities before they can ally with each other and become more powerful.*

Yes. He clenched his fists again behind his back. They would be easy targets.

Part Four:
Dreadnought

Chapter
Eighteen

A DAY PASSED AS I LEFT the others to their work. Lancombe continued the Triestrian defenses, and soon a work crew installed a new station in City Control: Trieste Defense. They showed me the setup, which was remarkable: a display of the region with launchers on all sides of the city, near fish farms so they were indistinguishable from the other pens, and controls which allowed the operator to select individual stations, select the type of torpedo, select targets, and fire. There were also numerous countermeasure launchers disguised as geologic features—but really fiberglass—in a two-kilometer radius around Trieste. And to top it off, should a USSF crewman ever enter the command center, the operator could press a button and camouflage the controls into something far less threatening—'Fish Farm Operations.'

Johnny and I spent some time together, discussing the dreadnought and the information that Lazlow had provided. We had been longtime partners in Trieste City Intelligence, infiltrating other cities and working to increase Trieste's power in the oceans, and he and I were no strangers to what I was suggesting. However, we had never infiltrated a vessel while it was moving. My suggestion had shocked him, but thankfully he hadn't objected during the meeting. Once we were in private, however, he told me about his concerns and wondered exactly how we would get onto a warsub—

perhaps in supercavitating drive—and sneak through an airlock without anyone on board noticing.

We spent hours talking, but just could not come up with a logical strategy. We'd keep trying.

He was happier than I'd seen him in weeks. He truly loved the city, loved working with me again, and was finding a purpose after so many years without feeling as though he had a home. He had fled Trieste years earlier and had ended up at Sheng City, but had confided in me that it never felt like home, that his superiors there had never trusted him, and they were always watching him.

It was a past that Johnny and I had struggled with, but we had persevered and moved past it.

Renée Féroce was also happier than I'd ever seen her. She was working the kelp farms—volunteering really—and spent most of her waking hours working. It was a tough job, grueling even, but still she pressed on and worked hard for the city.

I had other plans for her, however, and I called her to my office two days later.

She entered with a grin on her face, but with dark circles under her eyes. I studied them for a bit, and her expression grew concerned. "What is it, Mac?"

I noted her use of the name. "You can leave at any time, you know."

She frowned. "But why?"

I shrugged. "You're not a prisoner."

"But of course I know that."

"You really want to help us?"

She sighed. "Mac, I really do. I see the danger out there. I know that the dreadnought presents a serious problem. I want to help destroy it."

"And afterward? If we survive? There will be other threats to face. I have a big task in front of me."

She snorted. "I used to think you were a crazy man. Then I saw what you've achieved." She shook her head. "You're not crazy. You're *driven* to succeed. I think your dad played a big part in that."

I shot a look at the hatch, which was closed.

She continued, "Your father is famous. He's basically the founder of this city, although technically he came later. But the independence movement is *his*. Many people share this dream."

I was staring at her. I didn't know what to say.

"What is it?" she asked.

"I know all these things. But they're . . . hard."

"Why?"

"For so long I lived with the notion that he'd been a total failure."

"But why?"

"Because he was naïve. Because he didn't expect the assassination."

She nodded. "I understand, but—"

"And I had to live with that, Renée. It's a burden to believe your father a failure." I shrugged it away. "But then I discovered that I had it all wrong."

"You mean, that independence is what you should fight for?"

I shook my head. "That he hadn't been dumb. That he knew the attack had been coming. That he allowed it to happen, to move more people toward his dream."

She was frowning. "So that's what you meant."

"Pardon me?"

"Before, when you held me captive at your secret base, you told me Frank McClusky had 'sacrificed himself' for the cause. Did you mean that he let the CIA kill him so it would drive you to do what you're doing now?"

It caught me off guard. She knew exactly what I'd meant. "Yes."

"So, for your whole adult life—and more—you've lived under his shadow. Regardless if you believed him a failure or a hero, it's always put pressure on you."

I took a breath, and it caught in my throat. "Yes. I guess. It's hard to explain."

She studied my eyes for long moments. "I understand you better now."

"I'm an open book."

"Hardly." She winced. "You're very difficult to figure out." Then she stared at me for a while. "Are you really intent on going through with this?"

"With what?"

"The dreadnought. Infiltrating it. Sabotaging it."

"We have to."

"But why not just direct the USSF fleet toward it? They'll take each other out."

"Russia would still target us. This is the only way. I've thought a lot about it." I pointed outside, toward City Control. "I have something I'd like you to see, Renée."

We left my office and moved into the control area just outside. Nearby was the map of the Caribbean and Gulf region, and above was the skylight with a view of the surface high over our heads. It was a cloudy day out there, stormy perhaps. Weather didn't affect us much, although high waves could.

There was a bold, clear label on the consoles directly before us, and it took a moment for recognition to register in her face. "Your people finished the defenses?"

"Some of them. This is the station."

She eyed it, moving her fingers across buttons labeled TARGET ACQUISITION, HOMING, IMPACT DETONATION, and many more. "Looks fantastic."

I said, "After this mission, I'd like you to take this over, Renée."

She blinked. "What?"

"You're a captain in the FSF. You should be controlling a warsub and directing crews. However, we just don't have that as an option for you here. Yet." I gestured to the station. "I thought this would be a good alternative."

A smile twitched at her mouth. "You trust me to do this?"

"Yes, absolutely."

"But—but I wanted to kill you just a little while ago."

I sighed. "Both of our lives have taken paths we didn't expect. I'm trying to help you."

She hesitated. "And what did you mean, 'after this mission'?"

"I'd like you to come with us."

Now her face grew pale, and her voice lowered. "You mean, the dread-nought?"

"I need capable people. You're military. I want you with us."

It visibly shook her. She shot a look around to see if anyone was listening. "Mac, it sounds like a suicide mission."

"It might be," I conceded. "But what other choice is there? The other options lead to all-out war on the surface as well as the oceans."

She eyed me for a moment. "I see your point."

—••—

RENÉE SAT AT THE CONSOLE AND, working with Jessica Ng, began to get up to speed on the controls, how to operate each individual launcher and countermeasure station, and how to multitask during simulated battles.

I left her for the day to train, and retreated to my office to continue planning. The mission to the dreadnought meant I had to set aside important Triestrian business until a later date. Issues related to kelp production, mining missions, and so on.

I hoped I'd be able to pick it up where I'd left off.

I set the paperwork in a pile on the corner of my desk.

That night my dreams were different. They weren't of Kat asking me about the continuing fight or about her seacar. They weren't about submarine battles.

They were of my dad.

It was that night, thirty-one years earlier, when the family had been arguing about independence. Meg and I were only fourteen years old, but we could see the dangers of his efforts. He had spoken about fighting the USSF, and as a result, troop presence had increased in Trieste. Blue uniforms were everywhere. But still he continued to speak about it in open conversation. He had even suggested building an independent navy to fight them.

It was insanity.

Not to actually do it, but to speak so openly about it.

We knew it could only lead to one thing.

And so, we argued.

Our mom had gotten involved as well, the night before he died.

In our living compartment, in the only family module that existed at the time, we'd raised our voices and I was sure our neighbors could hear what was going on.

My dad was saying, "The USSF will increase their control until they have absolute power over us! I don't have any say over them, and I'm the mayor. Neither does the city council. We won't earn anything for our exports. It'll all just go to the mainland, which is almost what's happening right now. This Benning person is taking our produce for himself! Himself!"

"But you can't say these things in the open," Meg said. "You're putting a target on your back!"

I glanced at my sister. Somehow I knew this was a dream—I'd been having a lot of them, lately, and subconsciously I wondered why—but Meg looked as she did in my memories of her from that time. Her blonde hair was even lighter, even more curly, and her face was thinner. But her eyes were lasers as she glared at our dad.

She continued, "The USSF will kill you!"

"Then they kill me," he said in a clipped tone.

"You can't mean that!" I snapped. "You're the mayor of the city. You have a family!"

"Some things are more important, Truman." He stared at me. There was something behind those eyes, but I had been too young to interpret it.

"What the fuck does that mean? Do you seriously not care?"

"Truman!" mom yelled.

"What? You think this is a joke? Everywhere he goes, he's talking about fighting the USSF. It's not even a secret! He's too open about it."

"I'm doing what I feel is best for the city!" Dad bellowed. He was a large man, strong and powerful, and veins in his neck bulged. His face was red. "I've been working for Triestrians for a decade now! I know what I'm doing."

"Until you end up dead! Then where will you be?"

"Others will take my place."

"But you have us," Meg snarled. "Or don't you care?"

"This is about the future of the oceans. It's about our colonization efforts. If we fail, and let the topsiders take over, we'll just be their slaves. We'll work for the failing economies on the surface. We'll exploit the oceans for *them*. We'll pollute the oceans in the same way they've destroyed the surface. Only they won't care, because they don't live here! We need to be in control, because we live underwater, and only we can take care of the oceans responsibly."

"By starting a war?" I yelled. "Are you insane?"

He sighed and lowered his voice. "Maybe I am, Tru. Maybe I am."

Now my mom was staring at him, her jaw hanging open. "You can't be serious."

"It's the only way, Joanne. The USSF is growing powerful. We're getting weaker. I won't stand for that."

Then *she* started yelling.

The entire argument continued for another solid hour, none of us letting up. In the end, Dad stormed from the cabin. I'm not sure where he stayed that night, but the attack happened in the morning.

The travel tube, the bullet, the flood.

We'd been right, and he'd been wrong.

Later in my dream, after the funeral, he appeared to me again. He was older, older than he'd ever looked while alive, and he smiled at me.

I couldn't tell where we were, if it was even in Trieste.

Something told me this hadn't happened, it was all just a fantasy, but I let it continue.

"You're doing a great job, Tru," he whispered. His hair was gray, even his eyebrows, and I studied the lines in his face.

"How can you be here?"

"I'm not."

"You're dead."

"Yes."

"But—"

"I died for you. For this movement."

"You didn't even say you loved me. You left without a hug. You knew what was going to happen." A choking sob worked its way up my throat.

He hesitated. "Yes. I knew the attack was coming."

"But why?"

"Because the things that happen in our youth make us the men we become. Do you understand that?"

"No."

He frowned. "You're a great man, Truman. People respect you. They want to follow you now."

"Because of the things I've done."

"Or maybe also because of the things *I've* done. Or both."

I glared at him. "You destroyed our family."

"Trieste is too important."

"Mom hated you after. She never recovered. Meg left."

"She's back now."

"Mom's not."

His eyes fell. "She never understood either."

"You didn't even say goodbye to us . . ." I whispered.

"It's made you a better man."

A shudder coursed through my body. "Are you really that callous? Were you really that callous?"

He shrugged, then turned to go.

"Don't—" I started.

"Good luck on the mission, son. Hopefully it won't kill you. But if it does, it'll be good for the independence movement." He began to walk away. Shadows fell over him.

He disappeared.

I woke up, drenched and breathing sharply. I raised myself onto an elbow, careful not to bang my head on the low shelves.

It was dark in my living compartment.

Chapter
Nineteen

The following day, the nightmare was still in my thoughts. The way Dad had looked. How he *would* have looked, had he lived long enough.

But I had to thrust it aside, along with everything else I wanted to avoid just then. Compartmentalize it, just like in a warsub. Keep it separate.

I'd deal with it later.

There were other things to attend to first.

I knew that I needed more information. Benning was expecting me to contact him. If I didn't keep him satisfied, he was just going to launch his own mission, one which would likely fail, and then we would be in the crosshairs. Or he would use a nuke, escalating things. It was a delicate balancing act, trying to move forward and at the same time hold him back.

Irena Rostilov had moved into the lab with the other nuclear researchers whom I'd spoken to earlier. She was sitting hunched over a keyboard, staring at a series of monitors before her, and looked like she hadn't slept in days.

More equipment and supplies cluttered the cabin than had earlier, but the other three scientists were not there.

Irena turned to look at me as I entered. "Hello, Mac."

"Hi." I sat beside her. "Can we speak frankly?'

"Sure." She lowered a pen and pushed her notes aside. "I have some interesting information for you after."

"Great." I hesitated, wondering how to broach the topic, but decided to just go for it. "Mayor Winton sent you to me. She implied that you were part of the intelligence service over at Ballard."

She blinked and hesitated for a moment. "Sorry. It's not something I'm used to speaking about so openly. We keep it guarded over there."

"I head up Trieste City Intelligence. You can speak freely."

"Grace told me, otherwise I wouldn't have come."

"We desperately need your help."

"I'm not a field agent, if that's what you mean, but I'm part of the movement there."

"To fight for independence."

"Yes. Although we don't have quite the ambitions that you do over here. Until now, anyway. Whatever you arranged with Grace, she's totally on side with you."

I nodded. "I offered her an alliance to work together. I've built ships with new technologies."

"The SCAV drive."

"And more. I've given them to her. And now things are coming to a head, again."

"The dreadnought."

"Yes."

"And you need to know about it. That's why I'm here."

"There's more to it than that."

She raised an eyebrow. "Such as?"

"I need to know how to take that ship down."

"Torpedoes and mines?"

I frowned and told her the concerns that Meg and Cliff Sim had shared with me. "No, we have to take her down from the inside. What I need from you is help in sabotaging her."

Realization dawned on her features. "Because of my expertise."

I winced. "Irena, I want you to come with us."

She paled and searched for a response. "But I'm not a field agent. I'm a—"

"You understand fusion reactors. You can help us destroy it."

She blinked. "But fusion reactors are remarkably safe. It's not realistic to sabotage it to trigger an explosion."

I sighed. "That's what I thought. I do have a backup plan, but I wasn't sure—"

"But I don't have experience in infiltrating subs, or fighting, or anything like that," she interrupted. "I just don't." Then her face flattened and she rose to her feet. "But I should tell you something important first. Before we speak about going on the mission."

I leaned back, dejected. "I'd been hoping that there was something you could do to the reactor to cause it—"

"Not fusion reactors. When power is lost, the plasma simply expands and the reaction stops. No more neutrons. No more heat. That's why the world switched to fusion decades ago. It's much safer."

I swore. "Yes, you said that, but I'd been hoping—"

Then she pointed at the monitors. "The news I was going to share with you, Mac, is shocking."

My heart thudded. "What?"

"This dreadnought doesn't have a fusion reactor."

I frowned. That didn't make sense. "But it has a SCAV drive. It flash-boils seawater to steam. That's how they work."

"It's nuclear, you're right, but it's not a fusion reactor. It's *fission*."

—••—

I MUST HAVE LOOKED CONFUSED BECAUSE she was staring closely at me. I said, "But a SCAV drive needs a fusion reactor. It requires too much energy. A fission core of the scale needed would be unsafe. It's—"

"Obviously Russia doesn't agree."

"But—but—"

She pointed again. "The engine room in that warsub emits particles that no fusion reactor should. All indications are that it's a fission reactor. It doesn't make sense, it's dangerous, but that's what it's doing. Russia clearly couldn't miniaturize a fusion reactor for this sub, so they substituted the only thing they knew. Yes, it's crazy and yes, it's dangerous, but they must have felt rushed into doing this. They must have felt that they were running out of time. For what, I'm not sure. It's right here." She pointed at the schematic of the dreadnought, near the bottom of the hull at the stern. There was a red dot that hadn't been there before.

"How sure are you of this?" I whispered.

"Damn sure. Nearly a hundred percent."

"Because of the emissions?"

She nodded.

"And fission reactors are easy to sabotage."

She frowned. "Well, I wouldn't say that. There will be immense security. Safety protocols and backup systems to prevent tampering. But you're right, essentially. Fission reactors can go critical."

"And melt down."

"Yes." She gave me a sly look. "And they definitely wouldn't be expecting it."

I stared at the schematic on the screen. The reactor was next to the hull, but compartmentalization meant that causing a meltdown wouldn't have much effect. And it probably had backup power systems—diesel engines or banks of batteries.

"You have to come with us, Irena."

She didn't say anything; she simply stared at the dreadnought.

"You're part of the independence movement. You know more about nuclear reactors than anyone else in the struggle."

"You're saying it's my duty."

"More or less." I sighed. "I've sent a lot of people on missions in the past. Some have died. But I'll be with you on this one." I snorted. "And something else has happened that I never expected."

Her brow crinkled. "What?"

"You're Estonian."

"By birth, yes, but we immigrated to Ballard when I was very young. I told you that."

"But you understand Russian?"

Now her eyes turned cold and she fixed me with a glare. "Yes." Her voice was quiet. A few long seconds passed as she thought it all over. "I'm just a nuclear engineer," she whispered again. But it wasn't a refusal. She was still processing this information.

"I'll let you think on it for a bit. But we need to start planning in earnest now. And I have more information that you don't know yet."

She eyed me. "Go on."

"My backup plan to take down this warsub. I set it in motion a week ago."

She listened to me, eyes wide, for five more minutes.

Then she swore.

—••—

WE HELD THE MEETING IN *SC-1*. It seemed the safest place—we were inside the docking module still—and added an extra layer of security. I looked at the team I had assembled: Johnny, Lau, Irena, Meg, Renée, and Admiral Benning. It was an interesting mix of people—Benning didn't even know that he was going on the mission yet!—but it was missing one still.

I hoped he'd return soon.

Benning said, "You better have some information for me now, McClusky."

We were facing each other on opposite sides of the living area in the seacar. We'd be riding it to intercept the dreadnought soon, and I'd have to get them used to the close quarters. Meg was glaring at the admiral; I could tell what she wanted to do to him, right then and there.

"I do," I answered him finally.

"I am anxious to attack," he continued. "I've only held off for you."

"I appreciate that." I sighed. "Okay, here's the deal. Irena here has come up with more information about its powerplant. She'll fill you in. Then I'll tell you how we're going to take it out."

"We're going to sink this thing with torpedoes and mines," Benning snapped. "Plain and simple."

"No, we're not. It's too compartmentalized. It has the fastest SCAV drive in the oceans. It can just run to fight another day." I shook my head. "It's too risky. Just listen to our plan first, will you?"

His jaws clicked shut and he glared at me. But he remained quiet.

"Go ahead, Irena," I said.

She nodded and turned to the others. "This vessel doesn't have a fusion plant."

Meg's face erupted into surprise. "But how—"

"It has a fission plant."

Waves of shock passed over their faces. "But that's insane," Lau muttered. "For the output needed, they're too dangerous, too unstable. Especially the Russian variety."

"And we have a plan for it," she continued. She looked at me. "Mac has an interesting idea. Shocking even. And it might actually work." She hesitated while she mulled over how to lay it out in a clear and understandable manner. "Fission plants use a large amount of uranium or plutonium that decays naturally. As it does, it releases neutrons. Within the reactor chamber is a substance known as a moderator. This slows the neutrons down, allowing them to interact with the uranium, increasing the rate of reaction. Heating it up. If it weren't for the moderator, the neutrons would speed away, and not collide with enough uranium to continue the chain reaction."

"What's the moderator?" Johnny asked. He was confused, because it sounded so much more complicated than fusion, which was relatively simple in comparison.

Irena went on to explain that in fusion, reactors used immense heat and pressure to join atoms of hydrogen to form helium and energy. In fission, however, uranium atoms split to form U-236, neutrons, gamma rays, and other 'fission fragments.' These emissions were easy to spot. "Moderators are usually water, heavy water, or in some Russian cases, graphite. But it's vulnerable to attack. Which is what Mac is suggesting."

"Meaning we infiltrate the dreadnought and sabotage the reactor," Johnny whispered.

"Exactly."

Benning snorted. "But we can just use a nuke on it, I told you that."

I said, "And I told you why we can't do that. If you use a nuke, it'll escalate to outright war. We need to prevent that from happening."

"But they've already attacked us, McClusky!"

I tried to keep from raising my voice. "I want to prevent the land nations from getting involved in a third world war. There's already a cold war going on in the oceans—in many places a hot one. But I *will not* contribute to the use of nuclear weapons going off all over the world as well as in the oceans."

"You're proposing sabotaging a nuclear reactor here!"

"*One* nuclear reactor to prevent a larger-scale conflict with nukes." I turned to Irena. "Go on, please." I took a deep breath to keep myself calm.

Benning looked outraged, but he said no more.

Irena said, "The trick here is to create a situation in the reactor that will cause it to go critical." She grinned at that, staring at the rest of us, and paused for effect.

I found it amusing. She was a nuclear engineer who had spent her career taking care of reactors so that they *didn't* have accidents, so they continued to generate power without unfortunate side effects.

But here we were, asking her to intentionally force one to go critical.

"Wait a minute," Meg interrupted. She didn't look so angry anymore— she was curious now about my suggestion—but she was not exactly enthusiastic about all of this. Yet. She continued, "I may not be a nuclear engineer—I work on sub hulls and control systems—but even I know that a fission reactor won't just *blow up* if there's a problem."

"Just wait, Meg," I said, "and listen to Irena."

She huffed but remained quiet.

Irena turned to her. "You're right, it won't explode. But Mac has another idea. An incredible idea. He's proposing a *meltdown*. To make the core go supercritical, to melt the support structure, and to create a runaway reaction that will damage the ship beyond repair."

"But they'll have backups. Diesel engines. It would damage the dreadnought, but they'd still be able to fight and escape."

"Not likely," Benning grumbled.

"We're going to cause more than damage here," I added. "I want to cause a meltdown of the sort the world saw at Chernobyl. I want to cause a *China Syndrome*."

Silence. Their faces were blank.

Lau said, "What does China have to do with it?"

"It's a saying in the nuclear industry from the Twentieth Century,"

Irena said. "Basically, a reactor, should it go critical and coolant fail, will melt everything in the core and the core materials will melt out of their containment downward. It'll continue to melt through the base of the powerplant, into the ground, and all the way through the Earth until it hits China. But it's only a metaphor, for it would hit groundwater eventually and the entire thing would explode upward in a cloud of radioactive steam."

They were still confused.

She hesitated slightly at their expressions. "Nuclear plant engineers designed the structures to prevent this from happening. Underneath the core would be layers of concrete and thick metal barriers. The melted core materials—called *corium*—would hit those layers and the reaction would stop and the material would cool."

"Why would the reaction stop?" Johnny asked.

"The corium would melt the barrier, in the process diluting it, slowing and eventually stopping any reaction. It would eventually cool before it could penetrate the base of the reactor and make it to the water table."

Benning's eyes were wide and he lurched to his feet. His face was red and there were veins in his temples. "This is outrageous! You're talking about causing a meltdown to destroy the reactor! I can do the same thing with torpedoes! With a large enough force—"

"I'm not done yet," I said. "Yes, I want to cause a meltdown. But it gets better." I nodded at the nuclear engineer. "Keep going."

Benning looked flustered, but Irena began before he could keep yelling.

It was time to outline the multiple steps in our mission.

Chapter Twenty

IRENA WAS DOING A FANTASTIC JOB, I thought. She still hadn't committed to joining the mission, but I needed her on it. She was calm and collected, already part of the independence movement, so I knew that she would be reliable. Grace Winton wouldn't have sent her to me if she didn't completely trust her. Irena was highly intelligent and obviously capable. She was almost like a professor as she explained what we needed to do.

We *needed* her in that reaction chamber on board the dreadnought.

She continued, "We have to get into the reactor room and perform a series of steps. First is to fully remove the control rods. These control the reaction."

"So why remove them?" Lau asked.

"The control rods are composed of a material that absorbs neutrons. In these old-school reactors, if the reaction turned into a runaway event, the controllers would trip the control rods. Gravity would pull them back into place, *inside* the core. Their purpose is to stop the reaction. It's like taking the oxygen out of a fire. It prevents the chain reaction of fission from occurring. Boron or cadmium make up the control rods. In Chernobyl, just before the meltdown, controllers withdrew the rods for a test. When they realized there was an event in progress, they couldn't get them back in to stop the reaction. The heat dissolved the containment structure and the corium melted downwards into the lower levels of the facility."

"Why weren't the control rods inserted to stop the reaction?"

"They fractured during the overheating. They got stuck and wouldn't lower."

"But I thought gravity was supposed to pull them down quickly?"

"Yes, you're right." Irena frowned. "In the States, controllers would have hit a button marked SCRAM. It means to release the electromagnetic hold on the control rods. It was a failsafe. Also, should power to the plant fail, and there was no way to control the reaction, the control rods would automatically slide downward into the core, stopping the reaction. This didn't happen at Chernobyl. They found the corium in a massive hardened sculpture in the basement. They called it 'The Elephant's Foot.' Engineers who went looking for it died soon after. It's still there today, entombed by concrete. It was even highly radioactive ten years after the incident. A few minutes of exposure was still fatal."

Johnny said, "Mac, I'm behind you on this one hundred percent. You know that. But I still don't know how this is going to sink the dreadnought. The reactor is in one of the lower levels, near the hull." He pointed to the diagram, which once again was circling before us. The red dot that Irena had added was still there. "Say we manage to pull the control rods, stop a SCRAM, and cause it to go critical. This reactor might not be as large as Chernobyl. It might not melt down."

I shot him a sly look. He didn't know yet.

"There's more. I know what you're saying might be true, but the reactor must be huge in order to generate enough power for the SCAV drive. But just in case it's not, the solution is to add to the reaction, just in case. Make it more violent. Hotter."

More blank faces.

I pressed on. "I went to speak to three of our nuclear engineers here at Trieste and came up with an option for this. It's simple. All we have to do is add more uranium."

Creases appeared in Johnny's forehead. "But we don't have any."

"There's a way."

"You can't just order it, you know," Meg said. "It's controlled by the US

Department of Energy."

"There's a way," I repeated. They stared back at me now. "Thorium. It's an alternative. It's radioactive and decays naturally. It has other uses that don't set off alarms, like arc welding, so no one will think it's odd that we're using it."

"Do we have thorium?" Johnny asked.

I grinned at him. "We're in the process of getting some. We've opened a mine. We should have our first refined batch soon."

"And will injecting thorium into the core—"

"No. But part of what makes it special is the Thorium Fuel Cycle. In essence, if we bombard Thorium-232 with neutrons, it'll produce Uranium-233. U-233 is fissile. The US has even used it in some nuclear bombs. We can use it for this, to take down the dreadnought."

My suggestion echoed in the close confines of *SC-1* as the group looked at each other. Irena looked enthusiastic at the suggestion, while it had perplexed the others.

"But where will we be able to expose the thorium to neutrons?" Meg asked.

"We have a fusion reactor here at Trieste that generates 1,110 megawatts of electricity. Fusion creates neutrons." I shrugged. "We just have to expose enough thorium to neutrons and we'll have our uranium."

They couldn't believe what I had come up with. Their expressions shifted from the mystified to confounded, and Benning's bordered on rage. It had astonished Renée, however; there was a look of admiration in her features.

Meg closed her eyes. "Let me get this straight. You want to infiltrate the dreadnought, march to the reactor room, remove the control rods, and somehow insert more uranium into the core. Uranium which we'll manufacture, using thorium, here at Trieste."

"You're right so far. But there's more."

She frowned and gestured for me to continue.

"We're also going to introduce oxygen to the core. Remember Irena said that Russians like to use graphite as their moderator? Well, oxygen and graphite don't mix under heat. It'll cause a graphite fire, to really start things moving."

"So, the core will melt . . ." she prompted.

"Hopefully. It'll turn into a liquid hot mass of radioactive metal. It'll dissolve through containment. Meanwhile, our USSF, Sheng City, Triestrian, and hopefully Cousteauian fleets will engage the dreadnought to keep it occupied."

Benning at least nodded at this. He wanted to fire some torpedoes at this damned ship, but it would all just be for show. The meltdown would be the real weapon.

"But Mac," Johnny said, "you're not hearing me. This won't be enough." All eyes turned to him. "Look at the location of the reactor. It's too close to the hull. Maybe two or three decks away."

Meg nodded. "He's right. It's why the reactor is there probably. If it melts down it'll plunge toward the lower hull and out into the ocean. But designers no doubt compartmentalized engineering. Those areas will flood, but it won't be enough to sink the dreadnought." She snorted. "It's the same as punching holes in it with torpedoes. No real effect, and they'll just fight us off and use conventional methods to escape."

I said in a quiet voice, "I'm not done yet, Meg. You're assuming this ship is going to be floating, neutrally buoyant and upright during the battle." I shook my head. "No way. I'm going to do something unique to this dreadnought." I paused and then, "I want to turn it upside down."

—••—

NOW I REALLY HAD THEM CONFUSED. Then all at once a babble of voices hit me and I had to raise my hands to fend them off. "Listen to me, we're going to get the ship inverted. And *then* we're going to cause a meltdown. They won't be expecting any of this. They'll be fighting a battle *outside*, but we'll be *inside* causing shit. It's the last thing their captain will expect. And once we get the ship upside down, the corium will really cause some damage. It's twenty-seven decks or so to the *top* of the hull. When it melts out and into the ocean, *voila*. Water will flood all the way to the engine room, breaking containment in multiple areas of the ship. There's no way that fucker will stay afloat."

—••—

MEG SWORE. "IT'S INSANE. YOU'RE SUGGESTING a . . . a *multi-stage plan*. If any one of the steps doesn't work, we'll be in serious trouble. And we'll be on board, inside an enemy warsub!"

"That's right." I ticked the steps off on my fingers. "*One*, we get on board and damage the trim and ballast tanks to make the ship list to the port or starboard. We'll do this from either engineering or the bridge. The fleet outside will focus on one side of the ship to help us along. They'll be flooding compartments and distracting the command staff in battle. *Two*, we then make our way to the fission plant, eliminating any security along the way. We remove the control rods and cause a runaway chain reaction. Irena here will be with us because she's a nuclear engineer—she'll know how to do this. *Three*, we have to destroy the coolant system and simultaneously insert our created U-233 into the core, along with oxygen to start the graphite fire. And *four*, we'll then have to make sure the dreadnought is fully inverted, possibly by using the control surfaces on the warsub itself, which means we'll have to have some people on the bridge. Then the corium will dissolve its containment, and melt its way to the top of the warsub. Compartmentalization will be lost and the warsub will sink."

Jaws were hanging open at my list.

Lau said, "But the corium will dissolve metal and become diluted, which you said earlier was a failsafe. It might cool before it hits the hull."

I shook my head. "The corium will be moving through the corridors and will hopefully drip through hatch openings. It won't melt much at all except for hatch frames and some bulkheads near hatches, further destroying containment."

"This is insane," Benning growled. "Absolutely crazy."

I turned to him. "It's going to work. It has to." I paused and took a deep breath. "And if it doesn't, Benning, then you'll get what you want. Use all the torpedoes you want. Use a nuke if you want. Just give us a chance first."

Meg said, "Mac, do you realize we're going to be in a capsized ship with a mass of radioactive core material moving around, melting its way through bulkheads?"

"Yes, of course."

"In the dark most likely, as torpedoes pound away at the warsub."

I nodded.

Their mouths were still hanging open. I knew I had to appear confident with this. I had thought long and hard about it, and this was the only thing I could think of to fatally destroy this vessel, and not just damage it for a short amount of time. "The Russians will think the reactor went critical during battle. After all, it's a fission plant and dangerous to begin with. They might not question how the meltdown occurred."

"How did you know we'd need thorium?" Johnny asked. "Did you know it was a fission reactor?"

The truth was that I'd messed up. I'd been hoping to cause a meltdown by putting uranium into the *fusion* core, getting neutrons to hit the radioactive metal and somehow create a runaway reaction. I'd been wrong, and Irena told me it never would have worked.

But the news that it was a fission reactor had been fortuitous.

Instead, we would use the uranium to cause a China Syndrome in the dreadnought's fission chamber.

Benning was now looking calmer than he had earlier. Back to his normal self. In fact, he appeared as though the plan appealed to him, if only because if we failed, he'd still get to do what he wanted.

"And who is going on this mission?" Lau asked.

I motioned at the group there, in *SC-1*, with me. "We are. All of us in this cabin. Johnny, Meg, Lau, Renée, Benning, and Cliff, once he returns from his mission." I glanced at Irena. "I asked you to think about it. What's your decision?"

The nuclear engineer stared at me for long heartbeats. Then she took a deep breath. "It sounds like I'm crucial to the success of this." She glanced around. "I guess I'm in."

"That's eight," Lau said with a grin. "In China, it's lucky number eight."

"We still need a pilot though."

Benning said, "Wait a second, McClusky. I'm the commander of the USSF fleet. I'll be outside, leading the attack, dammit."

I spun on him. "Why? I need you with me on this. We'll be in Russian uniforms. Once we sneak on board, they won't even suspect." I narrowed my eyes. "We're sacrificing *everything* for this, Benning. Triestrians are. And you're saying here, in front of a group of people who are putting their lives on the line, that you're not willing to do it too?"

He looked around and sank to the couch. "I wanted to lead the attack."

I stepped toward him. "Think about this, Benning. We're going to be the cause of that warsub's destruction. We're going to be *inside* during it." I grinned. "What better claim on your résumé than that? It'll get you anywhere you want in the USSF. Hell, you could use it to move upward and beyond, even."

He was staring at me and his eyes narrowed slightly. "You're trying to manipulate me now, McClusky."

"I need you with us. Let's do this together. Let's take the fight to Russia for what they did."

And then a smile slowly crept across his face.

I pressed on, "Let's do this, *Admiral*."

He grunted. "It might be a good way to die as well."

I glanced at Meg and Johnny. I realized that he now knew too much about us and, afterward, should we be successful, he would likely cause increasing problems at Trieste when all this was done.

That would not be an issue, however.

—••—

THE GROUP DISPERSED FOLLOWING THE MEETING. They were quiet and reserved, mulling over what I had suggested. There was still the problem of how to get on board the warsub, but Cliff would help with that. He was a former USSF sailor. I just hoped he'd return safely, and soon.

Another issue was the thorium enrichment. It would take twenty-eight days, and I was still waiting for the batch from Laura Sukovski. Once we got it, my three nuclear engineers and Irena would expose it to the core in our own fusion reactor, bombarding it with neutrons, and begin the conversion process to uranium.

Hours later, I was in my office when security contacted me. I still hadn't been able to take care of any administrative work—I was busy with the mission plan—but knew I had to take the call. Kristen Canvel had transferred it to my desk.

"Go ahead," I muttered as I stared at the image of the dreadnought that Lazlow had given me. I was taking notes about possible infiltration sites. Closer to the fission plant would be better, but we did need a team to tamper with the ballast and trim tanks. Perhaps two infiltration sites with two different teams would be better, I thought.

"Mac, it's Jamieson down in security."

He was filling in for Cliff. "Go ahead."

"We're having some trouble with the USSF."

I looked away from the diagram. It had been too good to be true. The troops on furlough had been relatively well-behaved until this. "Continue."

"There have been a few fights. Drinking was involved."

"Of course."

"I haven't bothered you with things before now because we've handled it. Escorted the offenders back to *Devastator* to allow their own people to deal with them."

"So what's the—"

"We just had a fight in a pub. There's been a death."

Chapter
Twenty-One

THE NEWS MADE ME THROW A notepad to the deck. "Aw, *shit*. Triestrian?"

"Yup. Tried to break up the brawl. Got hit over the head."

"Who did it?"

"A USSF crewman. Big guy. He's in a cell over here."

I frowned. "You kept him here?"

"Until we heard from you. Yes."

I sighed. "I'll call Benning and get back to you."

"Thanks, Mac."

A minute later I had Benning on the comm. He stared at me, but his face was calm and collected. "What's the problem, McClusky?"

I considered what to say. In addition to the fight, I still had to speak with him about the mission. "You gave me a couple of days to research this more. Now I have a plan. What are you going to tell your people?"

He frowned. "I'm going to go ahead with it. We'll announce a major search effort. To attract the dreadnought. We'll set out and hopefully they'll attack us."

I grinned inwardly. "Pick some place deep so the ship won't cause contamination. Over a trench somewhere."

He nodded. "I'll have to inform my superiors that Russia is the culprit."

He leaned forward. "But I'll tell them the plan." He shrugged. "Who knows what they'll do with Russia. Maybe we'll attack them, bomb a few cities. Or maybe wait to see what happens with the dreadnought."

"Announce that the search will begin in one month, once the ships are ready."

His eyes grew hard. "Don't give me orders, McClusky."

"I need time to get things together here."

"I'm still considering this mission."

"Look at it this way. It's a two-pronged attack. All we need is for one of them to succeed. Either the nuclear meltdown, or the battle that you're going to arrange. Where will the best place be, do you think, to do this? Atlantic or Pacific?"

He frowned. "I can get the largest fleet together in the Pacific."

"Good." I would ask Lau to contact Sheng City to send their ships, and Renée to ask Piette at Cousteau. We also had twenty-eight *Swords*—no, *twenty-seven* now, for we had given one to Ballard—and would send those.

I brought my attention back to Benning. "Can you get some Russian uniforms for us?"

"I'll put the request in. We should have a department on the mainland that can take care of that."

It was the best I could hope for, at least. "I have another problem, Benning." I hesitated to gather my thoughts. "One of your people killed a Triestrian today."

His face went blank for a few moments. Then he sighed. "What happened?"

I filled him in on the information that Jamieson had provided. The admiral's face remained flat during the entire story.

He said, "Send the man back to us. We'll deal with it."

I leaned forward. "That's not good enough. This man killed one of my people."

"Not on purpose. It was a bar fight."

"Does that mean a Triestrian life is less important to you? He tried to *stop* a fight. And now he's dead. He's got a family."

Benning's eyes flashed. "Don't make me think that Heller had you pegged, McClusky."

"What does that mean?"

"You believed that Heller was a tyrant, a dictator. That his crew behaved poorly over there."

"That's exactly right. And so far, your people have been marginally better. But I won't stand for USSF troops causing fights and killing Triestrians."

"Watch yourself, now." His face was like steel as he stared at me over the comm. "The USSF is in control at Trieste. Not the other way around. Maybe the problem from day one was that you thought *you* were in charge." Then he sat back in his chair and swore. He mulled the situation over for a long minute. "Send the man over. I promise you that we'll deal with it here."

"What does that mean? A week in the brig? For taking a life?"

"He'll get a fair trial. At most it's manslaughter, but we'll investigate and prosecute."

I stared at Benning. There was no escaping it, especially if I wanted him to come with us on the mission. In fact . . . "Maybe we should try him here. In public. Televised."

His reaction was instant. "Don't even dream of it!"

"Tell me, are you committed to joining the mission? Infiltrating the warsub with us?"

He stared at me for a moment. Then realization dawned on his features. "You asshole."

"What do you say?" I pressed.

He exhaled. "I'll be coming with you."

"I'll send the man right over." Inside I was thrilled, but clamped down on the surge of emotion. I couldn't show it.

I didn't envy that prisoner. Benning would likely kill the man himself.

—••—

Two days later, the thorium shipment arrived. Laura Sukovski supervised the crates as crew carried them from the mining module to the nuclear plant.

The plant was in the southwest quadrant of the city, more than six hundred meters away from the main modules. We had recently buried it; during the battle one year earlier, USSF forces had hit the fusion reactor module with a torpedo and cut power to the city. Following our surrender and the USSF occupation, I had ordered the plant, once reconstructed, buried.

The travel tube was so long that there was a high-speed conveyer in it, and a hundred meters out from the reactor it angled down and disappeared beneath the sandy seafloor. The airtight reactor structure was inside the bedrock, twenty meters under the seafloor. The hard basalt protected our power source.

I rode the conveyer with Laura and three crates of thorium. Her people had worked fast, setting up a remote site initially, followed up with a manned station, and they had mined the ore and processed it in under the two weeks I'd given her.

She had come through.

"We won't reach the aluminum quota this quarter," she said. Turns out she'd had to pull workers off that mine to take care of this. "Do you want us to keep the thorium site up and running?"

I pursed my lips. "Keep the equipment there for now. I'll let you know in six weeks. But you can move your crews back to where they were."

She stared at me. "This is for the dreadnought that you were talking about?" Her voice was a whisper; her two crewmen were meters behind us, standing on the conveyer, and looking at the solid gray bulkheads of the travel tube as we moved. Few Triestrians had ventured to the fusion plant before. "Is that why I was at the meeting?"

"The thorium was crucial, and I wanted you to know that Trieste is in great danger. I owe you."

She blinked and then flashed me a smile. "Good to know." And then, "Good luck, Mac. You've got guts."

The conveyer came to an end at an airtight hatch with two security guards on sentry duty. Also standing with them were Irena Rostilov and my three nuclear engineers: Doctors Walls, Li, and Williams. They sported anxious expressions and their eyes focused on the crates at our feet.

It was time to start the great experiment.

The neutron bombardment would take twenty-eight days.

——••——

I WAS ON MY WAY BACK from the fusion reactor when a page for me echoed in the travel tube. It was Kristen Canvel. Back in my office, she transferred what she described as an 'incredibly important' call to my desk.

On the screen, Mayor Piette appeared.

I greeted him and thought briefly about how timely it was; after all, I had wanted to discuss the upcoming mission with him. But before I could continue, he said, "Your man Cliff Sim is on the line."

I blinked. I had sent Cliff to retrieve the syntactic foam from the base in the Indian Ocean. I had last seen him at the French base in the guyot where we'd met the mayor and picked up Renée. All I could manage was, "Go on."

"I'm going to add him to the feed."

An instant later, Cliff's face appeared in a split screen next to Piette's. "Cliff! Status report?"

He grinned. "I'm on my way back."

I noticed belatedly that there was a cut on his temple and his right eye was swollen and would likely be black in a matter of hours. But his expression implied something other than failure.

"Did you . . . pick up the package?" I asked.

"Got it. Mayor Piette helped. He had an 'in' at the . . . resort."

"Interesting." I stared at the mayor. "Does this mean you've made your decision?"

"Yes, I have." He offered a sly smile. "We are all in agreement here."

"And the other two French cities?"

"They are still mulling things over."

It was the best I could have expected, anyway. "I'd like Cliff to come to Trieste now. Can we return the seacar he's in at some later date?"

"Of course."

"I also need something else from you." I leaned forward. "We'll need Cousteau's help. Do you have any warsubs?"

He frowned. "A limited number. They're small but they're armed. We'll assist in any way we can."

"Great. Send them to Trieste within the next four weeks. Then we depart."

"Where are they going?"

"We're going to sink the .... the *target*, Mayor. And we need every bit of help we can get." I paused. "I need something else too."

"Go ahead."

He listened in rapt silence while I made my request. His face exploded into shock.

But he agreed.

—••—

CLIFF ASSURED ME THAT HE WAS okay and that he'd fill me in upon his return. I breathed a huge sigh of relief after the call. The mission to that French research dome in the Indian Ocean had killed two operatives just weeks earlier, and the FSF had used them as bait to lure me in. Following my escape, Renée had had a change of heart and had provided the exact coordinates of the facility. I had sent Cliff, and he had retrieved the foam for me. When we figured out how it allowed vessels to dive deeper than earlier iterations, we would adapt it to our own ships and our own deep-sea ventures, such as Triestrian mining stations.

I decided to check in with Lazlow to see how his research was going, and walked over to the research module. Inside, audio-processing devices and a multitude of screens and readouts surrounded him. His headphones were on and he hunched over a control panel of some sort tracing digital images with his finger. His face had filled out and his limbs no longer looked like twigs. His skin was still translucent, his beard was growing unkempt, and his spider fingers were still long and bony, but he looked better.

"Hi, Mac." He turned to me and grinned.

A sudden thought occurred to me. "Hello, Doc. Thanks for the new information." He had provided me with more detail of the dreadnought's hull. Of note were the probable sites of airlocks—potential locations for us to infiltrate the warsub.

"I have been studying the sonar traces in more detail. The 3D modeling has given a better idea about the skin of that sub."

"That's great." I glanced around his lab. What had once been relatively barren was now full of equipment and stacks of papers and books, headsets and screens and cables.

"I should have more for you soon."

That startled me. "Where is this info coming from?"

"All four sonar traces we have of the sub."

I frowned. "Four?"

"Agent Lau provided me with the CSF records of their attack. I know where the Russian torpedo tubes are now too. I'll add them to our model soon."

"That's fantastic. I'd like to see a workup of the battle."

He shook his head. "Lau didn't give me one. Just a sonar recording."

"Can't you—"

"But I can work up a computer simulation of the entire event." He grinned.

I stared at him. We owed him so much, and not just because he had given us the Acoustic Pulse Drive. "It'll give us an important idea about their strategy in combat. I'd like to see it ASAP. We should provide it to Benning as well, just in case."

"In case of what?" His brow crinkled.

"In case we fail."

"Ah."

"Lazlow, I have an idea." He stared at me and I simply paused. Then, "Can you come with me?"

"I guess. Why?"

—••—

I BROUGHT LAZLOW TO THE CENTRAL module and to the moonpool on the seafloor level. His eyes were wide as he stared at the rippling sea water in the rectangular pool in the deck. Along the bulkheads on all four sides were masks, tanks, flippers, and weight belts. Then his face lit in realization, and he stared at me in wonder.

"Care to take a swim?" I asked.

He had come to Trieste to fulfil a dream to live underwater. He'd spent eight decades on land, always wanting to live in the colonies, but had never been able to. Since he'd arrived, a childlike joy of being in the colony had filled him with obvious glee. We had pushed him hard, and he had struggled but persevered. And we would likely not have defeated the FSF and Heller's USSF force without his APD. Now it was time to show him something special.

He didn't even answer me; he marched to the scuba gear and began to put it on. I showed him the basics, how to use the regulator, how to reach the backup easily—even if he couldn't see—and stressed the importance of not floating to the surface. Of course he knew this already, but he humored me.

We gave each other thumbs up, grabbed our facemasks, and jumped into the moonpool.

——••——

Outside, the water was warm and the sun was high in the sky and the area well lit. The weights on our belts brought us to the sandy bottom, and we adjusted our vests until we were neutrally buoyant and could swim away from the module. Fish darted in to investigate the visitors to their realm, and I noticed a sparkle dancing in Lazlow's eyes as he swam leisurely. I watched to make sure he wasn't having difficulty, but he performed well.

It was satisfying to see him experience the outdoors with a childlike fascination. I'm happy he had come to Trieste to live and to help us with our struggle for independence. At first, I had resisted—he was eighty years old, after all, and it had worried me—but now I knew that Meg and Kat had been right in recruiting him.

I watched him float horizontally over the seafloor, poking his mask into sea grasses and rock formations and exploring the myriad forms of wildlife that lived around our colony. A seacar powered near us, passing overhead as it performed routine maintenance on the nearby module, and Lazlow looked up in awe as the sounds of its thrusters caught his attention. The pilot glanced out, recognized me, smiled and waved.

We stayed out until the tank alarm warned us that we were running out of air.

I think it was the greatest experience of Lazlow's life.

Chapter
Twenty-Two

WHEN I RETURNED TO CITY CONTROL, Mayor Reggie Quinn of Seascape City was there, waiting.

Part of me felt guilt at having spent valuable time with Lazlow outside the city, showing him the joys of scuba diving and why people of the colonies loved living underwater. After all, I could have been preparing for the upcoming mission. But Lazlow's gratitude had been effusive, which had made me smile, and I told him we'd do it again sometime soon.

Reggie offered me a sullen look and shook my hand as we walked into my office. He glanced around, taking in the sparse nature of the cabin. His was large and opulent and even had a wood desk and a massive viewport overlooking a water park. A bubble of glass surrounded the park, and Seascape tourists could swim and enjoy slides and a wave pool *underneath* the ocean above. It really was a marvelous city, but I could see in Reggie's eyes that things were not well there.

He was black, bald, and fit. He had a goatee and broad shoulders. His handshake had been warm and genial. It was a very different greeting than he'd offered last I'd seen him.

It was almost as if he could read my thoughts. "Once again," he said in a soft voice, "I'm sorry about how I treated you when you came to Seascape."

We sat facing each other across my desk and I said, "Tell me, what's the problem?"

He filled me in on the declining number of tourists to Seascape, that the city relied on them for revenue, and people were even canceling trips they had booked years in advance. The modules and travel tubes were empty. The city was suffering. "You were right, Mac. We're in serious trouble."

"San Diego and Norfolk?"

He nodded. "The US is in a dire situation. Even the wealthy—if there is such a thing now—are hurting. The rising water and the destruction of arable farmland. I had been hoping that we could sustain the number of visitors. But the USSF might just shut us down. Take over. Change our city into something else, for their uses."

My blood turned to ice. "What did he say?"

"Who?" But his eyes showed that he knew who I was referring to.

"Benning."

Reggie sighed. "He's looking for a place to set up a complete USSF operation. A new HQ for both the Atlantic and Pacific. He suggested Seascape because our revenue has crashed."

"But that would put the entire fleet, for both oceans, right in our backyard," I grated.

Reggie's face was tight. "Yes. And where would we go?"

Silence descended on us for long moments. The development was horrifying.

I said, "We can't control what's going on up on the mainland. And now these attacks . . ."

"You were right," he repeated.

I paused and stared at him. "You told me you weren't interested in joining us."

"I assumed you were going to ask me to join your fight for independence. That's what the battle was last year, right?"

I nodded. "We're more powerful together, Reggie. We can find alternate sources of revenue."

"And how will you deal with the USSF? What's your plan?"

I've already proven that I can deal with them, I wanted to say, but I still wasn't sure how much to reveal. I decided to appeal to his need for prosperity. "Where do your tourists come from?"

He shrugged. "Mostly from the southern states. Texas, California, Nevada, and so on. We do get some from the eastern seaboard too." Then he snorted. "Not many now though."

"But Americans, right?"

"Yes, of course." He was staring at me.

"But why not from Brazil, Colombia, Europe, and Africa? Central America? It's right next door to us."

"But a trip to Seascape would be too expensive—"

"Maybe. But if you take a global approach to it, you've just expanded your pool of people to draw from, haven't you?"

He stared at me for several long heartbeats. "You're suggesting independence and then opening up to other nations?"

"Why not?" I shrugged. "And to other undersea colonies. This is what your city specializes in. I want independence. I want to earn money from as many sources as possible, and not rely on the United States. It could be your goal too."

"But the USSF, Mac."

I smiled. "We won't have to worry about them for long."

—••—

TWO DAYS LATER, WHILE TOSSING AND turning restlessly in my bunk, Meg called me. I was having difficulties falling asleep yet again. I had to admit, the job was wearing on me. The USSF troops in Trieste, planning for the upcoming mission, and preparing the city defenses were all tasks that a mayor generally didn't have to take on. My position as Director of TCI put more demands on my shoulders—but ones which I had willingly accepted.

I rarely had a good night's sleep now, however, especially since Kat's death. The dreams were bothering me. Nightmares.

I'd been in bed, staring at the low shelf over my head, issues roiling through my mind. The countless administrative demands from the city's divisions—mining, repair, aquaculture, and more—were constant. There was no escaping them. Each day I was putting out fires. I was debating visiting the doctor to ask her for sleep meds when Meg's signal arrived.

"Go ahead," I muttered after hitting the ACCEPT button—AUDIO ONLY.

"Mac," my sister said, breathless. Her tone made me immediately hoist myself onto an elbow. She continued, "There's an issue."

"What is it?"

"Can you come to my quarters?"

She lived in the same module as me and was only a minute or two away.

"It can't wait until tomorrow?" I probed. But from her tone, I knew I'd be going. I was already pulling on a pair of loose-fitting pants and a t-shirt.

"Nope. I have a video feed you need to see live."

"On my way."

I marched into the corridor and turned toward the ladder.

———••———

TWO MINUTES LATER, I KNOCKED ON the sliding door of her living compartment. Inside, she was sitting on her bunk with a video screen on her lap. Her cabin was the same size as mine, about four square meters, and contained only a recessed bunk with drawers above it and a desk across from it.

I sat next to her. On the screen was an image of a moonpool with seacars moored to docks along one side. There were hoists on the ceiling. Two were empty, but three had vessels in harnesses hanging two meters over a platform. The scene looked oddly familiar.

I frowned. "Where is this?"

"Blue Downs."

Of course. The Australian undersea city in the Tasmanian Strait. It had been Meg's home after she'd fled Trieste. She'd worked in the repair docks at the city. I had been there a year earlier when she had repaired *SC-1*, and then returned with me to Trieste.

We'd had to blow our way out of there with a torpedo.

A man's face appeared in the view. He was leaning over a desk.

Meg said, "This is Mason Lunwick, one of my managers when I worked there. He's running the business now." She said to him, "This is my brother.

Tell him what's going on."

Mason opened his mouth to speak and the audio, which had been muted, began. Alarms were blaring in the background and I noticed a flashing light against the far bulkhead. "We're under attack!" he yelled.

I leaned forward. An electric prickle traced down my spine. "Who is it?"

"— have no idea." It was difficult to hear him over the din. The comm system was muting the feed whenever he wasn't speaking because of all the noise. "The alarms started sounding and an instant later there was an implosion event. I can't raise the mayor or City Control. I think it was the central module. I sent one of my crew out into the water to check." He pointed to the moonpool behind him. "Down there. He's got a tank and a weight belt, and should be back soon."

"Why not a travel tube?" I asked.

"Tried that. The airtight hatch has sealed automatically on the far end." That would be the end that connected the repair facility with the central module. "Emergency protocols slammed it."

Damn. "Do the travel tubes have viewports?"

"There are viewports on the sides and the ceiling is transparent, just like at Trieste. But the water is murky, can't see anything. Something's churned all the sand from the seafloor."

His face was drawn and sweat beaded his forehead.

I felt his anxiety. If modules kept collapsing, there was no escaping to the surface. Even though it was only thirty meters up, it would mean certain death.

I glanced at Meg. We were both thinking the same thing.

"Do you have a tank nearby? Weight belt on?"

He nodded. "Yes, just in case."

"What about a seacar? Is one of those seaworthy?"

He winced. "Unfortunately, no. They're all in the middle of repairs. Hull plates on all of them. If we lose pressure in this module, I'll have to swim and find something at four atms."

I thought the situation over. Why Blue Downs? Why an undersea colony? Unless . . .

Unless the captain of that dreadnought was making a point. And they'd

FATAL
DEPTH

been nearby. They'd recently battled the Chinese fleet just to the northeast.

I swore and glanced at Meg. "No place is safe from that warsub. They're declaring war on *everybody*."

"*If* it's the dreadnought. It could be a natural disaster of some sort."

There was a rumble from the speaker and Mason grabbed the sides of the console. He thrust his face to the camera, creating a fishbowl effect. He yelled, "Another explosion!" He peered around. "I think another module just went!"

"Any idea which?" Meg said. She'd clenched her fists. That had been her home for over a decade. For her, it was probably like me watching Trieste go down.

"No, can't tell. But—" He cocked his head to the side. "I heard a detonation followed by a big implosion. Now there are more tremors, smaller ones. Probably airtight hatches giving way under pressure. Water crashing through a module destroying one compartment after another."

"Damn, I hope they have a place to evacuate to," Meg hissed.

We had decided to create an underground bunker for just such an instance. We hadn't started work on it yet, and it made me worry.

I pulled myself back to the transmission.

"Something's happening!" Mason cried. "I hear a loud noise. It's echoing all around!"

The audio kept muting whenever he wasn't speaking, and Meg pressed a button on the controls. Now the sound reverberated from the speaker. It was a dull drone that was growing in volume.

"It's a SCAV drive," she whispered.

"Leaving?"

"I think approaching."

The sound reached a crescendo and Mason rammed his hands against his ears. "It's so damn loud!"

It ceased abruptly and the image shook crazily. Mason desperately hung on to the console. Behind him, in the moonpool, a massive wave surged upward and roared into the module. It was a fountain of green water complete with seaweed, sand, and even fish. It rose so high it hit the ceiling and crashed down onto the docks with a roar. It cascaded across the deck and washed up to Mason's waist. His knuckles were white where he gripped the desk.

In the background, the seacars on their hoists swung back and forth, crashing into each other. The ones at the docks had broken their moorings and were floating free, waves cresting over them as they collided with each other and crashed into the bulkhead. They were listing to the side as water flooded into them. Their top hatches had also been open.

"Get your workers out!" I cried.

I wasn't sure if he could hear me. Behind him there were people swimming frantically, flailing to grab onto something, *anything*, to avoid vessels from crushing them.

"Mason!" Meg yelled. "Get your tank on! Your mask!"

He was looking around wildly, but the water was up to his knees, waves cresting as high as his waist. It washed over the camera several times. His face was now white as he continued scrambling around the deck, keeping one hand on the console. "It's gone! The wave washed it away!"

"Is the pressure falling?" I asked.

He glanced around. "No pressure alarm."

Behind him, the water was descending back down the moonpool. The four atmospheres in the facility were forcing the water back out to sea.

But the repair docks were a mess. Equipment was everywhere, seacars half sunk, and curls of smoke hung in the air.

New alarms were sounding now, adding to the chaos—probably fire alarms.

Mason stopped and peered around him. "The sound . . . it's there again, but going away now."

I realized what was happening.

Oh my god.

"They're using the tsunami plow," I hissed. Then to Mason: "Get your tank on! Another wave is coming!"

Chapter
Twenty-Three

MEG WAS STARING AT ME. "WHAT do you mean? Creating a tsunami against . . . *against an undersea city?*"

"They can create a tremendous wave displacement either on the surface or *under* the surface. Blue Downs—or any undersea colony—can't withstand that type of water impact. It'll cause implosions and force water *up* every moonpool in every module."

"But the city is only thirty meters—"

I knew what she was thinking. The dreadnought had a hundred-meter height, so how could it attack such a shallow colony? "It's likely at the surface, maybe scraping the bottom." I recalled that there was a ravine next to the city descending into the depths; perhaps the Russian warsub had approached from that direction. Hell, the underwater ravine likely funneled the force of the wave up toward the colony, like a shotgun blast directed right at the modules.

"The noise is getting louder again!" Mason cried from the video. He was still looking for his tank.

"Come on, come on, come on," I muttered as I watched the scene before me. The seacars that had broken loose had disappeared beneath the surface of the moonpool. The water had retreated from the docks and the deck, but it was still crashing in the pool, cresting the sides. There was a lot of white water there. A moonpool was usually calm and still.

The sound grew in intensity.

My heart was thudding. My breathing was short.

I had clenched my fists in my lap.

"Is there anything we can do?" Meg asked.

I shook my head. "They're on their own. They have a security force, if they managed to launch it in time."

I recalled their subs that had tried to sink us as we'd made our escape. They were small, fast, and armed.

But against that dreadnought, there was no hope.

It was like watching a train wreck, and we couldn't tear our eyes from the screen.

The sound increased until it was one constant howl from the speakers. Mason disappeared as he searched for his tank. The noise halted with another geyser of water blowing upward from the moonpool. There was more this time; the fountain splashed into the ceiling and sprayed out in all directions. The seacars fell from their harnesses and disappeared in a foaming mass of green froth. Meg screamed for Mason but he wasn't anywhere in the view.

The video pixelated for a moment and water rose completely over the camera. Everything was a churning mass of bubbles and green. Debris and oil and tools.

Then it subsided and fell below the camera.

"Mason!" I yelled.

The water was foaming and boiling, but it was lowering slowly.

The containment was still there, but it probably wouldn't last for long.

Mason lurched back into the view. He was soaking wet and wiped a hand across his eyes. There was black oil smeared on his face. He was gasping. He pulled something into view and slid his arm through a strap.

An air tank.

He didn't have a mask though.

There was a *sucking* noise as the water finally receded out the moonpool. Mason reached back for his regulator, but couldn't find it. He glanced down and swore. "Torn off," he muttered. "The backup too." He stared into the camera, and his face was blank, his eyes dark and glassy. "Meg, I think this might be it. The sound is growing again. Whatever it is, they're not letting up."

"You have to find a tank!"

He shook his head. "The damage in here is severe."

"Get to an airlock then. Swim to someplace safe! Keep the weight belt on."

He sighed. "I'm guessing there's no safe place right now, but I'll try." He shot a glance to his left. "The hatch is ten meters away. I'm going now. Wish me luck, Meg." He flashed one more look at us before he darted away. The water was at his ankles, and I could hear the splashes as he ran.

I held my breath as the whining noise of the SCAV drive escalated.

It stopped.

There was a pause—everything seemed silent for just an instant, though it could have just been my perception of the incident, a stretched reality due to my own adrenaline—and then another eruption of water *exploded* up the moonpool.

But it didn't crash back down.

Instead the water rose over the camera.

Then a muffled thud rattled the speaker and a flash of steel appeared in the view, moving *downward*. More churning bubbles followed, clouds of sand, and the image strobed, pixelated, then turned blue.

CONNECTION LOST.

"Oh my god," Meg hissed. "The module imploded. Pressure failed. The weight of the ocean overcame the structure."

I took a deep breath. Blue Downs was gone. Regardless of whether Mason had made it to the airlock or not, he didn't have a chance.

We sat in silence, staring at the blue screen. Then I hit the comm and called City Control. "Alert Australian authorities," I muttered to Zira Miller, on duty at the communications station. "Notify them that there's been a disaster at Blue Downs."

She frowned. "Pardon me? What kind of disaster?"

"Implosion of multiple modules. They need to get submarine rescue there immediately." I cut the call and leaned back.

Meg and I stared at each other.

We needed to kill that weapon.

—••—

THE NEXT DAY IN TRIESTE, THE USSF troops were worse. There were more of them than the single shift of seventy that Benning had promised. There were several fights and the blue-uniformed presence in Trieste kept our security forces on their toes. It infuriated me. Benning was escalating. He was intentionally demonstrating that despite me having manipulated him successfully, *he* was the one in command. *His* troops oversaw Trieste and would dictate processes and procedures at the city. The next time I saw him, he even spoke of making Trieste a regular pit-stop for USSF crews in not just the Gulf and Caribbean region, but in the entire Atlantic. It made me think that he was moving forward with his plans regarding Seascape.

I growled inwardly and didn't say anything in response. It would just make things worse.

The attack on Blue Downs had likely contributed to the increasing USSF presence as well. Everyone had now realized that any ocean colony could be a target.

The Australian city was gone. Search and rescue crews had arrived, and the images they broadcast were devastating. Explosions and water displacements had flattened each module. Some travel tubes were intact with a few survivors huddled within, but the loss of life was immense. Numbers were still coming in, but things didn't look good. Rescue teams had only saved a few hundred people from the tubes. The rest of the city consisted of shattered modules and flooded wreckage.

And the population of the city had been over a hundred thousand.

Scuba divers had hung outside the travel tubes with nowhere to go. They'd drowned as the survivors watched, unable to bring them inside. When the rescue subs arrived, there had been thousands of drowned swimmers resting on the bottom surrounding the wrecked city.

Mason had most likely died quickly.

—••—

JOHNNY, MEG, AND I MET EACH evening for dinner to discuss the mission. Lazlow had provided us a new and very detailed diagram, which included every hatch he could identify, and we pored over it as we ate, pointing out possibilities and strategies. Sometimes we'd bring in Lau and Irena to add to the discussion. Irena was the more nervous of the two, but I assured her that she wouldn't have to fight. The rest of us were going to get her to the reactor and secure it so she could take over. It made her feel better, though not by much.

Lau, on the other hand, was prepared and didn't show an inkling of nerves. He confided in us that this mission was going to get him back in the good graces of the elders at Sheng City, and he was going to use it to advance his career. He felt no more animosity for me and Johnny—in fact, he had embraced this adventure. I was beginning to like him as well. He was knowledgeable about naval strategy and good in a close-quarters fighting, which I knew from firsthand experience. He was skilled with weapons.

When he wasn't with us preparing for the mission, he was visiting the family in Trieste with whom he had some sort of relation. Cousins, perhaps. I had security follow him from a distance, just to be sure that he was not doing anything underhanded. He knew about them—he was observant and effective as a spy—but didn't try to avoid them.

The fate of Blue Downs hung over all of us.

The stakes were higher than ever.

During one of our meetings, with just Meg and Johnny in my office, I sat back as the image of the dreadnought revolved before us. On the desk were three items: a one-inch drill bit twelve inches long, an oxygen nozzle tapered to slightly under one inch, and a black steel cylinder roughly half the length of a cigar. I stared at Meg until she noticed. Then I looked away.

"What's on your mind?" she asked.

I turned my gaze to the ceiling. "Dad, I guess."

Johnny immediately stopped what he'd been doing—making notes about the warsub—and watched in silence.

"What about him?"

"I wonder if he knew something like this would ever happen."

"I doubt it. He was really only concerned with Trieste."

"He was concerned with *every* undersea colony. He had a world view."

"But he was just fighting for this city at the time." She snorted. "Some fight. He didn't get much done."

I watched her for a moment. "You still don't believe that he did something worthwhile?"

"I can't believe that he knew it would come to this." She pointed at the dreadnought. "Technology like that. Or the battle over the rift. Huge undersea conflicts with us as victors. It's too much to believe."

Johnny said, "He was a remarkable man. Don't underestimate him."

"There you go falling into the trap," she snapped.

"Which one?"

"This myth that other undersea people have built up about him. *We* lived with him. We know how much is true. We argued with him all the time." She swore. "It wasn't a great way to live. Our family life was in turmoil."

I said, "It does seem like he knew what was coming, Meg. In a way, he predicted all of this." She was about to snap at me again but I cut her off. "Not the specifics, like this warsub here, I'll give you that. But the need to keep ahead of the other nations and cities, the need to have the best technology, the need to keep the USSF off our backs. He was right about all of it."

"He destroyed our family, Tru." Her voice was a whisper. "Mom was a wreck after. She didn't make it much further than he did."

Johnny appeared uncomfortable now, not wanting to intrude on family business, I supposed.

"I know that," I said, "but look at the situation in the oceans right now. Look at what's going on topside. Dad predicted it all."

"At what expense?"

"He didn't cause it, if that's what you mean."

"If you say so."

I frowned but didn't know how to respond to that. Then Johnny said to me, "Is this what's been bothering you, Mac?"

I blinked. "Say again?"

"For weeks you've been a different person. Sullen. Not as open."

"Kat just died. It's been hard coping."

"I know." He waved it away. "But not just that. Something's been weighing on you."

I thought immediately of my nightmares. Of the crews drowning and ships sinking to crush depth. Of sailors screaming my name the instant before they died—and they weren't calling for help. I also thought of the dream of my dad, and of the argument we'd had the night before his death. And how he'd aged. How could Johnny have known about all of that? "How—"

"The bags under your eyes. The terse responses. I had thought it was the pressure of what's coming, but there's more, isn't there?"

I offered him a slight smile. "You know me better than I thought, Johnny." Then I hesitated. "In the battle at the rift, I—I—" Meg was staring now. She tilted her head as I stumbled over my words. "I gave an order that I immediately regretted. But it was an order I had to give. Something we had to do." I exhaled and closed my eyes. "I'm having a hard time with it."

Johnny said, "The order to destroy the USSF ships."

"Yes," I said in a whisper. I could barely hear it myself. Heller had come with a hundred warsubs. We had sunk many, but twenty or more had survived the battle and had been heading off to the west, back to port perhaps, to lick their wounds.

Back to Trieste, to cause more trouble and continue the occupation.

I knew I had to stop them.

I also knew that I couldn't let them get word out about what I had done. About the APD, the *Swords*, the base we had built in the Mid-Atlantic Ridge.

We destroyed them all. Fired at them until each ship sank below crush depth.

I squeezed my eyes shut now. The crews had felt and heard the explosions—some distant, some near—and had known what was coming for them.

"I killed them all," I said, my voice husky, "to protect Trieste."

"You had to do it," Johnny said. "We all agreed with it. It was the whole purpose of the base, right?"

"Still. It doesn't make it easier. I wonder . . ."

"What?"

I opened my eyes and stared at them. My gaze was cold, my face like steel. "I wonder if Dad had predicted something like that. Did he push us on this path to lead Trieste to independence? Or did he push us to become killers? Because some days that's what I feel like."

—••—

CLIFF FINALLY RETURNED FROM HIS MISSION a few days later. I met him at the docks and gave him a sharp salute followed by a firm handshake. Escorting him back to security, I sat in his office while Jamieson updated the chief on everything that had happened during his absence. Then the assistant left, and we were alone.

Cliff was happy to be back; he kept looking around as if he were soaking it all in.

"Must have been a tough trip," I muttered.

He nodded. "It was interesting, Boss, I'll say that. How long have you been going on similar missions?"

"About twenty-five years, give or take. I stopped for a while to work the kelp farms when it got to be too much for me."

"And how long have we had an intelligence agency?"

I had always kept this from him, despite his increasing curiosity about it. It was only because I needed this mission completed that I had finally brought him into the fold. I shrugged. "Since I arrived."

He frowned. "But you came here—"

"In the early 2090s, yes. My dad led TCI, and George Shanks took over after him." I told him the whole history, about how there had been multiple groups vying for independence, and that Dad had convinced them all to band together. I also told Cliff the truth about the assassination.

He blinked at this. "That's a lot to carry on your shoulders, Boss."

"It is." I sighed.

"There's something I've never told you." He stopped and sat in his chair. "I was there, you know. During it."

"During what?" I couldn't grasp what he was saying.

"The assassination. I was in the USSF. I was serving on Benning's ship at the time. I was in the Gulf."

"You didn't—"

"No. I didn't do it." He had blurted it, almost in reflex to keep me from thinking that he had played a role in my dad's death. "I didn't even know what was happening. We performed our duties on our warsubs and followed orders. But afterward . . . when we found out what they had done, it infuriated me. I didn't stay in the fleet long after."

I stared at him. At the obvious guilt on his face. "You came to Trieste after."

"To work for the city. Yes. I was carrying a lot of guilt because of it."

"But you didn't actually do anything wrong."

"I was on the wrong side, Boss. It caused a lot of pain. I felt much better once I arrived here." Then he exhaled and stared at me. "And I've never mentioned it to you. Each February is difficult because of it."

That was when we celebrated my dad's life.

Emotions cascaded across his face for several moments. I said, "Thanks for telling me, Cliff. I appreciate it. But it doesn't change anything between us. You've served Trieste admirably for many years now."

"And I want to do more." His expression was intense. "I want into TCI. More missions. More to help the city."

I offered him a sly smile. "Then have I got something for you."

—••—

TEN MINUTES LATER, AFTER FILLING HIM in on the upcoming mission, he leaned back in his chair and swore. "Jesus Christ. That's some crazy shit, Boss."

"Are you in?"

He stared at me for long heartbeats. "I just said I wanted more, right?"

"Good. Because if you had said no, I don't know what I would have done. I need you to get us on board that ship."

"It's a crazy plan."

"Can you think of something better?"

"No."

"Then let's get on it. We only have a bit of time left."

Chapter
Twenty-Four

CLIFF HAD RETURNED TO TRIESTE WITH a small section of hull. It was only a foot square, but it was *heavy*. There were two obvious layers of titanium, and between it one inch of cream-colored plastic.

It wasn't plastic though. It was the syntactic foam.

Sprayed between hulls during assembly, it hardened to form a solid intermediary between the two titanium hulls. Our version—similar to the original invention in the Twentieth Century—consisted of microscopic ceramic or glass spheres bound with an adhesive. The intense pressure of deep water would squeeze the hulls together, but the spheres of the syntactic foam withstood the pressure better than the hull on its own could. Spheres had much greater crush depths than any other hull configuration.

But the French had an improved version. We needed to know why.

Meg started work on it—while we weren't preparing for the mission that is—and told me she'd let me know how it was going.

I forgot about it.

—••—

THREE WEEKS LATER, WE WERE READY to go.

Benning had planted several stories in the world media about a fleet going out into the Pacific to find the mysterious warsub that had attacked the United States. It was all anyone on the news was talking about. There were hundreds of USSF ships involved, and as I'd suggested, he casually mentioned where the search was going to take place.

"We have reports of the Chinese Submarine Fleet engaging a mysterious vessel in the Pacific, east of the Philippines," he said during one broadcast. Apparently, the US had agreed to 'his' plan, had given the go-ahead, and he allowed a news crew to speak to him via comm from his ship, *Devastator*. "We have a few reports and we're going out to sink it."

"And what nation operates this vessel?" the reporter asked, worry clear in his features. He worked for a major news network, and every other major station had paid for the feed to show to their viewers as well. "Are we at war with the country responsible? Thousands are dead and the damage to the US is immense. And now Blue Downs . . ."

Benning nodded. "The damage to the USSF, to property and civilians in Virginia and Southern California, is incalculable. We have some ideas, but for now we're treating it as a rogue vessel."

"And once you've sunk it?"

Benning offered an oily grin. "If there is a nation behind this, they'll pay for what they've done. Don't doubt it."

—••—

WE WERE IN *SC-1*'S LIVING COMPARTMENT: myself, Meg, Johnny, Lau, Renee, and Cliff.

Crates of equipment for the mission surrounded us. They contained uniforms, scuba gear and radiation scanners. There were weapons—machine guns, pistols, and blades—along with boxes of grenades. There were two types: the first could be strapped to an object and detonated remotely; the second was the more conventional variety.

There was also one especially heavy crate, smaller than the others. It was eighteen inches long and twelve high.

Lined with lead.

I had also brought Manesh Lazlow with us, although he would not be boarding the warsub. He was our pilot on this mission, and it thrilled him. He couldn't believe his good fortune. I reminded him that he would likely be attempting to avoid a major battle, and to simply hang back and wait for our communication.

He had some tricks up his sleeve for the confrontation.

Benning was also on board the seacar. His expression was tight. He still presented his usual persona—tough, mean, and cruel; a force that others shouldn't mess with—but I could sense his underlying tension. I'd manipulated him into this, and I hoped he wouldn't back out.

I needed him on that sub.

My suggestion that he could parlay the mission into far more politically may have played a part. Or, perhaps it was my threat to put his USSF soldier publicly on trial. Whatever the case, he was there, and we would have to work together.

Until I didn't want to anymore.

Meg glared at him from the second he stepped off the ladder and set his bag down, but he either didn't notice or didn't care.

I sealed the top hatch and turned to them. "We've prepared for this. We know a great deal about that dreadnought. Now it's time."

Johnny and I sat in the command cabin and activated *SC-1*'s systems. He glanced at me with a grin on his face. It made me shake my head. "This is the most dangerous thing we've ever attempted," I muttered.

"But at least it's a plan. Better than waiting for the dreadnought to take us out."

"We don't even know what the interior is like. Where to go. How to fit in." I kept my voice low so the others wouldn't hear.

"We have uniforms. Irena can interpret for us." He shrugged. "We don't have any other choice, do we?'

"No, we don't." My throat was dry.

I had called my people from The Ridge together. They had enjoyed a break of slightly more than a month—as they'd requested—and I'd asked for their help on the mission. To a one they had agreed, and they would follow in the *Swords*. The vessels were armed and ready to go. With the

SCAV drive and the APD, they would offer incredible resistance once the battle began.

I shifted ballast to negative and navigated out the docking tube. Once in the ocean with the twenty-seven *Swords* collected around us, I spun the seacar around to stare at Trieste. The others clustered at my back to look out the canopy with me. *Devastator* was there as well; she had undocked and was beside us, though she was powering away and leaving Trieste behind. The French city, Cousteau, had also sent some armed seacars. There were eleven of them, each about the size of a bus, and they trailed behind, letting us take the lead.

The city was quiet. We could see Triestrians through the viewports in the modules as well as the travel tubes. Scuba divers and seacars and scooters moved about their daily activities, along with the usual collection of fish and bubbles and wildlife, as well as wranglers in their bright-orange scuba gear.

There were also brand-new fish fences set up, bubbles rising slowly to the surface. Benning didn't seem to notice them.

"Do you think we can save her?" Meg asked, staring at Trieste.

I glanced over my shoulder at my sister. "Of course."

"You realize that this dreadnought could just power away from the battle and come here to destroy everything, right? She has the highest top speed in the oceans."

"I know that. But we'll be inside and will bring her down."

Renée said, "The city has protection. Richard and Jessica can operate her defenses."

"Not from that dreadnought," Meg whispered.

The tension in the seacar was palpable. No one could respond to that.

Then Benning cleared his throat. I noticed absently that the rest of my people, although the cabin was tight, had given him space. They didn't want to be close to him.

We powered toward Panama at conventional speed, entered the pass-through, and navigated through it to the Pacific Ocean.

The search was on.

Or, to be more precise, we'd set the bait.

———••———

ONCE IN THE PACIFIC WITH OUR fleet of ships—us, *Devastator*, twenty-seven *Swords*, and eleven warsubs from Cousteau—we set course westward, toward Hawaii. It was slow going, for among the collected vessels only Triestrian forces had the SCAV drive. We kept our conventional thrusters turning at roughly sixty-five percent, speed forty-six kph. That was the fastest Benning's ship could move. His was the largest warsub in the USSF fleet, a Terminator Class missile boat, intimidating and extremely powerful, but it was relatively slow as a result.

Kat's invention had changed the seas. Soon every nation in the oceans would be putting SCAV drives on all their subs, just to keep up with us. Now Russia had one too. I knew the US had the technology—stolen from us following the battle in the Gulf—but I had yet to see it on any USSF sub in the ocean. They were still either retrofitting theirs, or were engineering new designs.

We had to always stay ahead of them, I knew, with technology like the SCAV and the Acoustic Pulse Drive. Now we had the syntactic foam too, once Meg could figure out how the French had improved it.

We spent two days powering westward with our motley fleet of ships. Things on *SC-1* were calm and quiet. We knew, however, that soon we were going to have to transfer over to the dreadnought, likely in the middle of a giant battle. It made us all uneasy.

I glanced at the smallest crate on the deck.

———••———

LAZLOW WAS IN THE PILOT'S CHAIR; I'd been giving him lessons on how to maneuver the seacar and adjust the ballast. I'd shown him the warning indicators, demonstrated the various alarms—depth, pressure, flood—and had him run a few exercises away from our accompanying ships. The smile on the doctor's face was obvious, and it also made me grin. "This is Kat's seacar. Don't hurt her, please."

"Got it."

"Now, let me show you the SCAV controls."

We ran through exercises on and off in the days leading up to our meeting with the US fleet.

And then it happened.

A communication sounded from Benning's belt and he reached to grab his PCD. "Go ahead," he growled, staring at me.

"Captain, *Devastator* here. We have the fleet on our scopes."

I glanced at Johnny and he stared at our sonar. He shook his head. They still weren't showing on ours; the USSF likely had better passive equipment than we did.

Benning said, "We'll rendezvous with them. What's the ETA?"

"Slightly more than sixty minutes."

"Understood." He keyed off.

It meant *Devastator*'s passive sonar range was roughly fifty kilometers. Ours was only thirty.

When they finally appeared on our scope, my eyes bulged. They showed at the top of the screen first. Tiny points of light on the circular screen. Thirty klicks out, and as we moved toward them, more and more kept appearing. Johnny called out the numbers as the hour counted down. "There are almost four hundred warsubs of various classes here, Mac."

Benning offered a tight grin. "I told you I could get a good-sized fleet together for this."

"Now up to 455." A minute later: "Four hundred and seventy now. There are some Chinese ships here too. I count about thirty."

Lau said, "Those would be from Sheng."

"There are CSF ships too. Almost a hundred of them."

I blinked. "In addition to the USSF vessels?"

"Yes."

"That's . . . that's almost six hundred warsubs."

"That dreadnought doesn't stand a chance," Benning rasped.

"Nothing can keep up with her," Meg said. "This isn't *Bismarck*."

"We'll see about that." Benning had thrust his head into the control cabin and was peering over the chairs at the sonar. On it, *Devastator* was clearly in the lead and headed for the mass of contacts directly before us.

"Send out a comm signal to the fleet." He reached for a headset and put it on.

"Go ahead," I muttered.

"This is Admiral Taurus T. Benning," he growled, "in command of *Devastator*. I'm assuming command of this fleet."

A heavily accented voice responded. "This is Captain Leong of the CSF forces. What is the plan?"

I suspected that they wanted to know what the USSF was doing before they threw themselves in with us. After all, it was a rare thing for the two sides to work together, especially following the tensions in the Iron Plains and the battle in the Gulf.

"This is Captain Shih of the Sheng City fleet," a female voice added. "We stand with Trieste to aid in any way we can."

This brought a smile to my face, but it only served to irritate Benning. I keyed my mic. "This is Mayor Truman McClusky. We stand with the USSF fleet as well. Thank you for joining us, Captain Shih."

A second later the French captain signaled, pledging his support for Trieste.

Benning looked like he was about to explode. He wanted to be the sole person in command of the fleet.

"Don't worry," I muttered to him. "You're leading this stage of the attack. I'm following you."

He gave me a sharp nod and clicked his mic back on. "Set course to bearing 213 degrees. Use active pulses, everyone. Make some noise." He bared his teeth. "Let's attract that bastard."

A quick glance at the charts showed me what spot he had chosen. We had traveled 3,500 kilometers into the Pacific. Now he was heading toward a location between American Samoa and the northern tip of New Zealand: The Kermadec Trench. It stretched more than a thousand kilometers between the two locations, connecting with the Tonga Trench to the north.

He was taking my advice.

It was one of the deepest locations on Earth, at more than ten kilometers down. Explorers had attempted to investigate it in the past with mixed results: In 2014, the immense pressure at 9,900 meters had imploded *Nereus*.

"Thanks," I muttered to Benning. "It'll be a good spot to send it to the bottom."

"This is my decision, McClusky," he growled in response. "Mine."

I glanced at him. He wanted desperately to remain in control of this situation, which I was happy to grant him. For now. "It's still more than seven thousand kilometers away though." I performed a quick calculation in my head. We were moving so damned slowly. "It'll take us almost six days to get there at this speed." I wondered if I could survive living with him in *SC-1* for that amount of time. I hated this man. My father's murderer, right next to me, and here I was, willingly working with him.

Then again, I had a plan for him, though I had to admit that I was beginning to waver.

I wanted my nightmares to end.

Our sonar started to light with active pulses. The pings echoed through our seacar as the fleet turned toward the deep trench.

—••—

THAT EVENING WE SET THE AUTOPILOT and continued cruising at a slow pace of forty-six kph. Dinner was rations and water, not very appetizing but good enough for where we were currently, and we sat in the living area, on the couches and on the carpet, eating in silence. The fleet was still sending out active pulses; they rang around us constantly.

"How long do you think it'll be before that dreadnought makes a move?" Lau muttered between bites. He had picked a meal of dried beef of some sort.

"Hard to tell," I replied. "It could be following us right now."

"Do you think they know what we're doing?" Irena asked.

"That we're here? Or that we're just trying to lure them toward the trench?" She shrugged. "Both, I guess."

"Their superiors will have definitely informed them that we're looking for them. They just have to listen to our pulses to figure it out. Sound travels far in the oceans . . . and we're making a hell of a racket."

"Do you think they will?"

"Yes."

"Why?"

I hesitated. "It seems to be their goal. Destabilize. Announce their presence. This would be the perfect opportunity." I gestured at Lau. "The CSF suffered a major loss. According to Lau, they didn't put up much resistance."

Lazlow spoke up at that point. "Would you like to see the battle?"

Benning frowned. "What? You have a recording of it?"

"Reconstructed only. From their sonar records. I've pieced it together."

We sat around the holographic display, eating as we watched the battle. It was as if we were viewing a film. After a few minutes, all had stopped eating and were staring at the events in utter fascination.

The dreadnought hovered in the center of our living space. Even when it maneuvered to evade torpedoes, kicked on its SCAV drive, or dove deep to escape mines, it remained at the center. The CSF ships surrounding it were in constant motion.

Most of them suffered enormous hits during the fight, however, and soon began plunging down into the deeps.

"Look at the torpedoes," Meg gasped.

The dreadnought launched weapon after weapon which churned angrily toward targets. There was a cloud of cavitating and bubbling water surrounding the ship on three sides, preventing most torpedoes from making it to its hull and detonating. Its missiles, however, sailed through them easily before arming.

Some of the Russian weapons were supercavitating, which accelerated quickly to 1,000 kph. And since the CSF didn't have a SCAV drive . . .

They were easy targets.

"How many torpedo tubes does that thing have?" Renée whispered, watching the battle with rapt attention. The ships were outlines floating in transparent space, with torpedoes crisscrossing the scene and leaving glowing trails behind. There were so many objects cluttering the view that it was growing difficult to see what was happening.

"Sixty-eight."

Eyes turned to me. Jaws hung open.

"Sixty-eight?" Cliff repeated.

Most warsubs had eight or ten at most. But this ship was something else.

"Not including mine ejection hatches."

He shook his head. "There will be at least three people manning each one, just to keep them up and operating. That's over two hundred people, on torpedo duty alone." He frowned. "How many crew on this ship?"

"There's no way to know for sure," I answered. "But with that many on torpedoes, there might be upwards of six hundred at least. Probably more."

Irena's face was white. "And we're going inside it. To try and blend in."

No one replied.

Chapter
Twenty-Five

WE MAINTAINED COURSE AND HEADING FOR another five days. It grew monotonous after a while, and our morale began to slide. We spent our time cleaning weapons under Cliff's watchful eye. He taught the others how to use the safety, reload quickly, and use the laser sight to aim. They did everything but pull the triggers. He wanted them to feel comfortable with the small machine guns, with their weight and controls. He wanted it to become second nature.

There were more weapons in his bags, but he didn't spend time on them. That would come later, he told the others. There was a rare glint in his eyes when he said it.

—••—

JOHNNY, LAU, MYSELF, AND LAZLOW TOOK turns in the pilot chairs during the voyage. At one point, while Lau and I were in the command cabin late in the evening and the others were sleeping, he said to me, almost in an offhand manner, "I think this mission is insane, Mac."

It startled me, and I stared at him. The lights were dim, there was loud breathing behind us, and I said quietly, "But you're here right now."

"I support Sheng City. They're on your side. I'm not entirely sure why they've chosen this, but I have to fall in line." He shrugged. "And you've proven yourself. I just think this is . . ." He trailed off.

I finished for him, "A suicide mission?"

"Maybe." He winced as he said it.

"It might be. But suicide missions are *necessary* missions, wouldn't you say?"

He frowned. He didn't know how to respond.

"It's important enough for us to go. That vessel is a menace."

He nodded. "After Blue Downs, I'd have to agree."

"Sheng could be next. Or Trieste. Or the Chinese mainland."

He paused for a long moment, and we listened to the sigh of water as *SC-1* cut through the ocean. Then, "I'm surprised to be sitting here with you right now. After what happened last year."

He was referring to our fight. He had been trying to steal the supercavitating technology from Trieste, along with Johnny Chang. "Do you forgive me for that?" I asked.

He blinked. "Do you forgive me for stabbing you?"

I grunted. "It hurt like hell."

"I did it in a place to avoid serious injury."

"I recall," I muttered. Still, it hadn't felt like it at the time. He'd pushed the blade into my back, near my kidney in the lower right side. He'd barely missed my liver. "But I'm happy you're with us. Sinking that ship isn't just a choice. It's something we *have* to do."

"I know. But I love my city, the same as you love Trieste. I'll do anything for her."

I didn't know how to respond to that. I stared ahead and piloted the ship.

—••—

SOON WE WERE APPROACHING THE TRENCH. As I stared at the depth finder, a jolt suddenly shot through my body. A revelation had occurred to me. I said in an ominous tone, "What if . . . what if *they're* waiting for *us*?"

"What was that?" Benning asked. He was standing over my shoulder, watching the screens. Johnny was copiloting with me.

"I said, maybe they're here already."

Benning scowled. "How?"

"We've been making a lot of noise. Our course is obvious. Maybe they heard us, noted where we were going, and set course for the trench. They have a SCAV drive." I realized belatedly that we could have gone on ahead and just waited for the fleet to arrive. But had the battle occurred behind us, we would have missed our opportunity.

"Why would they do that?"

"An ambush." I pointed out the canopy. "That trench is ten kilometers deep. We picked it because it would be a good grave site for them. The problem is, it'll be a good grave site for our fleet as well."

"So what? Why would they care about it? We picked it because you want to release a bunch of radioactive sludge into the ocean, and this will bury it for you. But—"

"Listen to me!" I snapped, staring at the readouts. The depth had suddenly dropped off. One second it had been at 4,000 meters, now it was showing 9,000 and still falling.

We'd just sailed over a sheer cliff leading straight to hell.

Lazlow didn't think the APD could get us to the bottom. Eight kilometers was the max, but he hadn't tested it yet.

I continued. "If they sink our ships here, there will be no salvaging them. The Chinese, the USSF, Sheng City . . . the warsubs will be gone forever. Maybe this is *their* plan, and has been all along."

As I said it, a silence fell over everyone in the seacar.

The sonar alarm blared. A large white light appeared on the screen, coming fast from the north, along the trench at a depth of 350 meters.

Calls were coming in now from the rest of the fleet, frantically requesting orders.

The dreadnought.

—••—

"At bearing three-five-six," Johnny said in a level, calm voice. "Depth three-five-zero."

"I see it." I turned to Benning. "It's time to get the fleet in action." As he keyed his mic and started to address the ships—*six hundred of them!*—I motioned to Lazlow.

It was time to put our plan in motion.

We were going to kick on the SCAV drive and power away from the fleet until we were out of passive sonar range.

Then we would try something we'd never attempted before.

Something very dangerous.

Benning finished his orders—he had commanded the ships to break into four distinct groups and surround the dreadnought if possible—and it made me snort. He was taking a standard approach to naval combat; he hadn't even attempted a ploy or subterfuge of any sort. I had ordered my *Swords* to avoid the conflict until further orders, which Benning didn't realize. I didn't want them to engage the dreadnought. It would be a waste of armaments and effort, and could even lead to more Triestrian casualties.

"Okay, we're out of here," I muttered as I kicked on the SCAV and pointed our nose to the west, farther out over the trench.

It was very deep beneath us now, I thought. My guts slithered.

Soon we were moving at 450 kph, and I watched the sonar screen, breathless. The dreadnought had come to a stop and had begun ejecting a flurry of countermeasures. These powered away from her before coming to an abrupt halt. They began to bubble and churn.

It was a wall of noise between it and the enemy.

Then there was a second round of launches—more countermeasures, closer to the dreadnought this time.

Smart, I thought. If any torpedoes got through the first line of defense before arming, then they would hit the next group of countermeasures and detonate far enough from the dreadnought to prevent any damage.

"Attack from the depths . . ." I muttered. "Program your torpedoes to go *down* first, and then shoot up from below."

Benning stared at me, not understanding.

"There are no countermeasures below the dreadnought," I rasped.

He nodded and moved the mic to his lips.

I continued, "But remember . . . port side only. We need to get that beast tipped over." Inwardly, I swore. Benning was useless as a tactician. He was likely good at administration, pushing papers and handing out assignments, but had never faced a situation like this before.

I had.

A wayward thought intruded at that point, and it nauseated me. *To think this is the man who had killed my father.*

It would have insulted Dad.

—••—

IT ONLY TOOK TEN MINUTES TO get us out of range. I turned to the north and said to Lazlow, "It's time, Doc. Work your magic."

He had a device set up on the deck just behind my chair. Cables led from it into the control console before me—into the Acoustic Pulse Drive sytem. The newly installed generator in *SC-1*'s bow would broadcast whatever sounds Lazlow wanted, and he had created a unique program for this situation, for this battle.

He tapped at a keyboard and stared at a tiny monitor on his equipment. A droning hum began to echo throughout the seacar. It sounded oddly familiar.

It sounded like a warsub.

It was broadcasting the noise into the waters around us.

"Now take us back to the dreadnought," he instructed. "Don't go faster than sixty-five though. That's a *Vostok*'s top speed."

Benning looked outraged. "But it'll take us nearly an hour to get back! The battle—"

I said, "We have to appear as though we're a Russian warsub. We can't go faster than their top speed, for fuck's sake, Benning."

"And keep your voice down," Lazlow interjected. Then, at the admiral's glare, the doctor looked abashed. "Sorry. But if we're going to sneak into its defense sphere, we need to make them think we're on its side. This is complicated . . ." He started murmuring to himself, "Have to make sure the noises we broadcast merge with the sounds of our own seacar to simulate a *Vostok* . . . there has to be a harmony between the two different sounds . . . a synergy . . . to create a third predicted sound . . ."

Cliff rose to his feet and said in a soft voice. "It's time to get ready." He looked at me. "Mac?"

I exhaled and looked at Lazlow. "It's your turn to pilot now, Manesh." I slapped his shoulder as I moved past him. "Good luck. You know what to do."

—••—

THIRTY MINUTES LATER, WE WERE STANDING before the airlock. It made my heart flutter. Despite all the missions I'd been on in the past, I had never been part of *anything* like this before.

Irena, Lau, Johnny, Meg, Benning, Cliff, and myself wore Russian naval uniforms. Benning and I wore officer's insignia; the others were in crewmen's overalls. The fabric color was slate gray with crimson trim. We looked smart in them, I had to admit, but it brought home exactly what we were about to do.

As we powered toward the ongoing battle, distant thuds reverberated our hull: explosions, implosions, and the whine of torpedoes.

People were dying.

"Now for the wetsuits," Cliff said in a clipped, quiet voice.

We couldn't arrive on the dreadnought soaking wet. That would not be *blending in.*

Unless they had suffered a hull breach or two, I thought.

The wetsuits were several sizes larger, to go over the clothing. It had been part of our planning over the past four weeks. Our preparations had covered everything from Lazlow's strategy to get us close, Cliff's plan to get us on board quietly, and the Russian clothing to help us blend in with the personnel.

Soon Cliff, myself, and Benning were in the airlock. It was a tight fit; we had bags of gear and weapons slung over our shoulders.

The inner hatch began closing. I caught a glimpse of Meg; she was staring at me, fear in her eyes.

I shot her the hint of smile as the hatch ground shut and the locking mechanism slid into place.

"Get ready," I muttered.

Water began to flood in, and I checked my air supply to make sure it was ready for our depth. The pressure would be great, but not insurmountable.

We had successfully maneuvered through the countermeasure barricade from below and had positioned ourselves off the dreadnought's hull.

This had to happen *fast*, before they grew suspicious.

The outer hatch opened and we hauled ourselves outside.

I swore to myself.

Explosions and bubbles and torpedoes lit the sea everywhere I looked. The countermeasures continued to work, churning and moving and emitting sound, and torpedo after torpedo hit the wall and detonated in massive balls of steam and bubbles that rose in torrents toward the surface. The concussions pounded us, and I thought belatedly that earplugs would have been a good idea.

There was now a wall of countermeasures below us as well; the Russians had adapted to my earlier suggestion.

We scrambled out of the airlock and closed it behind us.

And waited.

Cliff was staring at the dreadnought. It was the largest vessel we'd ever seen up close. It was a skyscraper lying sideways in the water. Four hundred and fourteen meters long. I craned my neck to look up . . . it was a full football field high.

The hull was studded with anechoic tiles and there were too many hatches to count. Torpedo tubes, mines, airlocks, cargo bays, scooter hatches, and more. Cliff was scanning them quickly, trying to find one that we could use to gain access. He reached to his waist and removed a black metal weapon.

It was a grapple. Portable. Magnetic.

He aimed . . . and fired.

Chapter
Twenty-Six

THE WARSUB WAS TWENTY METERS FROM us. Cliff had just fired a flat metal projectile toward its hull. Drag with water slowed it, however, and nearby explosions were causing turbulence. *SC-1* was bucking about, nearly tossing us off, and the grapple lost depth as it moved.

He'd missed.

Cliff's eyes narrowed as he realized what had happened. He pushed a button and the reel began retracting the thin cable.

Behind us, the airlock opened and Lau, Meg, and Irena appeared. The nuclear engineer's eyes were wide in terror. She looked around at the explosions and torpedoes and backed deeper into the airlock. I gestured at her and then gently pulled her out. She didn't want to come.

We clung to the seacar's skin as the hatch closed.

Cliff fired again, only this time he pointed upward on a sharp angle. The projectile soared out on a parabolic course toward the dreadnought.

I held my breath.

This time, as the grapple descended, it hit the hull and stopped. He retracted the cable until it tightened.

He connected the weapon to a rung on *SC-1*'s hull. He turned to me.

It was time to cross.

I sent Benning first. He looped his legs around the wire, latching onto it with a carabiner on his belt, and began pulling himself across. His bag hung low off his shoulders, weighing him down, and the cable drooped with him.

All our bags contained heavy tools—equipment and supplies needed to sabotage the dreadnought. There was just no way we could swim with them on our backs.

I hoped Lazlow was watching this over the monitor. We needed him to keep the cable taut during this stage.

As I thought it, a maneuvering thruster pushed the seacar slightly away, tightening the cable.

Lau went next, then myself. I motioned to Irena and as I began pulling myself, hand over hand, the airlock opened.

It was Johnny and Renée. At their feet was the crate of uranium.

—••—

RENÉE WAS ON THE CABLE NOW. She seemed confident and sure of herself as she'd latched herself to it and looped her legs around it to steady herself. Her face was set like stone.

Johnny brought up the rear. He'd attached the crate to the cable and just as he was about to hook it with his own carabiner—

SC-1 lurched to the side as a tremendous explosion lit the water around us. The concussion was gargantuan and I closed my eyes involuntarily. I lost track of what was going on; bubbles churned around us and a current of water hit with enormous force.

The seacar moved away—

The cable detached.

The weight of seven people on the cable, along with the heavy crate on the very end, fell into the abyss.

I nearly screamed. I think Irena did; she was right behind me, and I reached down to grab her outstretched hand. We were hanging freely over the immense canyon. The purpose of a carabiner was to keep us on a *horizontal* cable—they slid freely across it as we moved.

But now we were sliding downward, toward the abyss.

—••—

WRAPPING MY LEGS AROUND THE WIRE, I squeezed with everything I had. I gestured at Irena to do the same; I couldn't hold her as well as myself at the same time. She nodded slightly, eyes through her facemask still bulging in fear, but she managed. She was breathing heavily; bubbles surged from her regulator.

We stopped, drifting back and forth in the current, as *SC-1* powered away.

A detonation had come close. Perhaps the Russians had realized what we were doing, or maybe it had been an errant torpedo meant for the dreadnought. It didn't matter now. If we couldn't get to the warsub, we were done for.

Hand over hand, I pulled myself up. I kept glancing down; Irena was still there. Below were Renée, Johnny, and the crate at the very end, swaying in the rough turbulence. For its size, it was quite heavy—twenty kilograms, or forty-five pounds. But we didn't have far to go—less than twenty meters. The bags across our shoulders also held us back, but we managed to make it to the warsub.

I reached out to touch its hull. It was surreal . . . the ship I'd first seen on my sonar weeks ago, a mystery which we had struggled to unravel, was now only inches away.

I touched it.

A surge of elation filled me. There was a rung nearby, and together we latched ourselves to it. I focused on Irena to get her over, then Johnny, and finally the crate. Together we hauled it over to the hull and attached it to the same rung with a short stretch of cable and a carabiner.

The magnetic grapple hung down now and disappeared into the depths. Cliff tripped the magnet loose and it dropped from sight.

We were hanging onto the skin of the dreadnought, but we needed desperately to get in.

Each second we spent out there meant more time decompressing in an airlock. We couldn't afford to wait.

Cliff was scanning the hull, looking for a lock. He'd gestured to one earlier, before he had latched onto the cable, but now we had to find it.

Soon he'd located it and together we began to move. The dreadnought was stationary and it was more a matter of climbing toward it than anything else. It wasn't difficult. The crate, however, would present a problem.

Cliff and Lau made it to the lock. I watched, holding my breath, as Cliff worked the outer panel.

If he couldn't get in, we were dead.

There was nothing we could do. We'd likely hold on until an explosion dislodged or killed us, or until the dreadnought kicked on its SCAV drive and left us, floating in the ocean, waiting for our air to run out.

He pushed a button—

Nothing happened.

Shit.

I could see it in his eyes. He was angry.

He quickly withdrew a tool from his belt and began unscrewing the panel. I took a moment to look back at Irena; she was moving away from me. She didn't seem to understand where she was anymore. Her full-face mask showed her fear. She was scrabbling toward the hull, floating free from the ship, and had lost her bearings.

"Irena," I whispered.

She snapped her head around, looking for the source.

"It's me," I continued. We hadn't wanted to speak out there, in case they picked up the transmission, but I'd had no choice. "Stay calm. We're almost in. Cliff is at the airlock."

She stopped thrashing and floated, looking up at me. I reached out to her, my other hand on the hull. "Come, grab it."

She didn't do anything; she simply stared with wide eyes.

A noise attracted my attention. A grinding, grating sound.

Above me and to the right, the hatch had slid open. Cliff was in the airlock, gesturing toward us.

"Look," I said. "We're in. Swim to me."

She was drifting away from the sub now, still not moving.

Johnny's eyes showed worry now too. We couldn't lose Irena.

I pushed off and swam toward her.

As I reached out for her, a different sound hit.

And then a current.

The dreadnought had started its thrusters. It was maneuvering.

Oh, fuck!

—••—

I TUGGED ON IRENA AND TURNED to the warsub. Johnny was still on the hull and he was reaching for me. I had to get to him, but the dreadnought was beginning to pull away.

Distant explosions were rippling the water, and the flash of detonations lit everything around us. It was like being in a thunderstorm at night, with lightning *everywhere.*

I strained to reach him . . .

But I was drifting down as the warsub ascended. I wasn't going to make it.

The warsub was blowing ballast as well; huge fountains of bubbles had begun to pour from the hull just below Johnny, engulfing him.

But still he held on; his arm was protruding from the stream and I kept pulling for him, dragging Irena behind.

My vest was the last option. I could use it to help lift me toward him. Pressing a button on its side injected a bit of air into it. It altered my buoyancy slightly—

I realized with a pit of hot fear in my gut that if we didn't get in that airlock, and the warsub went shallow, we would all suffer from The Bends, for the warsub could carry us up too quickly.

I swallowed and kept my eyes on Johnny's hand.

I screamed with everything I had at the last moments, straining to reach it. I was wearing boots—not flippers—making it more difficult to swim. Irena was pulling me down—she had no idea how to adjust her vest—and I was hauling on her to get her toward the hull.

Johnny's fingers wrapped around mine and he pulled us in.

We'd made it.

Scrambling toward the airlock, the three of us joined the others inside. It was large enough to fit us all, and we lurched in and collapsed, drifting slowly to the deck. Then we remembered the crate, and began to pull the cable attached to it. Hand over hand, we slowly reeled it in.

The dreadnought was picking up speed, however, and the crate stretched back toward the stern, making it more difficult.

Finally, it hit the airlock's lip, and we hauled it in.

A powerful shriek hit and we pressed our hands to our ears to block it. *Damn!* It penetrated deep into our brains and I clenched my teeth in agony.

The hatch closed and the water lowered.

We stared at each other, shock on our features.

We were in.

Interlude:
Sheng City
Warsub *Houju*
Over the
Kermadec Trench

Location: Sheng City Warsub *Houju*
                     Over the Kermadec Trench

Latitude: 30° 15′ S
Longitude: 178° 49′ W
Depth: 249 meters
Time: 2138 hours
Date: 14 June 2030

CAPTAIN LO SZUAN STARED AT THE sonar, mouth hanging open and stunned into a brief silence. Never in his wildest dreams—or nightmares—had he thought that he'd ever be involved in a battle of this magnitude. There were so many contacts on the display that it was difficult to see exactly what was happening. The largest target was the only one they were worried about destroying, but there were a multitude of other signals on the screen, including torpedoes, countermeasures, and hundreds of warsubs. To make it more confusing, surface ships and planes had arrived on the scene within the past few minutes, and mines had started to fall on the dreadnought as well.

Planes were also dropping torpedoes in the water, which were angling down and spearing toward the warsub.

Friendly fire was becoming a real issue. Szuan watched in horror as one of their own torpedoes, set to HOMING, accidentally locked onto a CSF ship. The impact was horrendous, and the Chinese warsub immediately imploded and spiraled downward into the abyss.

"This is too much," he muttered to his bridge crew. There were five of them sitting at consoles—one was the pilot; others were manning weapons and ballast; the remaining eight crew were in engineering and the torpedo bays. "There is too much clutter."

"This is the warsub that attacked the US and the CSF fleet," his executive officer said. "We must sink it."

"Casualties are going to be huge." As he said it, three more subs suffered catastrophic implosions and, spewing bubbles and debris, plummeted into the depths.

The canyon below was daunting. A hull breach they couldn't overcome would mean certain death. There were no safe places to bottom the boat here. Perhaps that's why their superiors had chosen this location.

The dreadnought had appeared suddenly, powering faster than any undersea vessel Szuan had ever seen. It had come to a stop, set up a defensive perimeter with a veritable *wall* of countermeasures, and had then launched weapon after weapon toward the fleet of six hundred warsubs.

The captain did not fully understand what was happening. The American admiral who was in charge had run away in one of the fast, little seacars. He had given one order—to program torpedoes to find a way through the countermeasures, possibly from *underneath* the dreadnought—then had left.

It was odd.

Now a commander on *Devastator* was issuing orders, but they were having little impact against this huge Russian vessel. The man had ordered the fleet to target only the port side, and it was making things even more difficult, for the Russian commander seemed to realize what was happening and had strengthened his countermeasures there.

Then the surface vessels started dropping mines, and the dreadnought finally started to move.

"Thrusters on that beast are powering up!" one of his bridge crew yelled.

Szuan also couldn't believe how huge this ship really was. He had only seen a few torpedoes make it through the countermeasure net, and when those finally impacted the hull, the explosions had seemed miniscule against the mighty warsub.

Pinpricks on a giant's skin, he thought.

"Stay with him," he ordered. "Continue firing."

"We're depleting our complement of weapons, sir, and I can't tell if any have even gotten through!"

The ship was shuddering with enormous blasts. Concussions were throwing their small warsub about, each echoing in the tight confines of the bridge, and the turbulence was like nothing they'd experienced before. Already two of his crew had vomited on the deck. The smell was disgusting.

Detonations had continued uninterrupted since the battle had begun. The sea was alight with flashes and frothing bubbles and hulled vessels soaring downward toward sure implosion.

"There goes another!" his sonar operator said. "And another! Already the enemy has taken out twenty of our warsubs!"

Twenty.

The captain wanted to scream. And only a few torpedoes had even made it through.

Hopefully the mines would have better results.

—••—

THE DREADNOUGHT'S TWO THRUSTERS WERE SLICING the water as it powered away from the cloud of countermeasures. It seemed to maneuver quicker than something that large should be able to, the captain thought. It didn't have large control surfaces. Perhaps gimbaling thrusters?

It banked slowly to the port and left a wake behind, causing even more turbulence.

"It's moving to escape the mines," he said. "Follow."

"There are torpedoes everywhere though," his exec said. "And falling mines. We have to avoid them."

The captain merely nodded in response and the XO hovered over the pilot's station to give direction. Szuan swore to himself. Surely there was some other way to destroy this vessel.

Explosions rocked the warsub; they even rattled his teeth. He had to hold onto the railing above his head to remain standing.

An alarm screamed from the sonar station. He snapped his eyes to it and swore yet again.

There were more contacts arriving.

Unknown contacts.

"Could they be with us?" the operator said.

"Not sure." He continued to watch the screen. They were still thirty kilometers out, but were approaching at just over sixty kph. Fast for conventional warsubs. "How many are there?"

"Twenty-four so far. More coming into range though."

"Tell me the configuration of those ships—French? American?" The captain was wondering if they were friendly and would join the battle to sink the Russian.

The response came a few moments later. "Double hull struts connect the thruster pods." The woman turned to look at the captain. "Same as the Russian dreadnought."

"Damn." Reinforcements had arrived.

But not for their side.

—••—

T<small>HE</small> R<small>USSIAN</small> <small>TORPEDOES</small> <small>WERE</small> <small>A</small> <small>MIX</small> of conventional and SCAV. They were set on HOMING, and most of them seemed to find targets. There were so many ships surrounding the dreadnought that there was no shortage of targets. And the SCAV weapons were just too fast for them. Each powered out, accelerating quickly on a plume of rocket exhaust, before hitting a Chinese or American ship. They barely even had time to accelerate before detonating.

The USSF, Cousteauian, and Chinese fleet was like a swarm of bees surrounding a victim, Szuan thought. Only this 'victim' was doing remarkably well. Now that it had moved out of its countermeasure blanket, however, more torpedoes were starting to strike.

A voice came over the comm. "Remember, just the port side. Hit just the port hull of that beast."

The captain shook his head. They had barely been able to even scratch the thing so far, let alone—

His sonar screen flared white.

"What is it?" the captain barked.

His sonar operator had ripped her headphones off and was grimacing in obvious pain. "A loud noise sir. It's disrupting *everything*. No weapon can acquire a target."

"Is it going away?"

She glanced at the panel. "It's a sustained tone, high frequency." She mumbled something under her breath.

"What's that?"

"I feel sorry for the wildlife in the area."

The captain stared out the viewport at the dark water around them, with the flashes of detonations strobing all around. "I doubt there's anything living other than us within fifty kilometers right now." He could hear the tone even through the hull of the ship. High pitched. Annoying.

The sonar was solid white. The Russians had effectively blinded everyone in the theater of battle. "The acoustic generator must be immense," he whispered. "We'll have to switch weapons to IMPACT only. We'll need to line up before we fire. Move us around to see if we can get a clear shot."

"The vessel is powering away at sixty-four kilometers per hour! Banking to the port."

Damn. Its top speed was faster than theirs. "Turn the ship to the port. Bring that vessel in front of us."

But inside, the captain was cursing. The chances of them hitting a moving target with an impact-only weapon were slight. They would have to fire *in front* of the vessel, aim by 'leading it,' and hope it continued the same course and the two trajectories intersected.

Captain Lo Szuan wondered why the city elders had assigned them this task. It seemed pointless, and might even end up with them dying. As far as he was aware, the Russians hadn't even attacked them. The Chinese Submarine Fleet, yes—but not the Sheng City fleet. And lately the people's mood in the city had been growing dour. There was an undercurrent of resentment toward the Chinese mainland and her submarine force. Sheng City citizens were growing weary of their demands.

Soon the mysterious vessels were in range, but the captain didn't know it by the sonar display, which the noise disruption still blanketed in a white cloud. His sonar operator had said, "The other ships should be here by now. I counted thirty of them before the screens stopped working."

As if on cue, all hell broke loose.

There was a detonation at the stern of his vessel, and flood alarms started screaming. Lights began to strobe. There was a muffled cry of warning over the comm from the engineering cabin, which cut off almost immediately.

Szuan looked behind him, at the open hatch and the corridor that led toward the stern of the ship.

The last thing he saw was the watertight engineering hatch blown off its hinges. It ricocheted through the corridor and a flood of water rapidly exploded toward him.

The bridge hatch automatically slammed shut, but the captain knew it wouldn't matter.

Part Five: Meltdown

Chapter Twenty-Seven

WE STRIPPED OFF OUR WETSUITS AND shoved them in the bags. Irena was breathing heavily; she was sitting on the deck, arms wrapped around her legs with her forehead on her knees. She glanced at me when I checked her. She wasn't catatonic, at least. "The hard part's done," I mumbled, not fully believing it myself. But being outside under that immense pressure had been foreign to her. What was coming, at least, was in her wheelhouse. Once we were in that reactor room, anyway. Hopefully she'd bounce back.

The ship was at four atmospheres, and we'd been out at over thirty atms; now we had to depressurize. The automated airlock was slowly lowering the pressure for us. The readout indicated that we had a forty minute wait.

The muffled sound of commands was echoing in from outside. Something floated to our ears that made Irena perk up.

"What was that?" I whispered.

"They announced . . . they said to prepare for something. A type of drive I think. I didn't understand the word."

I glanced at the others. "SCAV probably. They're running from the battle."

Meg said, "It was inevitable. Once they started taking hits, I knew they'd run."

"We have SCAV torpedoes," Benning said. "They can't escape those."

It made me shake my head. Even if some made it to the dreadnought, there wouldn't be nearly enough. But another thought worried me: if the dreadnought ran and the fleet couldn't sink it with conventional weapons, would they try a nuke? I asked Benning.

He looked grave. "Only I can give that order." He held up his PCD. "If need be, I'll send it. But I'm going to give your strategy a chance first."

I blinked. "And USSF command gave you this power?"

He nodded.

—••—

THE SHIP WAS BANKING TO THE port as the acceleration mounted. It was hard to believe that a ship this size could reach 467 kilometers per hour, but I'd seen it with my own eyes. The course evened out, and we continued at a constant bearing for several more minutes. Then there was a sharp bank and another wait.

A command echoed in the corridor outside.

We all looked to Irena. Her face was blank. "Something about a—a big wave? A tsunami? I don't fully under—"

"Everyone get against the forward bulkhead!" I rasped. "Stand up!"

Looks of confusion met me, but Johnny understood. "They're going to use the tsunami plow. But against what?"

"Against the fleet," I said. We were now standing against the airlock's steel wall.

This was going to hurt.

"What does that mean?" Irena asked.

"The dreadnought is going to deploy its plow at maximum speed. We banked to port and came around in a one-eighty. They created some distance and now they're coming back. Get it?"

Benning scowled. "They're going to use it against our subs?"

It was a brilliant tactic. It would send a massive shock of water toward whatever ships were remaining. Every torpedo in the water would likely detonate, their onboard computers interpreting the wave as an impact with a solid surface. The wave's turbulence would toss our ships like toys, probably causing broken bones and concussions on board.

Bridge crews would be in chairs—except the captains and executive officers—and if they were heading into the wave, the shock of impact would hurl them into the forward bulkheads. There were no seatbelts in a conventional submarine without a SCAV drive. It might even cause implosions in some of the smaller warsubs. And as for the crew standing about, working at their stations . . .

"Prepare yourselves," I said between clenched teeth. "Press your head against the steel. It'll snap our necks if we—"

The shock of a sudden stop hit us.

—••—

A RAPID DECELERATION *SHOVED* US TO the bulkhead. From 467 kph to nothing in only a second. More than ten gravities forced the air from our lungs and pressed us against steel. Rivets in the bulkhead tore through our clothing, puncturing our flesh in multiple places.

As we lurched away following the abrupt halt, I struggled to catch my breath. I pressed my hands to my knees and bent over, breathing heavily.

The others were gasping too. Then Cliff motioned to us. "Wait. Do you hear that?"

In the distance, explosions and dull thuds reverberated the water and hull around us.

Torpedoes were detonating. Mines as well, most likely.

"This ship has many tricks up its sleeve," he muttered to himself.

The alarm on my PCD sounded softly from its place in my pocket. Decompression over. Cliff glanced at the airlock controls and gave me a tight nod.

It was time.

Johnny and Lau were calm and collected. They were intelligence operatives, after all. They were used to this type of thing, as was I. The fact that they were Chinese had not caused us any worry at all; there were many Chinese in Russia, especially due to the Soviet Union's close ties with the communist country during the first cold war. Those ties had not disappeared in the past century.

"Ready?" I stared at them. Irena still looked terrified. Benning appeared visibly shaken, but he was trying to hide it behind his rigid posture. Cliff, however, was steady and determined. I continued, "Remember not to speak. Don't walk together. Johnny and I will lead the way. Irena and Benning behind us. Hang back, but don't let us get out of your sight. Lau and Meg will be next. You two will carry the crate between you. Cliff and Renée will bring up the rear."

They nodded in response.

Cliff added, "Keep your weapons in your bags for now. Don't pull anything unless we get into trouble."

We stood before the hatch and I nodded to Cliff.

He pressed the OPEN button.

———••———

ALARM LIGHTS BATHED THE HALLWAY IN a bloody glow. Warnings were blaring and commands from the PA system echoed around us. Signs on the corridor bulkheads directed crew around the ship—in Cyrillic, of course. It made no sense to me.

We knew the general location of engineering and the nuclear plant. Stern, near the bottom decks. We would march as a loose group aftward, and descend several decks until we were in the correct vicinity. Then we'd use the Geiger counter.

As part of our plan, we also had to gain control of the ballast control area of engineering. We had no idea where that was.

First, we'd locate the reactor and take over. Then we'd worry about the ballast tanks.

I snapped a quick glance at Johnny—he in his crewman overalls, me in officer's garb—and he eyed me. Taking a deep breath, we stepped into the corridor and turned left, toward the dreadnought's stern.

We didn't look back. We needed to rely on the others and not appear nervous or worried about them.

We had to seem *confident*. Like we belonged there.

We stopped at a cabin next to the airlock and deposited our scuba tanks and masks in the racks that held Russian gear. There was always such a cabin near an airlock—to store wetsuits and scuba equipment. Then we departed as quickly as we'd entered.

Johnny and I had infiltrated countless undersea cities before. We marched side by side, in the center of the corridor, and barely glanced at the crew we passed in the hall.

Some were running quickly, clearly on a mission to deliver a part or a command of some sort to some other station on the warsub. Some were walking slowly—deliberately—down the corridor and passed us without question or comment. Thankfully. We had learned a few words in Russian— *yes, no, on my way*—but did not want to risk anything by speaking to someone before we'd made it to the reactor.

But I noticed something almost immediately.

Their uniforms were different than ours.

—••—

THERE WERE SOME GENERAL SIMILARITIES, SUCH as the slate gray and the crimson trim, but there were insignia on theirs missing from our outfits. Patches on shoulders and upper chest. There was an image of the dreadnought with RSF APAKOH underneath it.

Apakoh?

Eventually we hit a ladderwell, turned smartly and descended. I could hear the others above us, also on the ladder, following.

"How many levels?" Johnny whispered.

We suspected the reactor was not on the bottommost deck, but two or three above it. We'd decided to go right to the lowest level near the stern, then scan for emissions to figure out our next steps.

"Until we can't go any more," I replied.

The internal sounds of the ship were like other warships, but the constant orders over the PA indicated something major was going on. There were explosions outside, overlapping and cascading through the hull and rumbling down the corridors of the ship, and a steady *hissing* of launching torpedoes.

I wondered absently if we might be able to stop some of the launches, to try and protect the fleet outside.

Finally, we hit the bottom of the dreadnought. It was darker there than the other corridor we'd been in. Cables snaked across the deck, some branching off and disappearing below the grating at our feet or into conduits that protruded into the hallway, and other cables appeared from openings in the bulkheads to join the snaking mass on the deck. It was almost as if engineers had rushed the ship through construction. Perhaps these cables were just temporary—but it simply wasn't smart having electrical wires running along decks. If any flooding occurred . . .

We knew it wasn't safe to collect so close to the hull of the ship. If a torpedo punched a hole here, we wouldn't even know what had hit us.

The dreadnought would likely survive the conventional battle.

And then the USSF might try a nuke on it, escalating things further.

And Trieste was always in the crosshairs, it seemed.

The bulk of the cables led into a cabin twenty meters ahead and to the right. I motioned to it and Johnny and I entered. It was a small chamber with electrical boxes lining one entire wall. Cables entered and exited the panels. The hatch wouldn't close because of all the wiring.

We waited.

A second later, the others had all followed and were in the chamber with us.

Irena's face was still white as a sheet. She seemed to be a zombie; Benning had been forced to grab her under the elbow and force her along.

"Get the Geiger counter," I said to Johnny.

He removed it from his bag and turned it on. The device's clicking was silent; it led to his wireless earpiece. He began sweeping the device back and forth, pointing it in different directions, attempting to settle on which way it would take us.

I said to Irena, "Apakoh? What does it mean?"

She didn't respond and I shook her by the shoulders. "Irena! Focus on what we're doing."

She blinked and turned her eyes to me slowly. "Sorry—I'm—"

"It's okay. We're almost at the reactor." I paused and stared at her. "Now, what does Apakoh mean?"

"Yes . . . yes—I saw that too. It means *Drakon*. Dragon. I only know because of the fantasy books I used to read as a child."

Benning's eyes were wide as well. He was not used to this type of thing. Meg, Johnny, Lau, Renée, and Cliff were all managing admirably though. They were prepared for this.

Johnny said, "It's in that direction." He was pointing upward and toward the ship's stern. Made sense. We had entered from an airlock and had only moved downward and aftward since. The reactor would not be so close to the ship's starboard side.

"Ok." I nodded. "Let's go."

—••—

As I said it, a tremendous explosion rattled the hull near us and alarms started to ring out. We reached out to brace each other as the reverberations rang through the chamber.

A torpedo had made it through their defensive net.

Benning swore. "Christ! That was close!"

"Shut up!" I hissed. We were in mortal danger on that dreadnought. He couldn't be so undisciplined.

He looked angered at my reaction and opened his mouth to retort—

When Cliff stepped up to him and put his finger in the admiral's face. "You will follow orders on this mission, Sir." His voice was a growl between clenched teeth. "You're not in charge here. Mac is."

Benning's jaw snapped shut, but he was glaring at Cliff. Then he turned his eyes to me. They were embers.

"No harm done," I whispered. "Just don't forget where we are right now."

He didn't respond.

—••—

Johnny held the sensor near his thigh and marched down the corridor. I was next to him and followed his lead. We came to a ladder and marched up three levels. The ladders were steep staircases with two steel railings that typically crew would hold as they navigated them. They were so steep—not quite vertical though—that a slip or fall was possible on any sub. Johnny could only use one hand, for his other gripped the scanner, making it more awkward for him. Eventually, however, we came to a landing and his face flattened. He moved the sensor up and down, and then nodded. "It's on this deck." His voice was a whisper.

We turned into the corridor and continued marching.

Deck three.

A hatch in front of us slammed open and a crewman came tearing out of it, sprinting up the hall. He passed us without a second look. I peered into the chamber he'd just bolted from. There were torpedoes lined up on the deck, secured by brackets, and two crewmen were using a hoist to place one of the four-meter cylinders into the tube in the exterior bulkhead. A small shutter in one of the walls opened and another torpedo slid into the room.

The warsub's complement of torpedoes were likely in an armory in a central compartment of the ship, away from the exterior. A conveyer system was transporting the torpedoes to chambers like this.

As I watched, the two men slammed the hatch shut on the tube and slapped a large red button. There was a hiss of air, and then an instant later a surge of noise as the engine revved up and compressed air shot the weapon from the tube.

On the cabin's hatch was a large yellow sign with Cyrillic lettering. There was an explosive symbol below it.

I turned and caught up with Johnny, who was still leading. He had turned into a wider corridor that led toward the interior of the warsub.

—••—

THERE WERE MORE CREW HERE AND I kept my expression stony, my eyes straight ahead, as we marched deeper into *Dragon*. Lights were flashing on the bulkheads—different colors representing different emergencies, I assumed—and the commands over the address system were continuing unabated. The fuselage was fifty meters across—not including the thruster pods—so the reactor had to be near. Large fluorescent-orange hatches every ten meters were clearly a watertight system in case of breach. The bridge crew could seal entire portions of the ship if needed.

It made me swallow. If they discovered us, and they closed those hatches . . .

Finally, Johnny slowed and I stopped with him.

He glanced at a hatch beside us.

There was a radiation symbol on it.

And a keypad beside it.

We could not get in.

Chapter
Twenty-Eight

WE WAITED OUTSIDE THAT HATCH. JOHNNY and I stared at each other, grim, not speaking. He tucked the sensor into his belt. Neither of us spoke, we simply waited.

I had expected something like this. There would be heavy security at the reactor room of any warsub, even though the entire crew would be Russian. It was in case of a catastrophe, or if a hostile power somehow commandeered the vessel and got on board, or perhaps to prevent a traitor from stealing secrets for a foreign government. Or, if the vessel sank, officials wanted another layer of security separating sensitive compartments from the rest of the sub, to buy some time until they could salvage the wreckage.

A crewman approached and stared at me for an instant before turning to the hatch.

My heart strobed.

I followed him.

He slid a card into the reader under the keypad and an audible *thunk* sounded as the locking mechanism slid aside.

I tapped the man on the shoulder and he turned to look at me once more, confusion on his features.

I slammed my palm into his throat and shoved him against the bulkhead.

With my other hand, I grabbed the handle and pulled the hatch aside. Johnny entered in one smooth motion and I held the man, pinned, as he gurgled in agony. His eyes bulged as he stared at me. They shifted left and right, as one by one the others passed behind me and stalked through the hatch.

I swung around and, hauling him by the throat, pulled him into the secured corridor.

The hatch clanged shut and locked behind us.

There was a shout—something indistinguishable—and the sounds of a fight broke out around me. The crewman I had manhandled finally overcame his shock and surprise and tried to kick me. Simultaneously, he pushed my hand to the side with a forearm and it came loose.

His kick was weak, however, and did no damage. I spun my body to the side and my other fist clipped his jaw. Then an uppercut to his chin and an elbow to his temple.

He slumped to my feet, out cold.

Beside me, Cliff and Lau were struggling with two other security crewmen, but it didn't last long. Both were on the deck within seconds. Cliff pulled out plastic ties from his bag and quickly secured the three men, hands behind their backs, ankles together.

The corridor was clear.

I took a second to study my surroundings. It was different in this area of the ship. The bulkheads were white and it was narrower. There were warning signs everywhere and the lights recessed in the ceiling. In the other corridors, they had been bare bulbs, swinging as the dreadnought maneuvered during the battle.

There was another hatch at the end of this corridor, with another keypad. The two men Cliff and Lau had subdued were likely there to guard it.

"Did anyone see us come in here?" I asked.

"Hard to tell," Cliff said. "There were two walking away. Depends how much noise we made. But the sounds of the battle might have masked it."

"How are we going to get through that hatch?" Meg hissed, staring at it.

I gestured to the man at my feet. "He must be an engineer here. His keycard should do it." I glanced at Cliff. "It's time to split up." Our plan had several components. Not all of us could stay in the reactor area.

"Agreed," Cliff said.

"I have a new target for you and Lau."

A frown. "Altering the plan?"

I shook my head. "The battle is not going well."

Benning said, "How can you be sure? Listen to all those explosions." They were continuing to echo through the hull. More distant now, since we were farther into the ship, but they were still there.

"How many torpedoes have hit this ship since we've come aboard?" I snapped. "*One*. Only one. When we were in the electrical room. The other explosions are from *our* fleet getting hit. Some of the sounds are implosions." I snorted. "That tsunami plow probably hurt."

"What are you suggesting?" Cliff asked.

"You and Lau go to the port side. Remember the yellow sign that was on the hatch to that torpedo room? Find as many rooms as you can with that sign. Kill the crew inside. Disable the launchers."

Lau pursed his lips. "According to Lazlow's diagram, the tubes were two decks apart. Since we saw one on this level—Deck Three—they must be on odd-numbered levels."

"Sounds right. Go to the port side and take out as many launchers as you can. They'll figure out what's happening pretty soon though, so be ready to run."

"But Cliff was supposed to stay here, in the reactor, and set up a defense for us," Irena said.

"Yes. I'll give you thirty minutes. Then get your butts back here. Use your PCD to contact me. We'll let you back in." *Just don't forget how to get back*, I wanted to add.

Cliff and Lau didn't even blink. They nodded and turned to leave. They opened the hatch and marched out.

It locked behind them.

Meg spun on me. "Are you sure about this?"

"We need to help our fleet. This vessel is still level in the water. It's not even listing." I gestured to Renée and Benning. "Ready?"

—••—

Renée and Benning were the next step of the plan. They were to find the ballast controls in engineering. It was also the most dangerous part of the mission, for there was no way to locate the ballast station as we just had with the reactor. No sensor to help lead the way. They'd spent weeks studying the Cyrillic symbols for 'Ballast' and possible images that might indicate the path to that section of engineering.

The ballast controls would be on the bridge, but every vessel had manual valves to also adjust the trim tanks. We needed to flood the port tanks.

To start turning the warsub in the water.

— •• —

The next hatch opened and Johnny and I marched in. There were consoles and displays on every flat surface. Readouts and blinking indicators on control panels.

There were also five crew in the room.

They looked at us, casually at first. Then their eyes narrowed as they tried to place our faces, unsuccessfully.

To a one, they turned from their displays. One of them spoke; there was no mistaking it as a question.

I shook my head.

The three unconscious men were on the deck in the corridor behind us. One of the controllers peered past me and noticed the bound bodies on the deck. His eyes widened and he opened his mouth to yell—

"Shut up," I growled and raised my gun. I clicked the safety off.

Their expressions went blank. Some of them spoke to us but I put my finger to my lips. "I said shut. Up." My tone was clear if the words weren't. Irena stepped beside me and said a few Russian words haltingly. She wasn't fluent, but she got her point across.

I gestured with the gun for them to raise their hands.

These were not security guards. They were nuclear engineers. Some were in their fifties.

Their faces showed complete and utter shock at what was happening.

"Johnny." It was a simple word, but its meaning was clear.

"Got it." He stepped toward them with the plastic ties.

One of the men swung at Johnny as he grew near. Johnny dodged the swing easily and elbowed the man across the temple. He dropped to the deck like a rock.

The other Russians were staring at the scene in horror. Johnny tied the man and soon the four were lying next to him, wrists and ankles also bound. We dragged the other three men into the room, and soon the eight of them were together.

"Tell them not to speak or we'll gag them," I said to Irena.

She was looking at the controls, trying to decipher them. Her face showed anxiety. "I don't know if I can say that."

"Try."

She had spent the last few weeks reading Russian texts on nuclear power, trying to familiarize herself with the terminology and what the Cyrillic equivalents looked like. She turned to the prisoners and said a few words. Then a pause, then a few more.

They looked at her and turned back to me. I held my finger to my lips and then gestured with my gun.

They understood.

"Johnny, watch the hatch to the corridor. If anyone comes in here, wait till that hatch closes before you move. Take him out."

"Dead or unconscious?"

"Whatever is easiest."

"Got it." He exited the chamber, machine gun at his waist.

Now it was Meg, Irena, and me in the reactor control room. I turned to Irena. "It's time for you to get to work."

—••—

S<small>O</small> <small>FAR, SO GOOD</small>, I <small>THOUGHT</small>. We were in the warsub. We'd successfully made it to the reactor. Cliff and Lau were on a new mission to stop as many of the thirty-four torpedo launchers on the port side as possible. Renée and Benning were out searching for the trim tank controls.

Leaving the reactor to us.

I flashed a tight smile at Meg. "Having fun yet, sis?"

She swore. "This is scary as hell. You've done this for how many years?"

"Over twenty. But I've never done anything quite like this."

Irena was studying the displays. She was moving with purpose now, going from console to console, peering at the readouts. The prisoners were staring at her, foreheads creased. One of them muttered something to another, and I took a step toward him. I raised the machine gun and leveled it at his face. "Do you get my point?" I growled.

He stared at me, then after a second lowered his gaze.

I said to Meg, "Come and search them. Remove their ID tags and any communication devices they have."

"Watch my back, Tru," she muttered.

Irena said, "We're in trouble."

"What's the problem?" I answered, not taking my aim off the men on the deck.

"This isn't the reactor control room."

My blood turned to ice.

"What the hell do you mean?"

"Oh, we're in the right general area, but the reactor controls are not here. They must be farther in. This is a monitoring chamber only."

There was another hatch in the room, leading deeper into the dreadnought. And there might be more security within.

—••—

I GESTURED AT THE PANELS. "YOU mean this is all just for . . . *monitoring?*"

"Exactly." She sighed, exasperated. The one positive was that she did seem more engaged in what was going on around her. She was becoming an active participant in the infiltration. "This panel is for the control rods. That one over there is for the fuel rod system. Over there—" She pointed. "—is the coolant system. There are the backups for coolant over there. All just displays though . . . no buttons to actually change anything."

I grunted and turned to the eight crewmen bound and on the deck. Four of them were still unconscious, two of them with saliva and blood dribbling from open mouths. The others were awake and aware, staring at us with wide eyes.

Meg said, "We're going to have to go deeper into this section."

It was going to spread us very thin, I thought. Johnny was at the main entrance and someone was going to have to stay in the monitoring room to watch the prisoners. Meg had collected their belongings in a pile: keycards, watches, and IDs. I frowned as I stared at their uniforms. We were going to have to do something about that as well.

"You two stay here," I said. "It's time to gag them. I'll continue on."

Meg stared at me, horrified. "But Mac—"

"There's no other choice," I said. "I'm the only one who can do it."

Then one of the Russians said in a thick accent, "Please don't."

We snapped our eyes to him. "Why?"

"Why do you want to get to the reactor?" He snorted. "To sabotage it obviously. That will kill us all." He was small and slight with salt and pepper hair.

"You've killed thousands already with this ship. What did you think was going to happen to you?" I crouched before him. "What's your captain's name?"

His face tightened and he looked from me to Meg to Irena and back again rapidly. I pressed my gun to his hip. He was lying on the deck at my feet, and I pushed hard. He grimaced.

"I will shoot, I promise. It won't kill you immediately, but it'll shatter your hip. Bone fragments will pierce your intestines. You'll be immobile, stuck in this room because you won't be able to walk. Your intestinal contents will spill into your insides causing massive infection. All I'm asking for is a name." I tightened my finger on the trigger.

His face exploded into terror and he gasped rapid breaths. "Please— please don't—"

"Three seconds."

Over my shoulder, I could feel Meg's disapproving glare. She had no idea the things that I'd done in TCI. For her it had just been a *concept*. Not reality. Now she was seeing me in action.

The man blurted, "Ventinov! Ivan Ventinov!"

I frowned. I'd heard the name before. Despite the relative lack of involvement in the oceans, the Russians had settled two conshelf cities and did have a submarine force. It was minor compared to the fleets that other nations had put to sea, but every nation had a cast of characters that were famous in the intelligence business. Ventinov was the child of government officials, raised around aristocrats and powerful political figures. He had climbed the naval ranks rapidly and had commanded multiple classes of warsubs. He was a known warhawk who longed for the days of Russian and Soviet power.

Benning had said that the Russians had been focusing on the nations to their west, exerting more control and seizing land from Belarus and Ukraine. Ventinov was clearly part of their plans in the oceans.

I rose to my feet. "Gag them, even the four who are unconscious." I turned to the hatch that led toward the reactor control room. "I'm going in."

A keycard opened the hatch. The lock disengaged with a *thunk* and I grabbed the handle. Looking at Meg, I flashed her a wink. "Don't worry about me, Sis. I'll be fine."

Her face was pale. "Love you, Tru."

I grinned at her, then yanked the hatch open and stepped through.

Chapter
Twenty-Nine

THIS ROOM WAS MUCH LARGER. THERE were more consoles and displays around the chamber, an island in the center, and a large angled viewport stretching across one whole bulkhead, looking down on a cabin I couldn't see.

There were seven people in the room.

Two were security officers.

I turned to them first.

They were staring at me with creases on their foreheads. One of them asked a question. I pushed the hatch shut behind me until it clicked and marched toward him. "*Da*," I grunted. "*Ty videl eto?*"

I held the keycard in my left hand as I approached them. I stared at it.

It was a simple strategy. I'd learned a few basic things in Russian. *Did you see this?* Their eyes flicked to the keycard and watched it as I approached.

They inherently knew something was wrong, but I'd distracted them with a simple question.

I dropped the card at their feet and moved quickly.

I grabbed the first man around the head and pulled him down to my upraised knee. It crushed his nose in a fountain of blood and he fell back with a yelp and a gurgle. The second cried out and I hit him with an elbow followed by an uppercut. I hit his nose as well.

TIMOTHY S.
JOHNSTON

It was one of the first things my trainers had taught me in my early months with TCI. *Hit the nose.* The victim's eyes would instantly water, obscuring his view. The psychological impact of such a strike also had an enormous effect. Blood would pour out; he would feel the heat spilling down his chin and into his mouth.

And it hurt like hell.

The two men stumbled back, arms outstretched as if to ward me off.

For an instant, it had stunned both.

My shin connected with the first one's temple in a powerful roundhouse kick. It was like a bat hitting with full force. He spun away and hit the deck hard, face first, blood splattering in a circular radius around him. The other man was shaking his head and trying to clear his vision.

I stepped toward him.

There were shouts around me, and I knew I had to act faster. There would be an alarm button in there, and I couldn't let one of the scientists trigger it.

Three quick punches and another kick to the guard's gut. He doubled over and I spun with a savage spinning kick. My booted heel connected hard and he twirled away, teeth flying. Without stopping, I pulled my machine gun from behind my back, strap still over my shoulders, and sighted one of the other men—a scientist?—who was running across the room.

He was the only one moving, the only one who realized what was happening.

I pulled the trigger, hoping not to damage any equipment.

The sound echoed loudly and the man fell face first to the deck, instantly still.

The others were staring at me.

"Don't move." I'd said it in Russian.

—••—

THERE WAS ANOTHER HATCH IN THE control room that led somewhere else. I groaned when I saw it. I'd just fired the weapon, and it had been *loud*. There had been no other option though. I gestured to the four remaining controllers to lie on the deck. They were barking questions at me and I ignored them. Ramming a knee into each back, one at a time, I quickly bound them with ties around ankles and wrists. *"Shut up,"* I growled in Russian. I held the barrel next to their eyes, which were wide with fear.

The other hatch opened. Three security officers burst in, all carrying weapons.

—••—

I <small>DOVE FOR THE ISLAND AND</small> slid underneath it. Lifting my weapon, I sighted for the only thing I could see—their feet. My weapon rattled in my hand, close to my face, as the bullets shot only an inch over the deck. Boots *exploded* in a gory mass of blood and flesh as the projectiles tore into them. Without waiting, I rolled to the side as a shower of bullets sprayed the deck where I had just been. Lurching to my feet, I stumbled back and peered over the island.

They were there, hiding where I had just been only a second earlier.

They were groaning in agony but were still very much in the fight.

Some of the bullets had ricocheted off the deck and hit a panel behind me. It was smoking and buzzing. I didn't have time to curse about it; I had to eliminate the threat first.

More bullets sprayed out toward my feet now, but I had anticipated the tactic. I jumped onto the central island and thrust my machine gun over the far side, aiming downward.

I squeezed the trigger and fired blindly under the console.

The men cried out and a pool of blood spread across the deck.

I moved again. It was the best strategy. Never stay in the same place.

Jumping down from the island, I crouched and peered under it. One man remained. He was searching for me and our eyes met. His machine gun was turning toward me—

I pulled the trigger.

Click.

Out of ammo.

"Shit!" I lurched away and dove to the side as bullets traced across the bulkhead behind me, hitting the large viewport. It shattered and exploded out into the room below.

The man yelled something unintelligible and rose to his feet. I scrabbled at my bag to grab a magazine for the gun—

And the hatch from the monitoring room slammed open.

It was Meg.

She held her machine gun before her.

She fired.

—••—

THE BULLETS LANCED ACROSS THE MAN'S stomach and chest and tore his internal organs to shreds. He arched his back as the impacts hurled him against a console. He lifted his chin and screamed involuntarily.

He slumped to the deck, now a carcass of meat and blood.

Meg's face was fixed like stone. I quickly checked the bodies on the deck to make sure all were dead. The security officers were wearing a different uniform from the other crew: they were also steel gray, but the sleeves were crimson and there was a different patch on the right shoulder.

There were also the two others I'd fought at first entry to the control room; they were still unconscious.

The four remaining scientists had pressed together, curled into fetal positions as they'd tried to avoid the bullets spraying everywhere.

"Thanks, Meg," I grunted.

"I couldn't listen to the fight without helping."

"I'll thank you properly later. For now, help me move these Russians."

Together we grabbed them by the ankles and hauled them through the hatch out into the monitoring room to join the ones we'd already subdued. There were now *fourteen* nuclear engineers or security bound and on the deck. Meg and Irena had gagged eight of them already; we worked on gagging the newcomers.

Irena entered the control room and glanced around at the shattered displays. "Jesus, Mac." There was a haze in the air from the shorted console, but the shattered glass had helped ventilate the room. We peered over the edge and down into the chamber.

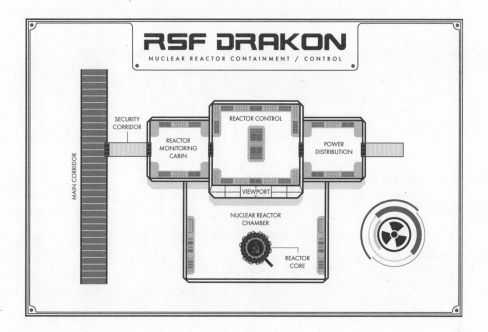

The Reactor Core.

I couldn't quite believe we'd made it.

My heart felt like it was going to explode.

There was a large metal chamber in the center, one deck down, with myriad wires and tubes leading into it. Radiation symbols were obvious on the bulkheads, and there were valves and dials on the pipes leading into the chamber. It was a big room, but cramped because of the sheer multitude of pipes, cables and tubes that snaked across the deck and dangled from the ceiling. A metal framework in the room held the pipes in place as they led from the bulkheads on all sides to the reactor.

"Those pipes are the coolant," Irena whispered. She pointed at the deck where the core disappeared below it. "The seawater pipes for the SCAV drive are probably just under there. There must be an immense boiling system." She blew her breath out. "We made it." She studied the consoles and traced her finger along the Cyrillic labels, trying to decipher it all.

"One of the men had been running for this console here." I pointed. "I assumed it was to hit the alarm."

She shook her head and pointed. "No. He was trying to push that." A large red button the size of a drink coaster was in the center of the panel. There was a red label on it. "SCRAM," she said. "He was trying to shut down the reactor."

"But we'd be able to start it up again, right?"

"Had he hit that button, it would take time to get it running and back up to temperature again." She looked at me. "It's a good thing you stopped him, Mac."

"I thought he was trying to signal the bridge."

"The smoke might have triggered an alarm already," she muttered. "Hope not."

As she studied the controls, I checked on Meg. She was watching our prisoners in the monitoring room. I had asked her to stay there and keep her gun on them.

A minute later I tilted my head. Something suddenly seemed off. "Do you feel that?"

She glanced at me. "What?"

I stared at the chamber around me. But I wasn't *looking* at *anything*. I was feeling something.

"We're listing to the port."

She frowned. "Are you sure?" She paused and held her arms out. Then she blinked. "You know, I think you're right."

Benning and Renée had done it. They'd made it to the ballast trim tank valves.

—••—

AN ALARM STARTED AND A VOICE burst from the public address system. We'd blocked the hatch to the control room open, and Irena's voice floated to us. "The bridge just ordered an engineering crew to the ballast control room."

We had considered flooding *all* the tanks and sending the ship to the bottom, but there were several problems with that. First was that if the ship didn't implode, the Russians might be able to salvage it and put it back into operation. The second issue was that if the ship still had power—even just conventional thrusters—control surfaces and gimbaling thrusters on the dreadnought might keep the negatively buoyant ship afloat.

The only way to ensure destruction, without nukes, was to cause a meltdown and damage the watertight capabilities of the dreadnought, then puncture its hull.

"They think it's a mechanical issue," I muttered.

"How do you know?"

"They would have called security otherwise. They still don't realize what's going on." I stared at the hatch where the security crew had stormed into the control room. I had to get it locked.

Irena noticed my gaze. "It should be easy. There will be a way to secure the hatches in case of intruders." She searched the consoles before her eyes settled on a control switch. "Here. LOCKDOWN."

I hesitated. "Will it also set off alarms?"

"There's a chance, yes."

"Then we'll wait." I cracked the hatch and peered around into the opening. There was another equipment room beyond with more controls and displays. Irena looked over my shoulder. "That's the power distribution room."

"You mean we can adjust the power output to different systems on the sub?"

"Yes. But it doesn't make much difference. We're about to cause a meltdown anyway, right?"

"I suppose." I considered cutting power to the bridge or the SCAV drive, but that would cause an immediate response. At the moment, they might not even be aware that intruders were on their warsub.

I closed the hatch and stared at the keypad. There was a LOCK button on it, which I pushed. A security card could likely override it, but it would hopefully give us some warning if someone tried to enter.

The button flashed and nothing happened.

"You probably need a key card," Irena said.

I picked one up from the deck and tried again. This time it worked.

I turned to stare at the control room. There was blood and glass and four bodies lying on the deck. Shattered consoles and even crimson splatters on the ceiling. It was obvious there had been a major battle there. "Okay, Irena, let's get to it."

She blew her breath out in a rush and pointed to one of the units against the bulkhead. "We have to remove the control rods completely. The panel is there. But first we have to drill into the core and add uranium to make sure there's enough fissionable material to cause meltdown. We also have to shut down the coolant system. Permanently would be ideal."

I nodded. We also wanted to add oxygen to the core to help the graphite fire along, once the runaway reaction started.

According to the plan, Lau and Cliff were going to take care of those things, but they were still gone. They'd left the bag of tools, however. I checked my watch. They'd left twenty minutes earlier. I withdrew my PCD and sent Cliff a silent notification.

Then I waited.

More voices came over the address system. Irena was studying the control rod system and lifted her head. "They just called security to the ballast room."

"Damn."

"Also to a torpedo room."

I glanced at my PCD. I pressed the signal button again. An instant later, Cliff responded. "Go ahead, Boss."

"They just called security to your location. The torpedo rooms. They know we're here."

"We've taken out seven so far. Damaged beyond repair."

"We need you back here for the next step. We're ready to drill into the core."

"Got it. On our way."

I notified Johnny to expect them and then peered over the broken viewport into the reactor chamber. I had to get down there. The deck was five meters below and I searched for somewhere in the control room to secure a rope. The center island would work perfectly. Johnny had a coil in his bag and I wound it around the console and used a climber's knot to secure it. Then I stood on the edge of the viewport and rappeled down in one smooth motion. Meg was staring at me in shock.

"Where are you going?" she called from above.

"Getting ready," I grunted. I pointed at the reactor chamber. "That's a radiation and heat barrier. Time to drill."

—••—

I <small>PICKED A SPOT BETWEEN ALL</small> the tubing and wiring and drew a large X with a black marker. Then I prepared the drill. It was heavy, especially with the tripod. Lau had carried it across from *SC-1* on the cable, another reason why it had been difficult to swim. It took only a minute to set up, and I positioned the bit against the black mark I'd made.

When I penetrated the shielding, I would leave the drill bit in place to keep the radiation locked in.

Until we began the next step, that is.

I set the oxygen tank nearby and glanced up at the control room where Meg was watching me. "Are they back yet?" I asked.

"No."

I swore. I'd have to do it myself.

—••—

M<small>Y HEART WAS POUNDING.</small> I <small>KEPT</small> telling myself that it was just business as usual—just a regular mission—but the reality was that this was far from normal. There were over six hundred crew on the sub who would kill us in an instant should they discover us. There was a major battle going on outside; I could feel the ship lurching during maneuvers, and reverberations from detonations or implosions occurred every few seconds.

And, of course, I was about to drill into a fission core.

The drill bucked under my hands as I pulled the trigger. The deck shook at my feet.

It was *loud*. I pushed the bit to the containment structure, and it whined as metal slivers crawled from the hole. It cut into the shielding at a steady pace, and an acrid odor hit me within seconds. We had brought a radiation suit as well, and I'd have to put it on when transferring the uranium pellets.

The drill continued. I applied pressure evenly, but not too quickly. A broken drill bit would be a disaster. We had extras in case it happened, but every second counted.

Meg yelled something from the control room and I snapped a look back at her.

She repeated, "They just called security!"

"To where?"

"Another torpedo launcher. Also to the ballast room. Again."

We were running out of time.

I continued drilling when abruptly the machine rattled beneath my hands and before I could pull back on it or stop it, it began to spin freely, shuddering and vibrating.

The drill bit had snapped.

"Shit."

I reached for another when a hand gripped my shoulder.

Chapter Thirty

"I've got it, Boss," Cliff Sim muttered. He grabbed the drill and, with a deft hand, removed the bit. The broken piece had jammed in the shield, and he used vice grips to remove it. The muscles in his arms flexed as he wrenched the broken piece of diamond-tipped steel counterclockwise.

I noticed that there was blood on his uniform—splatters of it across his sleeves and chest.

"It's not mine," he muttered.

The bit came out and he quickly inserted a new one, positioned the drill again, and started it up. He clenched his jaw as he worked. The drill chewed into the radiation shield and smoke poured from the hole.

"Are the torpedo rooms you attacked permanently out of use?"

"We disabled the conveyer in each one that was carrying in new torpedoes. They can't reload those launchers unless they physically carry more weapons there."

I clasped his shoulder. "Good job." I withdrew my PCD and marched to a corner, away from the drill. I keyed it on and a voice floated to my ear. "Go ahead."

It was a *Sword* pilot, in charge of our fleet. I'd ordered them to hang back and wait. I didn't want to lose any ships unnecessarily before we had a chance to take down the dreadnought.

Now, however, it was time.

"Port side is more vulnerable," I said.

"The ship is listing that way but she hasn't taken many hits yet." The voice sounded distant and distorted. "A few mines have connected. Maybe four or five torpedoes. Their countermeasure shield was effective. Then the tsunami plow knocked a bunch of weapons out. Some of the fleet's vessels are just sitting motionless. I think the water impact really hurt some crews onboard."

I cursed. Then, "Go deep and fire your weapons. Port side only. Flood as many compartments as you can. Avoid their weapons by staying deep."

"Got it." The pilot clicked off.

We have to get this beast tipped over, I thought, grim.

Everything counted on it.

—••—

AN INSTANT LATER, A VOICE BURST from the PA system. It seemed more frantic than previous announcements. There was a long burst of unintelligible yelling.

Afterward, Irena thrust her head over the edge of the control room, peering down into the reactor area. "Mac!" She searched for me and I moved toward her. She said, "They just sent out a 'Repel Boarders' order! They're closing the watertight hatches." She paused, and then, "They're preventing us from moving freely around the ship."

I took in a deep breath. Time was ticking.

The lights suddenly turned off and emergency ones activated.

It was likely their protocol in case of invaders. Turn off the lights. I'd been on the receiving end before; one city I'd infiltrated had tried it. The security forces had used night-vision goggles to try and trap me. I'd only had a flashlight at the time.

But I'd made it then.

And I hoped to survive again.

"Are Benning and Renée back yet?" I yelled out.

Meg's face peered down at me. I couldn't make out her features; she was in silhouette with an emergency light just above and behind her. The drill was loud and we had to raise our voices so we could hear each other. She said, "They haven't come back from the ballast control room yet."

I swore. The watertight hatches had trapped them in another section of the warsub. And since the bridge had called security to that area twice now, there was also the possibility that the Russians had captured or killed them.

Using my PCD, I sent a silent signal to them.

No answer.

I turned to Cliff. "What's going on in the corridors?"

"Crew moving about. Everyone's in battle mode. No one really looked twice at us, even though our uniforms are slightly different."

"Any resistance?"

"In the torpedo rooms, once we started, yes. Otherwise, no." He glanced at the dark light fixtures and the warning lights flashing on the bulkhead. They had changed colors. "Things will be different now. They'll be looking for us."

"Are you good to continue here?"

"I've got it." His words were clipped and confident.

"We don't have much time. We have to remove the control rods and insert the uranium."

"Give me another five minutes."

"Keep at it."

I moved toward the rope and realized that the ship was listing even more. I pulled myself up and swung a leg over the ledge into the control room. Lau was on his knees reloading weapons. He had also spread out some grenades. There was a cut over his eye and an angry bruise on his cheek. "You okay?" I asked.

He nodded curtly. "Yup. They got a few lucky hits in, that's all."

"Good job on the torpedoes. You'll give our people outside a chance."

He rose to his feet and put a machine gun strap over his shoulder. There was a long knife strapped to his thigh now as well. "How's the battle progressing?"

"Not great." I collected the others with me in the control room for the next step. Johnny came in; there were more blood splatters on his chest.

Meg, Johnny, Lau, and I watched over Irena's shoulder as she described the control rod system to us.

It was nearly time to withdraw them and start the runaway reaction.

"Now just be aware," she said, "that once the control rods are out, the neutrons are going to start hitting more uranium in there. Especially once we *add* to the pile. That will cause more fission, more neutron release, and it'll quickly get out of hand. The temperature will spike. We're going to have to turn off the cooling system to *really* let it get out of control." In the reactor room there were numerous pipes leading into the containment chamber. Those had valves on them to control the water circulation through the reactor. It kept temperatures from skyrocketing. "Now, I can press a few buttons up here to shut down the coolant. But that won't be permanent."

"Can we turn those valves off down there?" I asked.

"Yes. But they can just get in here and turn them back on. The best thing is to cut them completely. Once we lift the control rods and add the uranium, is there a way to damage those pipes beyond a repair team's ability to fix them?"

I glanced at Lau and Johnny. "What do you think?"

Johnny said, "We can cause some explosions, sure. Turn that piping into broken pretzels." He frowned. "But repair crews might be able to get in here and weld temporary pipes into place. How long after the control rods come out will the meltdown start?"

Irena wrinkled her forehead. "After the coolant is gone, about thirty minutes perhaps. Give or take. The graphite fire will speed things along."

"Sounds like it'll give us some time to get out of here," I said. "But once the core melts and escapes confinement . . . we can't be *anywhere* near here. There's no telling which way it'll go." I looked at the ceiling. I was hoping it would go up that way once we managed to invert the ship, but for that we needed to make it to the bridge or a backup control station.

"When shall I start?" Irena asked. She was now in total control of herself. In fact, she seemed excited to be *causing* a nuclear disaster, instead of preventing one.

"We need to give Cliff a little more time. Then I'll add the uranium and oxygen. Then we'll do it." I pointed at the LOCKOUT button. "We'll have to hit that soon."

The others stared at it. "It'll prevent keycards from gaining access to this section?" Lau asked.

"Yes. It'll give us time to do what we want, but it'll probably trigger some alarms on the bridge too."

"Will it lock us in here though?"

Irena shook her head. "We'll be able to leave. The protocols will be to keep people out, not in."

Cliff's voice floated to us from below as the drill powered down. "It's done, Boss."

Time for the uranium.

———••———

THE RADIATION SUIT WAS IN MY bag. I had already decided that I was going to be the one to perform the next step. I moved to where I'd left it and yanked the yellow suit out. It was heavy, lead lined, and included foot coverings and a helmet. It was one of the reasons that it had been nearly impossible to swim over to the dreadnought when we'd boarded. We'd needed that cable to help us cross.

I put the suit on. Johnny and Lau hauled the crate over the ledge and lowered it to the reactor room deck. As I was opening the lid, a sudden cry followed by a gunshot echoed from above.

Then another.

I stopped and stared up at the broken viewport. The shield across my face made it difficult and I had to adjust the helmet slightly. Meg poked her head out. "Security just checked in on us. Johnny took care of them."

I swore. "Did they get a call out?"

"No. But I'm guessing the bridge will want them to check in soon."

Most likely. We probably only had ten minutes before they sent another team.

I turned back to the uranium.

The ingots were heavy. Each was half the length of a cigar. Roughly the size of my pinky finger. The drill hole was double the width, so all I had to do was slide each one through the hole and drop it into the reactor vessel. Cliff had removed the drill bit from the hole and immediately plugged it with a lead stopper that we had brought with us.

Once the steam made it into the reactor room, it would set off a radiation alarm.

But Irena had isolated the circuit and switched it off.

I hoped.

I took a deep breath and held it. The first ingot was in the palm of my hand. It was warm; I could feel the heat radiating from it and through my lead gloves.

Sweat was dripping from my forehead. I'd forgotten to tie something around my head to keep it from happening. *Stupid mistake*, I scolded myself as I shook the drops from my eyebrows.

In one fluid motion I pulled the plug from the hole and inserted the first ingot. Holding it in place, I grabbed the next one. When I dropped the first in, I'd immediately place the next one in the hole and get the third one ready. We had practiced this back at Trieste. The purpose was to keep an ingot and my hand over the hole as much as possible to keep the radioactive steam in the core. It was under pressure, however, so some was leaking out as I inserted each ingot, but the pressure wasn't tremendous. The ship's four atms might have kept the steam from firing out like a kettle. Or, perhaps the coolant system was just doing its job.

One by one, I inserted the ingots.

There were 153 of them.

All converted from Thorium-232 to Uranium-233.

Hopefully we'd be adding enough mass to the pile so that when the reaction really started to go critical, there would be enough uranium in the molten corium to cause an impressive meltdown.

China Syndrome.

Only this one would go *up*.

—••—

A FEW WISPS OF STEAM ROSE from the drill hole as the ingots slid in. It made me swallow. It was highly radioactive and was escaping into the reactor room.

The viewport to the control room was no longer intact. If the steam got into that room, it would irradiate the others.

The reactor had a ventilation system and Irena powered up fans which began to suck the steam into its filtration systems. They would have started automatically when the radiation alarms went off, but Irena had already locked them out.

I moved as fast as I could. One by one each ingot went into the hole and fell into the containment structure. They'd collect at the bottom, and when the control rods came out . . .

The neutron reaction would rapidly spiral out of control.

Finally, I slid the last one in. I had already prepared the oxygen canister before I'd begun the transfer, and I rammed the nozzle into the hole. We had arranged it to fit perfectly, to also act as a plug.

We'd planned it all out in the weeks leading up to the mission, with the help of my nuclear engineers at Trieste.

The nozzle was in, and I cranked the feed to full.

Oxygen.

Fed directly into the containment vessel.

To fan the graphite fire, once it started.

Graphite lined the insides of the core to slow down neutrons and help the reaction along. It was the *moderator* in Russian fission plants. I hoped the Russians hadn't changed their plant design, but it was doubtful. The rest of the world had moved on to fusion power, but Russia had clung to Twentieth Century technology, when they had been at the peak of their military might and control across Eastern Europe. Perhaps they still used the same plants because they were struggling economically. Or, maybe it was a psychological issue for them. Since Russia had been at its peak during the fission era, had they decided to stay with the technology despite its limitations?

"I've started the oxygen," I called up to Irena. "Send Lau down."

A minute later he was on the deck next to me. He glanced at my radiation suit with worry in his eyes. He wasn't wearing one.

"It's okay," I muttered. "I've plugged the hole. Radiation contained."

He nodded and looked at the mass of pipes leading to the core. Blue valves marked the coolant feeds. There were valves where the pipes emerged from the bulkheads, and then another set where they entered the containment vessel. We would turn all valves to the off position, then sever all the pipes with explosions.

Meg stuck her head into the reactor room. "Mac! The comm is blaring like crazy."

"What are they saying?"

"They're asking for a response."

"Shit. They know about us." I gestured to Lau. "Plant the explosives. And get ready for a fight."

Chapter
Thirty-One

WE PULLED THE HATCH TO THE monitoring room shut, as well as the one that led to the corridor where we had entered the reactor section. "Hit the LOCKDOWN button, Irena," I snapped. "Johnny, get ready!"

The hatches simultaneously *clunked* as the security latches slid into place. Lights on the hatch panels burned red.

The PA kept blaring; it was a rapid-fire stream of yelling.

Irena muttered, "They just called security to this section."

"It's time," I said in a grave voice. "Raise the control rods."

She nodded, grabbed a handle on the control console, and pushed it up. On the display before her, the diagram of the reactor showed the rods rising slowly. The nuclear pile of uranium fuel was pulsating with a yellow glow. As the rods withdrew, the color began to darken.

The temperature of the core was increasing.

"They'll try to cut power here," she said. "It'll trip the rods down into place."

And that would cause a SCRAM. It was a failsafe of fission plants. Electromagnets lifted and held the rods in place. No power meant no magnets, and they would fall into the core where they would absorb neutrons. The analogy Irena had made earlier was that inserting the control rods into the core was like sucking the oxygen out of a fire.

We had to damage them so they wouldn't go back into their slots and descend into the core.

Like Chernobyl.

I glanced down at the containment vessel. Above the structure, a mechanism was moving upwards, pulling long cylinders from the core.

The control rods.

I pointed. "Lau, put a grenade under those rods! Just a small one—we don't want to crack the vessel."

He looked where I pointed. "Got it." He was nearly done; the bombs were strapped to multiple pipes labeled with blue throughout the chamber. "I'm ready to turn off the valves."

"Do it."

On the control before Irena, warnings began to flash. "Temperature is increasing rapidly! It's happening!"

In the nuclear core of the dreadnought *Drakon*, neutrons were colliding with uranium atoms and splitting more neutrons outward. These found more uranium, generating even more neutrons. And since we had added more U-233 to the core, there were now more neutron collisions occurring.

The uranium in the fuel rods and the ingots would begin to glow red soon, and the entire structure would melt into a molten mass of burning metal that would liquify anything it touched.

Someone began pounding at the hatch to the corridor.

—••—

"YOU HAVE TO DAMAGE THE CONTROL rods!" Irena yelled. "Before they cut power!"

I turned back to the reactor room. "Lau! Hurry!"

He was moving from valve to valve, twisting them closed. Each one took thirty seconds. He was sweating and moving quickly. "Working on it," he muttered. "Never sabotaged a fission reactor before. There are a lot of pipes."

Alarms were beginning to blare in the control room. Lights were flashing, and combined with the red emergency backups, the effect was surreal. The banging continued at the hatch to the corridor. I glanced at a monitor that showed the hatch. Sparks had started from the top of its frame, lancing inward toward us.

Lau's head appeared over the shattered viewport's edge as he hauled himself into the control room. "Ready," he gasped. Then he fell to his knees and held a control unit before him.

He glanced at me and I nodded. "Do it."

He pressed the button.

One by one the grenades detonated. Each tore a coolant pipe to shrapnel, which flew through the containment chamber and ricocheted off the ceiling and fell back to the deck in twisted shards of smoking steel. Pieces flew into the control room and we hurled ourselves away from the shattered viewport and fell heavily to the deck. I threw my arms over my head to shield my face, but I realized dimly that I was wearing the radiation suit and helmet.

Pieces of hot metal rained down on us. I pushed myself to my feet and lurched to the ledge to peer into the reaction chamber.

The coolant pipes were gone. Loose tubes and conduits hung from the ceiling and drooped from the bulkheads. Lau had turned all the valves off though, so there was no water leaking into the area.

I turned my gaze to the control rods. They were bent and twisted but still suspended over the containment structure. There were some broken pieces littering the deck nearby.

The power went out.

With the electromagnets no longer holding them in place, the broken rods fell. It startled me and I jumped backward from the crash. They hit the containment unit and shattered, pieces skittering across the deck, rolling amongst the other debris.

They were highly radioactive.

I turned to Irena and found her sprawled on the deck. I pulled her up and checked her over.

"I'm okay," she whispered. She pushed the hair from her face. She looked at the consoles, which were dark. "They know what we're trying."

"The rods are broken."

She offered me a grin. "Then the chain reaction has started."

"And the graphite fire?"

"Did you add the oxygen?" I nodded and she continued, "Then it'll start soon. When the coolant that's left in the reactor has boiled away, the temperature will skyrocket." She hesitated and looked at me with fear in her eyes. "There's no stopping it now, Mac. It's going to melt out of containment."

"How long? You said thirty minutes . . ."

"Once all the coolant is gone, that's right. I've drained what I could from the vessel, but there's still some in there. It'll take a while for it to boil away. Say . . . fifteen minutes for that, give or take."

So, we had just under an hour to capsize the ship, otherwise the corium would melt downward, pierce three decks, and then drop out of the hull at the bottom of the sub. The lower three decks in this section only would flood, but it wouldn't be enough to sink the dreadnought.

But if the ship was inverted, the corium would penetrate twenty-seven decks and drop out of the top of the warsub, flooding a much larger portion of the vessel.

"Okay, time to go." At the hatch, the sparks were still shooting inward and the cut was now at the bottom, near the deck. I pulled my helmet off and threw it into the reactor room. "Grab your bags, load your weapons."

"Which way?" Johnny asked, his eyes on the sparks.

I pointed and they followed my finger with their eyes.

Into the power distribution room.

It was the only exit now.

—••—

WE EXITED EN MASSE INTO THE adjoining chamber and pulled the hatch shut behind us. There was another one leading out, and we followed it. There were several cabins off it, with rows of radiation suits hanging from hooks. It was a changing area for reactor maintenance crews. I stared at the suits for a moment, then glanced back at my people.

I smiled.

—••—

WE PULLED THE RUSSIAN RADIATION SUITS over our uniforms. We still had to carry our bags—they held weapons, ammo and our wetsuits—and we followed the corridor out of the reactor area. We were breathing heavily and moving quickly. Every second mattered.

The hatches locked behind us, and when the Russians finally arrived on the scene, it would only take them a few moments to realize what had happened. The coolant pipes were gone. The grenade had shattered the control rods and they would not be going back into the core. The uranium reaction was accelerating and nothing could stop it. A graphite fire had started in the containment vessel and would be raging out of control, preventing repair crews from getting near. The heat would crack the structure, and radioactive smoke and steam would fill the chamber.

There was a chance they could get some coolant to this area by rigging up a new piping system, or dumping a 'poison' on the core to soak up neutrons, but Irena felt that it was too late. Security had to get through two locked hatches still, and by then the reactor would have already melted down.

The corium would have begun moving.

And we needed to be out of there.

We reached a hatch that led to a corridor; there was a stream of sparks shooting inward from it as well.

—••—

I GRABBED IRENA AND THRUST MY mouth to her ears. I hissed instructions to her and she looked at me in shock. "Do it now!" I rasped.

She nodded and stepped up to the door, avoiding the sparks. She turned her head to the side and shielded her eyes. She slammed her palms against the door again and again.

The sparks immediately ceased.

"*Pomogi nam!*" she cried. "*Vypustit nas!*"

"Pomogi nam!" I repeated.

Help us! Let us out!

There was a chatter of voices outside and the sound of something grinding across the deck. I turned to the others and mouthed, *"Here we go."*

I punched the open button.

The hatch slid aside.

We stumbled into the corridor hacking and coughing. Irena fell to her knees muttering something in Russian and I slumped against the bulkhead, pretending that my lungs were heaving.

There were eight security officers there and two crewmen operating the welder. The lights were dim in the corridor—a ghastly red glow hung over us—and there were blinking alarms strobing up and down the level. I pointed through the hatch and toward the reactor chamber as I continued to cough. Their eyes followed my fingers and they nodded, yelling something unintelligible.

They pushed past us and entered the section we'd just come from. The two crew with the welder followed the security team, lugging the tanks with them.

They disappeared, and the hatch closed behind them. The others' eyes were wide as they realized what I'd just done.

Time to run.

"This way," I muttered as I pointed toward the bow of the ship. We needed to go as far as we could before we hit a watertight security hatch. Then we'd decide what to do.

We had to move on to the next stage in the plan, and to do that, we needed to get to a control system to maneuver the ship.

Using torpedoes to flood one side and force the dreadnought to invert had not worked. Time for a new strategy.

One that was far more dangerous.

The six of us ran through the dim corridor, wearing Russian radiation suits and carrying duffle bags, and plunging deeper into the warsub.

—••—

CLIFF AND I LED THE WAY. Lau and Johnny were in the rear. As we rounded a corner, we stumbled into another security team. They were poking their heads in each hatch they passed, yelling something within, before moving to the next.

They were following the 'repel boarders' protocols and were sweeping the ship.

We came to an abrupt halt and they stared at us. There were four of them.

I raised my finger as if I wanted to speak to them and marched forward confidently. My weapon was in my bag and there was no time to pull it.

Instead I just walked right up to the four of them. They continued to watch with questioning eyes. Their gaze flitted over our radiation suits and their brows furrowed.

As soon as I was within striking distance I lashed out. Cliff was next to me and had taken the one nearest to him. I hoped Johnny and Lau had recognized what was happening and would grab weapons to assist. I knew Johnny would, at least. That was how we'd trained for such a situation.

The Russian I hit first staggered back from the blow. It was a right cross to his temple and his head jerked to the side, dazing him. Then I stepped forward and swept his legs out from under him with a low kick.

A gun went off and someone fell heavily to the deck. Then there was another series of shots.

It was Johnny, firing at a security officer.

Lau also had his weapon out and was squeezing rounds off. He'd reacted quickly and with a level of training that spoke to Sheng City Intelligence's abilities.

I knelt over the man I'd leveled, preparing to knock him out, when he caught me with a palm-strike to my neck. I pulled back, gasping, and he rose to his feet. I kicked again and he blocked with a forearm. Then I swung to the side, twirling, and kicked with my other leg. He raised his arm to block—

And I lowered my leg and instead swung with a backhand.

I connected with his nose, which exploded in a shower of frothing blood.

He uttered a single, simple grunt and fell heavily to the deck.

There were shouts now, coming from the cabins the team had been checking on. It must have seemed obvious to the crew what was happening. One second a security team had stuck their heads in, asking if everyone was okay and if they'd seen any intruders, and the next there was a raging fight in the corridor directly outside, complete with machine gun fire.

Beside me, Cliff clutched his man in a sleeper hold. The Russian's eyes were narrowed and glaring with hatred. He groaned in agony as he struggled against Cliff's powerful grip.

After a few moments, he grew limp and slumped downward.

I flashed Cliff a tight grin. This type of work perfectly suited him.

"We have to keep going," I said. "Hurry!"

We continued down the hall, leaving the four on the deck, all badly injured or dead.

Irena's face was pale. She was gasping and staring around her at everything that was going on. She'd done her job in the reactor room well, but now I had to get her out. I wanted her to survive this. She was way outside her realm of expertise here.

A bright orange door blocked the way around the next turn.

Watertight hatch.

Meg slid to a stop next to me and stared at the control panel.

"Is there a way to open it?" I asked.

"Likely not," she said, chest heaving. "It's controlled from the security station. The bridge, probably."

Beside the hatch was a sign with a diagram of a crewman on a steep ladder. "In here," I gestured. I kicked it open and grabbed the railing. I was moving fast, desperate to get off that deck. They knew intruders were there, knew we'd sabotaged their fission plant, and they would shoot to kill as soon as they saw us.

I *threw* myself down the ladder, three flights until I hit the lowest level. The lights were dimmer there, the cables snaking across the deck, and the corridors narrower than they had been three levels up.

"Where are we going?" Meg asked.

"An airlock."

She stared at me in shock. "We're leaving?"

"Not yet. Not even close, Sis." I pointed at a hatch in the deck. "There."

She peered at it.

We were at the bottom of the ship but not at either port or starboard; we were in the middle of the dreadnought near the keel. The hull was directly below us. There was an emergency airlock hatch in the deck. It swung upward and I looked down into it.

"What's our depth?" Johnny asked.

The lock was big enough for the six of us. The grating at my feet clanged as I landed heavily. I studied the control panel as the others peeled off their radiation suits. According to the display, the pressure outside was nine atms. Since we were already at four, it was a negligible difference. "We're only at eighty meters," I said. "Find some tanks. There must be an airlock changing station up there somewhere."

In the distance, I could still hear explosions and the whine of screws as torpedoes cut through the water. The dreadnought heeled from side to side at times as it maneuvered.

Shouting reached my ears as I scrambled back up to the deck. The others were searching for scuba gear—ours was back in the airlock we'd entered, but the watertight hatches had sealed it far away from us—and I cocked my head, listening to the sounds.

They were coming from the ladderwell we'd just exited.

Another security team.

They'd followed.

Chapter
Thirty-Two

I THOUGHT FURIOUSLY. WE WERE IN the lowest deck of the dreadnought. It was tight there. Cramped. It would be a difficult fight in that area. Friendly fire was a real possibility.

It was dim; the red glow of emergency lighting did not provide much detail. There was a haze of smoke in the air from an equipment malfunction or perhaps a nearby fire. I glanced at the deck. The footing was poor as well, because of all the electrical cables.

More shouts.

I glanced at the ladderwell. They were one deck up now.

Only seconds left.

They were on the steel ladder, *flying* downward toward us.

Then it hit me.

I shouted at Lau. "Give me that knife!" He was at my side in a second and handed me his long blade. I slammed it down on a cable and sparks flew. Grabbing the rubber insulation, I yanked savagely, tearing it from its clamps and pulling it from the deck. I hauled it toward the ladder and, peering upward at the security team only a few steps above me, jammed the sparking edge against the metal railing.

Sparks flew.

There was a hissing, buzzing sound as the electrical current arced through the ladder and upward, deep into the bowls of the ship. Men and women cried out as, in unison, they jerked to a stop and collapsed, quivering and trembling from the current flowing through them. There was more yelling, and bodies started to tumble down the ladder in uncontrolled falls. Smoke rose and the smell of burnt insulation and meat met my nose.

I pulled the cable back and craned my neck to look up. There were eight people on the ladder, lying with limbs intertwined haphazardly. Some were moaning, some twitching, some completely still and silent.

Farther up, there were more footsteps and I pushed the cable back to the rail. More screams.

An instant later there was a clang of metal as something fell downward. I thought it was a gun at first, perhaps released by a convulsing hand, but I was wrong.

It was a grenade.

I hurled myself backward with a cry and buried my head in my arms on the deck.

The explosion shook the corridor and shrapnel ricocheted around the ladderwell and rained down.

It had exploded on a step above me and hadn't made it all the way down to the lowest level.

I searched through the smoke and debris and located the cable. It was still sparking and I pressed it again to the ladder steps. I wedged it through the grating so it wouldn't move. It would keep the ladder electrified and should buy us some time.

"You okay?" Johnny muttered. He was lugging air tanks from a cabin into the corridor and setting them beside the airlock hatch in the deck.

"Still here," I grunted. "That was fun."

He flashed me a quick smile. "Enjoying this? I am too."

So far things had gone to plan. More or less. We'd made it into the dreadnought, found the reactor, triggered the meltdown, and escaped back to an airlock.

We weren't done yet though, and we had lost two people, so not everything had gone perfectly, but the meltdown had been the most critical goal, and we'd started it.

We still had to turn the ship—something easier said than done.

I pointed at the airlock. "Grab your tanks and get down there. We're going outside."

—••—

We'd stripped off our radiation suits and pulled our wetsuits on over our uniforms. The tanks and masks were of Russian design, but they worked the same as any other. I took a few quick breaths and pulled the mask into place. The others were with me, and we closed the hatch above our heads. I gave them the thumbs up and they returned it. Irena was shaking again, and I gave her shoulder a squeeze.

Water flooded in.

The outer hatch opened.

The scene outside was shocking.

Torpedoes lanced through the depths. Each left an expanding trail of bubbles. Explosions lit the sea all around us, flashes of red and white and geysers of bubbles churning upward. There were warsubs powering around us, launching countermeasures and evading missile fire. The whine of screws overlapped in a multitude of layers—Cousteauian, USSF, Sheng City, and Triestrian—each a unique pitch and volume. Lazlow could have separated them all in his mind and identified each, but to me it was a buzz of different noises all indistinguishable from each other.

"The acoustic shriek. It's gone," Cliff muttered into his facemask.

I frowned. He was right. The sonar screens were probably clear now. Perhaps our forces had targeted the Russian acoustical generator and destroyed it.

"Which way are we going?" Johnny asked.

I pointed toward the bow.

—••—

THERE WERE RUNGS ON THE DREADNOUGHT'S skin and we hauled ourselves along the steel, fighting the current as the dreadnought maneuvered and turned during the ongoing battle. We came to several areas that had been hit by torpedoes. There were gaps in the hull, jagged steel jutting inward, and we could peer into interior cabins and corridors, now flooded. There were even some bodies within.

We had to haul ourselves around the damage as we continued toward the bow. It was agonizing—a marathon before us. We'd been near the stern of the warsub and the bow was *four hundred* meters distant, and we had to pull ourselves along the hull to get there.

The one positive was that we no longer carried the uranium crate, the drill, and other tools that we'd brought with us to sabotage the reactor.

I just hoped the ship didn't jump to SCAV drive and throw us off.

However, as I thought it, I realized it might not be possible. The reactor was spiraling out of control at that moment, and I doubted they could go to SCAV after meltdown.

I checked my watch. Fifteen more minutes, then the corium would start moving.

I swallowed. I wanted to be as far away from that section as possible when it started.

A low vibration began in the hull beneath my hands and I jerked to a stop suddenly. *What the—*

"SCAV drive!" Meg blurted.

Oh, shit.

—••—

THE SHIP'S SPEED WAS INCREASING. THE meltdown obviously hadn't occurred yet. I searched my gear frantically, hoping to find a latch that we could use to secure ourselves to a rung. The ship would be going 467 kph soon, and we'd never be able to hold on.

The dreadnought banked and powered away from the battle. I searched the scene behind me and gasped into my mask. There were hulks of broken warsubs drifting motionless, dropping debris and oil as they took on water. Others were sinking slowly into the darkness. There were little ships flitting about—our *Swords*, dodging torpedoes and powering down into the depths to avoid them, and the black Russian warsubs were also there, highly agile and maneuverable thanks to their gimbaling thrusters.

And we were leaving it all behind.

Then a shock of fear jerked down my spine.

I scrambled to find a cable or belt in my bag—*anything* to help secure us—and the others followed suit next to me. Johnny pulled some carabiners from his duffle. We hurriedly connected them to the straps on our tanks and latched ourselves to a rung on the hull. Where we could, we connected to *each other* using more carabiners, latching our tanks together until we were one solid mass of scuba divers desperate to stay together.

I pressed my face to the hull as the speed mounted.

The current threatened to pull my mask off . . . and since the regulator connected to it, if that happened, I'd drown.

The acceleration continued. The water was pulling us back and the straps were digging into my shoulders and chest as the water friction attempted to drag me off the ship.

Breathing was growing difficult as well. I was gasping for air.

A unique feeling came over me abruptly and I lifted my head with trepidation. There was no more tug of water, no more current.

Oh my god.

We were *inside* the supercavitation bubble!

I glanced right and left to check the others. They too were looking around, dazed. Lau had lost his facemask and was breathing from Johnny's backup regulator.

Surrounding us, the bubble distorted the ocean and it appeared as a hazy mirage of blue, black, and white. It was like being in hyperspace, I thought.

We stopped banking and nearly leveled off—we were listing to the port more than ever.

I held a hand out before my mask. Water was dripping from it.

I was in a bubble of air *underwater.*

At over four hundred kph.

Incredible.

Then another vibration reached my ears.

The tsunami plow.

—••—

WE SLAMMED TO A SUDDEN STOP and everything went black. I think I lost consciousness for a second or two. There was a jerk at my air tank and a snap, and then the group of us were floating free.

The dreadnought's plow had caught the water and the friction hauled the ship from SCAV and *shoved* it to a stop. The force of movement transferred to the water in front of the ship and generated a massive wave toward the theater of battle.

We had detached from the hull, but were floating free as the ship came to an abrupt halt. Friction slowed us abruptly as well, and when I blinked my vision to clear it, I realized that my mask was full of water. I couldn't breathe. I hastily cleared it and glanced around me. We were still strapped together, and the dreadnought was twenty meters next to us.

We were near the bow!

Irena's mask had come loose and she was scrambling to find it. There was a look of terror on her face, but Meg grabbed her and put the mask back on. She pressed the button on the regulator; bubbles streamed into the mask to force the water out.

Irena was still trembling in fear, but she could breathe again.

The rest of us started to swim toward the dreadnought.

Beside us, detonations were going off and the crush of imploding water shook us.

I couldn't believe what was happening at that moment.

Cliff pointed and we followed his finger, pulling with everything we had for the dreadnought. We couldn't let it leave us behind. There was an airlock near an expansive viewport.

It was the dreadnought's bridge.

We were there.

—••—

THE AIRLOCK DRAINED AND WE STARED at each other in horror. None of us wanted to speak, however, for fear of giving ourselves away. Johnny checked the display and motioned to me. Ten minutes of decompression.

I leaned back and closed my eyes for a long moment. My limbs were trembling. I had to calm my breathing.

And my heart felt like it was going to explode.

We were still alive.

But there was more to do.

—••—

TEN MINUTES LATER THE AIRLOCK SLID aside and we stepped out into a wide corridor. There was an open hatch to our right, and we stepped through and onto the dreadnought's massive bridge. Above and beside us was a viewport that showed a panoramic view of the ocean and the battle surrounding the dreadnought. There were control consoles spaced around the long and wide chamber, and a central aisle led toward the bow. The illumination, as in the rest of the warsub, was a red glow.

There were three people standing there, staring at us with mouths agape.

I studied them for an instant before I raised my machine gun and marched toward them.

One of them was my former deputy mayor and a traitor to Trieste.

He was working with the Russians, something I had wondered about earlier.

It was Robert Butte.

Interlude:
RSF *Drakon*,
SSBN Over
the Kermadec
Trench

Location: RSF *Drakon*, SSBN
                   Over the Kermadec Trench

Latitude: 30° 19′ S
Longitude: 178° 31′ W
Depth: 84 meters
Time: 0318 hours
Date: 15 June 2030

CAPTAIN IVAN ARKADY VENTINOV AND *DRAKON* had arrived at the Kermadec Trench just northeast of New Zealand and south of the Tonga Trench a full day before the fleet searching for them had appeared. The enemy had been rather obviously causing so much noise that Ventinov had realized their plan immediately. They wanted to drag *Drakon* into deep water and sink them.

It made Ventinov chuckle in derision. There was no way they could sink *Drakon* in a conventional battle. He'd already proven the ship's effectiveness against the CSF fleet in a—by his standards—*minor* skirmish, and had shown what damage the plow was capable of inflicting on his enemies by destroying the Australian undersea colony Blue Downs.

No one could stand up to him.

However, not all had gone as planned in this battle over the trench.

Firstly, a small number of faster warsubs were a part of the attacking fleet. They had SCAV drives, were highly maneuverable, and they could dive *deep*. Deeper than any sub he'd seen. Over five kilometers, using some sort of unique sound pulses to force the water back upon itself. Ventinov's engineers had first noticed them, and had requested one captured so they could study it. The captain wasn't sure it was possible, but he was trying.

Secondly, armed infiltrators had successfully managed to board the dreadnought. They had penetrated right to the ballast section, damaging the *trim* tanks before security had arrived on the scene. It almost made Ventinov laugh. Why they had damaged the trim tanks was beyond him. It would make no real impact on the dreadnought. They were listing to the port now, but that was about it.

Thirdly, there were also reports coming in about armed combat in the torpedo rooms, also on the port side. The fighting had somehow damaged many of the launchers, and he had ordered security to find the culprits.

Following these reports, Ventinov had immediately called his security chief to the bridge. The man was standing before him now, clearly frightened, as the captain demanded answers.

"Just what the hell is going on down there?" he asked with a finger jabbed at the man's chest.

"We neutralized two invaders in the ballast section."

"And the torpedo rooms?"

The chief hesitated. "Still searching, Captain. They've evaded our teams."

"Don't you think it's time to seal the ship? Prevent them from wandering around freely?"

"Uh, yes, sir."

Ventinov scowled at the man. He seemed incompetent and unprepared for such an incident. They trained for it regularly though, did they not? Ran drills? Apparently, the man had never expected something like this to happen, despite the training. "Close the watertight hatches. *Now.*"

"Aye, aye, sir." He motioned to a nearby controller, who carried out the order.

"Is there anything else?"

The chief opened his mouth to speak, then closed it again.

"Well?"

"Sir," he said finally, "we've reviewed the logs from over the past hours. Near the start of the battle—"

"Go on." The captain's voice was ice.

"The computer intercepted transmissions from outside the hull."

"From other warsubs?"

"No. From divers. They entered through an airlock near the stern."

"Didn't it alert you?"

"We—" His voice faltered. "We were busy with the battle, sir. It did notify us, but my people overlooked it."

Ventinov wanted to tear someone's head off. He clenched his fists and stared at the scene over his head. The sky above was black, and they were currently battling numerous warsubs. His fire control team was targeting warsubs and launching countermeasures when needed. They were doing extremely well. What had once been six hundred enemy subs was now down to just over two hundred.

Ventinov considered the situation for another long moment. This dreadnought had proven its ability to extend Russia's grasp far into the oceans and make the world tremble in fear, as the country had during the Soviet era. More warsubs like her would follow, and no one in the oceans would be safe.

He marched to a schematic of *Drakon* on a nearby display. "Show me which airlock," he growled.

His chief pointed near the stern of the warsub. "This one."

"Have you sent a security team?"

"Yes. The airlock was wet. Someone had—"

"Wetsuits?"

"We found scuba gear not belonging to us in an adjacent cabin."

Ventinov swore. "How many tanks?"

"Sir?"

The captain turned to the man and once again jabbed him with his meaty finger. "The number of scuba tanks will indicate how many invaders there are!"

"Oh, yes, sir." He looked abashed. "Eight. There must be eight intruders."

"From where?"

"They were American, sir. To be more precise, we identified Triestrian markings on them."

Ventinov exhaled harshly. "Trieste, is it?" He paused and thought about what their visitor had recently told him about the city and its mayor. "Perhaps that should be our next target then." He stared at the schematic. What was near to that airlock? What important system was close to where they had entered? He pondered the dilemma. Surely the invaders would have entered close to whatever they—

He stopped abruptly and swore. A chill worked its way down his spine.

"The reactor," he hissed. "They're close to it." He spun toward his communication person. "Contact the reactor room!"

A minute later: "No response, sir. I'm still trying."

Ventinov said to his security chief, "Send a team there to check it immediately."

He nodded and turned to march away.

To his back, the captain yelled, "And send our guest up here. I want to talk to him."

—••—

TEN MINUTES LATER, THERE WERE A series of heavy steps clanging on the deck, moving toward the captain. The command bridge was so large that it took some time for the man to reach him. There were two guards trailing; they glided quietly behind their guest, not making much noise at all.

As they approached, the sound of several torpedo blasts shook the ship. The captain had to brace himself slightly against them.

The hull around them vibrated.

Ventinov stared at the large man before him.

It was Robert Butte, former deputy mayor of Trieste City.

—••—

VENTINOV CONTINUED STUDYING THE AMERICAN. WEEKS earlier, they had discovered him in the Atlantic Ocean, piloting a small vessel toward Europe and had decided to just let him go. Then Butte had contacted them, and told a rambling yet remarkable story of subterfuge and betrayal by Trieste's mayor, including mention of a secret manufacturing base in the Mid-Atlantic Ridge, powerful seacars with new technologies, and a man intent on going to war with the USSF as well as the other superpowers of the world to bring freedom to the undersea colonies.

Ventinov wasn't sure he believed Butte, but he had humored him and sent a small group of warsubs through the Ridge to see if they could locate this base. Butte provided the depth of the facility and an approximate bearing from their location, and sure enough, the *Vostok* Class subs had come across a well-hidden dome on a ledge over the rift zone. They had attacked and flooded the dome, but most of the inhabitants had escaped using ships powered with SCAV drives.

Butte had also spoken about a new technology that allowed their subs to go deeper than any other in the world. He had said something about them diving deeper than five kilometers even.

Ridiculous, Ventinov had thought. Only a madman would make a claim like that.

But now, during this battle, these tiny ships had proven it possible. Butte had been telling the truth after all.

And there were these mysterious intruders on *Drakon* . . . and *Triestrian* intruders at that.

Robert Butte was a conundrum. He had not fully explained why he had been on the run, or what Mayor McClusky had on him. But to his credit, he had been willing to work with the Russians to destroy the Triestrian forces.

But now there was something else going on, and the captain wanted answers.

The captain said, "Are you still interested in working with us?"

Butte glanced around him as if perplexed by the question during a major battle. "Of course. I have no home right now."

"Not Trieste?"

The other winced. "I told you, I can't go back there."

"But why?"

"I just don't want to go. I hate those people. What they did to me."

Minutes passed as Ventinov oversaw the battle going on around them. Butte simply stood nearby, silent and watchful. As Ventinov glanced at the ocean above, several splashes drew his attention. An alarm sounded at the sonar station, and he yelled at his pilots, "Take us down and move us away from those mines!"

"Depth, sir?"

"A thousand. Keep us away from the surface. Get ready for another tsunami run." The last one had been very effective. They'd done it shallow to eliminate surface ships. Several had capsized and were at that moment on their way to the bottom.

He turned back to Robert Butte. The man would not meet the captain's eyes, which Ventinov thought odd. His lips twitched. "I think you are not telling the entire truth."

"Let me prove myself then. Let's go to Trieste. Destroy the city." His face had twisted into a mask of rage.

"We don't work for you. We're hosting you here. Kindly, I might add." He sneered. "You could be in a cell right now, and not walking around freely."

Butte snorted. "I have these two guards following me everywhere. I'm hardly free."

"You boarded willingly," Ventinov snapped. Then he collected himself and stroked his bushy moustache. "I will consider what you want, but you have to give us something too."

The other shrugged. "I really don't have much. I've worked in City Control at Trieste for years. I wasn't in the military."

"But you know about the politics in the region?"

"Of the undersea colonies? Somewhat." Then he faced the captain. "But what does it matter? We can just go and level them all at once. Why do you want to know about them?"

"We tested our weapon on the Australian city. It was closest and, according to you, Trieste has been recruiting other cities to join them."

"But I don't know which cities McClusky has convinced."

The captain sighed. More was going on than this man revealed. He had told a story of McClusky and an independence movement, but claimed not to know much else.

Butte looked like he wanted to say more. He was angry, almost straining at a leash that didn't physically exist.

During the exchange, the XO had left to consult with another officer. But now he had sprinted back, breathless, and said, "Sir! Reports have come back from the reactor."

Ventinov turned to the man. "Go ahead."

"Intruders have infiltrated the area. The reactor's power is spiking, as is the temperature." He hesitated, his face pale. "Sir, I think they've sabotaged it!"

The captain growled under his breath. Then he stared at his first officer, who was obviously growing frantic. "Calm down. You know there's not enough fissile material there to cause a major meltdown. Our engineers designed it that way."

"But—"

"It's okay. Send a repair team. And tell security to capture or kill the Triestrian invaders."

Robert Butte frowned. "What was that? They're here? Triestrians?"

Ventinov ignored him. The battle continued, and the captain remained ramrod still as he issued orders and listened to reports. Butte paced back and forth, breathing heavily.

Ventinov watched him through narrowed eyes.

There seemed to be a running battle through a corridor and ladderwell, but that was all the captain knew. Eventually they heard nothing more.

He ordered another tsunami run, aimed at a pesky grouping of CSF warsubs that continued to launch SCAV torpedoes at the dreadnought's water intakes.

It was successful.

Ventinov and Butte watched a sonar display as three of the warsubs—each with over a hundred sailors aboard—plunged toward crush depth.

The captain smiled; his teeth glowed red.

The battle continued to rage, and Butte said, "What was that about Trieste? You said something about Triestrians here?"

Before Ventinov could respond, footsteps rang on the deck behind them. They turned to look.

Ventinov frowned. Six people in wetsuits had appeared on the bridge.

They were holding machine guns.

Part Six:
Crush

Chapter Thirty-Three

I LOCKED EYES WITH ROBERT BUTTE and leveled my weapon directly at his face. He was staring at me with an equal intensity.

"Cliff," I muttered, without taking my eyes from Butte. "Take control of the bridge. Get the operators away from their stations. Check for security."

Around us, people were beginning to take notice. The controllers were wearing headsets and sitting at consoles, and they had begun to rise slowly to their feet. Cliff, Johnny, Lau, and Meg leapt into action and started yelling, motioning with their weapons.

The captain took a step toward me and I shifted my aim to him. "Hello, Ventinov."

He stared at me for a long moment. It was a battle of wills. His eyes were dark and his glare fiery. "You infiltrated and damaged my ship. I am not going to treat you kindly." His voice was deep and coarse, like gravel.

"You've attacked nations, unprovoked. Did you think no one would act? Let you run around and kill innocent people?"

He snorted at that. "Unprovoked. That's laughable."

"You destroyed Blue Downs. You're on a rampage around the oceans. I'm putting a stop to it."

"You are in a far more difficult position than you think. This ship is not going down. We've destroyed over half the fleet out there. And we're not done yet."

I watched him silently. "We'll see about that." Then I said to Irena, who was standing behind me, "Seal the bridge."

There was no response.

I didn't take my eyes off the three men in front of me. "Irena! Snap out of it. Go to the hatch we just came through. Press the red LOCKOUT button."

Finally, "Got it." Her footsteps receded toward the hatch.

Within two minutes, Cliff had returned. During that time, Butte hadn't said a single thing. He was still glaring at me.

The other man there was, I presumed, the first officer.

Cliff said, "There are close to forty people on this bridge. We have them corralled in the central aisle, sitting together."

"Security?"

"A few. We separated them from the others, tied them up."

"One of them likely activated an alarm. I asked Irena to seal the bridge. Can you check on it?"

"Got it."

"And Cliff—" He turned to look at me. "We won't be able to hold this. Security will be here soon. Find an alternative way out for when the time comes." There was only one obvious hatch leading onto that bridge, but I knew there had to be another exit.

"Got it, Boss."

He disappeared behind me. I checked my watch. Meltdown would be happening any minute.

"Now," I ground out, shifting my attention to the man. "Butte. What the hell have you been up to? What are you doing here?"

"It's pretty obvious, McClusky, don't you think?"

"I sent you out with a seacar. I let you live. And now you've joined up with *the Russians?*"

"You hardly gave me a choice. You told me not to return to an American undersea colony."

"For being a traitor. You were working to expose us to the USSF. To give

Trieste to them. I did what I had to, but I let you live. I figured you'd try a European city."

"I've also done what I had to do." His expression was acid.

"Attacking the United States? That's ballsy."

He blinked and his façade cracked just a bit. He turned to Ventinov. "You? The mainland?"

I snorted. "Come on, Butte. You've thrown your lot in with this bunch here. They've declared war on the world! Are you claiming you don't know anything about it?"

"I knew about your secret base. I was aware of the Chinese fleet."

"And Blue Downs?"

He finally looked away. "Yes, I knew about that."

"And you led it?"

"I'm just a guest here."

That made me snort. "Right. You're just enjoying their hospitality as they destroy underwater cities and attack nations."

He had nothing to say to that, but his icy stare didn't let up. I found it pathetic.

I turned to the captain. "You. Ventinov." I shifted my aim to him. "You have some explaining to do as well."

He squared his shoulders and spoke in a deep voice, "What's to explain, Triestrian? I've made our point clear."

"That you can attack a nation? That you can destroy a highly vulnerable underwater city?"

He frowned. "And you? Claiming resources in the ocean that aren't yours? Mining ore deposits that belong to us?"

"We rightfully claim any deposit in the open ocean—"

"Such as the Iron Plains?"

That stopped me. "I'm Triestrian. You're talking about an American and Chinese claim." The two nations were still arguing over mining rights to the large area just east of the Philippines.

"You're American," he snapped. Then he cocked his head to the side and stared at Robert Butte. "Robert was telling me about this independence movement in the undersea colonies. That's why you don't feel responsible for claiming resources that aren't rightfully yours."

"Any nation can claim any resource in international waters. That's been the law for centuries now," I said. "And don't tell me that's why your nation built this beast." I gestured around me.

"It's part of it. For too long Russia has lagged behind the other nations of the world. No longer. We're proving to the world never to underestimate us again."

"Like the Soviet Union. The Russian Federation." I snorted. "Those experiments turned out well. I wonder why you want to reenact them."

His expression turned poisonous. "You will die for saying that."

"And not because I sabotaged your nuclear reactor?"

He offered a slight laugh. "You think that will slow us? You have a lot to learn, McClusky." He pursed his lips as he stared at the consoles around him. Then he turned back to me. "Trieste will be our next target. I'll do to it what I did to the Australian city."

"Soon this ship will be at the bottom of the trench, and you with it."

Now he offered an oily grin. "If you say so, *Mister Mayor.*"

I hesitated and watched him for a long heartbeat. He was confident, I had to give him that.

—••—

WE TIED UP THE THREE MEN and put them with the security crewmen away from the rest of the bridge crew. They were all watching us, wondering what we were going to do. Outside, the hammering of explosions continued. The battle raged on. We were on autopilot, circling a mass of countermeasures churning away at a depth of a thousand meters.

I glanced up at the viewport over our heads that covered the entire bridge. It was massive. Sixty meters across. If a torpedo made it through their countermeasure shield, and it hit that port, we'd die instantly.

"Status?" I asked Johnny. We were standing at the pilot's station. It was at the bow, facing forward, and to either side were navigation and control stations.

"There are some two hundred vessels surrounding us. They're still firing torpedoes. The odd torpedo is coming from the surface as well. Helicopters are dropping them."

"I wonder what happened to all the surface ships," I muttered.

"Likely the tsunami plow took care of them."

"Security is at the hatch!"

I jerked around and stared at the source of the cry. Cliff was there, listening to the sounds on the other side. He yelled, "They're going to blow it with an explosive!"

I checked my watch. More than forty minutes had passed since we'd sabotaged the reactor. "Take this station," I said to Johnny. "Get ready." Then I called Irena. "Can you find the nuclear consoles? I want to see what's happening."

She glanced around and, after a few seconds, pointed. "Over there." We marched to it and stared at the readout. There were blinking red lights *everywhere*. Emergency warnings were flashing, and a display screen was showing a rapid scroll of Russian text. She scanned the readout. "According to this, the reactor is completely out of control. Temperature has rocketed to over 2,000 degrees Celsius."

"When will it escape containment?"

"Nothing can hold a liquid mass of corium that hot."

The temperature readout she indicated was climbing rapidly. From behind me, the captain said, "That won't happen, McClusky."

I turned to him. "And why not?" I pointed. "I'm watching it right now."

"There's not enough uranium. It'll get hot, but not hot enough for what you want."

I smiled. "You might be correct. Unless, that is, someone added more uranium to the pile. Enough to cause a total breach of the entire area."

His face went blank and his brow furrowed. "You didn't—" Then he stopped and snapped a look at Butte. Cliff had tied their hands behind their backs, and they were sitting cross legged in the central aisle. "You wouldn't have known though!" he snapped.

Robert Butte turned slowly to the captain. "I told you, he's clever. If he's saying that's what he did, then I would trust him."

More alarms started to blare from the console. I said, "Irena, see if you can pull up a video feed of the core."

While she was doing that, I studied a schematic of the dreadnought. I noted the location of the reactor core and the compartments it would melt on its way through the ship. I was searching for one in particular. It took me only a minute, and I burned it into my memory.

Irena studied the console before her. It was massive. Five meters long against the starboard bulkhead. While she was searching, I called Lau over. "Find the controls to open the watertight hatches. They'll be at a security station. Grab a guard and make him tell you."

"How much force can I use?"

I glanced at the guards currently tied up and lying face down on the deck. "As much as you want. This is a doomed vessel anyway. Get it done."

He stared at me for a second and then nodded. "Very well."

He continued watching me for a moment and I said, "What?"

"I'm just thinking that maybe the elders were right about you all along."

His expression was steel. He seemed sincere. "What does that mean?"

"I wasn't sure about the path Sheng City wants to take. They've thrown in with you."

"They want independence. That's what you told us."

"I wasn't sure you could take on our enemies though."

I frowned.

"I'm loyal to Sheng. But now I see that maybe I should be loyal to you as well." He shrugged. "You've surprised me, Mac. Let me just say that." Then he turned to do what I'd asked.

I watched him leave, then faced the reactor core readouts again. Irena was pointing. "Here's the video feed." She pressed a button and an image popped up on a screen. I immediately recognized the reactor room. The camera was in a corner of the chamber, on the ceiling, and showed the containment vessel. There were crew in radiation suits attempting to do something near it.

Irena swore. "They're about to make this even worse." She was shaking her head in disbelief.

"What?"

"Trying to get coolant in. See—they're bringing a hose. But that's insane."

"Why?"

"Mac, if any water touches that core right now it'll vaporize instantly. Probably cause a massive explosion."

"How massive?"

Her forehead wrinkled. "They tried this at Chernobyl. The explosion blew off a containment lid."

I frowned. "So? What's—"

"It weighed *four million pounds*. Two thousand tons."

I watched the images, my heart pounding.

The containment vessel was glowing red. Waves of heat were distorting the air around it. The people in orange radiation suits were backing away from it slowly. One was motioning at a man with the hose and pointing toward the core.

"Oh my god," Irena whispered. "They're really going to try."

The temperature had passed 2,500 degrees. The core was glowing brighter.

The man pushed the hose into a makeshift pipe that led inside the containment structure. It hadn't been there when we'd left. They must have welded it into place to allow coolant direct access to the fuel rods. He turned the nozzle several times to tighten it then threw himself back from the incredible heat. Another crewman stepped over to a lever on the hose and pulled it.

"Oh no . . ." Irena said.

There was a sudden flash of light and the image shook crazily. The last thing I saw was an incredible force throwing the group of men and women in orange suits backward. The entire structure disintegrated in an expanding ball of steam and—

The image went dark.

Simultaneously, every light on every console flickered momentarily.

The dreadnought shuddered from the explosion. It felt different from the torpedo blasts. This one had come from *within* the ship.

Its heart had just exploded.

And the meltdown was on.

The reactor was no longer generating electricity. Automatic backups must have tripped on to continue supplying power to necessary systems. The SCAV would no longer operate either; hopefully it would strand us at that location, where the dreadnought would plunge into the trench at battle's conclusion.

There was a sudden blast behind us, an explosion, from the hatch we'd used to enter the bridge. I thought for an instant that the core explosion may have caused it—the fear of radiation contamination crossed my mind—but that wasn't it.

This was security, finally blowing their way onto the dreadnought's bridge to regain control.

I spun on Johnny and cried out, "Now! Do it, Johnny!"

He grabbed the yoke and twisted it savagely to the left.

Below us, at the stern of the warsub, the nuclear fuel had melted the containment vessel to slag. It had begun to drip onto the deck below, melting the steel there. The temperature rose as neutrons hit more uranium atoms, releasing more neutrons. It had spiraled out of control.

The temperature kept increasing.

It hit 3,000 degrees Celsius.

Anything the molten mass touched would melt and join the liquid metal as it burned its way through the ship.

The dreadnought began to capsize. It tipped to port—in the direction it was already listing—easily. Johnny gritted his teeth as he held the yoke as far as it would go.

The captain screamed, "What are you doing!?"

"Get ready!" I yelled.

Behind us, security was sprinting through the bridge, leaning to the side as the ship turned.

Johnny held the yoke firmly in his hands.

As I began skidding down the deck toward the port, I yanked my PCD from my pocket and frantically signaled my *Sword* pilots. "Target the dreadnought near the vertical stabilizer! Put some holes in the top of this beast!"

The bulkhead was rushing quickly toward me.

I held my arms out to break the fall.

Chapter
Thirty-Four

IT WAS TOTAL, UTTER CHAOS. As the warsub continued to turn, I rolled along bulkhead consoles, banging against displays and switches and levers and suffering countless cuts and abrasions. People everywhere were screaming. The crew we'd tied up—security guards, the captain, Butte, and the XO—fell heavily to the bulkhead. The others—the ship's controllers—slid along the deck and grabbed consoles to save themselves from injury. Debris was sliding along the deck and crashing through the bridge. Everything from coffee mugs to headsets to chairs and clipboards and bulky equipment fell from one side of the bridge to the other. Loose wires hung from consoles like delicate fingers reaching to caress the crew with a dangerous touch.

The ceiling had been five meters over our heads. I continued to roll and tried desperately to get my feet under me. I failed. I tumbled head over heels as Johnny held the yoke in place. My hands slapped down onto the deck beneath me, but it was no longer steel.

I blinked. *It was the viewport, now on the bottom of the ship*. It faced into the fatal depth of the abyss—the deeps of the Kermadec Trench, ten kilometers straight down. Torpedoes and warsubs were only a few hundred meters away. My face was pressed against the port as debris continued to rain down on me. It was like a glass-bottomed bridge suspended over the Grand Canyon, only the seafloor at the Kermadec Trench was five times deeper.

I rose to my knees and looked above me. Johnny was sitting in a chair, buckled in, and staring at the controls before him. He was upside down.

It made me shake my head. It looked like he was stuck to the ceiling.

Others were hanging from console islands, their knuckles white, as they tried to prevent themselves from falling five meters—*fifteen feet*—to where I was kneeling. Some had pulled themselves up and were bracing themselves atop the control stations, and were staring down at me with shock clear on their features.

I realized that there was a large security team currently on the bridge with us. I'd seen at least twenty of them running in as Johnny began the maneuver.

"Keep us here, Johnny!" I cried as I pulled my machine gun from around my back. The corium would be sinking through ceilings at that precise moment, ruining the watertight integrity of the warsub.

Below me, a torpedo shot past and hit the dreadnought just behind the bridge. There was a massive shudder and a vibration coursed up my legs.

I knew that at that moment, everywhere on the dreadnought, the incident had left crew reeling. There were probably broken bones and concussions and massive injuries. They might even believe their vessel was in the process of capsizing and sinking.

A red glow still illuminated the bridge. I pressed the machine gun to my shoulder and sighted along the barrel, searching for crew wearing the distinctive security uniform with the crimson sleeves.

I found them.

They had clustered together on the viewport, looking around and trying to figure out exactly what the hell was going on.

I fired.

The shots rang out in the bridge and more people screamed. The security team immediately pressed themselves to the clear acrylic port and scrambled for their guns, but they had no chance against me. It was dark in there and they couldn't get their bearings. This was the last thing they'd expected. We, on the other hand, were prepared.

More shots rang out from the far side. I thought for an instant that the bullets were meant for me, but in my sights another security officer fell back, blood spurting from a neck wound.

We had the Russians in a crossfire.

I kept squeezing the trigger, watching the bullets tracing paths across crimson-sleeved uniforms. It was incredibly dangerous; if I hit the viewport . . .

Instant death.

A figure darted across my view, ducking behind debris and sliding. Above, a console exploded, sending a shower of sparks down. The figure rose to a knee with a rifle to his shoulder . . .

It was Lau. He was taking aim at a security guard near the hatch. The sparks lit Lau from behind, putting him in complete silhouette.

And a bullet slammed into his chest.

I searched for the shooter and put two rounds in him. He fell back, screaming in agony.

Crawling to the bulkhead and crouching behind a now-upside-down console mounted there, I searched for Lau. He was on his back, writhing in obvious pain.

He shuddered as more rounds pounded into the side of his ribcage. He twitched and arched his back. Then he opened his mouth in a soundless cry.

A final breath hissed out.

—••—

THE DREADNOUGHT CONTINUED TO ABSORB TORPEDO strikes. Our forces were taking advantage of the upturned vessel and were following my orders. The corium was melting through the warsub and carving through airtight bulkheads as if through butter. People in those sections were probably trying frantically to escape, but moving about an inverted ship would not be easy. They'd be running from a 3,000-degree mass of slag in the near dark. It would be a thing of nightmares. We had opened the watertight hatches—hopefully—so it would allow them an escape route, if they could overcome the confusion of being upside down. The ladders would be difficult to overcome.

I wound my way through the debris, staying low, until I was directly below Johnny. I glanced up at him. "Can you lock the controls like that? Keep us upside down?"

He hesitated. "Yes, I think so, but they'll be able to get up here eventually."

"We only need an hour. Maybe not even that long. The corium is moving right now. Lock them in place." I paused. "How the hell are you going to get down?"

"I got it. Don't worry."

He pressed a few controls on the console before him and reached to his side. His bag was there, jammed under his arm against the armrest. There was a rope in it, which he tied off on the chair and lowered to me. I looked toward the bridge hatch, sixty meters away, as I sighted along the barrel, searching for security.

I couldn't see any. They were staying low perhaps, or Cliff had finished them all off. There was also no sign of Ventinov or Butte. I didn't envy what they'd just been through: tumbling around on an inverted bridge with hands tied behind their backs.

Meg was lying nearby, also staring along the barrel of her weapon. Soon Irena joined us, followed by Cliff. Johnny lowered himself and grunted as he landed on the viewport.

"Tell me you have a way out of here," I muttered to Cliff.

He gave me a tight nod and pointed to the starboard side about thirty meters back from the bow. "Over there. There's an emergency egress. A watertight hatch."

"Okay, then that's where we're going."

I filled the others in quietly on the plan and we threaded our way through the debris toward the hatch. We came across several crewmen laying in the wreckage. They were not armed, we were carrying weapons, and they said nothing. They simply watched us file past them slowly.

The hatch was half the size of normal and it opened manually. It was far up the bulkhead—close to the deck, but we were upside down. It was going to take a while for me to figure out the layout of the ship now, I realized. We had to hoist each other up to reach it. It was clearly meant for evacuation in the event of a catastrophic disaster. One by one we entered, half crouched, and closed it behind us. Then we began to work our way through the tight confines. There were pipes bracketed to the bulkheads and low-hanging wires, which at one point had been on the deck. The light fixtures were now at our feet, and we had to step around them as we moved.

We passed a branch in the tunnel—an inverted sign signaled an escape vehicle of some sort.

We were as silent as possible as we negotiated the tight chute.

All but Lau.

We'd left his body behind.

—••—

TEN MINUTES LATER, WE HUDDLED IN a corridor aft of the bridge. The ship was in chaos. There were distant screams and yells as crewmen tried to figure out what was going on. The corridors were difficult to navigate. Each hatch was *above* the deck by thirty centimeters, which we had to step over to enter each new section. The lights were in the decks. Alarms pierced the ship.

The rattle of detonations continued, each one shaking the dreadnought. The Russian warsub was taking huge damage.

A large crash and bang startled us from just around the next corner. The yelling was growing in volume.

Someone was coming.

We ducked into a cabin and slammed the hatch shut. I leaned against it and held my breath. A group of crewmen ran past. They were headed for the bridge.

They would get the warsub turned around in just a few minutes.

I willed the corium to move faster. *Make it to the hull. Just get there.*

Meg said, "What are we going to do, Mac? We don't have much time left here."

I turned to them. Cliff was looking to me, waiting for the next order. Johnny was studying the cabin. Broken furniture lay strewn across the 'deck.' It was a lounge of some sort.

Irena was looking calmer now, but was also waiting to hear our plan.

I tapped the PCD in my pocket. It wasn't time yet.

"We need to go to the brig," I said finally.

The statement hit like a bomb. Even Johnny turned toward me with a look of shock.

"What?" Irena hissed. "What are you talking about? We're a thousand meters down right now! The corium is melting—"

"We can't leave our people here. The Russians have Renée and Benning. We need to get them. At least try."

Meg said, "But Mac." She hesitated. "This is our chance."

I paused and said nothing to that. Cliff was staring at me, then to Meg, then back to me. "What does that mean?"

I ignored him. "Renée's in trouble. She's risked everything for us. She turned her back on the FSF to join us. She helped get Cousteau on side with us."

Meg leveled a laser-like glare on me. She knew the others were listening and her next words were a hiss. "But our plan. We're almost done."

"Before we leave we need to get Renée."

She looked confused. "You're suggesting going all the way to the security section while this ship implodes around us? While the core dissolves the interior?"

"That's exactly what I'm saying."

"But the plan." She looked desperate.

The exchange had confused the others. They were silent as they watched brother and sister debate something they didn't fully understand.

"Trust me, Meg." I grabbed her shoulders. "Please."

—••—

THE ENGINEERING SECTION WAS IN THE ship's stern—back the way we had come. That area occupied ten decks near the keel. Directly above it was security and the brig.

But now the ship was upside down . . .

Meaning the core was melting its way near the brig at that very moment.

The others looked at me with horror in their eyes. They knew the location was incredibly dangerous.

But I was intent on getting there.

We were still in our Russian uniforms—we'd ditched the wetsuits while on the bridge—and could move through the warsub in the dark without much trouble. I led the way and we started to wind through the central arteries of the vessel, working backward toward the stern. There were crew in the corridors, trying their best to also move to duty stations. They were finding it just as difficult to get around. The ladders were the most challenging aspect of our journey. We had to go *up* to get to the lower decks. The ladders, however, were now upside down and the first step was two meters over our heads. We had to reach up to grab it and pull ourselves to the bottom of the first step. One by one, Cliff boosted us up. Then Johnny and I turned and grabbed his outstretched hand and hauled him up.

The ladderwell was tight and only lit by dim red bulbs in the deck.

"How many levels do we have to go?" Johnny asked, keeping his voice low.

I reviewed my mental map of the dreadnought. There were thirty decks in the ship. The brig was fifteen decks below the top deck.

Irena had stopped talking and was on autopilot, going in the direction we pointed. Meg was tightlipped and obviously furious with me. At least she was sticking with us on the trip, and hadn't left to find her own way off the ship. I hoped, when this was all over, she'd understand what I was doing. Johnny and Lau were directing us and assisting the others as we negotiated the challenging task of ascending an inverted staircase.

The ship shuddered and a blaring announcement echoed in the ladderwell. It was difficult to make out, but Irena's face suddenly burst into shock. "They've got control again! They're going to turn the ship!"

Chapter Thirty-Five

As she said it, things began to tilt.

The crew had reached the controls and were forcing the ship upright.

I stared at the ladderwell above, stretching up more than twenty decks, and realized with a jolt that in a few seconds it would be *below* me, and if I didn't move immediately, I'd be dangling over the center of a long and dangerous drop. "We have to get onto the other side of this!"

There were five of us on the same section of ladder—a very steep staircase. The ship started to roll back to the port. The hull was popping and creaking, and more detonations thundered in the distance. As the ladder turned, we scrambled over the edge, holding on for our lives. Irena slipped, and a cry escaped her lips. Johnny reached out and grabbed her around the wrist. Cliff pulled himself around the lip of the ladder as the ship continued to roll.

More explosions reverberated from the port and screams echoed through the nearest corridor.

There was an obvious sound of rushing water.

Oh, shit.

An alarm blared as the ship rotated.

I stared at the nearest hatch. It was open and beyond it water was pouring into the dreadnought. It was pooling on the bulkhead because the dreadnought was still sideways—

And it had stopped moving.

They couldn't rotate the ship any more.

It was flooding now—foundering.

The ladder was horizontal, and I stared in the direction we wanted to go. At least it would be easier now, I thought. To go *down*, we had to go *left*.

The hatch to the corridor abruptly slammed shut. Safety protocols.

"Run!" I yelled. "Get up—now's our chance!"

We half ran, half stumbled along the bulkhead with the ladder beside us. We had to zigzag as we moved—to avoid the ladder steps—but it was far easier than it had been a few seconds earlier.

Alarms continued to blare. The hull was cracking . . . *snapping*.

Another announcement echoed from the speaker as we hit the hatch to Deck Sixteen. Only one more to go. We pulled to a stop and Irena cocked her head as she listened to the voice. She was frowning. I noticed absently that she had multiple cuts on her face and a monstrous bruise under her left eye.

The lights in the stairwell began to flicker. But they weren't getting darker—*they were growing brighter.*

"What is it?" I asked.

"I think—I think—"

Another announcement rang out and we collectively held our breath. Then she turned to me. "It's another 'repel boarders' command." Then a different crewman came on the speaker. Her jaw dropped. "Mac, they're activating the SCAV drive. They're leaving the battle."

I stumbled over my words. "But the reactor is gone. We destroyed it."

She shook her head. "They're powering a backup." She stopped and stared at me in horror. "Mac, they have another fission reactor. They mean to go to Trieste and destroy her."

—••—

I SLAMMED MY HAND AGAINST THE bulkhead. Dammit. There was no way we could have known, for only one was ever active at a time, and that's the one whose emissions we'd intercepted.

And now they were going to abandon the battle to go destroy our city.

Avenge what we'd done.

There was a roar building through the ladderwell. The bulkheads were vibrating. I put my hand on the railing and felt it shudder under my grasp.

"It doesn't seem right," I muttered.

"The ship is partially flooded," Johnny replied. "It'll hold it back. The top speed will be much slower. Maybe it'll rattle itself to pieces."

A bullet abruptly rang out and we ducked behind the ladder steps.

—••—

I READIED MY MACHINE GUN AND sighted along the barrel. There were figures behind us, advancing from the upper levels of the dreadnought. The hatches back that way had slammed shut due to the flooding and had trapped them in the ladderwell with us.

"Mac!" a voice called out. "This isn't over yet!"

It was Robert Butte.

I pulled the trigger and sprayed the area behind me. Bullets ricocheted and sparks flew. Lights blew outward. Glass shards pierced flesh.

"Keep going," I muttered to the others. "Get to the brig." I realized how crazy it sounded as I said it. The brig was in the center of the security section—the source of the very people hunting us!

I could only hope that the ongoing chaos would offer some protection.

Benning was there, and I was going to have to make a grave decision.

We backed away from Butte and his team of people in the ladderwell and I continued to fire.

"You can't survive this, Mac!" he called. "You're going to pay for what you did to me!"

"Do you have a grenade?" I asked Johnny.

He handed me one and I pulled the pin and threw it down the narrow tunnel. "Go!" I turned and sprinted toward the hatch to Deck Fifteen. Behind me, the grenade rattled along the steel ladder. Its sound was distinctive and there were yells from the Russians as they realized what

I'd just done.

The hatch was at our feet because the ship was currently sideways in the water. We hauled on the lever, attempting to open it. It was heavy.

Before we could jump through, however, a familiar whine pierced the ship. The tsunami plow.

Ventinov was activating it!

I glanced around frantically. "Get against the bulkhead, now!"

He was trying to take us out through sheer force. Trying to shake us around his ship, knock us senseless and kill with blunt force trauma.

The grenade exploded ten meters from us, hot steel spearing through the ladderwell. It sounded like a can filled with stones. Smoke surged through the area, making us gasp and cough.

The ship jerked to a sudden stop and slammed us against the bulkhead. My arm twisted behind me as my body collapsed into the steel. I groaned against the agony and fell to my knees, cradling my left arm in my right.

The tsunami plow had hurt Butte's team as well. They were groaning and coughing.

"Give me another grenade," I whispered. Johnny passed it to me and I pulled the pin. I winced against the pain in my arm as I did so.

I threw it.

A shower of bullets sprayed across the ladder. Behind me, Johnny and Cliff struggled with the hatch, lugged it up and jumped through it.

I followed just as the device detonated.

The hatch slammed shut behind me.

I peered around us. We were on the correct deck. The sub was still once again, but the roar was building. They were trying to get back into SCAV drive. As we accelerated, the ship slowly rolled upright.

The corium was probably burning a hole in the center of the warsub. I wasn't sure how close it had come to the outer hull, but while the ship had been rolling, it had been shifting directions. First downward toward the bottom of the sub. Then upward and toward the top. Then the ship had turned on its side, and the core would have melted toward the port.

Toward the flooded compartments.

"Where's the brig, Mac?" Johnny hissed. His machine gun butt was against his shoulder and he was sighting up and down the corridor.

I pointed and we jogged toward security. Alarms were ringing out and there was smoke in the hall. Debris littered the deck and there were even some bodies, limbs twisted at odd angles and smears of blood on the bulkheads and ceiling.

A group of security guards came into view ahead of us. They were armed and standing outside a wide hatch.

"Are you sure about this?" Meg muttered at my side.

I glanced at her but said nothing. Instead I fell to a knee and took aim.

—••—

OUR BULLETS ECHOED DOWN THE CORRIDOR, sparked against the bulkhead and cut down several of the troops ahead of us. They cried out and turned their weapons, but our aim was precise. We hit each of them, center mass, where they stood.

Things were chaotic on the ship, and they clearly had no idea what was happening.

They hadn't expected *us* to attack *them*.

The bodies were lying in a heap on the deck, limbs intertwined as they groaned in agony. They were bleeding out.

"Protect this position," I snapped to Johnny and Cliff. I turned to Meg. "Let's go in, Sis."

—••—

THE HATCHES WERE HANGING OPEN AND there was debris everywhere. Papers, drawers, furniture. More bodies. The maneuvers had turned the entire section upside down and had shaken it. We threaded through the damage and examined the geography of the chamber. There was a smaller area at its rear with a narrow hatch and a glass viewport.

Cells.

I pointed and together we sprinted toward them.

Outside, where we'd left Johnny, Cliff and Irena, gunshots rang out.

Shit. It was Butte. He'd survived and was still pursuing us.

We didn't have much time.

We peered through the viewport. It was a cell with a narrow bunk and a toilet and nothing else. There was no one in it.

Damn.

There was a long corridor with eight more viewports. We moved to the next.

We examined each.

The first six were empty.

The last two held our people.

—••—

THEIR CAPTORS HAD BEATEN THEM BADLY. Their faces were bruised and lacerated. There was blood on their clothes, but their eyes lit up when we appeared and unlocked the hatches.

Renée threw herself into my arms and I held her tightly.

"You didn't leave me," she whispered.

"Of course not," I replied.

Benning was staring at me. He was limping and looked like he'd been through hell. "Thanks, Mac," he said. "I didn't expect you to come."

I stared at Meg. She had her weapon aimed at the Admiral. Her face was tight.

I separated myself from Renée and moved her to the side. She studied Meg and glanced at me. "What—"

I ignored her. "Meg."

Meg's face was set like steel. "This is our chance, Tru."

A silence descended on us. It was absurd. We were standing in the dreadnought's security region, a firefight raging in the hall, we were in a desperate situation and needed to get out as soon as possible, and there we were, in a standoff.

"Don't do it," I said.

She snapped a look at me.

Benning's face had gone blank. He was looking at her, then back to me, then back to Meg. "What are you—"

"We can do it now," Meg said. "Look at what he's done to us. His troops will continue to harass us."

"That's going to happen regardless," I said. "It doesn't matter who's in charge. Heller, Benning, or someone else. They're going to choke us until we achieve independence."

"He killed Dad! He deserves to die." She pressed the weapon against her shoulder.

Her finger tightened on the trigger.

Chapter Thirty-Six

BESIDE ME, RENÉE GREW TENSE AT the rapidly escalating situation. She knew what was happening. I'd told her, while I'd held her at The Ridge, about Benning and how he'd killed my dad.

And how I wanted to kill him.

"Meg," I said. "This isn't you. You don't want to do this."

Her face grew hard. "This is something we wanted. It's something you were going to do. This is our chance. If you don't do it, *I* will!"

"You'll regret it."

"Dad deserves it!"

"Dad allowed himself to die, dammit. He let Benning do it."

Benning finally realized what was going on. His expression showed understanding.

I continued, "I've been living with the guilt of what I did for weeks now. I killed innocent people. It'll haunt you, Meg."

"The USSF is not innocent! They harass and assault our people! They've raped before! They deserved what you did!"

Benning was staring at me. "What did you do, Mac?"

"Don't call me that," I snapped. "I'm trying to save your life. Shut up." Then I turned back to my sister. "Listen. We can't rescue just Renée and leave Benning behind."

"I thought we had both decided that! You were going to kill him!"

"He came with us when he didn't have to. He's fought with us on this ship."

"And now he's made up for his sins? Is that what you're—"

"I didn't say that."

"He killed Dad! You manipulated him to get him on this dreadnought."

I winced. She was right. But something seemed off about all this now. It felt like a betrayal. I sighed. "We have to at least try to move on, Meg. It's the right thing to do."

"You forgive him for murder?" Her eyes flashed and she tilted her head.

"Never. That day will torture us forever. It's affected more people than you can imagine." Cliff was in my thoughts. He'd been there, the day of Dad's murder, and had quit the USSF because of it. "We have to try because it's who we are, Meg. We're Triestrian." I swore. I'd been dealing with more guilt than I could ever have imagined because of what I'd done to the USSF fleet over the rift. I'd destroyed them all, killed hundreds of sailors. Their only crime had been to serve on a USSF vessel. Some were cruel and heartless— we'd endured our share of them at Trieste, that was for sure—but not all. And I'd killed them all indiscriminately.

Here was one that I could save.

And possibly forgive myself for the things I'd done.

Maybe stop the nightmares.

I continued, "I know he's evil. He's been stealing from the underwater cities for more than three decades. He murdered Dad. But it's not right to leave him to die here, in a Russian vessel that he helped us infiltrate."

Benning had gone white. "You were going to kill me?"

"You murdered my dad, Benning."

He hesitated. "I didn't know . . . didn't know you knew."

"I was going to kill you."

"But not anymore?"

I gestured at Meg. "You're still in a bit of trouble right now."

"I was following orders."

"Orders to harass our people? To kill the mayor? To assassinate the entire city council?"

"Yes!" he bellowed. "Your dad was clamoring for independence. The US relies on the undersea cities. It's all falling apart topside! The land is turning to dust and blowing away. The oceans are flooding coastal cities. And during it all your dad was announcing his intention to separate from the United States! What did he think was going to happen?"

I snorted. "You're right. I expected it."

"Then why are you upset?" he growled. "Why so surprised that it happened?"

I sighed. "It's not every day you come face to face with the man who murdered your dad, Benning. And Meg's right. We have a chance to kill you right now and be done with it."

"You think it'll make Frank McClusky happy? You just said he let it happen. Why? That doesn't make sense."

I exhaled and turned back to my sister. There was no point explaining to him. If he made it out of here alive, I didn't want him to know about our independence movement. I wanted him to think that it had ended with George Shanks and the battle a year earlier, and that I now had nothing to do with such a thing. "Meg. We don't have to do it. We're working with the USSF right now to destroy this dreadnought. Maybe it'll help get them off our back. We've partnered with them on this. We can't betray them."

"Betraying them was the plan." Her voice was a whisper, but she gripped the weapon firmly. It didn't waver.

"This is the new plan. I'm sorry I didn't say anything earlier. This is a better way. To build a bridge of peace with the man."

"I'm not sure I can forgive him like you can, Tru."

I understood what she was saying. The assassination had destroyed our lives, but hers especially. She'd run from Trieste. Mom had died soon after. Our family had fallen apart.

"I'll never forgive him. But I'm saying there's a better way here. One that will improve things for Trieste."

She didn't say anything. She just stared at Benning. The barrel was only inches from his face.

It began to drop.

Then she swore and lowered it. "You better be right about this."

I put my hand on her shoulder. "You'll see. And I'm sorry I didn't tell you. I only just realized it myself."

She shook her head and stepped back. "It doesn't matter." Then she swore again. "I couldn't bring myself to do it."

"You don't have it in you, Meg."

Tears began to spill down her cheeks. "I wanted to do it for Dad."

"He's long gone," I whispered. "He gave himself up for this."

"Still. Benning destroyed everything. He destroyed Mom too."

"We have to move on together. Get through this as a family. It's the only way, Meg." I swore. "Hell, I just lost Kat! I've lost everything too. All except one person, and I need us to move on. Together."

She stared at me. "You'll always have me, Tru." Then she blew her breath out and nodded. "I got it. I'll try."

Benning had watched the entire exchange in silence. "Listen, if I didn't do it, someone else would have."

It wasn't a smart thing to say to me. "You wanted to advance your career, is that it?" I snapped.

"No. But I didn't want to get court martialed for disobeying a direct order! The CIA demanded it!"

"He was an innocent man."

He snorted. "The US government thought he was a traitor. And they killed him because of it."

I grabbed him by the lapels and shoved him against the bulkhead. "You shot him in the head, you sick fuck! Don't tell me that you had a right to do that!"

Then I realized what I was doing. I stepped back. "We're running out of time. We have to get out of here." I pulled the PCD from my pocket. "This is Mac."

"Go ahead." It was the *Sword* pilot, still in the battle outside.

"Report."

"The dreadnought is listing badly. She's slow too. SCAV is still functioning, but their top speed is only just over 155 kph. We can keep up with her easily."

"What's the course?"

"Due east."

"Shit. They're heading toward the Americas."

"Seems like it. What's their plan?"

"Trieste. They want to destroy Trieste." I hesitated. "Do any of the remaining warsubs have grapples?" It was possible that we could drag the ship back, but it was a long way from the trench.

There was a pause. "I think so. There are only a hundred left though."

A hundred left, *from over six hundred warsubs*.

The dreadnought had devastated the fleet.

"I still have a surprise up my sleeve. Keep working on the ship's upper hull."

"Got it."

"Is *Devastator* still seaworthy?"

"Barely. She's taken a lot of damage. She's fallen behind. Still over the trench."

Benning looked shocked.

Then I signaled someone else.

"Go ahead."

The voice made me smile. "How are you, Lazlow?"

"Great!" His enthusiasm was contagious. "The battle has been one for the ages. It's been going on for hours now!"

"Get ready to extract us. Are you following?"

"Yes. I'm at four kilometers depth and matching speed with the dreadnought." He couldn't go any deeper otherwise he'd have to activate the acoustic pulse, and for that he'd have to slow to fifty kph.

"Okay, I'll be in touch."

Afterward, I contacted one more person. It made Benning, Renée, and Meg blink in surprise.

— •• —

THE GUNFIRE WAS CONTINUING FROM THE hall. I poked my head out. Johnny and Cliff were there, crouched in the hatchway, peering around the corner and continuing to fire at the security team that had been chasing us.

They were both using Russian weapons now; theirs were out of ammo.

I grabbed a knife and holster from my bag and strapped it to my thigh. "Report," I ordered.

Johnny filled me in. There were only a few security crew remaining; they were well armed but pinned down. Butte was still alive.

"Damn," I said. He was proving to be a bigger problem than I'd ever expected.

A low rumble met our ears and I pulled back from the corridor and cocked my head. "What is that?"

Renée, crouched next to me, said, "The SCAV? Or the tsunami plow?"

"Neither."

It was an odd rumble. The deck was vibrating too.

Then I noticed the ceiling.

It was glowing red and smoking.

I exploded to my feet and screamed, *"Get out of here! Now!"*

It was the corium.

———••———

IT HAD MADE IT UP SEVERAL decks, but once Ventinov had righted the ship, it had started back downward. It hadn't hit the hull at the top of the ship, but it had churned a massive and circuitous pathway through the dreadnought.

And now it was melting the deck of level sixteen, right over our heads.

The radiation it gave off would be massive.

"RUN!" I screamed. We bolted into the corridor and a hail of gunfire met us. Benning immediately took a round in his leg and fell to his knees, but he hauled himself back up and kept moving. As we ran, we glanced over our shoulders at the ceiling. It was red hot and slag was dripping to the deck. Behind it, Butte was advancing with a rifle to his shoulder. "You can't run!" he yelled. "You're going to die here, Mac!"

Then he noticed the ceiling and his expression went blank.

We rounded a corner and kept moving.

Screams peeled out from behind us.

——••——

JOHNNY AND I SUPPORTED BENNING AS we sprinted through the hall. The dreadnought was shuddering now as multiple missiles slammed into it. A haze of smoke hung in the air and alarms pierced the corridors.

There was a continual stream of commands over the PA system. Crew were sprinting down the corridors, paying us no attention. The looks on their faces were frantic. They knew their ship was in trouble.

They'd done well against the fleet, but torpedoes were finally scoring consistent hits on her hull, punching holes and flooding decks.

There were intruders on board who had sabotaged torpedo tubes and ballast tanks.

The primary core was gone, melted away, and the corium was now moving through the warsub, dissolving everything in its path and releasing fatal levels of radiation.

The dreadnought was listing severely to the port—so much so that we were leaning to the right as we ran through the corridor.

Ahead was a ladder and Johnny pointed to it. We ducked in and started down. A waterfall was streaming in from the decks above. It made my gut twist in fear.

The water was green and salty.

One flight lower, a shot rang out and we ducked against the sparks that erupted near our faces. I raised my weapon and squeezed off some rounds at a security team running up the ladder.

Someone must have told them we'd just been at the security offices on Deck Fifteen.

"Grenade?" I muttered at Johnny, and he shook his head.

Above us, a hatch opened and footsteps clanged on the ladder. I glanced up, squinting against the falling droplets of water.

"Mac!" Butte screamed. "If I don't survive this, then you don't either! We're both going down!"

I swore. "This guy doesn't let up."

Meg said, "He's obsessed. He thinks you ruined his life."

We spilled out of the hatch onto the next deck. I shut it behind us, but there was no way to lock it. It was meant for emergency access to the ladder.

I glanced down the corridor and an idea occurred to me. We moved twenty meters aftward and stopped, turned and took up positions in hatchways.

We waited.

Cliff and Johnny had Russian machine guns. "How many rounds do you have?" I hissed.

"Two clips each," Johnny said. He paused and looked back the way we'd come. Then he turned back to me. "Where are we trying to go?"

"To an airlock at the lowest deck. For extraction."

The clatter of feet on steel deck plates met us and we sighted along barrels. Russian security appeared and skidded to a halt when they saw us.

We fired, hitting two immediately. Their bodies jerked as bullets tore into them and they fell to the deck, bleeding. The others ducked into hatches, like us, and hid from view.

Robert Butte was among them. His face was red, veins popping on his neck as he screamed instructions at the group of Russians who probably didn't understand a word he was saying. They stared at him, confused, wondering why he was so frantic to kill us.

I glanced at the ceiling and then back to the security team.

They were poking their barrels around hatchway corners and spraying the corridor with fire. We ducked back. Shrapnel and bullets ricocheted around us.

"What are we waiting for?" Renée yelled from my side. "Let's run!"

"One minute," I said calmly, glancing again at the ceiling.

She followed my gaze. "Oh. My. God."

It was steaming and glowing orange.

Directly above the security team.

Butte was motioning at us angrily and screaming at his companions. They were yelling back at him in Russian. Neither could tell what the other was saying.

I squeezed another round and clipped Butte in the knee. He fell to the deck, screaming in rage. I fired again—

And the gun clicked. Empty.

"Get ready to run," Cliff said. He too was staring at the smoldering scene above the Russians. They hadn't noticed it yet.

Then slag started to drip down. They glanced up in shock.

Molten metal slithered in drooping threads from above. They held their hands over their faces to protect themselves from the incredible heat.

"*Chto eto?*" voices called in wonder and bewilderment.

What is it?

I bared my teeth. *It's your death, motherfuckers.*

Chapter
Thirty-Seven

MORE LIQUID METAL FELL TO THE deck before them. Butte was staring at it, horror on his face.

Cliff fired again and hit him in his uninjured leg. He screamed.

The entire ceiling above them gave way. *A mass of glowing slag fell in a hissing and gurgling pile right before them.* Scalding uranium and steel hit them and they howled in fear and surprise and pain.

Waves of heat radiated down the corridor.

"Run!" I yelled again. I'd been saying it a lot in the past few minutes, I realized.

We needed to get to an airlock.

Sprinting down the hall, I grabbed my PCD and called Lazlow. "The bottom of the dreadnought! Starboard side, near the stern! We'll exit there!"

His voice sounded distant. "The depth is 1,500 meters. Do you have gear for it?"

I swore as our feet pounded the deck. We didn't.

"We'll have to try an umbilical. Get *SCAV-1* ready!"

"But it's on the wrong side! The airlock—"

I clicked off. We rounded a corner and hit another ladder. We flew down it, two or three steps at a time. Even Benning was moving fast, despite the bullet in his leg. His face was pale and dripping with sweat, but he'd gritted his teeth against the pain. He wanted off that ship too.

Eventually we hit the bottom deck.

Nowhere else to go.

"Get to the starboard side. Find a lock," I grated. I was gasping for air. My left arm was aflame from the tsunami plow. Water flooded the port side compartments; we couldn't go there. We continued to move along the dark corridor. The cables on the floor made running more difficult and there wasn't much room to maneuver. We were moving uphill, for the ship was listing in the opposite direction. We had to go in single file. Johnny was in the rear, watching behind us, and Cliff was in the lead.

I had no more ammo.

I grabbed the PCD again. "Starboard side," I repeated. "We don't have any scuba gear." I hoped he could connect the umbilical, but *Dragon* was currently in SCAV drive at 150 kph.

Minutes later we'd arrived at the end of the corridor. The dreadnought was rattling as its SCAV drive powered the sluggish vessel through the water. Seawater had flooded large compartments and multiple punctures in the hull had increased friction, slowing it.

We stopped.

Cliff was staring at an airlock hatch. "Here's one," he muttered, "but it doesn't have an umbilical."

"Let's keep going," I gasped.

We turned toward the bow and continued moving.

If we didn't find one with an umbilical to extend to *SCAV-1*, we were through.

We staggered through the corridor as more torpedoes pounded away at *Dragon*. The impacts were not occurring on this side, however—I'd directed fire to the vessel's top, where I'd been hoping the corium would have melted a hole and compromised the entire ship's watertight integrity.

There was a noise behind us.

We stopped and spun to look.

There was a rattle of footsteps on uneven deck plates. A nearby torpedo strike had twisted and warped the interior deck sometime earlier.

A figure appeared in the smoke behind us, in silhouette with an emergency light behind.

He stumbled forward toward us, and my blood ran cold.

Robert Butte.

"Keep going until you find an airlock," I whispered. "I'll follow."

"Are you sure?" Renée said.

"I've got this."

The group moved on, continuing the search as I stood my ground and waited.

He was dragging his left leg behind him. His knee was a shattered ruin. Blood drenched his right leg—it was leaving painted bootprints behind him.

I gasped, but it wasn't because of the blood.

It was his face.

My god, his face.

The slag had burned and seared it into a distorted and curdled mass of bloody flesh and twisted meat.

The corium had dripped through the ceiling and he hadn't been able to escape fast enough. Radiation and temperature had dictated his fate.

This was a dead man lurching toward me, I thought.

He just didn't know it yet.

—••—

HE CAME TO A STOP THREE meters away, his features a ruined mass of coagulated and burned blood and flesh. There were char marks on his neck and arms, and his hair was a mess of matted burns and sweat.

"Robert," I whispered, staring at him. "Give this up. You're done."

"—I'm done, so are you." His voice was a quivering rasp.

"The radiation . . ."

"You did this to me. You're going to pay."

"You did this to yourself. You betrayed Trieste. You betrayed me. You were giving secrets to Heller. I could have killed you when I found out, but I let you live. And you led the Russians to our base. They ruined it. That was your fault."

"Because you banished me!" he screamed. He had bared his teeth while yelling, and they were a shocking white against his black and red flesh. His lips were bloody and cracked, and his tongue flicked over them.

"You could have started a new life for yourself. Instead you chose to join the Russians. That was your last mistake, Robert."

"It was no mistake. They're making their move now, Mac. They're going to take the oceans. They're going to rise to the top of the heap. Claim the Iron Plains and all the other resources. The undersea cities are nothing compared to them."

I gestured around me. "Like this unsinkable warsub? Look at it now."

"It's not sunk yet." He coughed and a mass of bloody phlegm spilled out. He hacked and rasped again and this time a fibrous piece of flesh ended up in his palm. He stared at it for a moment before hunching over, convulsing spasms wracking his body as he retched onto the deck.

I stepped back.

He was vomiting pieces of his stomach lining.

He straightened and stared at me. There were stringy bits of flesh on his chin and bloody clots in the whites of his eyes. He staggered toward me.

I kicked him in the gut and he lurched backward and fell to his knees. My knife was in my thigh holster and I grabbed it. "Don't make me do this, Robert."

"You're going to have to." He pushed himself back to his feet. "I'm not going to let you get out of here."

I steeled myself and took a deep breath. "So be it." I stepped toward him and struck out with the blade. It plunged into the former deputy mayor's chest and he gasped.

He reached for it and I let go and stepped away. He fell into the bulkhead and slid down, leaving a bloody trail on the steel.

"I'm sorry, Robert," I whispered. "You made the wrong call. I had to deal with it."

He opened his mouth to say something. I couldn't make it out. I leaned forward. He gasped, "Don't let them destroy Trieste, Mac."

It made me frown. "I won't. I'll never let anyone hurt the city again." He had betrayed the city to the USSF and had given important information about me to Heller. His actions had hurt Trieste more than he had realized.

And now he'd asked me to protect it.

He was gasping sharp intakes of smoke-filled air. His eyes were half closed, only the whites showing. His chest shuddered and his limbs twitched.

There was no doubt he loved the city. He just had an opposing philosophy on *how* to protect her. He wanted to allow the USSF to take over and run things. Keep the peace through capitulation. It was like giving in to a bully hoping that it made your life better. I knew that would never work. They'd just keep demanding more from you.

You had to stand up to them.

Fight.

I watched him die at my feet.

— •• —

I FOUND THE OTHERS THIRTY METERS farther up the narrow corridor at an open hatch. It was an airlock with an umbilical. Cliff and Johnny were working the controls and hydraulics whined as the tube extended.

I put the PCD to my mouth. "Lazlow. The umbilical is extending. Do you see it?"

It took a moment but finally he responded with a loud exclamation. "I've got it! You're about 130 meters from the stern."

"Bring the seacar up. Match velocities."

"But Mac, the airlock is on the wrong side!"

"Don't worry. Just be ready." I pressed another call button on the PCD and waited.

It beeped. "Go ahead." It was the leader of our fleet.

"Do you have any SCAV torpedoes left?"

"A few. Not many."

"Are you still following?"

"Yes. But we don't have much hope of stopping the dreadnought."

"It's okay," I said. I hesitated. "I have a surprise coming. Don't shoot when you see them."

"What do you—"

I switched frequencies and made another call. "Are you there, Piette?"

"Right here, Mac."

It was Mayor Piette of Cousteau City. Weeks earlier I'd asked him for a favor. He'd carried it out.

"Did you rescue our man?" I asked.

"I've got him, he's right here with me."

I smiled. "Jackson?"

"I'm here, Mac! Mayor Piette and a team of his engineers arrived at The Ridge a few days ago. They repaired the hull and pumped out the water."

"And now you're here. In the middle of another battle."

"With thirty-three *Swords!* We've been watching from a distance, just waiting for your call."

I grinned and stared at the others. They returned my smile. The *Swords* could hit a max speed of 460 kilometers per hour and a depth of eight kilometers. And there were over thirty of them about to join the battle.

"We've got to knock this dreadnought out of SCAV. Can you do that, Piette?"

Piette said, "We'll target the water intakes. Maybe that'll do it."

"Just get it out of SCAV. We need to cross over to our seacar."

"Got it."

I keyed off and waited.

Meg was staring at me and shaking her head.

"What?" I asked.

"You just never cease to surprise me, Tru. You sent a rescue team to get Jackson and the *Swords* how long ago?"

"A few weeks." I shrugged. "I couldn't leave Jackson Train there any longer. He was all alone behind the collapsed ceiling, a flooded dome, and a watertight hatch. I sent Piette there with a team from Cousteau to rescue him and bring the *Swords* to the battle."

I recalled the earlier communication, when I had made the request.

"I've left some ships in the Mid-Atlantic Ridge," I had said. *"I need your help getting them."*

Francois Piette looked utterly perplexed. He was at Cousteau, I was at Trieste, and we were speaking over the video comm. "Say again?"

"How much experience do your people have with that Sword I gave you?"

"Some. We've taken it out. It's blown our scientists away, frankly. Its top speed is simply—"

"I have more, hidden away at a secret base."

His face exploded into shock and surprise.

I continued, "I need help getting them." I explained what had happened, about how Jackson Train had collapsed the tunnel and sealed the airtight hatch, but there were forty more subs just waiting for us to use.

"And this man is . . . still there?"

"Yes."

"For how long?"

"A few weeks now."

"By himself. Nearly four kilometers down." He shook his head. *"Remarkable."*

"There is a major battle coming. We need those ships."

He stared at me. "You're asking me to get forty people, train them on our Sword, and go get the others from your base."

"And save our man."

"And then meet you to help with this dreadnought."

My expression was deadly serious. "That's exactly what I'm asking."

I pulled myself back to the battle. "I guess we should hold on," I said to the others. "They're about to pound the SCAV intakes and haul us back to zero velocity."

They stared at me, their faces blank.

Then the torpedoes started detonating.

—••—

WE HELD ON AS BEST WE could, but it was difficult. The warsub shook and rattled as impact after impact slammed into the hull near the water intakes.

Within five minutes the dreadnought jerked to a stop and we fell to the deck heavily.

The SCAV torpedoes had done it. I triggered the PCD and yelled, "NOW! Lazlow, bring the seacar in!"

Because *SC-1*'s airlock was on her starboard side, she had to line up with her bow facing the dreadnought's stern. I watched the tiny screen on the panel controls as the ship appeared from the darkness and sidled up to the umbilical.

"Do you think he can do it?" Meg whispered.

"He only has to get close. We can do the rest," Cliff replied.

Two minutes later it was done. Lazlow had brought *SC-1* next to the umbilical and hit the station-keeping thrusters. Cliff maneuvered the umbilical out and there was a clang as it formed the seal against the seacar.

Pumps cleared the umbilical and a minute later we spilled across into the airlock, unconsciously holding our collective breath as we sprinted across the short tube.

Then we were inside the airlock and we shut the outer hatch.

I turned to face the others.

They were staring at each other, surprise on their features.

Grins split their expressions.

"We did it!" Irena yelled. "Holy shit!"

I laughed.

SC-1 separated from the critically wounded dreadnought and we powered slowly away.

Chapter Thirty-Eight

THE INTERIOR OF THE SEACAR BROUGHT an even bigger smile to my face. A part of me thought I'd never see her again. Cliff, Renée, Meg, Irena, Benning, and Lazlow sat on the couches in the living area. Johnny and I took the pilots' chairs. I studied the sonar screen. There was one major contact—the dreadnought—and fifty smaller ones. Our *Swords*. Thirty-three had come from The Ridge, piloted by the Cousteauian team led by Piette. The others were from our force that had come from Trieste.

I pursed my lips as I studied the map. We had moved from the Kermadec Trench, which was just over a hundred kilometers to the west.

I ordered our people to target the dreadnought's conventional thrusters before she could continue moving again. We needed this vessel dead in the water so we could finish it off.

Meg said, "Do you think the corium will burn through the bottom?"

Irena shook her head. "It was still fourteen decks above the hull. Each deck it melts dilutes the uranium more. It'll cool and solidify soon, if it hasn't already."

We piloted *SC-1* in a large circle and turned to look at the dreadnought. It was listing at a fifteen-degree angle to the port. The stern was listing as well, though not nearly as much. There were bubbles streaming from multiple impact points on the port side.

Despite this, there were still torpedoes lancing out from her, mostly from launchers on its starboard, though some were originating from the port as well. Her crews were still doing what they could to win this battle.

I signaled the *Swords*, which were now swarming at SCAV speeds and easily avoiding the weapons. "Target the torpedo launchers and let's defang this beast," I ordered. Then I checked the comm. I wanted to contact the larger warsubs, back at the Kermadec Trench, but they were too far away through simple comm signal, and they were also too far away from the common fiber optic lines or a junction for us to speak with them.

Instead I contacted Mayor Piette. "Can you pick a *Sword* to send back to the trench? I need to get a message back to them."

"What do you want to tell them?"

I filled him in and he nodded. "Got it."

A *Sword* would only take fifteen minutes to get my message to them. In the meantime, we would continue to hammer *Dragon*.

We still had eight torpedoes on board *SC-1*—four SCAV and four conventional. Johnny selected a torpedo tube on the dreadnought's starboard side and programmed a weapon to take it out.

He fired.

The weapon streaked from *SC-1*'s nose and churned toward the Russian vessel. I tracked it through the canopy as it plowed into the hull and a white flare blossomed. Thousands of liters of water instantly vaporized and shot upward in a flowering mass of bubbles. Surrounding water smashed back into the cavity and a secondary impact pounded the hull. It punched into the torpedo room, tearing and warping the hull inward. Water flooded into the dreadnought—filling the compartment instantly and converting crew within to bloody mush.

But it was just one tiny compartment and wouldn't have an impact on the overall buoyancy of the ship.

Meg and Cliff had been correct—no matter how many compartments along the hull of the dreadnought we flooded, it would still retain an overall positive buoyancy due to the inner watertight hatches.

There was also the fact that the dreadnought might be able to stay neutrally buoyant through sheer velocity and control surfaces keeping the ship angling *upward*. However, one look at the thruster pods indicated that this was not going to be an issue. The *Swords* had destroyed them. Impacts had twisted and warped the blades and there were bubbles streaming from the pod structures; fires raged within the battery compartments.

Weapons continued to strike multiple torpedo rooms, and one by one the launchers fell silent.

The dreadnought was no longer releasing countermeasures to distract weapons.

Their last-ditch effort had been to run, and we had stopped them.

I leaned back, exhaled, and stared for long minutes at the gargantuan ship before us. It was the largest vessel I'd ever seen. The fact that it was a submarine made it even more astonishing. Scars and holes pockmarked the hull, but they were pinpricks against the skin of that giant.

It still wasn't over yet.

We needed to drag her *back* to the trench, which was why I'd sent the message to the larger warsubs, asking them to follow and attach grapples to this beast.

I signaled the dreadnought.

Johnny stared at me for an instant before he turned back to the sonar to watch for incoming danger. "What are you doing, Mac?"

I checked my watch. "Buying us some time."

An instant later the comm lit. Captain Ventinov was on the display, scowling at me. He looked disheveled and injured; his right eye was swollen and there was a cut on his forehead.

"McClusky!" he raged. "How dare you! I'm going to make sure our forces target your city and turn it to rubble!"

My insides tightened at that. "Your plan failed, Ventinov."

"You will not be able to sink this ship. We're a new force in the oceans. We've made ourselves heard, and will continue to do so. The States, the Chinese, Blue Downs. Trieste is next. The world is trembling at our power."

"You attacked nations who are stronger than you. Even Trieste is more dangerous than the Russian Submarine Fleet. You underestimated the ocean powers. You thought *Dragon* was the ultimate weapon. It's big, I'll give you that, but it's vulnerable. Its design is a failure. You rushed things when you should have taken your time."

"What does that mean?"

"Russia isn't ready to play with the big boys, Ventinov."

He clenched his teeth. Behind him I could see the bridge of the ship. It was in ruins. Debris cluttered the deck and a haze of smoke hung over the controllers. I cut the feed for an instant and said to Johnny, "Take us to a hundred meters off her bow, depth nine hundred."

He nodded, and I reactivated the feed. Ventinov was in the middle of a rant. "— and you've stolen resources that belong to the Motherland. You flaunt your arrogance and pretend to be a shark when in fact you're a minnow."

"Your metaphor doesn't make sense. I want the people of the oceans to work together, but to avoid the land nations from taking advantage of us. We're not their slaves. We're not your slaves."

"You're weak and we will always be in control."

I shook my head. "You stormed into the seas and the seas struck back."

He snorted. "*You?* You think *you* defeated *me?* Pathetic."

"You used a fission power plant for your SCAV drive. It failed and melted down. And now you're in trouble."

His face grew harder. His tone was volcanic. "We have backups for all our systems! And now you're going to pay!"

He cut the signal.

Johnny said, "What did he mean by that, I wonder?"

"Who knows." I shook my head and checked my watch again. We still needed more time.

Johnny was staring at his controls. He pressed his headset closer to his ears and furrowed his brow. "I'm hearing something from the dreadnought."

"Implosions from within perhaps?" Water was currently flooding outer compartments.

"No. It's mechanical. Hydraulics."

I considered what Ventinov had just claimed. *We have backups for all our systems.* "Piette," I said into the mic. "Are you nearby?"

"Five hundred meters off its stern," came the prompt reply.

"Can you get under her? See what's causing this noise?"

"Give me a minute."

On our sonar, I watched as the white point of light moved toward *Dragon* before disappearing under her. I knew the mayor would be looking up through the canopy, peering at its underbody.

His voice came to me, clipped and urgent. "Another set of hatches just opened, Mac! Near the SCAV intakes that we destroyed. They look the same."

I swore. They had a backup fission reactor, and now they also had a backup set of intakes. He hadn't been lying.

And then Johnny blurted, "Mac! She's going back into SCAV drive! The exhaust is ramping up!"

As he said it, a stream of bubbles erupted from the exhaust port at the stern of the ship. The fission reactor was flash-boiling seawater and funneling the steam aftward to provide thrust.

This ship was bound for Trieste, and Ventinov was not going to give up.

This was far from over, after all.

Dragon was beginning to power away.

—••—

I STARED AT THE DREADNOUGHT'S EXPANSIVE bridge viewport. We had to take out this ship, once and for all.

"Johnny," I said. "Prepare a SCAV torpedo. IMPACT detonation. Target its canopy."

He clenched his teeth as he pushed the buttons. "Ready."

"Fire!"

The missile streaked out from *SC-1*'s bow and shot toward the dreadnought's bridge. The warsub was moving forward, on a course underneath us, and we were motionless and angled downward. The stream of bubbles traced the path of the missile as it lanced out.

It struck the clear canopy over the bridge and flared white.

The vaporized water churned upward as more seawater crushed into the void just above the dreadnought's command and control center.

The canopy cracked like brittle glass.

Water pounded into the sixty-meter long chamber, crushing everything and everyone within. Bubbles *exploded outward*. Debris and bodies drifted from the broken viewport as the ship continued to thrust away.

Johnny swore. "Do you think he made it out?"

An image of the escape tunnel we'd used only hours earlier came to me. He might have used it, but it didn't matter. The ship was powering away, still bound for the Americas and Trieste.

I had to do something.

I slammed the acceleration controls forward and the SCAV drive kicked into gear. The roar behind us built as *SC-1*'s fusion reactor began generating steam, forcing us through the water.

The dreadnought was trailing debris as it moved. It was shuddering, and the sonar was glowing white from all the noise. The ship was hardly streamlined anymore. There were punctures all over it. The canopy was gone and the bridge now open to the ocean at a depth of a thousand meters. All her controllers were dead, though I realized they most likely had a backup bridge as well.

Bubbles rose from multiple impact sites as the dreadnought lurched through the water.

Soon our velocity was great enough to overtake the Russian warsub. I brought us to the port side and began to move closer to its bow.

"Uh, Mac," Cliff muttered from over my shoulder. "What are you doing?"

"We have to get her back to deep water." The seafloor below had a depth of four kilometers—not enough for what we needed. "This ship just won't die. We have to finish her off." I was clenching my teeth as I piloted *SCAV-1* closer to the Russian hull. On the other side of the canopy, just beside Johnny, the warsub was only meters away now.

Still I brought us closer.

Three meters.

Two.

One.

Johnny was staring at it, right next to him. "Careful, Mac . . ."

"Don't worry," I muttered.

"Just what are you doing?"

SC-1 shuddered as our hull collided with the dreadnought. The supercavitating bubbles were overlapping and the resulting turbulence hit hard. I gripped the yoke tightly and swallowed.

I turned it to the starboard. Slowly.

Ever so slowly . . .

The sound of grinding steel screeched through the seacar. It pierced the control cabin and sent shivers down my spine.

Kat would be very, very angry with me.

I kept turning and hit the accelerator lever with my left hand. The growl from our engineering compartment rose to a howl.

Still I turned. The foot pedals directed us to the port or starboard, and I had the starboard one jammed down.

"Keep an eye on our bearing, Johnny," I grunted.

"You think we can turn her?"

"I don't think anybody's in control of her right now. Their SCAV drive is on but no one's at the controls."

We had obliterated the bridge, flooding it.

This was our only chance to change its course.

Chapter
Thirty-Nine

"It's working!" Johnny cried. "We're at ninety-nine degrees and still moving." He paused for a moment and then, "One hundred and five! One fifteen! One twenty!"

We were turning quickly now, and I backed off the accelerator slightly. The grinding from the bow continued and it sent shocks down my spine with each angry screech. I had to be careful not to damage our seacar; we needed to stay in this fight.

Finally, we were at a bearing of 270 and I pulled back on the yoke. It bucked in my hand and we bounced in the pilot chairs. "Hold on back there, everybody!" I cried. The turbulence of the supercavitating dreadnought was tossing us in its bubble, and I veered away.

I lowered speed until it matched *Dragon*'s and checked the display. One hundred and twenty kph.

I sent out a call to all nearby ships. "We'll be back to the trench in an hour. At that point we're going to finish this beast off."

Unless they had something else up their sleeves, that is.

—••—

I LEANED BACK AND CHECKED THE scope. The dreadnought was moving due west now, and there was no communication of any sort coming from the ship. It was shuddering angrily as it tore through the water; the turbulence it gave off was violent. It must be a very rough ride on board, I thought. It was probably shaking the crew to bits. Debris continued to fall from her, emerging from the puncture wounds and plummeting through the supercavitation bubble and down into the depths.

We were unconsciously holding our collective breaths as the minutes ticked by.

I stared at the map as the hour counted down.

Still no word from the dreadnought . . .

And then—

And then we were there.

We had a force of over fifty *Swords* and there were still numerous warsubs, most of them damaged but still seaworthy, and I immediately barked an order to fire on the SCAV intake pipes.

Five minutes later we'd scored numerous hits with SCAV torpedoes and the exhaust ceased abruptly, the surrounding bubble detached from the warsub, broke into numerous tiny mushrooms of air, and soared upward to the surface.

I stared at the crippled vessel, picking the best location to aim—

When on the outside of the hull, from stern to bow, numerous hatches opened.

I narrowed my eyes at that. "What the hell? More torpedoes?"

Simultaneously, the sonar began to blare. Smaller one-man subs began to stream from the warsub.

Fighters.

I swore. "Sink those ships!" I cried. Go to SCAV! Dive deep if necessary— don't let them get close!"

It was a last-ditch attempt to avoid the inevitable. Then my comm screeched to life. As I ramped up the SCAV drive and avoided three torpedoes on our tail, I shot my gaze toward the screen.

It was Ventinov.

———••———

"I'M NOT GOING DOWN!" HE SCREAMED. His face was red and there were streaks of blood across his chest and shoulders. There were veins popping on his temples.

"You've lost," I said in a soft tone. "You don't have the technology to defeat us. We can dive deeper than your ships. Your little fighters don't even have the SCAV drive. It's time to accept your fate, Ventinov."

He glared at me in silence. Behind him, on some sort of secondary bridge, people were yelling commands at one another. There were consoles along the bulkheads, sonar screens and fire control stations.

"Russia will never give up, McClusky."

"I'm not asking you to. It's too late for that. You've lost."

"Trieste is not safe. You've made an enemy today." He bared his teeth. "Trust me in this."

"You had your own agenda. *Everyone* was your enemy. We only responded."

They had no chance against Triestrian technology.

Behind me, Benning was silent as he stared at the sonar display. He watched the *Swords* diving below five kilometers to avoid torpedoes, and then ascend rapidly to unleash SCAV torpedoes toward the tiny targets.

One by one they scored hits and Russian vessels lost control, took on water and spiraled downward.

Implosion waited for them in the dark depths of the Kermadec Trench.

I wondered what was going through his mind.

It was impossible to hide our superiority from him.

The USSF now knew about our seacars. We had an advantage over them, and this would not make them happy.

He snapped a glance at me and then turned back to the display. "You've kept some secrets from us too, I see," he muttered.

"A few," I said after a moment. "With threats in the oceans, however, I believe in being prepared."

He nodded. "It's a good strategy to take," he said finally. He stared at the scene for a few more minutes as more of the Russian fighters sustained fatal impacts and plummeted downward. "I suppose I should thank you now, Mac."

"For what?"

"For saving my life. And . . ." He hesitated. "For not killing me. You had good reason to."

I shrugged. "My dad had been prepared. And like you said . . . if you hadn't done it . . ." I couldn't finish. A memory of Dad came to me at that point.

He'd walked away from me the night before his death. He hadn't even turned back.

He'd just . . . *left.*

But he'd had a plan. And it had worked.

I felt the power of *SC-1* in my hands. Its strength vibrated the yoke as we soared through the water, avoiding torpedoes and sinking Russian fighters.

It made me smile.

"What's so funny?" Benning asked with a frown.

"Just thinking about my dad, actually."

"Ah." He winced and turned away. He knew it would always be a wedge between us. I just hoped my goodwill wouldn't translate into a negative for Trieste. I didn't want to regret saving him.

Finally, there were no more fighters to sink and the dreadnought hung in the water before us, motionless. It was listing more than ever now. Bubbles continued to stream upward.

It had been a tough fight. Sabotaging the reactor, causing the meltdown, the fight on the bridge . . .

But we weren't yet finished.

I keyed the comm. "Listen up, all remaining warsubs. Target the top of that beast, near the stern. Just forward of the vertical stabilizer. Fire everything you've got."

The others clustered behind the pilot chairs, watching through the canopy as torpedo after torpedo slammed into the dreadnought's hull. The warsub was shuddering with each blast. *SC-1* shook violently.

The comm lit and Ventinov appeared once again. He was holding onto a console and screaming orders at his crew. Many of them were sitting silently, still, as they stared at their screens.

They'd accepted the reality of the situation.

The futility.

Each torpedo that detonated caused secondary implosion impacts as water flooded into the voids caused by energy release. Compression waves pounded *Dragon* and slammed into the hull at the top of the vessel.

Containment compartments prevented increased flooding from occurring, until finally a crucial bulkhead gave way and water flooded into yet another sealed compartment.

Sealed in name only, however, for the corium had melted close to the outer hull after we'd inverted the ship, and had burned through a nearby bulkhead.

The uranium slag had made it to within three decks of the outer hull.

And the last barrier between the cavity and the open ocean gave way.

There was a massive surge of water into the puncture on the outer hull. Debris spiraled around it as a thousand meters of water pressure shoved into the dreadnought.

It flooded twenty-four decks in only a second. The force *rammed* into the beast and other compartments instantly gave way.

The hull on decks three, four, and five bulged outward before rupturing and spewing titanium-alloy away from *Dragon*, bits of the hull shattering into shrapnel and bursting like a display of metallic fireworks.

The dreadnought shuddered, and the rear sank while the bow pointed up toward the surface.

On the comm, Ventinov fell heavily to the deck, then grabbed a console and held on for dear life as the crew dangled out above a long drop toward the rear of the backup bridge.

His ship was vertical.

Bodies started to fall.

I stared at *Dragon*'s final death throws. Explosions lit the inside now, their blasts reverberating the water and shaking *SC-1*.

More screams burst from the comm, and then cut out.

Johnny whispered, "She's imploding, Mac."

The ship was sinking now, leaving a long trail of bubbles, oil, debris, and bodies.

I checked the depth gauge.

It would fall for nine kilometers before hitting the bottom.

—••—

WE WATCHED THE SHIP; NONE OF us spoke. Implosions echoed around us as containment hatches gave way, one after another, on the gigantic warsub.

Eventually it disappeared from our sonar entirely, and we sat back and breathed a collective sigh of relief. I studied the display and saw only ships from our fleet. I turned to Lazlow. "Where did the Russian warsubs go? The *Vostoks?*"

He frowned. "They disappeared hours ago. They were taking heavy damage and fled."

"Which way did they go, Manesh?"

"East."

I swore and slammed the acceleration lever on my left to full. Making our depth two hundred meters, I began to power away from the Trench toward the Americas. I keyed the comm as the others stared at me. "Attention all *Sword* pilots. Set course for the Gulf of Mexico immediately. This isn't over yet.

"They're on their way to Trieste—to destroy her."

Chapter Forty

WE MAXED OUT THE SCAV DRIVE on the way back to the Americas. Every remaining *Sword* came with us, churning the ocean through our fusion reactors at 450 kilometers per hour, and we made quite a scene as we blew past merchant vessels and naval ships and cartography boats and civilian seacars.

It was essentially the Triestrian Navy on display, in all its glory—something that few even knew existed. And its technology was superior to all others in the world's oceans.

We didn't slow for anything; nor were we concerned with people hearing our collective noise as we flash-boiled seawater to steam.

We had announced our presence in a very clear and dominating fashion, though we hadn't calculated it that way. We all feared what we'd find when we returned.

Trieste was still there, however. Peaceful and serene, thirty meters down. The sun glittering through the blue water like light through diamonds. Bubbles rose to the surface languidly, kelp swayed silently in the currents, and seacars and scuba divers moved about without any concerns in the world.

But the threat was coming, I knew.

It had been an 11,500-kilometer journey to Central America, through

Panama at a slow forty kph, then around Cuba to the west and to Trieste. Traveling at SCAV drive had gotten us home in an incredible thirty-five hours.

We docked *SC-1* and sprinted to the central module. I sent Benning to see the doctor and he nodded in reluctant agreement. He was pale and weak. We'd stopped the bleeding and had given him intravenous fluids, but he needed proper attention, and probably some sleep. None of us had slept in days. I hadn't had a good sleep in months, for that matter.

Kristen Canvel was at City Systems Control and stared at me in shock when I burst into the chamber. I was disheveled with dark circles under my eyes. My Russian clothing didn't help matters. There were still blood splatters on it.

I was cradling my left arm slightly. I had wondered over the past day whether in fact the tsunami plow had fractured it while we'd been in the ladderwell aboard *Dragon*.

"Mac!" Kristen cried out. The other controllers rose from their stations and stared at us in openmouthed wonder. "You're back! What happened?"

I glanced at the rest of my team and realized that we looked like quite the motley bunch. We hadn't even told anyone where we were going; I'd left my assistants in charge with instructions to keep the city running, and had been gone for eight days.

I cleared my throat and began speaking.

I filled them in on the battle over the Kermadec Trench, about the Russian dreadnought—their eyes widened at that—and our belief that a Russian fleet would be arriving soon to destroy the city.

Waves of concern swept over them. I set up an immediate team of people to keep a close eye on the sonar screens for incoming warsubs, stationed a controller at the defense console, though Renée would take over eventually—for she had trained on it and knew exactly how to deploy our countermeasures and launch weapons—and called Lancombe to find out what he'd managed to do while we'd been gone.

In my office later, he listened to my story with a shocked expression. He couldn't believe what we'd been through.

"The runaway meltdown to destroy the dreadnought? It worked?" he asked.

"It was quite effective. Melted decks straight through, damaged watertight integrity. In the end we had to punch more holes in the hull to compromise compartments, but once we did it . . ." I trailed off.

He swore.

"Lau died."

"You're lucky you didn't lose more."

"Probably." Still, I was going to have to let Sheng City know what had happened.

"And now you're expecting a Russian fleet?"

"Soon. We need to be ready for it."

He exhaled. "We're as ready as we're ever going to be. Launchers are set. Countermeasures are out there—" he gestured to the oceans surrounding the city "— concealed and armed."

"I think our next step is to carve a bunker for people."

He nodded. "After what happened at Blue Downs."

The fact that we couldn't just swim to the surface was a major concern for us. We were prisoners in a saturation environment.

I leaned back in my chair and closed my eyes. When the attack came, I hoped we were truly prepared. *Devastator* was in the Pacific, days away still, but I didn't want to rely on the USSF for help. I didn't mind growing closer to them economically, and I didn't mind forging a new bond with Admiral Benning, especially after what we'd just been through, but when it came to Trieste, I didn't want the USSF in my thoughts.

If we were going to be truly independent, we'd have to be able to defend ourselves.

Lancombe said, "It must have been quite an adventure."

I snorted. "I've never been through anything like it. I've infiltrated cities before, but this was . . ." I didn't know exactly how to describe it. "They could have captured and killed us at any time. And the fission meltdown was terrifying, to be honest. I think we all took a big radiation hit."

He frowned. "How'd you get the uranium? It's a controlled mineral."

"We made some." I said it as a matter-of-fact, and he just stared at me, not understanding. "I'll fill you in later when—"

My comm buzzed and Kristen said, "Mac, call coming in from Admiral

Benning. Urgent."

Odd, I thought. He was down in the clinic. "Go ahead, Admiral."

His voice floated to me, and he sounded more assured and confident than he had in hours. The doctor's treatments were obviously working. "I just received a call from *Devastator*. The remaining fleet intercepted the *Vostok* Class vessels that took part in the battle over the Kermadec. Sunk them all."

Those Russian warsubs had departed early, bound for Trieste. They'd only had conventional drives, however, so they would have taken days to arrive. We had searched for them on the way back, but the collective fifty SCAV drives made so much noise it had been impossible to locate them, and we'd wanted to return as soon as possible in case there were other Russian warsubs in the Atlantic that might also pose a danger.

"Thanks for the news," I said. "But I still—"

Kristen's voice broke into the conversation. "Mac! Sonar alarm just went off! Thirty warsubs approaching around Florida!"

I rose to my feet. Before me, Richard's face paled. "Country of origin?" I asked.

"Russia," she said. "They're Russian warsubs, and they're coming."

———••———

I ᴀᴄᴛɪᴠᴀᴛᴇᴅ ᴛʜᴇ ᴄɪᴛʏ-ᴡɪᴅᴇ ᴇᴍᴇʀɢᴇɴᴄʏ alarm and announced the incoming danger. Renée Féroce arrived in City Control, looking refreshed after a shower and a change of clothes. The bruises were still on her face, but she flashed me a tight grin as she burst into the cabin and marched straight for the defense station.

"Time to see it in action," I said to her. Then I signaled Cliff down in security. "We have a major problem here, Chief. Be prepared for possible intruders."

"I've already posted guards."

"We're going to need the *Swords*."

"They're rearmed and ready to go. I had them dock in the storage module when they returned."

I released a sigh of relief. "I can always count on you, Cliff."

"Yes, Boss."

It made me smile. I sent out another city-wide page, calling all pilots to the storage module. Our French visitors from Cousteau were still in the city, whom I had likely just woken up.

But this wasn't over yet.

—••—

Soon all fifty armed seacars were in a defensive blockade southeast of Trieste. I had elected to stay in City Control, but Johnny was out in *SC-1* and in charge of coordinating their efforts.

Meg arrived and stood by my side as we watched events unfold.

The Russians continued to advance. There were the newer variant of the Vostok Class warsub, but their incoming force also included *Lenin*, *Devil*, *Revolution*, and *Gagarin* Classes, and there were even three *Kirov* Class vessels among them. Thirty warsubs in all. It was not a huge fleet, and it made me wonder.

I nodded at Kristen and she activated our comm. "Attention, incoming Russian warsubs," I said. "You are approaching Triestrian waters. What are your intentions?"

A second later, an accented voice replied, "We didn't start this, but we're here to finish it. You sunk our vessels in the Pacific Ocean, no? You're Truman McClusky of Trieste?"

"That's me. And yes, I blew your ships out of the water and sunk the pride of your fleet."

Lancombe, beside me, whispered, "Easy, Mac. Don't provoke him."

I ignored him. "I infiltrated *Drakon* and sank her. You'll be next if you continue. This is the first and only warning I'll give."

"I'm acting on orders, McClusky. And your warnings don't matter." He clicked off.

I turned to Lancombe and grimaced. "They don't know what they're getting into here."

"Perhaps a show of force? Warn them off that way?"

"Good idea."

The Russians were an escalating presence in the oceans. They had a belief that they were still this monumental power from the Twentieth Century.

It was time to show them the truth.

I called Johnny. "Accelerate to SCAV drive and cut right through them. Show them what we've got." Then I glanced at Renée, who was sitting at the Trieste defense console. "Prepare SCAV torpedoes, Renée. What's the largest warsub out there right now?"

She studied the targeting display before her, which was an echo of the main sonars in City Control. "The *Kirov* in the lead."

"Prepare a missile."

"Got it," she said in a curt tone.

I gritted my teeth.

Here we go.

———••———

THE *SWORDS* AND *SC-1* POWERED UP their fusion reactors, and within seconds, plumes of steam were erupting from the exhaust ports of our fast and agile seacars. Johnny led the mass of vessels as they sliced through the formation of advancing Russian warsubs. Their wakes tossed the larger warsubs behind them as our vessels circled for another pass.

At our sonar station, Jaden Kahn yelled, "I hear torpedo hatches opening!"

"Which subs?"

She hesitated. "*All* of them!"

I groaned. If just one torpedo got through, it would mean an end to possibly tens of thousands of civilians, if not all of Trieste. "Get ready on countermeasures," I muttered.

Renée nodded.

The Russians continued to advance. They ignored our fish farms, for they were simply harmless streams of bubbles rising to the surface, holding stocks of fish within.

Or so they thought.

The farthest one out from Trieste was fifteen hundred meters.

I stared at the sonar station, waiting for their next move. No doubt they were watching their own displays, openmouthed in wonder at the sheer speed of our seacars. They could not compete with them in battle.

But if they were intent on destroying Trieste, our *Swords* might not dissuade them.

A different alarm blared from the sonar console.

Torpedo in the water.

"Target that vessel!" I roared. It had come from the *Kirov* that Renée had indicated. "Take it out!"

They had fired a single torpedo at us, on a direct course for the Commerce Module and City Control.

I watched the red line on the sonar, my guts quivering. Johnny gave the order and ten *Swords* fired SCAV missiles simultaneously. They accelerated to 1,000 kph and lanced toward the *Kirov* from multiple directions. Renée also fired one; it appeared seemingly from nowhere, *exploding* out from a wall of bubbles and angling straight for the warsub.

The Russian vessel started blowing ballast and increased to flank speed, but it was no use.

Her max speed was seventy-three kph. It was incredibly fast by conventional standards, but nothing compared to SCAV technology.

"Countermeasures, Renée!" I said. She hit the button and from a nearby disguised position, a churning device launched, moved a hundred meters away and hovered five meters off the seafloor.

My eyes narrowed.

Beside me, Meg swore.

Then I groaned.

Richard glanced at me but said nothing.

The other Russian subs were turning. None of them had fired a shot.

The first SCAV torpedoes collided with the *Kirov* almost all at the same moment. The explosion was absolutely tremendous. The shock wave shook the ocean around it and every structure at Trieste trembled. The deck vibrated at my feet.

I studied the sonar, guts wrenched in fear.

The torpedo was still coming.

It veered slightly toward the countermeasures but didn't detonate. It soared through them, adjusted course, and continued toward Trieste.

I opened my mouth to snap an order at Renée—

But I didn't have to. She had already launched more countermeasures from locations closer to the city.

Even if they caused a detonation, it was close. It might cause some damage.

The torpedo veered toward the new targets—

And exploded.

A ball of energy and hot bubbles flowered in a massive expanding ball of fury. The ocean crashed back in and compression waves flooded outward.

It was as if a lightning bolt had hit the city.

The *CRACK* of the detonation pierced the travel tubs and modules and everywhere people pressed their hands to their ears and crouched involuntarily, half expecting a crush of water to spill in and kill them all.

I looked around unconsciously, expecting it myself.

But—

Nothing.

No damage reports were coming in.

I sighed. "Good job, Renée. Get ready for more though."

On the sonar, there were brilliant white flashes lighting the scope where the *Kirov* had been moments earlier. One after another, more SCAV torpedoes soared in, instantly replaced by angry detonations.

I watched the display, eyes shifting from warsub to warsub, waiting for more launches.

There were none, and I clenched my fists in realization.

"Mac!" Jaden cried. "They're continuing to veer off! Torpedo hatches closing!"

Richard swore. "You and I are thinking the same thing."

"Yes." They'd been testing our defenses. They'd probed, looking to see how strong we were, and we'd fired a torpedo, launched two sets of countermeasures, and shown our *Sword*'s capabilities.

They had sacrificed one warsub to learn our secrets—the defenses we'd built—and had likely recorded the entire incident.

Filed it away for future use.

Perhaps for the next attack, likely to happen at some point when they were more prepared.

But at least we had saved Trieste.

For now, anyway.

—••—

Meg visibly deflated and the hint of a smile crossed her features. She hugged me and someone in the chamber cheered. Then there were more cries and soon people were throwing their arms in the air and yelling in joy. Lancombe grinned and said over the din, "Looks like it worked, at least. Trieste is far safer than it was a few months ago."

I stared at the map of the Gulf and Caribbean on the bulkhead, at the three undersea cities there, at the points of light representing all sea traffic in the area—surface as well as submarine—and a feeling of pride surged through me.

I had protected the city and we were prospering.

Drakon was gone.

The USSF had suffered enormously, but we had forged a potential relationship that hopefully would continue, despite our quest for independence.

We'd built the foundation for a strong future for our city, and despite the immense dangers of undersea life, we'd proven that we could succeed.

For the time being, at least, our future was bright.

Interlude:
In Living Module C,
Trieste City

Location: Trieste City, Module C
                  In the Gulf of Mexico
                  Thirty Kilometers West of Florida

Depth: 30 meters
Time: 1523 hours
Date: 20 June 2030

ADMIRAL TAURUS T. BENNING SAT ON the bunk in the cramped living compartment. The city administration had arranged the berth for him while waiting for his command ship to return from the battle. He was recovering from the mission to *Drakon*, nursing a gunshot wound in his leg and getting much needed sleep, but he was basking in the success of the journey. He knew that McClusky had manipulated him into going, but he'd allowed it to happen. He could indeed use a success to help him pursue a rise beyond the admiralty, even into the ranks of politics not just in the USSF, but perhaps into the United States government.

Maybe even to the White House.

Over the past day, Benning had been in contact with multiple people in the USSF as well as the commanders of *Devastator*. The warsub had taken heavy damage as well as casualties, but it was limping back slowly. It should return in another four days. At that point, they would have to figure out where to make repairs. The *Drakon*'s attack weeks earlier had devastated Norfolk's repair berths.

Benning had been debating with himself over his next conversation, but he knew it had to be done. Despite the closer ties with McClusky and Trieste, he had to put the USSF first. The Russians had degraded USSF power substantially, and they had to start looking to the future. To rebuild their power, and make the USSF more dominant in the oceans.

He signalled USSF command at the Pentagon and sat back, waiting for the call to connect.

A minute later, he'd successfully bypassed multiple aides and assistants, and finally the overall Commander of the USSF was on the screen.

She was a five-star Admiral, the only *Fleet Admiral* in the United States, and a member of the President's Joint Chiefs of Staff. Her name was Lucille Quintana. The President of the United States was the only person with more power over the direction of the US military and its colonization efforts in the oceans.

She was seated in a large wood-adorned office in the Pentagon. There were aides behind her, conducting work and seeing to other matters.

She stared at Benning with an intensity he had seldom experienced. She was in her fifties and had gray-streaked brown hair pulled back into a tight ponytail. She looked smart in her form-fitting blue uniform, and the rank insignia and stars on her shoulders were as clear as day.

Benning swallowed. Despite his thirty-plus years in the USSF, and his powerful and respected reputation, she worried him. She had immense pull and stature in the fleet.

"I've read your report," she said in a clipped tone. "Well done, Admiral."

"Thank you, ma'am."

"It was bold, I'll say that. You refused to use nukes on it though. Why?"

He frowned and hesitated.

She continued before he could answer. "You could have saved many USSF ships."

"I knew that using a nuke would inflame an already intense situation. Possibly escalate into war on the surface." A part of him realized that he was parroting what McClusky had said, but he thrust the thought aside.

She stared at him in a painful silence before finally offering a tight nod. "You might be right. Our ambassador to Russia is dealing with this now. It will give us some political power in the upcoming treaty negotiations." She was referring to the conflict in the Iron Plains. The nations in the area were attempting to divide the region between China and the States, and now Russia wanted a piece of it too. The US would attempt to prevent that at all costs.

"They did use nukes in their attacks," she continued, "although they were tactical and small. We are . . . *pretending* not to know about them. We've avoided discussing that fact. For now."

"Really," Benning muttered.

"They're claiming an independent splinter group operated *Dragon*. They also claim to have no idea about what happened to Captain Heller and the hundred warsubs he had under his control in the Mid-Atlantic Ridge. Total bullshit of course. Not only that, but satellite reconnaissance has identified three more *Dreadnought* Class ships under construction."

Benning's guts twisted at that. His face paled.

"Yes," Quintana said. "They are pressing, and we will have to deal with them again. There is also a rumor that there were survivors from *Dragon*. As the ship sank, sonar may have detected escape pods."

He swore. He recalled that *SC-1* had left the scene quickly to return to Trieste. "But our fleet would have destroyed them."

"Unless sonar operators mistook the pods for wreckage. The ship was shedding debris as it plummeted to the bottom of the trench. Some of the 'debris' may have in fact been watertight." She shrugged. "It's a theory with no proof at this point."

Benning took a minute to process that. Then, "And how are the next generation of USSF warsubs progressing?"

She offered a tight smile. "They'll put to sea soon."

Benning shifted in his chair. "While on the mission, Admiral, I saw something . . . incredible. Unbelievable, even."

She frowned. "Proceed."

"The Triestrian forces are stronger than we thought possible. Their small vessels can travel 460 kilometers per hour underwater. We first saw these last year. They have SCAV torpedoes as well. Those can make upward of a thousand kph."

"What's unique about these vessels, since we already knew about them?"

"These can dive five kilometers. Maybe even deeper."

Her face went blank. "Are you sure?"

"I watched their sonar myself. During the battle. They have a new technology . . . something which allows them to make that depth." He shook his head. "I'll keep digging here. I'll find out."

She sighed. "Good. Our new classes of vessels will be ready in a few weeks. We've retooled our *Hunter-Killers*. They now all have the SCAV drive." She was referring to the *Houston* Class warsubs. There were over seventy of them in the fleet. "We also have outfitted a few *Cyclones*, *Typhoons*, and even a couple *Tridents*."

"They all have the SCAV drive now? Fusion reactors?"

She nodded. "Their top speed surpasses Triestrian models. Close to 500 kilometers per hour. With SCAV torpedoes." She glanced at her office ceiling. "No one will be able to stand against us. In total we have 145 warsubs outfitted and ready to go, not including the rest of our conventional fleet. And we'll continue refurbishing subs, getting them all upgraded. The supercavitating drive is the future, Benning. And we're not going to let it pass us by."

Benning swore. He had been debating whether to inform his superiors about the Triestrian ships, but now he was happy that he had done so. He wanted to be on the dominant side of the upcoming struggle.

"What of USSF HQ?" he asked. "Norfolk?"

She pursed her lips. "We've taken your proposal under advisement. The president likes the notion."

"Seascape is a failing city anyway. Tourism is down. It'll make a perfect HQ for us. We'll be close to Ballard and Trieste to keep our eyes on them."

"Good." Quintana reached out to terminate the call. "Keep up the strong work, Benning. Make sure those undersea colonies know the USSF is in control for now, as well as in the future. You'll be my eyes and ears at Trieste and Ballard."

Admiral Benning stared at the screen long after the call had ended. He felt the thrill of power surge through him. He clenched his teeth. Trieste had built a navy under Heller's watch. They were powerful now.

They were a true *force* in the oceans.

There was no way he was going to let it continue.

Epilogue:
Trieste

Epilogue

Two days had passed following the Russian's fleeting attempt at probing our defenses. I had no doubt that more would come of it, but for now, at least, we felt safe. I was in my office, staring at the pile of papers on the corner of my desk that had grown even larger since I'd originally put them aside. I wasn't looking forward to getting back to those administrative duties, but as mayor I had to do the job expected of me.

Before that, however, there were a number of other matters I had to take care of.

With trepidation, I contacted Sheng City and requested their leadership. We had already notified them of Agent Lau's death, but this was an important political matter. They had risked everything and thrown in their support with us, and I needed to thank them directly.

Within minutes, the city's highest-raking official—or *elder*—appeared. He smiled warmly. We couldn't say much over an open comm about our plans, but I arranged to visit within a few weeks, purportedly for a vacation but I knew it would be far more important than that.

It was hard to maintain my smile, for these were the very people who had captured and tortured me for four months before I'd rejoined Trieste City Intelligence, but we were beyond that now, and looking toward a joint future.

I said, "I wanted to commend you on Agent Lau. He performed

admirably. Although we had our difficulties last year, he put his issues aside for the good of Sheng City. If it hadn't been for him, the mission to sink the Russian dreadnought may not have succeeded. He was pivotal. He opened the watertight hatches and locked the Russians out of the controls. Saved our lives."

The elder smiled again. "We appreciate that."

"I will make sure to bring one of our new seacars when I visit," I said.

"Please do."

I hesitated. "Will there be representatives of the other cities there when I arrive?" There were five other Chinese undersea cities, and they hadn't yet joined our movement.

"We will try."

It was the best I could hope for. "Unfortunately, Lau's body is currently at the bottom of the Kermadec Trench."

The other nodded solemnly. "We'll notify his family."

I knew that his grandparents had played an important role in settling Lau Tsi City. I offered a sympathetic smile. "Good day to you, Elder. I'll see you soon."

I ended the call and stared at the pile of papers on my desk. Finally, with a growl, I reached out to grab them and start work again as Mayor of Trieste.

———••———

MAYOR PIETTE WAS PLANNING ON RETURNING to Cousteau City later in the day. He had been an enormous help and had joined our movement with an eagerness that would have been nice to see among the Chinese cities, but I understood their worries. The CSF was powerful, and their rule was dictatorial. It was a different society in China than in France. For centuries France had praised independence and liberty and freedom. It was a part of the fabric of their society.

I met Piette in the docking module. His team of forty who had rescued Jackson Train at The Ridge and joined us in the Battle at the Kermadec had already departed. Piette was taking a *Sword* back with him, personally piloting it. This vessel was fully operational, complete with Lazlow's Acoustic

Pulse Drive, which I had also promised the French cities of Conshelf Alpha and Conshelf Beta.

We shook hands warmly, and his smile was broad. "Thanks for bringing some excitement back into my life," he said.

"Being a mayor can be boring? Is that what you're saying?"

"If that's all you are, then yes. But you have shown me a more exciting way, Mac."

We embraced, and I watched him climb into the *Sword*.

"Take care of Renée," he said as he closed the hatch above him. "She likes you, I think."

I watched the seacar as its tanks flooded and it powered from the module.

I didn't quite know how to respond to that.

— •• —

IRENA ROSTILOV WAS ALSO THERE, PREPARING to journey back to Ballard City. I had decided to see her off as well. She'd been a necessary—*and crucial*—member of the team to infiltrate the warsub and had helped my own nuclear engineers to manufacture the uranium.

She grinned at me as we shook hands. "I guess I'm not quite field material, Mac."

"What are you talking about? You were incredible."

"In the reactor room, maybe. But not outside of it."

"I needed you for the uranium. You knew how to manufacture it. You also knew more about fission reactors than anyone else."

"I guess I enjoy antiques."

It made me smile. "You also speak and read Russian."

"Not well. I might have weighed the rest of you down."

I waved the notion aside. "If you ever want to come live at Trieste, become part of TCI, just say the word."

She smiled again. "Thanks, Mac."

"Give my regards to Mayor Winton."

"I will."

She boarded a commercial transport bound for Ballard, and departed a minute later.

—••—

J<small>ACKSON</small> T<small>RAIN WAS AT A CAFÉ</small> in the Commerce Module. He was sitting along the railing in the atrium, enjoying a drink and staring out at the wide expanse before him, lit from above by sunlight streaming through the skylight. As I approached, I noticed him close his eyes and turn his face to the sun. There was a hint of a smile on his face.

"Enjoying home?" I asked as I pulled up a chair. "It can't be the kelp beer making you smile."

He grinned. "After the weeks I spent alone in the pond back at The Ridge, this is paradise, Mac."

"Not to mention the year you spent there." He and forty-nine others had left Trieste to work at the facility building *Swords* without anyone knowing. Their families had even thought them dead. It had been an enormous sacrifice, but to a one they had done it for a full year, and had succeeded at everything I'd asked of them.

His smile faded abruptly. "I assume you're here to ask me something," Jackson rumbled. He took a swig of the beer, wincing slightly as the stuff burned down his throat. Around us in the atrium, Triestrians enjoyed the sights and sounds of the city, relaxing while off-shift, and some were also sitting nearby nursing drinks and socializing.

I smiled. "I'm here to offer what you requested. A vacation. You wanted two weeks, correct?"

"And then back to The Ridge?"

I frowned. "If it's okay with you. We need to keep building. We need more ships."

"You never let up, do you Mac?"

"I can't." I gestured around the module. "Look at this."

We were on the upper level; the atrium was nine levels down and surrounded by shrubs, vines, and trees. It was beautiful. A class of ten-year olds walked by, all carrying scuba gear. Jackson stared at them as they passed. Then he turned to me. "There's a lot to protect. You're right." Then he hesitated. "But can I have the month you originally offered? Those weeks stranded behind the cliff after you left, in the flooded dome, were a challenge." He sighed. "I didn't think I'd make it out of there. Thankfully, Piette and his team showed up when they did."

I grinned and offered my hand. "Deal."

He shook gratefully and took a massive gulp of beer. "I would have gone immediately had you asked, Mac. I love building those ships and living at The Ridge."

"Good," I said. "Because I'm going to ask you to do far more than build *Swords* for me."

"More?" His face paled.

"We have to keep pushing, Jack. We have to create more ships, better ones even, and new types as well. And you're all I've got."

He stared at my departing back. I knew it had shocked him, but I didn't care. Trieste was the only thing that mattered.

—••—

JOHNNY WAS WALKING FREELY AROUND TRIESTE and sporting the largest smile I'd ever seen on him. The USSF was gone—all except Benning, that is—and he was essentially a free man. He was enjoying his newfound freedom and exploring the city with an abandon that he probably hadn't felt in over a year.

I met with him in a lounge in the research module. I'd just visited Lazlow in his lab, where he had recovered quickly from our adventure and was working on new acoustic technologies to help protect Trieste from hostile forces. He seemed healthy and overjoyed to be back in the city. We'd arranged to go out on another scuba adventure, and afterward I'd planned to meet Johnny.

I had something important to ask him.

"What's up, Mac?" Johnny asked as we settled into a pair of comfortable chairs before a large viewport. Just outside was an incredible view of Trieste. We were facing the commerce module, and could see people strolling through travel tubes, walking within the modules, and there were even scuba divers outside, enjoying a mid-afternoon swim.

"I wanted to thank you for everything. You're dependable, Johnny. I can always count on you. It's why I wanted to talk to you now."

He frowned. "Go on."

I snorted. "In short, my former deputy mayor was a traitor who tried to get me killed. I ended up banishing and later arranging a mass of molten uranium to fall on him. I don't have a deputy mayor right now."

Johnny's face went blank for an instant. Then the hint of smile appeared. "You're serious?"

"I haven't asked you anything yet."

He looked confused. "But what are you—"

"Sorry, bad joke." I leaned forward. "I need someone I can depend on. Especially as we grow closer to these other undersea cities. We have to do this delicately, and I need you by my side."

"You're serious?"

"You already said that. Yes, I am. What do you say?"

He sighed and looked away. "I don't think I can do it again. I can't be away for a long time. I need a home, Mac. Trieste is all I've got."

I frowned. "I'm not asking you to leave. I'm asking you to *stay*."

"But you mentioned the Chinese cities."

Realization hit at that point. He was worried that I was asking him to go away to negotiate on my behalf, as I'd done a year earlier. He'd spent that time in the Chinese cities, trying to encourage them to join our quest for independence. "I won't ask you to leave for that length of time again, Johnny. I promise. If anything, I'll be with you. We'll journey together and try to build close economic and military ties with the other cities." There were twenty-nine major undersea colonies. I had a big job ahead of me.

And I wanted to ensure that Johnny would be at my side during it. "Trieste is your home. I want you to be deputy mayor. Do you accept?"

He grinned widely. "Hell yes, Mac!"

——••——

THE NEXT DAY, I FOUND MEG in her office in the repair docks. She was assisting with the repairs on the *Swords* that had been in the battle, and she was also overseeing long-needed repairs on *SC-1*. Its hull had a multitude of scratches and abrasions, any one of which could lessen the seacar's viability under great pressures. Already crews had lifted it from the water; it hung from a harness under the hoist, and I studied it as I entered the module. The seacar took my breath away whenever I saw it. We'd been through a lot, and it had been Kat's creation. Kat's memories would always surround the vehicle.

Meg smiled as I entered her office. She'd been examining the syntactic foam that Cliff had brought back from the French facility in the Indian Ocean. She had the piece of hull before her on the desk, and a set of electron microscope photographs.

She was shaking her head as she pointed at the photograph. "I've discovered why this foam is so much better, Tru."

Manufacturers sprayed the foam between the two layers of hulls in submarine construction. It consisted of microscopic spheres, which resisted pressure far better than any other geometric shape. The foam hardened into a filler between the hulls, and seacars or warsubs with the foam could withstand greater pressures than vehicles without it.

The question is, why was this foam better than the one we'd been using? It was an invention from the 1950s, with little improvement since.

"It's brilliant in its simplicity," she said. "The spheres withstand more pressure than ours."

"Are they made of something different? Aren't they all ceramic, glass, or metal?"

"Yes, but these have a hollow in the middle of each."

I frowned. "How does that help?" I imagined that it would make each sphere weaker.

She leaned forward, her features aglow with discovery. "Water!"

I couldn't respond. I didn't understand.

"Truman, at the center of each microscopic sphere is a tiny droplet of water. And water doesn't compress!"

"So . . . so it's stronger than a ceramic sphere without water?"

"Yes!"

I had thought that their spheres would be miniscule droplets of titanium or something along those lines. But to put water in the core of each . . .

I said, "They're using water to repel water?"

A smile had split Meg's features.

I sank into a seat. "Amazing."

"It is!" She shook her head. "I just have to figure out the manufacturing process. Shouldn't take too long."

I had nothing to say.

She simply stared at me. She was my twin, however, and knew why I was silent.

Finally, I said, "Listen, Meg. I wanted to apologize about Benning. I know what I told you when we left, but I just couldn't go through with it. I think in the long run it'll be better for Trieste."

She looked shocked at my change in topic. She put her hand on my arm. "Don't worry. You're right. I'm sure we'll manage. We just have to keep the USSF off our backs."

"And the Russians, now."

"Yes, there's that too."

"And the French."

She watched me silently for a long moment, then tilted her head. "Are you okay?"

"I'll get over it."

"No, not about Dad. About Kat."

"Ah." I winced. The truth was, she was everywhere I looked. She'd loved living in the undersea city. She'd given us the greatest gift to help us achieve independence. But every day she was in my thoughts less and less. I knew I would get over her death, but that didn't mean it wasn't difficult. "I'll be fine. I'll get over it. Everything I do is partly for her. I know that she would be proud of what we just achieved." I thought of the funeral and where we had put her body—in the depths of the Mid-Atlantic Ridge, where new crust was constantly forming. It was a fitting resting spot for her.

Meg smiled and gave my arm a squeeze. She looked away, and I could tell there was something on her mind. I didn't ask, however. I'd let her tell me, in time. I'd assumed it had been about Kat.

—••—

Josh Miller was right outside Meg's office, and I stopped for a moment to speak with him. He was happy that Meg was now working in the repair module, and I asked him if he knew anything about syntactic foam.

"Of course!" he said. "I used to work in a seacar manufacturing facility on the mainland before I came here. I worked for Toyota."

I gestured at Meg in the office. "Maybe you can help her out. She has a new type we need to build. Maybe even improve on."

He nodded. "Of course, Mac."

But there was something in his expression that triggered a concern. "What is it?"

He hesitated. "Is she okay?"

I shrugged. "She's fine, I think. Why?"

"Something's been bothering her. Everyone else has been happy since you returned from the trench. Overjoyed even. But Meg . . ." He trailed off.

I glanced through the clear port into her office. She was at her desk, staring at the electron microscope photos. Interesting. "Thanks, Josh. I appreciate that."

I left the repair module as I mulled over what he'd said. He would be a good asset to use at The Ridge perhaps, if I could convince him to sign up for a year-long stint there, cut off from family and all communications at the secluded manufacturing facility.

But Meg would get through it, I thought. We had both wanted to avenge Dad, but I hoped she would understand my reasoning. Another occupation was the last thing we needed. And I knew I had to get past this as well. Dad had had his reasons for why he'd done it. Maybe he'd been right. It had led us to this point, anyway. Our vessels were superior to all others in the oceans. We could go deeper than anyone else. Soon, with the syntactic foam, our mining settlements would be deeper than any others in the undersea resource extraction business. We had allied with Ballard, Cousteau, and Sheng City. The other two French cities had expressed interest, and Seascape's mayor, Reggie Quinn, had also offered to join our efforts.

In terms of independence, things had never looked brighter. We'd get The Ridge back up and running soon, and we'd start producing newer and even better vessels.

I felt positive about everything in Trieste at that precise moment.

—••—

I'D BEEN SLEEPING FAR BETTER SINCE the battle.

Since saving Benning's life.

The act had lifted the weight from my shoulders. No longer did I hear the cries of drowning USSF sailors at night. My dad had not visited my dreams again.

Things were settling down at Trieste. The Russians had backed off after their initial probe of our defenses, the people were happy, and everywhere there seemed to be a lessening of tension. The workers from The Ridge were on vacation and enjoying their time with families, after a long unexplained and seemingly bizarre absence, but they were also excited to return to the facility and begin production once again.

It was late at night, and Johnny, Cliff, Renée, and I had been out for a drink and a laugh at a local pub. Renée in particular was happy; she'd kept glancing at me with offerings of shy smiles. She had decided to stay and live at Trieste.

Afterward, just after midnight, on my way back to my living compartment, I decided to check in on Meg before settling in for the evening. She had agreed to join us at the pub, but had not shown up.

I knocked on her compartment. "Meg?" I whispered, conscious of the late hour. "Are you there?"

There was no response, but I could hear something within. A shuffling, dragging of some sort.

I frowned.

"Meg—I can hear you in there. Are you okay?" I grabbed the handle and prepared to slide it open.

"Don't open it, Tru! I'm—"

I thrust it aside and stared at the scene within. A gasp worked its way up my throat and I clamped down on it, not quite successfully.

Meg's right hand was soaked in blood. There were splatters across her arm and her upper torso. Her blond hair was disheveled, and her blue eyes flashed in anger. Blood droplets speckled her cheek. She stood over a body splayed across the deck, one leg on the bunk, one arm lying across its chest.

But the arm couldn't hide the gory stab wounds beneath it. There was blood everywhere around the body, across the bulkheads and the sheets, and it was pooling on the deck beneath it.

It was Admiral Taurus T. Benning.

There was a long, bloody knife in Meg's right hand.

She stared at me for a long moment; we stood in a frozen tableau as I struggled in vain to process the scene.

She said, her voice a quiet rasp, "I'm sorry, Mac. I just couldn't get past what he did. I had to kill him."

A Note from the Author

ANY ERRORS IN THE PHYSICS OF cavitation and supercavitation, the effects of water pressure, sound propagation underwater, sonar systems, nuclear fission and power plants, and SCUBA diving are mine alone.

I loved writing this novel. At its heart it's a "Men on a Mission" story, something I've been wanting to write for some time. I came up with the idea while working on *The Savage Deeps*, and it stuck with me, percolating in my mind for many months before I finally sat down to write it. The idea to sabotage *Dragon* by causing a meltdown of its fission plant led me to some fascinating research involving current nuclear power plants as well as the captivating story of Chernobyl, the disaster that occurred in 1986. I remember the incident quite well; I was fifteen years old and it had already been a memorable and tragic year in world news—Space Shuttle Challenger had exploded on liftoff a few months earlier.

I took some of the issues that had led to the Chernobyl meltdown and used them in this novel. I simplified the reactor substantially to make it more dramatic and easier to describe, and I apologize to those who might call details into question that don't quite jibe with reality. My apologies, but this is a thriller and a work of fiction, and sometimes as an author one takes liberties with such things to make a more dramatic, thrilling, and tightly paced story.

Syntactic foam was invented in the 1950s. It has many uses, but is most common in marine applications to increase buoyancy due to its low density. The microspheres can be hollow (microballoons) or non-hollow, and can increase both tensile as well as compressive strength. There is a large range in the size of the micro spheres used—from 1 to 200 micrometers (a micrometer is one-millionth of a meter). The aerospace industry also uses syntactic foams because they are lightweight but strong. They are also found in a multitude of other applications (including soccer and bowling balls!) but of particular interest is their potential for radar and sonar transparency.

The temperature of corium can more than double the melting point of steel, which is just under 1 400 ° Celsius. In this novel, I had the corium hit 3,000 °C. There are three incidents where a fission reactor's core has melted to corium:

First, Three Mile Island in Pennsylvania, 1979. The reactor core temperature skyrocketed when the coolant failed and nearly 20,000 kilograms of corium melted downward. Luckily, it did not escape the containment structure of the facility.

Second, Chernobyl in the Ukraine (then part of the USSR) in 1986. The reactor temperature reached almost 2,300 °C and the corium melted through containment, eventually reaching the basement of the reactor building, resulting in the famous "Elephant's Foot."

Third, the Fukushima Daiichi disaster following the 2011 tsunami. Temperatures in the core reached 2,500 °C and the corium pooled at the bottom of the containment vessel.

In my notes at the end of *The Savage Deeps*, I mentioned some of the movies and novels that inspired me to write this series. For *Fatal Depth*, I watched many "Men on a Mission" movies to provide inspiration. Some of them include: SAVING PRIVATE RYAN, THE GUNS OF NAVARONE, FORCE TEN FROM NAVARONE, U-571, THE DIRTY DOZEN, WHERE EAGLES DARE, KELLY'S HEROES, A BRIDGE TOO FAR, and INGLOURIOUS BASTERDS. There were others, but you may notice that they are all World War II films. It's a fascinating and exhilarating period in our history, a time where there is no better example of good vs. evil, and no shortage of heroes, and I would love to one day write a novel set during the war.

I am conscious of maintaining gender equality in my novels, though because I am a man there is always going to be a bias toward writing from a male point of view. However, I enjoy writing strong female roles. The strongest female character I have ever created (possibly the single most capable character I've ever written) to date is probably Shaheen Ramachandra from The Tanner Sequence (*The Furnace, The Freezer, The Void*), though in these novels Katherine Wells, Meagan McClusky, Irena Rostilov, and Renée Féroce are all highly intelligent, strong, well-educated, and capable women. I loved writing them. My intro to this novel, featuring a USSF character who does not respond well under stress, is not meant to be a slight toward the gender. The purpose was to contrast the Russian strategy with Cathy Lentz's vulnerable nature to further enhance the vicious nature of the attack.

Mac will be back in The Rise of Oceania Book Four: *An Island of Light*.

Please visit me at Facebook *@TSJAuthor* and Twitter *@TSJ_Author*. Also visit *www.timothysjohnston.com* to receive updates, learn about new and upcoming thrillers, and to register for news alerts.

The previous novels in The Rise of Oceania include: Book 1: *The War Beneath* and Book 2: *The Savage Deeps*. My futuristic murder mysteries include *The Furnace* (2013), *The Freezer* (2014), and *The Void* (2015), all published by Carina Press.

Thanks for investing your time in this novel. Do let me know what you think of my thrillers.

Timothy S. Johnston
tsj@timothysjohnston.com
1 August 2020

Acknowledgments

Thank you to Fitzhenry & Whiteside for acquiring The Rise of Oceania, publishing *Fatal Depth*, and showing faith in me and my writing. In particular, I'd like to single out Sharon Fitzhenry, Holly Doll, and Sonya Gilliss. I will never be able to express how truly thankful I am. Thanks also to my friends and family, who have always supported and encouraged me, and are without question my biggest fans. Thanks also to my followers on social media and my blog, Life After Gateway, for providing so much love and support. Creative souls are often tortured souls, and your kindness has been uplifting and most welcome.

Cheyney Steadman created the schematics within this book and she did an outstanding job. She is a true talent at graphic design, and her images exceeded all of my expectations. Thank you, Cheyney!

Coming Soon
from Timothy S. Johnston and
Fitzhenry & Whiteside

AN ISLAND OF LIGHT